P9-CLY-159

Murder on the Serpentine

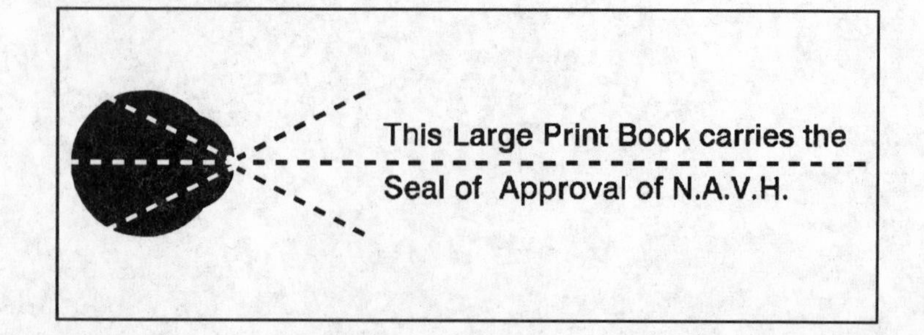
This Large Print Book carries the
Seal of Approval of N.A.V.H.

A CHARLOTTE AND THOMAS PITT NOVEL

MURDER ON THE SERPENTINE

ANNE PERRY

THORNDIKE PRESS
A part of Gale, Cengage Learning

Farmington Hills, Mich • San Francisco • New York • Waterville, Maine
Meriden, Conn • Mason, Ohio • Chicago

Thorndike Press, a part of Gale, Cengage Learning.

Thorndike Press® Large Print Basic.
The text of this Large Print edition is unabridged.
Other aspects of the book may vary from the original edition.
Set in 16 pt. Plantin.

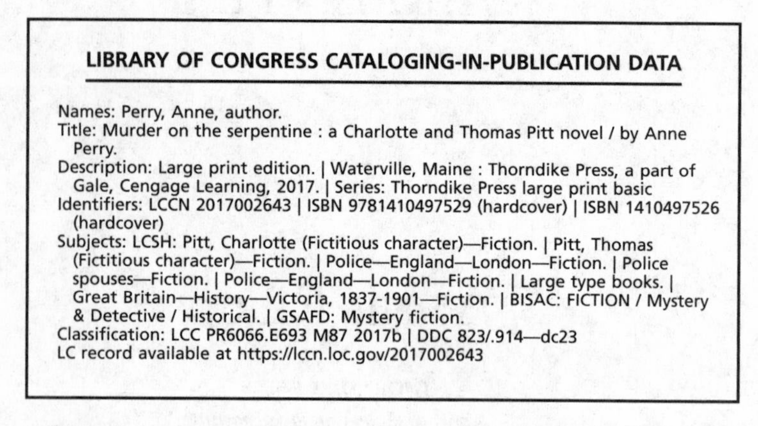
LIBRARY OF CONGRESS CATALOGING-IN-PUBLICATION DATA

Names: Perry, Anne, author.
Title: Murder on the serpentine : a Charlotte and Thomas Pitt novel / by Anne Perry.
Description: Large print edition. | Waterville, Maine : Thorndike Press, a part of Gale, Cengage Learning, 2017. | Series: Thorndike Press large print basic
Identifiers: LCCN 2017002643 | ISBN 9781410497529 (hardcover) | ISBN 1410497526 (hardcover)
Subjects: LCSH: Pitt, Charlotte (Fictitious character)—Fiction. | Pitt, Thomas (Fictitious character)—Fiction. | Police—England—London—Fiction. | Police spouses—Fiction. | Police—England—London—Fiction. | Large type books. | Great Britain—History—Victoria, 1837-1901—Fiction. | BISAC: FICTION / Mystery & Detective / Historical. | GSAFD: Mystery fiction.
Classification: LCC PR6066.E693 M87 2017b | DDC 823/.914—dc23
LC record available at https://lccn.loc.gov/2017002643

Published in 2017 by arrangement with Ballantine Books, an imprint of Random House, a division of Penguin Random House LLC

Printed in the United States of America
1 2 3 4 5 6 7 21 20 19 18 17

To Rita Keeley Brown, with thanks

CHAPTER 1

The man stood in front of Thomas Pitt in the untidy office, papers all over the desk from half a dozen cases Pitt was working on. There was no discernible order to the papers, except to him. The visitor's appearance was immaculate, from his discreet regimental tie to his crested gold cuff links. Not one silver hair was out of place.

"Yes, sir," he said gravely. "Her Majesty would like to see you as soon as possible. She hopes that now would be convenient." There was not a flicker of expression in his face. Quite possibly no one had ever refused him. Victoria had been on the throne since 1837, sixty-two years, and he was merely the latest in a long succession of emissaries.

Pitt felt a chill run through him, and his throat tightened.

"Yes, of course it is." He managed to keep his voice almost steady. He had met Queen Victoria before, on two occasions, but not since he had become head of Special Branch, that part of Her Majesty's Government that dealt with threats to the safety of the nation.

"Thank you." Sir Peter Archibald inclined his head very slightly. "The carriage is waiting. If you would be kind enough to accompany me, sir . . ."

There was no time for Pitt to tidy the papers, only to inform Stoker that he had been called away. He did not say to where, or by whom.

"Yes, sir," Stoker said, as if such things happened every day, but his eyes widened slightly. He stood back a little to allow them to pass him and head through the door into the passage.

Sir Peter led the way down the stairs and onto the street, where a very well-turned-out Clarence carriage stood waiting half a block away, outside a tobacconist's shop. There was no crest on the carriage's door to proclaim its owner. The coachman nodded in acknowledgment as the two men climbed in, and a moment later they moved into the traffic.

"A trifle cool for early summer, don't you think?" Sir Peter said pleasantly. It was a polite, very English way of letting Pitt know that there would be no discussion of why the Queen wished to speak with him. It was even possible that Sir Peter himself did not know.

"A little," Pitt agreed. "But at least it's not raining."

Sir Peter murmured his agreement, and they settled to riding in silence the rest of the way from Lisson Grove to Buckingham Palace.

As Pitt expected, they went past the magnificent façade and around the side. Pitt found his stomach knotting and had to make a deliberate effort to unclench his hands. They were in the Palace Mews. Coachmen and grooms were preparing horses and carriages for the royal family's evening visits, giving animals a final brush, trappings a last check and polish. A groom passed in front of them with a pail of water. He was whistling cheerfully.

It was barely dusk, just a slight fading of the light and a lengthening of the shadows. The carriage stopped and Sir Peter alighted, with Pitt a step behind him. Still nothing was said, no inkling of the reason for this extraordinary visit. Pitt tried to stop his mind from racing over the possibilities. Why on earth would the Queen send for him in this hurried and so very private manner? His was a government appointment, and there were official channels for just about everything. Too many of them. Sometimes he felt strangled by red tape of one sort or another.

He followed Sir Peter's stiff, upright figure — his straight back and squared shoulders. The emissary walked with a short, perfect military stride, as if he could maintain it for miles.

Once they had gained entry they went in silence up and down stairs, along passages decorated here and there with faded sporting prints, or perhaps these were the originals. As Pitt vaguely recalled being here before, Sir Peter stopped abruptly and knocked on a large paneled door. It was opened immediately and Sir Peter stepped in, spoke to someone just inside, then turned and gestured for Pitt to follow him.

It was a comfortable, private withdrawing room, high ceilinged but not very large, with windows onto the lovely back garden, curtains not yet drawn against the dusk. The walls were almost entirely covered by portraits, ornately framed. The carpet had once been patterned but was now fading gently with the passage of decades of feet.

Ahead of Pitt, in a chair to one side of the huge fireplace, sat a plump little woman who looked very tired. She was dressed entirely in black, which made her seem faded and quite old. She had little left of the vigor he had seen in her only a few short years ago when she had defied the men who had her hostage at Osborne House. Not that anyone knew of that, except Pitt and a couple of very close friends.

Pitt stood still. He knew better than to move or speak until invited.

He heard the door close with a slight click.

"Good evening, Mr. Pitt," the Queen said quietly. "I am obliged for your attention with so little notice. I hope I have not drawn you from urgent matters of state?"

It was merely a politeness, a way of beginning the conversation. There was a chair opposite her, but Pitt did not sit in it. One stood in the presence of the monarch, for however long the interview might last. Even when he was prime minister, Mr. Gladstone had not been granted the liberty of sitting. Only Mr. Disraeli had been offered that, because he sometimes made her laugh.

"Not at all, Your Majesty," Pitt replied, lifting his eyes a little but not yet meeting hers. "There are no unusual troubles at the moment."

She let out her breath in a sigh. "You choose your words carefully, Mr. Pitt. If you had said there were no troubles at all, I should have disbelieved you. I do not wish to be catered to, as if I were unable to grasp difficulties, or too old or too tired to face them."

There was a tone in her voice now that demanded he meet her gaze. Was he expected to answer her? From the silence, apparently so. What could he say? He could neither agree nor argue with her.

"It was not so long ago, ma'am, that I recall you facing armed men who held you captive, and defying them with some vigor. Time and griefs touch all of us but they have never broken your spirit."

She nodded her head, and there was a hint of a smile on her face. "Your new position has taught you a little polish, Mr. Pitt. Probably a good thing. I hope it has not made you evasive." It was more a challenge than a question. She did not wait long enough for him to reply. "I do not have time for polite euphemisms, going around in circles until nobody knows what anyone else is talking about."

"Yes, ma'am." He inclined his head very slightly. The burden of some deep fear was playing in the weary lines of her face. She was a very small woman, a foot shorter than him, overweight now, and the years of constant duty and the loneliness since Albert's death were written indelibly in her skin, the slightly beaky nose, the thinning hair scraped back off the bones of her brow.

She sat silently. Was she wondering whether he was the man she wished to trust, or merely gathering her thoughts for something that was more difficult to tell him than she had anticipated? With anyone else he would have asked, but with her it would be presumptuous.

She took a deep breath, and her attention, which looked to have been wandering, returned to the present.

"You may be seated, Mr. Pitt. I have much to tell you, and I do not care to look up at you. It makes my neck ache."

"Yes, ma'am." He nearly thanked her, then realized that that too would be inappropriate. He sat down on the hard-backed chair opposite her, his spine straight, both feet on the floor.

She smiled very briefly, only a ghost of amusement, as if some memory had stirred and then vanished before she could capture it. Her eyes studied his face as she spoke.

"The Prince of Wales has recently acquired a new adviser in certain matters, mostly to do with horses, I think, but the man seems to be everywhere, and involved in all sorts of other affairs." Her eyes sharpened, as if she had seen some surprise in Pitt's face. "Of course he has to have friends — we all do —" she said a trifle quickly, "but Edward will be king one day, quite . . . soon. He cannot afford to choose haphazardly." She stared at Pitt. She was not waiting for a response, she did not require his opinion, but she wished to see if he was paying attention.

Did she want to hear more about this friend, and from Special Branch? All his life the prince had loved horses, and horse-racing. It was to be expected that he would seek friends among those who shared his passion.

Satisfied that he was listening to her, the Queen continued. "I am concerned that Alan Kendrick is not an entirely satisfactory influence. He is a" — she searched for the right words — "forceful character," she finished. "And I do not care for his wife either. A woman who does not know her place. Sharp-tongued, occasionally of unseemly behavior. Or perhaps I am simply old-fashioned . . ." She looked away from him for a moment, and he realized that memory had intruded on her with painful clarity, perhaps of the happy years of her marriage. She had been an opinionated woman herself, but she had been queen —

since she was eighteen, awakened in the night to be informed that the old king was dead and she was his heir.

She brought her attention back to Pitt, blinking rapidly and staring at him again.

"I wish to allay my concerns," she said tartly. "I have few people I can trust with such delicate matters, and I was prepared to be told that my anxiety was unfounded. I considered whom I might ask to look into Mr. Kendrick for me with the utmost discretion, you understand?" It was a question. She required an answer.

"Yes, ma'am," Pitt said quickly, his heart sinking. This was not a matter for Special Branch. Was there a way he could tell her so without giving offense? Did one ever refuse the Queen? He was trapped.

"You appear uncomfortable, Mr. Pitt," she accused.

He felt himself flush. He had not realized he was so obvious.

"You know something of this man?" she demanded.

"No, ma'am."

She gave a little grunt, and it was impossible to tell if it was displeasure or merely impatience.

She looked at him intently, as if making an accurate judgment of him was of the greatest importance. Or possibly, at eighty, her eyesight was failing and it was merely an effort for her to see his face clearly.

"I asked my old and trusted friend Sir John Halberd to look into this man Kendrick and give me his opinion." She blinked rapidly, fighting some deep emotion, and stared down at her hands, folded neatly in her lap but gripping each other too tightly.

Pitt had a sudden desire to comfort her. He was waiting for her to say that Halberd had told her something that hurt her very much. But whatever it was, however badly Kendrick had influenced the Prince of Wales, it was not something in which Special Branch could interfere. It might be a disappointment to the Queen, even an embarrassment, but surely she was used to the prince's libertine way of life? Everyone else was. And he appeared to have calmed down a lot as he had grown older, less physically well and also, of course, as Victoria became more fragile and he came closer to the throne himself.

The silence grew heavy. She seemed to be waiting for Pitt to respond.

"Did Sir John give you his opinion, ma'am?" he asked.

"No," she said abruptly. "He sent me a message that he wished to see me urgently.

It came late in the evening. I was not well. I replied to him that he might attend me anytime he wished the following day. He always gives my well-being the utmost care." Again she stopped, and was quite visibly struggling with deep feelings.

Pitt dreaded what she was going to say. Had she been anyone else he would have attempted to make it easier for her, but one did not interrupt the Queen. He waited in acute discomfort.

"He never came," she said in little more than a whisper. Pitt drew in his breath sharply.

Now she was looking into his eyes almost as if they were equals, just an old woman deeply distressed and a younger man who might help her.

She nodded, her lips tight, then spoke with an effort. "He was found dead that morning. In a rowing boat in Hyde Park. At least, strictly speaking, he was in the water, shallow as it is. He appeared to have stood up, for some reason, then slipped and struck his head on the edge of the boat, fallen into the water, and drowned."

"I'm very sorry," Pitt said gently.

She swallowed with effort. "I wish you to find out for me if his death was the accident it appeared. And what it was that he intended to tell me regarding the man Kendrick. You are an excellent detective. This I know from our previous acquaintance." She did not refer to either incident specifically, but she had not forgotten their brief captivity at Osborne.

"And now you have the power and the secrets of Special Branch in your hands. I require to know the truth, Mr. Pitt, whatever it is. What did John Halberd find out, and was he murdered because of it?"

For a moment he was speechless.

"I trust you, Mr. Pitt," she said gravely. "Both for your skill and your discretion." She did not mention loyalty. Perhaps it was taken for granted. More probably, he thought, to question it was too painful at the moment. Halberd had died, possibly because of his loyalty. She was asking a great deal of Pitt, personally rather than through official channels. She had mentioned discretion. Was that a polite way of telling him he was to speak of this matter only to her? That was something he needed to know, and he felt that it gave him the right to be direct.

"To whom shall I report, ma'am?" He met her eyes and saw in them a grief so deep it startled him. And guilt? Did she fear she had sent an old friend to his death? Even as the thought came to him, he was certain it was so.

"To me, Mr. Pitt," she said very quietly. "Report to me. You will inform Sir Peter Archibald when you wish to see me, and I will have him fetch you immediately. You will keep the whole matter as discreet as is possible, not only for my sake but for your own. Is that understood?"

"Yes, ma'am."

At last she smiled very slightly, just an easing of her lips.

"I am obliged, Mr. Pitt. You have my leave to go. Sir Peter will take you to your carriage. Good night."

He rose to his feet and inclined his head in a bow. "Good night, Your Majesty."

Outside in the corridor he deliberately straightened his shoulders and had walked a dozen paces before Sir Peter appeared, calm and polite as before. Had he any idea what the Queen had just asked of Pitt?

"I will have the coachman called immediately, sir." Sir Peter said it as impassively as if this was a usual occurrence.

"Thank you," Pitt answered.

Sir Peter smiled very briefly. "If you would be good enough to follow me, sir . . ."

Pitt rode home with his mind whirling, completely unaware of his surroundings. He could not have refused her, yet he loathed the task. He recalled the brief piece in the newspaper mentioning Halberd's death. He had been a distinguished man, but not much in the public eye. It had said merely that he died in an accident, and left no family. It did not say what the accident had been. That was where he would have to begin.

Could the Queen be right? She was an old woman, worn out with grief from having lost two children and the husband she adored while he was still in the prime of his life. Many of her children had married into the great royal houses of Europe, and thus lived far away from her. She might have friends, but never equals. She was queen and empress of a quarter of the earth. She took the vast responsibility very seriously indeed. She could not live many more years. Perhaps she did not even want to. But she had no choice as to her successor. A millennium of history dictated that it be her eldest son.

She mourned the death of Halberd, and perhaps in a way she was bitterly reminded of death itself. Too much of all that she had loved lay in the past. She had asked Halberd to help her, and he had died trying to do so. Surely it was out of loneliness and imagination that she would feel guilty for that. If Pitt could prove to her that Halberd's death was a genuine accident, one that could have occurred at any time, then would she be reassured and at peace?

He had convinced himself of that by the time the carriage stopped in Keppel Street and let him off at his own front door. He alighted, thanked the driver, and went up the steps and inside.

A sense of warmth surrounded him immediately. It had nothing to do with the summer evening, but with familiarity, long memories stretching back through friendship, countless conversations, a few griefs — but above all, love.

He put his jacket on the coat stand in the hall. Charlotte had bought it in a junk shop and given it to him the first Christmas after their marriage, when money was scarce. The pewter candlestick had been his mother's. In this house he had celebrated victories, and recovered from a few losses. His dearest friends had sat around the kitchen table far into the night and talked about endless possibilities.

The sitting-room door opened and Charlotte came out, her face lighting with pleasure at seeing him. It was nineteen years since they had met, but he still found himself smiling, noticing the curve of her cheek, the grace with which she moved.

He bent a little to kiss her, holding her tightly for a moment.

She pushed him back. "What's wrong?" she asked quietly, her brow furrowed.

He glanced over her shoulder at the tall clock against the wall.

"It's not so late," he replied.

Her expression registered momentary amusement, then anxiety. He knew exactly what she was thinking. He had evaded the question. When he had been in the regular police he had often discussed cases with her. Indeed, they had met when a number of murders took place in the area where she lived. Her own elder sister had been one of the victims. Out of that tragedy had come the greatest happiness in his life. He had never imagined that he, the son of a laundress and a man convicted of poaching — wrongly, he still believed — could marry the daughter of a wealthy banker, not far beneath the aristocracy.

"Thomas!" She was looking at him steadily, the concern in her eyes deepening.

"I have just gained a delicate case I don't know how to approach," he answered. Since moving from the police to Special Branch, he could no longer discuss cases with her. At times he would have dearly liked to have her wisdom and knowledge of the upper levels of society, where he would always be a stranger. There were multitudes of small expressions, mannerisms, codes of behavior that he'd observed but could not copy without seeming clumsy.

They went into the sitting room, where the French doors onto the garden were closed against the evening breeze but the curtains were not yet drawn. Again, the familiarity wrapped around him, the calm, painted seascape over the mantelpiece, all muted blues. The carved wooden coal scuttle had been an extravagance when they bought it. On the shelves were photographs of Daniel and Jemima, aged two and six, and mementos like seashells, a piece of polished driftwood from a holiday on the coast.

"Stoker will help," Charlotte said with certainty. "Tell me when you are ready for dinner. Daniel and Jemima have already eaten, but I waited for you."

That happened so often it was hardly worth comment, yet he was grateful. He did not like to eat alone.

"I can't tell Stoker," he replied, easing back in the armchair and stretching his legs out. "But I might ask Narraway." Victor Narraway had been head of Special Branch when Pitt was first moved there from Bow Street. It was Narraway who had recommended Pitt to take his place, after the disaster of the O'Neill case had forced his own resignation, much to many people's surprise. Several in high positions had been against Pitt's appointment as Narraway's successor, thinking there were other candidates much more capable. But Narraway had prevailed.

Charlotte looked unhappy. Surely she understood?

"Thomas, you've forgotten," she said quietly.

"What?"

"Narraway and Aunt Vespasia are on a cruise to Rome and then Egypt. They'll be away for a couple of months at least." He had forgotten. Now he recalled it, and it was like a blow. He would need to have this matter resolved long before then. Perhaps Halberd's death had been the accident it had seemed, and he would be able to reassure the Queen. She would still grieve for him, and no doubt still dislike Kendrick.

That was not something that could be addressed.

Charlotte was waiting for him to answer,

and her anxiety was plain in her eyes.

He smiled at her. "I forgot," he admitted. "Perhaps I shouldn't be looking for the easy way out. Yes, I would like dinner, before it gets too late." He stood up, smiling now, willing himself to think of other things.

CHAPTER 2

Early the next morning Pitt began by going in to Lisson Grove and telling Stoker that he would be absent from the office for a few days on a case, but could always be reached in the evenings at his home, were it necessary.

"Yes, sir," Stoker said calmly. His bony face was almost impassive. "There's nothing out of the ordinary at the moment. I'll tell Jenkins and Doherty. Anything we can do to help?"

"Not so far. Probably not at all," Pitt replied. "I'll look in on Friday, if not before." He hesitated. There was a question in his mind that it would be foolish not to ask Stoker: He had been in Special Branch several years before Pitt had joined. "Do you know anything about Sir John Halberd?"

Stoker frowned. "I've heard the name. I'm trying to think where."

"He died recently," Pitt prompted.

Stoker nodded. "That's right. Stupid boating accident. You'd think he'd have more sense than to stand up in a boat, even in shallow water."

"What do you know about him, other than that?" Pitt asked.

"Nothing really. He's one of those people everyone knows slightly and nobody knows well. Never had government office. Don't know who he is related to. I'm sorry. Is it important? I can find out."

"No, thank you. Forget I mentioned him. And that's not a casual remark, it is an order."

"Yes, sir." Stoker looked puzzled, but he knew that Pitt meant what he said. He would not inquire.

The first thing Pitt did was to telephone the police station in Savile Row, some fifteen or twenty minutes' brisk walk from the place on the Serpentine where Sir John's body had been found. He was told courteously that the case had been dealt with by the station on Pavilion Road in Knightsbridge, roughly the same distance in a different direction. He thanked the man and ended the call.

The Serpentine was a decorative stretch of water that curved across the middle of

Hyde Park. The Queen's instructions to Pitt were clear. He was to be discreet. That in itself was difficult. Special Branch had no uniforms, so at least he looked like any other tall man in his late forties, with untidy hair and a well-cut suit that somehow managed not to sit comfortably on him. But he had been a policeman all his working life. Half the policemen in London knew him by sight.

He walked into the station and presented his card, still something he was not used to.

"Yes, sir," the desk sergeant said with sudden respect.

"I would like to speak to your superintendent, please." He did not have to give a reason: His rank was sufficient. Not everyone respected Special Branch, but everyone held it in some degree of awe. They dealt with secrets and violence, the hidden threats to a whole way of life most people held in common and largely took for granted, although in the last twenty years or so there had been unrest throughout Europe. There were whispers of change everywhere.

"Yes, sir. I'll tell him you're here, sir," the sergeant said. Five minutes later Pitt was seated in Superintendent Gibson's comfortable, cluttered office. Wanted posters were tacked on the walls, all very slightly crooked.

Law books and procedure manuals were heaped on the shelves.

"What can I do for you, Commander Pitt?" Gibson asked, his brows drawn down in an anxiety he tried to mask with a soft voice.

"Just tidying up a few details," Pitt replied, as if it were of no importance. "Your officers were called when Sir John Halberd was found in the Serpentine?"

"Yes, sir," Gibson agreed, biting his lip. "Very unfortunate. Don't get many accidents there. Usually just people getting wet. Fall in, feel like a fool, and one or two get angry about it." He gave a slight shrug. "Often young men, the worse for a few too many drinks. This was quite different. Poor man must've stood up for something, lost his balance, and hit his head as he went down. Chance in a hundred. Tipped the boat badly and slid into the water. Never came to." He shook his head, started to say something else, then changed his mind.

"You found him in the water the next morning?" Pitt asked.

"Yes, sir. Young gentleman walking his dog stopped, but there was nothing he could do to help. By then there were more people gathered, and someone came for us. Can I ask why you're inquiring, sir?" Gibson put his hand up as if to straighten his tie, then let it fall again.

"Details," Pitt repeated. "He was a distinguished man. Just want to have all the answers. No sign of anyone else there, I presume? Does anyone know what he was doing on the Serpentine alone? What time did the police surgeon say he died? Where did he hire the boat, and when? That sort of thing."

Gibson cleared his throat. "Is that what this is about, sir? It rather looks as if he took the boat out at night, having arranged the hire earlier." He was quite openly anxious now. What was wrong that he had not seen?

"After dark, then?" Pitt pressed.

"Yes, sir. Police surgeon reckoned he must have gone into the water about ten in the evening, most likely. Give or take a bit. But with the body lying in the water, which is still pretty cold even at this time of year, it's hard to be exact."

Pitt nodded. "Anyone got an idea what he was doing alone in a boat on the Serpentine, at ten in the evening?"

Gibson colored uncomfortably. "No, sir. Nothing to suggest there was anybody there. If there was a young lady, she left no evidence as we could find."

"Uncomfortable place for a rendezvous."

Pitt shook his head slightly.

"If it were a young woman of . . ." Gibson began. He did not finish the sentence, but his meaning was obvious.

Or a young man, Pitt thought, but he did not say it.

He changed the subject slightly. "When you informed his staff, butler, or valet, did they make any remark as to why Halberd was there?"

Gibson looked relieved. He did not wish to inquire too closely into the habits of the gentry, yet equally he could not afford to appear incompetent.

"No, sir. He must have let himself out after the house was locked up, which was a little before ten o'clock. He came and went as he pleased. Nobody knew anything about why he went out that night. Upset, they were, all of them. Held him in very high regard. My officers said it seemed more than just shock, or of course the loss of a position. There is no one else in the house for them to look after."

"I see."

"Sir . . ." Gibson was clearly uncomfortable. He moved awkwardly in his seat, and twisted his hands as if he had no idea what to do with them.

Pitt waited.

"Sir . . . if Mr. Halberd . . . I mean Sir John . . . made an indiscreet appointment and . . . and had an accident . . . Well, there's no one else hurt. Couldn't we just . . . close it up . . . let it be?"

"If that's what it was, then yes, of course we could," Pitt agreed. "Does the evidence suggest that?"

"Looks like it to me, sir."

"Nothing to make you think there was a quarrel?"

"No, sir. He stood up and overbalanced, hit his head on the gunwale, and fell into the water. Because he was knocked out, he drowned. If there was a young woman there, she must have taken fright and run off. Or maybe he stood up because she arrived, and when he fell she scarpered. Didn't want to be caught and blamed. Let it go, sir." There was no judgment in his face, only compassion for a man who had made a fool of himself and paid a terrible price for it.

Pitt stood up slowly. This was not an answer the Queen would like, but she did not need to know the details. Indeed, they were only speculation anyway.

"Thank you, Superintendent. It was more or less the answer I expected, but I had to be sure. Good day."

Gibson released a sigh. "Good day, sir."

Pitt went out into the busy street, filled with shouts and the clatter of wheels and hooves over the uneven cobbles.

Was that the answer? An accident, not investigated any further because it was part of an indiscretion that would have spoiled the reputation of a good man? A silence of kindness? He could allow the Queen to believe the assignation was with a woman of his own class, her name withheld because it would serve no purpose to disgrace her. But he had to be satisfied that was all it was.

He would check with Cornwallis, who had been assistant commissioner of police when Pitt was still at Bow Street. He was a man Pitt both professionally trusted and personally liked. He might also know more about Alan Kendrick. Halberd might have spoken to him on the subject already but not had the chance to report his findings to the Queen. Which would be what? That Kendrick was an ambitious man, keen to become a close friend of the man about to be king? It was what she expected. She must be more than familiar with such people. In her position, did one at least half suspect everybody's motives?

Pitt had already reached the end of the street, where it crossed the main road, and within a few moments he stopped a cab and

gave the driver Cornwallis's address. Cornwallis had retired now, and it was still early enough in the morning that he might well not have left the house.

Cornwallis was at home and delighted to see Pitt, but he knew that a call at such an hour meant Pitt needed advice or information. After the briefest of greetings to Cornwallis's wife, Isadora, whom Pitt also knew well, they retired to his study and remained uninterrupted.

Cornwallis sat back in one of his well-upholstered armchairs, and Pitt in the other. Pitt had seldom been to this house, but it seemed familiar because of the paintings of sailing ships before the wind, the ship's sextant, and the brass model cannon. Cornwallis had had those paintings in his commissioner's office since Pitt first knew him. He even recognized at a glance many of the books, some of them poetry.

Cornwallis was a lean man, usually of few words. "Well?" he prompted.

During his cab ride, Pitt had considered what to say, and how much to tell Cornwallis.

"John Halberd," he said simply. "Did you know him?" Cornwallis stiffened almost imperceptibly, no more than a slight increase in the tension of certain muscles.

"Yes," he replied. "We were friends. Why?"

"Your feelings about him?" Pitt asked.

A shadow crossed Cornwallis's face. "Stop studying me, Pitt. Why are you asking? The man died in an idiotic boating accident. Any fool should have known better than to stand up in a flat-bottomed boat like that. Let him rest in peace, man. The police surgeon said it was mischance. Why on earth do you want to rake it up? He's scarcely settled in his grave."

"I need to know something more about him," Pitt explained. "I am not looking into his death." Was that entirely true? He disliked being evasive, with Cornwallis particularly. "He was investigating a certain matter. That is all I can tell you."

Cornwallis relaxed a little. "He wouldn't discuss anything of that sort with me or anyone else. What do you need to know?" He was still guarded. It was in the steadiness of his eyes, the motionless hands locked together in front of him.

"Was he a good investigator? Where did he come from? What did he do? Who was his family?" Pitt asked.

Cornwallis thought for a moment. "Landed gentry. Lincolnshire, I think. He went up to Cambridge and read history. Good degree, Honors. Then he traveled.

Mostly Egypt, down the Nile and farther south into Africa itself. What the devil does this have to do with Special Branch? He's been here in Britain for decades since then."

"So an intelligent and well-traveled man," Pitt summed up. "But you didn't tell me if you think he was a good investigator."

"Of what?"

"People. If he wanted to find out about someone, would he be likely to succeed?"

"What the hell does it matter now? He's dead, poor soul. Barely into his sixties. He had probably the best part of twenty years left." Cornwallis's voice caught for an instant, betraying the depth of his feelings. That was probably the most powerful clue Pitt would gain as to Halberd's character. Cornwallis had been at sea, and he knew its demands and the price a single mistake could cost. His respect was not won easily.

Pitt would have liked to have left it there, but he could not.

"Was he a man to exaggerate?"

"Never." Cornwallis sat upright, then leaned forward a little. "For heaven's sake, man, tell me what it is you want to know. Was Halberd working for you? How did you come to employ somebody you know so little about? Didn't Victor Narraway teach you better than that? I certainly did!"

"He was investigating something when he died," Pitt told him. And that was possibly more than he should have said. "I have now been asked to complete it. And you would be wasting your time, and mine, by asking me more than that. Would Halberd have exaggerated anything?"

"No. If you'd ever met him, such a thing wouldn't cross your mind."

Pitt weighed his response only for a moment. "What do you suppose he was doing in a rowing boat on the Serpentine alone, at ten o'clock in the evening? And why would a man who'd been along the Nile stand up and overbalance on the water?"

Cornwallis's face paled and he sat motionless. "I don't know," he said finally. "But even if he had some kind of . . . assignation — which I find hard to believe — what the hell has that to do with anyone else? Let him rest in peace. We all have our . . . weaknesses. Does it matter?"

"Not if it was a genuine accident," Pitt replied, "but the more you tell me of Halberd, the less likely it seems he would have been so careless. Although if there was a woman and she lost her balance, he might have stood up to help, slipped, and knocked himself senseless when he fell."

"Then why the devil did she not help

him?" Cornwallis said angrily. "At the very least hold his head above the water."

"Have you any idea who it might have been — was he there with anyone?"

"None at all. I presume someone married, or they would not have been meeting at night in a rowing boat." Cornwallis blushed as he said it. He had been passionately in love with Isadora, and still was, but women in general were a mystery to him. He had spent most of his life at sea, ending as a captain of his own ship, before becoming a commissioner in the police.

Pitt moved the subject a little. "Where did Sir John's living come from?"

"Largely inherited, I think." Cornwallis was clearly relieved. "The land in Lincolnshire, or that direction, brings in a tidy sum. And I think I recall hearing that his mother brought a goodly fortune to the marriage. Halberd was the only son."

"Did he ever marry?"

"Not that I know of." Cornwallis's look dared Pitt to make anything of it.

"What did he do with his time?" Pitt continued. "Who were his friends?"

"As I said, I was one of them." Cornwallis leaned forward again, his face earnest. "Pitt, he was a good man. One of the best I've known. Maybe he had weaknesses. Who doesn't, one way or another? Please, leave it alone."

Could he? Pitt would have liked nothing better than to do precisely that. If Halberd had died during an indiscretion, ending tragically but without fault, then Cornwallis was right. It was both cruel and pointless to dig into it, and no matter how careful he was, it could end up becoming public. Would it be sufficient for the Queen if he undertook to learn about Alan Kendrick and complete the task Halberd had begun? It would be awkward, and perhaps futile, and he would have to put at least one other man on it. Stoker would be ideal, the very soul of discretion, but there were half a dozen others who could also make inquiries in the right places.

Cornwallis was watching him, waiting. He might be naïve about women, but he was an excellent judge of men. He could not have commanded a ship had he not been. The sea forgives nothing, especially when you battle it under sail, without the power of an engine to rescue you.

"You knew him well enough to be certain he was a good man?" Pitt asked, watching Cornwallis's face for even a brief shadow.

Cornwallis gave a very slight smile. "I did."

■ ■ ■ ■

Pitt had to steel himself to face the next person he decided to interview. It would have been so much easier simply to ask Vespasia, Charlotte's sister's great-aunt by marriage and the woman Pitt cared for most in the world after Charlotte herself. In her youth Vespasia had been the greatest beauty of her age, and — of far more importance — she had been brave and devastatingly honest at times with a wit that cut through all pretense. She had known almost everyone of any importance at all.

But as Charlotte had reminded him, she was out of the country. He must see Somerset Carlisle himself. At least he knew where to find him. He was a member of Parliament and took his office seriously, underneath the passionate, unorthodox beliefs and the occasionally outrageous humor.

Pitt did not find him until early afternoon, taking an after-luncheon stroll along the Thames Embankment next to the Houses of Parliament. Pitt walked rapidly enough to catch up with him just before he joined a group of his fellow members.

Carlisle stopped, slightly surprised as Pitt took his arm. He was a slender man, even a little gaunt lately. He had a sardonic face, too much laughter in it to be conventionally good-looking.

"You look ominous," he said with a smile. "But I will admit, you are never a bore."

"Thank you," Pitt said drily. "I need to talk to you privately, and without interruption."

Carlisle's expression was suddenly lugubrious. "Oh dear. This time, whatever it was, I did not do it! Or is it information? Yes, of course it is. Lady Vespasia is somewhere in the Mediterranean, I hope enjoying herself." He had been a friend of Vespasia's as long as Pitt had known him, which dated from his involvement in a particularly grisly and absurd case in Resurrection Row. Carlisle had been crusading for a cause, which he did rather too often.

Pitt had never been able to befriend a man simply for the sake of it. But Carlisle would have been interesting. He was the utmost eccentric but, in his own way, passionately moral.

"Did you know Sir John Halberd?" he asked.

Carlisle's remarkable eyebrows shot up. "Of course I did! We will all miss him, even if we don't know it is his absence that is hurting us. Why? Sorry. Silly question. No doubt it is all frightfully secret. He was a good man. What do you want to know?"

"Probably everything . . ."

"Oh! Then yes, a private place, and perhaps a halfway decent meal will be required. Small private club I know. I'll give you the address. How about dinner — in one of the side rooms? Waiters are chosen for their discretion." He took out one of his cards and scribbled a note on the back of it, then handed it to Pitt. He had written the address in a very elegant script, and the time of eight p.m.

"Thank you." Pitt nodded his agreement.

Carlisle gave a cheery wave and caught up with his colleagues as casually as if he had been asked directions by a stranger.

Pitt turned and walked back toward Westminster Bridge.

He spent the afternoon reading the coroner's report on Halberd's death, and various obituaries with remembrances of his life. Of course such notices very rarely said anything about the deceased except what was flattering. It was the custom to be generous. But they all agreed on his origins, his education, his exploration of Egypt and Africa, and that he had contributed quietly and consistently to the welfare of his countrymen. It was exactly what Pitt expected; he was reading only to be sure he had not missed something that might prove to be relevant later.

He arrived at Carlisle's club precisely five minutes after the time Carlisle had stipulated on the card. He did not wish to draw attention to himself by getting there first and having to explain who he was. Narraway would never have had to. He was a gentleman from birth, part of the Establishment, not needing to prove anything.

Carlisle was waiting for him inside the lobby. Either it was his normal courtesy or an act of particular sensitivity. In some ways he was an outsider himself — but by choice. He could have conformed, had he wished, and probably risen to high office.

Carlisle led him through the inner hallway with its high ceiling and ornately paneled oak doors leading off into cloakrooms, offices, and smaller sitting rooms for private meetings. Pitt had no time to look at the many portraits on the walls — to judge by costume, dating back at least a hundred years.

They passed the entrance to the main dining room before Carlisle stopped, opened a door, and ushered Pitt inside, then followed him in, leaving the door ajar. Possibly it was a signal to the steward that they were ready for him.

Pitt took his seat and tried not to appear as if he had never been here before. He was aware of the carved oak fireplace, the high-backed dining chairs, and the gleaming surface of the table. Then the steward arrived with the wine menu.

They were served an excellent meal, chosen by Carlisle beforehand.

Pitt began to speak the moment the steward had withdrawn and closed the door behind him with barely a snick of the latch. He had already decided how much he intended to tell Carlisle.

"I believe Halberd was making inquiries into Alan Kendrick shortly before he died," he said. "The task remains unfinished, and for various reasons I need to complete it."

"Really?" Carlisle did not disguise his interest, or his surprise. "Since you appear to know very little about Halberd, I assume he was not doing it for you. I also assume you are not free to tell me for whom he was doing it? No, I thought not. Perhaps it is better I don't know."

"Did Halberd make inquiries for many people?" Pitt asked.

"He had a great deal of knowledge," Carlisle replied slowly, now measuring his words. "I don't know how much of it he searched for and how much was incidental to his way of life, his natural curiosity, and his phenomenal memory. He observed relationships between facts that many other people missed. He was a natural scholar of human behavior, but one, I believe, of unusual compassion. At least that is what I have heard from several people. But the observations were general. Whatever was particular remained discreet."

Pitt thought about it for a moment.

"So if one wished to know a good deal of information about someone, then Halberd would be the man to ask," he concluded.

"Especially if it was not easily available," Carlisle agreed, his eyes still on Pitt's face. "Have you any idea what kind of information your . . . patron was looking for? I assume something Kendrick would not willingly reveal?"

Pitt sidestepped the answer. Given the slightest hint, Carlisle was easily quick enough to deduce it was the Queen.

"Who are Kendrick's friends, his associates? Where did his money come from?" he went on.

Carlisle took another mouthful of the excellent pâté and swallowed it before he answered. "I have no idea where his money came from, but he seems to have a great deal of it. Has stables in Cambridgeshire, and some very fine horses indeed. Word is that he has a couple of possible Derby winners in training. That doesn't come cheap."

Pitt made it easy for him. "So his friends would be others who care about horse-racing?"

"Exactly. And gambling in general. He likes to live well, when he's in town. He spends a while in Cambridgeshire. It's more than a hobby for him. He knows horses better than most men, even in racing circles."

"His friends?"

"The Prince of Wales is the most obvious. And Algernon Naismith-Jones, another lover of horses and gambling in general. Likable fellow, but a bit unreliable as far as money is concerned. Never quite sure whom he owes, and that can make a man erratic. Sod of a thing, owing people money you can't pay, even if the situation is temporary."

Pitt had heard the name before, as a member of the prince's circle. He was liked, if not trusted.

"Others?" he asked.

"Walter Whyte." Carlisle seemed to be turning over his answer in his mind, uncertain how to continue.

Pitt waited, finishing the last of his pâté and taking a sip of the rich dark wine Carlisle had chosen to complement it.

The door was closed and he could not even hear the murmur of conversation beyond.

"Decent chap," Carlisle continued. "Married Lady Felicia Neville — of course Lady Felicia Whyte now. She loathed Halberd. No idea why. Story behind it somewhere, but haven't heard any hint of what it is."

"Guess!" Pitt suggested with a slight smile.

Carlisle raised his eyebrows. "How totally irresponsible of you!" he said with satisfaction. "Moving up in society has done wonders for your sense of humor. Or perhaps I should amend that — your appreciation of the absurd. My guess would be an old affair that ended badly. Lady Felicia was once quite lovely but is not wearing well; time can be cruel to the very fair. Delia Kendrick looks ten years younger and I think they are of an age."

"And acquainted?" Pitt guessed.

"Of course!" Carlisle agreed. "Everyone in society is acquainted with everyone else. At least half of them are related, one way or another. That's possibly why nothing is ever entirely forgotten, good or bad. There's always a cousin or a sister-in-law who will recall it in ghastly detail. And Halberd knew hundreds of people, Naismith-Jones and Whyte included, of course."

"Did he use the information?"

Carlisle pursed his lips. "That's the curious thing. Not that I am aware of. But then, if people know that you know, you don't need to use it. It uses itself."

The next course was served: rack of lamb with spring vegetables. Pitt ate it with less pleasure than it deserved. Everything Carlisle had said suggested someone could have a motive for wishing Halberd to be permanently silent.

"Tell me more about Halberd," he asked after several minutes had passed. "What did he believe? What were his loves, his hates? He seems to have been acquainted with a huge number of people, but who did he like? What did he read? Listen to? Who did he support politically? Or perhaps more important, what did he fight against? He didn't marry — why not? Most men do, and he must have had ample opportunity."

"What did he believe?" Carlisle considered the first question thoughtfully. "Do you know what you believe, Pitt?" He took another mouthful of the lamb, as if he expected Pitt to need some time to weigh his answer, or even evade it altogether.

Pitt did not hesitate. "That without honor and kindness there are no rituals in the world that make any difference," he replied. "The rest is detail. Do whatever seems beautiful or of comfort to you."

Carlisle stopped with his fork halfway to his mouth and very slowly put it down again onto his plate. All levity disappeared from his face.

"I'm sorry. I should have taken you more seriously. Do you believe John Halberd's death was suspicious?"

"I don't know," Pitt admitted. "But I need to find out. If it was, then it matters very much. He seems to have been a man who knew a great many secrets. And when people are frightened, the most surprising ones can become dangerous."

Carlisle thought for a few minutes before replying. "It could be anybody, Pitt. All sorts of people are more than they appear at a glance. Halberd looked like a quiet man with many adventures in the past, now retired to study for its own pleasures, doing a little quiet good here and there as the opportunity arose. Only the occasional remark gave away that he was a man of extraordinary self-control and knowledge of people. I can remember vividly one occasion at a dinner party when someone made a damn silly remark about Africa in general, rather disparaging, actually. Halberd froze. I can still see the expression on his face. He was lean, suntanned. He didn't move, but everything within him altered. He became like a bird of prey that had seen its kill. He did not raise his voice, but in a few words he demolished the man. Then equally quickly, he was benign again. But I did not forget it."

Pitt imagined the scene and understood Carlisle's sense of shock. When he thought of some of the bizarre things that Carlisle himself had done — outrageous, crusading things when he perceived injustice — the fact that Carlisle was startled made Halberd all the more remarkable.

"What do you think he was doing alone in a rowing boat at night?" Pitt asked.

Carlisle's face broke into a broad smile, his eyes lighting. "Trust you to wrong-foot me, Pitt. You would have liked Halberd. You both have the same kind of tenuous idealistic innocence, and the ability to do the unexpected. I have absolutely no idea. Except I doubt very much that it was an assignation of a romantic kind, to put it politely. Nor do I believe he simply wanted to be alone on the water. It will have been to meet someone else who found that a convenient place. It is the only thing that makes sense."

"And that person killed him?" Pitt asked quietly. "And Halberd was caught completely off guard? Doesn't sound like the man you described."

"Or it was an accident," Carlisle said. "And whoever else was there had a pressing reason why they did not report it. Not likely an honorable one, but I suppose it's possible." They were interrupted briefly when the steward brought dessert, and resumed as soon as he had closed the door behind him.

It was Pitt who spoke first. "If Halberd knew something about anyone, would he make use of it against them, if he thought it served a higher purpose?"

"I presume that is what this entire conversation is about?" Carlisle lifted his remarkable eyebrows in an expression that was more amusement than any kind of disapproval. Pitt had never known how to determine Carlisle's exact beliefs. He was as bright, and as hard to pin down, as mercury. The moment you thought you understood him, he had eluded you again.

"Of course," Pitt admitted. "And you didn't answer me as to what he believed."

Carlisle shrugged very slightly. "Because I

hate to have to say that I don't know. He looked like an old-fashioned country gentleman, the sort of adventurer who built the empire, and gave all he had, because it was his nature and his belief to do so. But I have no idea if that was merely how he wished to appear. If it was an act, then it was a good one. So do I know if he used his extraordinary knowledge for his own ends, or even for the love of power? I do not."

Pitt declined brandy after dinner. He thanked Carlisle for an excellent meal, then walked out into the darkened streets and the gas lamps and the clatter of hooves, to find a hansom to take him home, all the while mulling over what he had learned. Had Halberd been the loyal friend the Queen imagined him to be? Or something quite different? Had he finally threatened or blackmailed the wrong person?

A hansom pulled up, and he gave the driver his address and climbed in. The questions haunted him through the lamplit streets.

Knowledge was power, but it was also a razor-edged weapon. The greatest test of all was to have power and yet refrain from using it. It was something few men could do. Sooner or later the mere fact that you could do something drew you to do it, as a precipice draws you to its edge, no matter how deep your sense of vertigo.

Did the Queen understand any of that? Since she was eighteen she had held extraordinary power, with far greater restraint than most people knew. She of all people must understand its lure, and its dangers. Did that mean she thought other people did too? He realized with surprise how much it would hurt him if she was disappointed in Halberd.

If she were young, he would have told her the plain truth, whatever it was. But now? She was vulnerable, facing the same human death as a beggar in the street. In the end death makes no difference, except in the courage with which it is met.

The cab pulled up at Keppel Street. He alighted and paid the driver, then walked up to his own front door, determined to cast all other thoughts aside.

He was sitting in the warm and comfortable kitchen at breakfast the following morning when the post arrived. Among the letters was one addressed to him in a handwriting he was vaguely familiar with, although he could not place it. More curiously than that, it had been delivered by hand.

Charlotte read his expression. "What is

it?" she asked. He gave her a quick smile, then opened the envelope.

It was an invitation to a party that evening, and with it was a quickly scribbled note.

"Might interest you. I suggest if at all possible you come." It was signed by Somerset Carlisle.

"An invitation," he replied. "To a rather grand reception this evening . . ."

"This evening?" she said in dismay. "But there's no time to get ready! Why have they asked you only now?" A sudden bleakness filled her face. "Why am I not included?"

He realized how seldom she had gone out to such an event lately. Long ago, when he was in the regular police, she had been instrumental in solving crimes of passion, greed, or fear in the high society into which she was born and to which he was such a stranger. But now that he was in Special Branch he could tell her almost nothing.

"It's a social event." He looked up at her again. "The note is from Somerset Carlisle." He watched her face, the half belief in her eyes. "I saw him yesterday," he added by way of explanation. "He knows there is going to be someone there I would like to . . . observe. He knows I will bring you."

She waited a moment to see if he would continue. "Oh. I see." She took a breath. "I have only one gown of this season. Will that be appropriate?"

He scrambled in his memory to think what it was. Charlotte was one of those rare women whose true beauty increased with age, as other women's began to fade. She was now just over forty, and the poise granted by maturity, and the confidence in her wisdom and humor, became her. Perhaps Pitt was the only person who knew she was still vulnerable beneath it.

"It will do very well. It is very becoming."

She gave a little laugh. "You can't remember it! But if you liked it, that's all that matters. What time do you wish to be ready?"

He glanced at the invitation. "Seven will be good," he replied.

Pitt spent much of the day at his office in Lisson Grove attending to urgent cases. There were reports of attempted sabotage and one rather awkward matter involving a foreign diplomat whose association with anarchists needed to be much more closely investigated. He had little time to consider the unfortunate and possibly embarrassing circumstances of the death of John Halberd, and whether there had been any crime in it. He did not want to accept that it was a rather juvenile assignation gone wrong, because even in so short a time he had gained much respect for the man. But it did look very much like that was the case, and it had not been reported at the time in order to save reputations. He did not want to have to tell that to the Queen. She had trusted Halberd, and Pitt was quite sure she had liked him. It was a shabby and rather absurd way to die.

But he had some time before he needed to speak to her again. She was worried that the Prince of Wales, charming and affable, dissolute in his ways, was not being wisely counseled by Alan Kendrick. Did it really matter, except to her? The prince was extremely good at the diplomatic work he did. His visits to Canada and the United States of America had improved relations there. His easy nature and clear enjoyment of life had endeared him to both the leaders and the public in general.

He had accomplished even more in Europe, in Germany, and, most particularly, in France, the centuries-long enemy of Britain. He loved their way of life, their appreciation of good food, good wine, good laughter. And in return they loved him. He spoke both French and German fluently.

And, of course, he was related to all the royal houses of Europe. Half the kings and emperors were part of his immediate family.

What earthly difference did Alan Kendrick make? The Prince of Wales, surely very soon to be king, would do exactly what he wanted.

Of course, when he became king he would have access to papers of state that it was rumored the queen had denied him so far. Did that matter?

There was no choice but to find out at least a little more about Kendrick. It was not only Pitt's wish to satisfy the Queen's anxieties; it was his job to know if Kendrick represented any future threat to the safety of the man who would become Edward VII, and therefore a threat to the state.

The reception was held at the home of Lord Harborough, in York Place, just off Regent's Park. Pitt and Charlotte arrived fashionably late, which meant not so early as to seem too eager, and not late enough to appear rude — or even worse, desperate to be seen to make an entrance.

It was a much more formal affair than Pitt had expected. Liveried footmen served champagne. The room shimmered with color: silk dresses in rich shades of plum, peach, and gold. The light from the chandeliers glanced off diamonds in hair, around slender throats, and hanging from earlobes. The evening black of so many men made the contrast even more dramatic. One or two wore scarlet or blue sashes across one shoulder, with orders of this or that distinction.

Pitt heard Charlotte's quick intake of breath and turned to look at her. It was enough to see the delight on her face at the splendor of the party and to wonder with a stab of regret how much she had missed such events in recent years.

If she had married someone of her own social rank, these things would have been commonplace.

He felt the pressure of her hand on his arm. It was an understanding. This was fun, but it was also business. She would not ask what Pitt needed to do there. He wished profoundly that he could have told her, but to do so would be to let them both down. She expected better of him.

Almost immediately they became part of the crowd. Pitt did not see Carlisle, and perhaps he was not even present, but he knew that Kendrick would be. Carlisle must have gone to some trouble to engineer the invitation at such very short notice.

Within minutes he noticed a tall woman with exquisite flaxen hair piled upon her head like a crown. In its beauty a tiara would have seemed superfluous. Only when he was closer to her did he notice that she was older than he had first thought. Her pale skin, fine as porcelain, was marked with lines — not gentle ones of laughter, but down-dragging ones of disappointment. Carlisle's description of Lady Felicia Whyte came back to him. Time had been unkind. Except that it was not really an unkindness, but time's cutting honesty. Every wound of the spirit was there.

She was staring at Pitt. Should he have recognized her? Charlotte was watching him.

Was this woman the hostess, wondering who he was and knowing that she had not invited him? He must say something.

"I beg your pardon for staring, ma'am," he said, "but I have never seen such beautiful hair."

She drew in a quick breath and the color rose in her face. She attempted to conceal her pleasure, and failed utterly.

He inclined his head. "Thomas Pitt," he introduced himself. "And Mrs. Pitt," he added.

"How do you do, Mr. Pitt?" she replied, smiling at Charlotte but not addressing her directly. "I am delighted you could come this evening. I am Lady Felicia Whyte. Our host, Lord Harborough, is my brother-in-law. But I daresay you know." It was not quite a question. She was attempting to find out if Pitt had been invited. She could not place him.

"So generous of you to make us welcome," Charlotte said warmly. "My sister has spoken so kindly of you. Her husband is Jack Radley." She let it hang in the air, with whatever suggestion one cared to draw from it.

Lady Felicia chose to take it as a compliment, and returned the smile. The next moment conversation proceeded on the usual themes of well-mannered people who did not know one another: the current social news, theater, recent books, places one might have visited. Charlotte was willing to listen, agree, and admire. Pitt knew how unnatural that was to her these days, but she fell into it as easily as if it had been only a matter of weeks since the last such party and it was mere coincidence that she did not know these people.

Pitt watched with curiosity and a degree of respect as she subtly flattered Felicia Whyte without for a moment losing her own dignity. Felicia seemed quite unaware of it. Or perhaps receiving compliments well was part of her own skill?

Within twenty minutes Pitt contrived to meet Walter Whyte, Felicia's husband and one of the men Carlisle had mentioned that Halberd had known well. Pitt was startled by how unlike his image of him Whyte was in the flesh. There was nothing remarkable in his appearance until he smiled; then perfect teeth and a vivid natural warmth made him extraordinary. He shook Pitt's hand with a strong grasp, then let it go immediately.

"Glad you could come," he said warmly. "Carlisle said you grew up on Arthur Desmond's land, or somewhere near it? Excellent man." He was either tactful enough not to add any more, or he already knew and might be waiting to catch Pitt in a self-protective lie.

Earlier in his career Pitt might well have explained that Sir Arthur had taken pity on him as a fatherless boy and used his enthusiasm to learn as a spur to urge on his own son, who was a highly unwilling student. But Pitt had decided not to offer unasked-for explanations. He recognized it as defensive in others; now he saw it in himself too.

"Indeed," Pitt said sincerely. "A beautiful part of the country. Do you know it well?"

"Not as well as I'd like to," Whyte answered a little ruefully. "Spent too much time abroad."

"Then we envy each other," Pitt said with a smile, noting incidentally that Charlotte was a few yards away now, and appearing to listen to another conversation. "Where?"

"All over the world. Mostly Africa. Marvelous place. So much of it still unknown. Thank God there is still somewhere left to explore!" Whyte said it with a sudden burst of feeling, then the moment after realized that he had laid an emotion bare within himself, and did not know how to conceal it again.

Pitt was tempted to probe this a little, but instead he moved the subject on as if quite naturally. "Well, there are still the North and South Poles. But I imagine they have little cultural history to offer. No great kingdoms, or races we hardly imagine, who built cities and created art when we were barely out of caves."

Whyte gave one of his sudden, dazzling smiles. "What an odd fellow you are. You would have liked John Halberd. He was an odd fellow too, full of sudden twists and turns, and a love of knowledge of every kind, from the habits of beetles to the patterns of the stars." Sudden grief filled his face. "Unfortunately he's dead, poor devil."

"Boating accident, I heard," Pitt replied as casually as he could. "You knew him?"

"As much as anyone did," Whyte replied. "He appeared to be completely open, but actually he was more like those Egyptian tombs where the doors are hidden and you have no idea there is anything but a blank wall."

"Then what makes you think there is anything?" Pitt asked innocently.

"Looking for hidden tombs?" Whyte raised his eyebrows. "Measurements. Space unaccounted for. Inside and outside don't match."

Pitt met his eyes, which were very blue, and wondered how many layers this conversation possessed. Did Whyte know perfectly well who Pitt was?

"And you think Halberd had some space unaccounted for?" he asked curiously.

"I'm damn sure he did," Whyte replied. "Part of what I liked about him."

"And the other parts?"

Whyte stared at him. "He understood what mattered, and what didn't," he replied. "And how to keep a secret, if it needed to be kept." He signaled discreetly to a passing waiter. "I say, you don't have a drink. Let me offer you some champagne."

Pitt accepted it as if he were delighted.

Actually, he did not like champagne; he greatly favored a good cider. If he was to have wine, he preferred red. He loved the rich aroma of it.

A few moments later Whyte introduced Pitt to Algernon Naismith-Jones, another agreeable-looking man of easy charm, whom Halberd had also known. He greeted Pitt as if they had only just missed meeting each other for years, and were making up now for the omission. He had a large, sprawling estate in Cambridgeshire and an indeterminate number of children and stepchildren, whom he spoke of with affection. However, his deepest interest was horses.

"Wonderful creatures," he said, enthusiasm lighting his face. "Nothing nobler in the world than a good horse! My God, Walter, did you see that filly in the last race at Newmarket on Saturday? What a gorgeous creature. Looking up her lineage. Something damn special there!" He turned to Pitt. "Know anything about horses? Yes, of course you do. Can't come from your neck of the woods and not care, what!"

"Caring and knowing are not the same thing," Pitt replied, trying not to sound too guarded.

Naismith-Jones gave a great gust of laughter. "Well said! Indeed they aren't. Hey! Kendrick!" He turned toward an elegant man with thick brown hair and a handsome face. "Come and meet Pitt here." He gestured with his arm. "Alan Kendrick. Here's a man who knows horses!"

Kendrick smiled but did not offer his hand. Closer to, his face was more interesting than merely handsome. The impression of good looks was added to by the intelligence in his eyes, but marred by a certain insensitivity in the line of his mouth.

"How do you do?" Pitt nodded to him.

"So you are interested in horses," Kendrick observed.

"I respect them," Pitt replied levelly. He was not going to be caught pretending a skill he did not have.

"An odd choice of word," Kendrick said, looking at Pitt more closely. Clearly the answer had surprised him, something he was not used to.

"I respect a man who can do something I aspire to." It was an opportunity to engage that Pitt should not ignore. "I respect any man, or animal, that does supremely well what it is designed to do," he explained. "The only horses I know are the shire horses, the Clydesdales. I worked with them as a young man. Racehorses I have seen only at a distance."

"You worked with horses?" Kendrick looked Pitt up and down. "And here you are at His Lordship's reception. How times change." His face was quite bland. It was impossible to tell if the remark was merely clumsy or if he intended the insult.

Pitt chose to engage. "They do indeed." He smiled back. "Something like a wheel, up one year, perhaps down the next. Its infinite variety is part of its charm."

"That was Cleopatra," Kendrick said with an edge to his voice. "And as I recall she ended rather badly."

"I was not quoting Shakespeare," Pitt corrected him. "It is so easy to get a word or a reference mistaken and make a fool of oneself."

Kendrick drew in his breath, then changed his mind. He returned the bland look, as if retreating a step. He turned to another man who had joined them. "Ferdie, come and meet Pitt, a man who respects horses." He gestured toward Pitt. "Ferdie Warburton. Not half such an ass as he pretends to be." He turned back to Warburton. "No idea who Pitt is, but he's a man who respects horses, and that should be enough for anyone."

Warburton was pleasant-looking in a

casual, slightly ruffled sort of way, as if making an effort would be too much bother. He smiled easily, offering his hand.

The conversation became general, and Pitt was having to listen far more than speak. The subject moved from horses to Africa to the latest European politics. Gradually he became aware that Kendrick also was listening. His only remarks were to spur others into declaring their opinions.

The unpleasantness began when Lady Felicia joined them. It was clear from the outset that she did not like Kendrick.

"Nice to see you in town for a change," she remarked to Kendrick, her eyebrows raised a little. "The prince not visiting your stables lately?" She turned immediately to Naismith-Jones. "And you, Algernon, always make the company a little lighter."

He gave her a quick smile that was bright and empty. "Thank you."

As if unintentionally, the conversation moved back to racing and upcoming major events.

"Think you'll run again?" Lady Felicia asked Kendrick. She was smiling but it was clearly out of amusement, not friendship. "That would please His Royal Highness."

"I'm surprised you still know so well what pleases him," Kendrick responded softly.

She stared straight back at him, but the color was high in her alabaster cheeks. She looked him up and down with an expression exactly like Kendrick's as he had looked at Pitt.

"Has he changed all that much, Alan? I don't believe it." Her eyes did not waver. "Ask Delia!" She gave a tiny shrug, an excellent and dismissive gesture. "Mr. Pitt." She held out one hand. "Come and tell me about the kind of horses you like. As long as they don't race . . . and lose."

Kendrick looked at her with an intensity that should have frightened her; then it was gone. Lady Felicia took Pitt's arm, and he was obliged to turn away.

Chapter 3

Sitting in the carriage on the way home, Charlotte was thoughtful. She had not really enjoyed the reception. She had known from the beginning that it was a professional occasion for Pitt rather than a social one. The invitation had been arranged by Somerset Carlisle at the shortest possible notice. She had looked at the note as soon as Pitt had left that morning. She knew Carlisle only slightly, and she liked him. He was amusing, unpredictable, and brave. But he had always been connected with mystery of the darkest sort, and usually violence as well. He was a man of passions, which he wore lightly, but they led him to crusade, at any risk, against what he saw as wrong. Very often he did it alone. He espoused the causes others disagreed with, or thought too dangerous or too unlikely to be won. That was partly why she liked him, and a good deal why he charmed her.

Whatever Pitt was doing must be desperate for him to have enlisted Carlisle's help. That was the part that alarmed her.

She had not asked Pitt about it, since she knew that if he could have told her, he would have. To put him in the position of having to refuse her would only hurt them both. It was clear from his preoccupation, and everything else in his manner, that whatever this business was, it troubled him. He did not enjoy formal society engagements, and yet he had leaped at the chance to go. He did not even complain about having to wear a dinner suit of immaculate black and a starched shirt. Even though he looked very distinguished, he felt out of place. The very fact that he did not try to evade going was enough to make her certain that he had no choice.

She had watched him carefully. If she could not help him openly, then she would do so without his knowledge. She had lost touch with who was important in society lately, or why: who loved or hated whom; who owed or wanted something. She would have to pay a great deal of attention and try to recall the skills she'd had in her single days, and a few she had still practiced when Pitt was a regular policeman.

Charlotte had entered the party on Pitt's

arm, but not fought against their separation when courtesy required it. She knew that he was unlikely to do whatever he had come for with her beside him. Also, she wanted to watch, observe, see the unspoken emotions that are betrayed by the expressions on faces, the angles of the body, the tensions that people themselves were unaware of.

Was Lady Felicia Whyte of any importance? She certainly had the air of a woman who thought she was in danger of losing the place she felt was her right. There was an edge to her voice, a stiffness in the way she moved. Watching her through the evening, Charlotte saw the hard lines appear on her face now and then, just fleetingly, before she mastered them. But never did she see her at ease, even when her husband stood beside her. Once he reached out, as if to touch her, then changed his mind.

She looked at Pitt as their hansom passed under a streetlamp and the light illuminated his features for a moment. He was deep in thought, unaware of her. Now it was she who reached out to lay her hand on his sleeve, and then changed her mind. He could not tell her anything — that she already knew. She was being childish merely wanting him to talk to her.

A few moments later they reached Keppel

Street and the hansom pulled up at the curb. Pitt came to attention with a sudden awareness, climbed out, paid the driver, then helped Charlotte to alight with grace. Together they went to the front door. He unlocked it and they went inside. The late summer evening was chill. Daniel and Jemima would be in bed, almost certainly asleep. The maid, Minnie Maude, had left the hall gas lamp on, burning low. The gleam of light on polished wood and the faint smell of lavender polish was comforting, like the smile of a friend.

"Thank you," Pitt said quietly to Charlotte. "It cannot have been much fun for you."

She wondered whether to say that it had been but decided to preserve the honesty that was so precious between them. "It had its pleasures," she said simply. "But it's nice to be home."

Pitt turned the one gas bracket even lower, barely a glow. Charlotte led the way upstairs, stopping on the landing to very quietly open the door of eighteen-year-old Jemima's room. She stood for a moment listening to the quiet breathing, then closed the door again. She did the same with fourteen-year-old Daniel. He stirred very slightly but did not awaken. She did it out of habit. She had not expected anything different, yet could not rest until she had assured herself. All was well. Still, she remained awake later wondering why Pitt had gone to the reception at Lord Harborough's house, and why Carlisle had arranged it so precipitately. Who had Pitt gone to see?

The only person she had noticed him deliberately approach was Alan Kendrick. From the expression on Felicia Whyte's face, there had been a very sharp exchange between Kendrick and herself. It appeared sudden, but such emotion does not arise out of nowhere. They knew and disliked each other. Several times after that she had noticed Pitt looking at Kendrick. He had done it discreetly, but she knew him too well to mistake it for chance. Perhaps she should learn more about Kendrick.

Normally she would have been quite frank about it and asked Aunt Vespasia. But then, so would Pitt, were Vespasia in London. Perhaps there was no choice but to go to her younger sister, Emily? But discreetly, without telling her anything, if such a thing was possible? She only asked Emily's assistance when it was absolutely necessary.

Emily's first marriage had made her Lady Ashworth, and extremely wealthy. When George had died — or, more exactly, been killed — Emily had remained a widow for a while, then married Jack Radley, a charming and handsome man who had done little with his life up to that point. He had since become a member of Parliament, and was gaining a reputation of some value. Charlotte was not unaware of how hard he had worked at that, even if he pretended that it came easily.

Emily was still the delightful, highly skilled, and observant lady of society that she had always been. But she was bored with that and looking for some of the old adventures.

Accordingly Charlotte called upon Emily a little after ten o'clock the following morning. It was not a suitable hour for a visit, but she chose it in order to have a better chance of finding Emily at home and not yet receiving anyone else. She was fortunate to succeed.

Emily's house was far larger than her own, but Charlotte had long ago become accustomed to it. Her own house in Keppel Street was perfectly comfortable, and filled with memories, almost all of them happy in one way or another.

Emily had a very different life — wealthy, glamorous, but without the danger or victories of Charlotte's. Charlotte would not have exchanged her life for anyone else's. She knew there were certainly times when Emily would have.

The maid showed her up to Emily's boudoir. This was not a bedroom but a smaller and very much more feminine and personal sitting room upstairs off the main landing. It was decorated in muted shades of cream and pink and gold, lots of florals, cushions like giant heaps of roses — an undisciplined side of Emily she showed hardly anyone else. The chairs were extraordinarily comfortable. There were books chosen for interest and pleasure on every shelf of the case — lots of novels, several collections of poetry, and scrapbooks she had made . . . and never looked at since. Three separate bowls of flowers sat on tables: roses in golden yellow; irises, their dark purple giving form and shape to more complicated arrangements.

Emily was a couple of years younger than Charlotte, just reaching forty, with no gray visible in her lovely hair. But then, as fair as it was, the gray probably would not show for years. She was dressed in pale green, the color that flattered her most.

She came forward, her face alight with pleasure, and gave Charlotte a quick hug.

Then she regarded her more closely, and with interest.

"Something has happened," she observed. "A concern, but not a disaster, at least not yet." It was comforting to be known and understood without explanation. It was also disconcerting to be read at a glance so accurately. But Charlotte had seldom been able to hide her emotions for very long.

"As usual, you are right." She sat down in her favorite chair, and Emily sat on the one opposite her. "There are some people I would like to know more about."

"A case of Thomas's," Emily deduced. "I suppose you can't tell me about it. I find these secret matters such a bore." She gave a slight shrug. It was an elegant, very feminine gesture. "It used to be so exciting. Who is it?"

"I saw them yesterday evening. Alan Kendrick and his wife, and Lady Felicia Whyte and her husband," Charlotte replied. "And, of course, their circle in general."

"Why?"

"I don't know! That's why I need to know more." Charlotte felt that was a very reasonable explanation. Regardless, it was the only one she had.

"You are detecting behind Thomas's back," Emily concluded.

Charlotte bit her lip and moved uncomfortably on the soft, embracing chair. "Not . . . detecting, just learning a little more. Being prepared . . ."

"Then I will be prepared with you," Emily responded. "Give me an hour or two and I will find out where we should go. I presume you want to begin as soon as possible?"

"Yes, please." Charlotte hesitated. Should she say more? Emily was obviously waiting. Could she trust her discretion?

Emily continued to wait, but the brightness slowly faded in her eyes.

Charlotte took the risk. "Somebody important died. Watching Thomas yesterday evening, I think that may be what he is concerned with . . ."

Emily's fair eyebrows went up. "Died? Do you mean was killed? Who?"

"An accident on the river," Charlotte answered.

"Oh! You don't mean Sir John Halberd, do you?"

Charlotte was taken aback, but perhaps she should not have been. She sometimes forgot how wide Emily's acquaintance was. "You knew him?"

"I met him a couple of times." Emily's voice dropped with a note of dismay. "I liked him."

"Why?" That came out more abruptly than Charlotte had intended, but it was a relevant question. Everything about Halberd mattered now.

Emily must have appreciated that because she answered without arguing, just a moment's hesitation for thought. "There was something very direct about him. He seemed never to play for effect. Society is so full of . . . posing. But I do think he was much cleverer than some people thought. I was surprised that he should die in an accident, and on the Serpentine, of all places. It just doesn't seem like . . . who he was. But I suppose many of us are not what we seem. I would hate to be as light and uncomplicated as some people assume I am. Nothing to me but the latest fashion, and a few predictable causes. Does Thomas think Sir John was murdered?"

Charlotte heard the sadness beneath the words, and she understood perfectly. She had glimpsed that void herself. But this was not the time to acknowledge it. Now, at least, they had a purpose.

She answered more gently. "I don't know. I don't know anything except that Thomas went to a party last evening, at very short notice, and met people he would never normally wish to meet. He hates dressing up, then standing around talking about nothing much, except where people have been and who they met."

There was a bleak look in Emily's face for an instant, almost a sense of fear, as if she were lost; then it vanished.

"It isn't what is said. It's the tone of voice, and all the things that are left out. Have you forgotten so quickly?"

Charlotte did not bother to answer. "Can you help?"

"Of course. There is a garden party tomorrow afternoon." Emily pursed her lips thoughtfully. "It will be high fashion. You had better borrow something from Aunt Vespasia. It may not suit you, since you are of such different coloring, but nobody will be able to find fault with your style."

"Aunt Vespasia is in Europe."

"Oh, yes, of course. Never mind. Her maid will find you something, if you explain the need to her. Her name is Gwen."

"I know. Aunt Vespasia calls all her maids Gwen, regardless of what their names really are. I don't think they mind."

"Borrow the dress anyway. I'll let you know about the party. Now I must begin." Emily stood up, suddenly alive with purpose.

■ ■ ■ ■

Charlotte felt rather self-conscious wearing one of Aunt Vespasia's gowns, in spite of the fact that it fit her well and was exactly the right length. It was a shade of deep, warm ivory she had never dared to wear before, and she was not certain it became her. It was clearly expensive and in the very height of fashion. Its style all lay in the cut of the shoulders and the fall of the very slight fullness at the back. It was extraordinarily lovely. She hoped Vespasia had not been saving it for a special occasion. She had asked, and Gwen had assured her that was not the case.

She straightened her shoulders and reminded herself that a man Pitt was concerned with had died, and she knew from a dozen little signs that he was worried about it. Nothing trivial would have taken him to the reception two days ago — or kept him awake last night. She knew it every time she had stirred; and even when half asleep herself, she was aware of his restlessness.

Now she crossed the pavement beside Emily and entered under a garlanded gateway into a large, formal garden with lawns, its flight of shallow stone steps flanked by huge stone urns with scarlet and orange nasturtiums trailing over their edges. Lush herbaceous borders were filled with spires of lupines in full bloom and splendid, gaudy poppies.

"Looks like an army, carrying its spears and banners aloft," she murmured to Emily.

"Doesn't it!" Emily agreed. "Prepare for war! Enemy approaching from the left!"

Their hostess welcomed them, skillfully hiding the fact that she had no idea who Charlotte was, but her wide, rather pale blue eyes reflected unmistakable admiration for the gown.

Charlotte felt herself blush, praying it was not also recognition of it. On the other hand, if Vespasia had not worn it yet, how was Charlotte going to explain wearing it before its owner had had the chance? But there was no time now for such considerations. She banished it from her mind, smiled with all the charm she could manage, and allowed herself to be introduced to the first group of women.

For several minutes the conversation was polite and meaningless. Then a stout woman in a floral dress glanced sideways and Charlotte could see Lady Felicia Whyte talking to one of the few men present.

"I used to envy her so much," the woman said with a smile. "He had such an air about him. So dashing, Major Whyte, don't you think?"

"I thought him rather quiet," her friend in green replied. Then she lowered her voice conspiratorially. "I think something happened. But of course I have no idea what . . ."

"Some dark adventure," her companion said in a whisper. "Sometimes I think safety is so tedious . . ."

Charlotte shivered. So easily did gossip begin. Like a hat pin plunged between the ribs, she thought. You don't even feel it at the time; only afterward do you wonder where the blood came from.

"You know who would tell you?" Emily said with an unreadable expression in her face. "Sir John Halberd. He has the air of knowing everything about everybody. I find him fascinating. So polite, and says everything, and when you come to think of it afterward, he told you nothing at all."

"Oh dear," the first woman said in dismay. "Didn't you know? The poor man died a couple of weeks ago . . ."

"Oh no!" Emily gasped, putting on a mask of shock. "What happened?"

"Apparently he drowned . . ."

Charlotte bit her tongue to stop her first reaction. She dared not meet Emily's eyes. "Where? I didn't hear of a boat going down," she said innocently.

"It was hardly a . . . a major sinking . . ." the floral woman answered.

"You can't sink very far on the edge of the Serpentine," her friend said a trifle waspishly. "Not literally, anyway." Charlotte looked at her with interest. She was a handsome woman in a lean way, marred at the moment by a flicker of malice in her eyes.

"Do you mean morally?" Charlotte asked, then wondered if she had been too direct. "I always think of little boys playing with sailing boats. Sort of Sunday afternoon thing to do."

The woman stared at her as if she had noticed her for the first time.

"I beg your pardon?" Her tone dared Charlotte to respond.

"If not literally, then in some other way," Charlotte said with a sweet smile. "One may drown in several senses of the word."

The woman was not deterred. "Are you suggesting he was morally . . . lost?" she said with incredulity.

"Is that fatal?" Charlotte was not going to be beaten so easily. She just managed to keep the edge of laughter out of her voice, and sound innocent.

Now everyone was watching, waiting for the next response. Emily moved a little closer to Charlotte, in a tacit mark of loyalty.

"Lots of things can be fatal — at least to your reputation in society," the woman answered. It was clearly meant as a warning.

Charlotte did not alter her expression in the slightest. "And it would seem that boating on the Serpentine is one of them."

The woman hesitated this time before lifting her chin a little and replying, "I still think very highly of him." She closed her mouth in a hard line.

"I gather that," Charlotte said meekly.

There was a titter of laughter, stifled quickly.

"I wish I had known him," Charlotte added. "He seems to have been remarkable."

"You have a taste for night boating on the Serpentine?" the lean woman retorted, this time instantly.

Charlotte knew exactly what she meant. It was a not very subtle suggestion that she conducted a string of affairs behind her husband's back. Night boating, after the manner of Halberd, was going to become a standing joke.

Charlotte opened her eyes very wide. "Is it fun?" This time the laughter was less well concealed.

Quite a few people conducted affairs of one degree of seriousness or another; it was just not mentioned, for one's own protection. The façade was too valuable to be broken. Certainty took some of the entertainment out of speculation.

It was Emily who changed the subject, and then decided it was imperative that she introduce Charlotte to Lady Something-or-other.

"You are outrageous!" she told Charlotte with satisfaction as they moved past the bed of lupines and began up the shallow steps. "Nothing new to learn of Halberd's death here, maybe?"

"It was Alan Kendrick whom Thomas seemed interested in at Lord Harborough's." They were passing a large urn of geraniums in hot pinks, the scent of them sharp. Bees hovered around, a mass of blue flowers sprawling across the edge of the steps above.

"I don't think Delia Kendrick is here," Emily answered very quietly, at the same time nodding and smiling to an acquaintance coming down the steps. "We will have to find another party for you to shine at. I don't know whether to tell everyone you are my sister — or no one at all."

"No one at all," Charlotte said immediately. "Because I don't promise to behave graciously. I have to learn what I can. Aunt Vespasia knows everyone, but she's probably crossing the Alps, or on the Orient Express, or on an island in the Aegean. I miss her."

Emily tightened her hand on Charlotte's arm. "I know. But we will just have to manage by ourselves. We could try Felicia."

"I met her briefly at the reception," said Charlotte. "I find it hard to decide exactly how old she is. She has the figure of a woman much younger than sixty, yet —"

"Never say that!" Emily grasped Charlotte's hand. "She's only just passed fifty. Or are you being deliberately . . ." She let out her breath. "You're right. She's not wearing so well . . . the fine skin . . . oh, buckets of mud! Am I going to do that? Look sixty and be only fifty, do you think?"

Charlotte understood Emily's fear. She had seen it before, and it was real and painful. Beauty mattered far more than it should. But she had no time for it now. "Ask Aunt Vespasia what she does, because she still looks marvelous," she advised. "Instead of watching her when she enters a room, watch everybody else admiring her. You'll see. Does Felicia care?"

Emily considered for a moment. "Yes, I think she does," she answered as they left the steps behind and reached the shade of a huge elm tree soaring into the sky, leaves whispering in the slight wind. "She is afraid of something, and that may be it. Her mother was beautiful too, in the same way, and she lost her looks comparatively young. I don't know what happened to her. When I first stepped into really high society" — her voice dropped — "with George . . ." She took a sharp little breath. "It seems like ages ago. Felicia's mother, I think she was the Countess of something. But she was lovely, and at almost every party or ball. Then in the space of only a few years she seemed to age, and then to forget things. Then we didn't see her anymore."

Charlotte tried to imagine it and found it both painful and frightening. What happened that someone lost everything, lost themselves, in the space of a very few years? It would not be surprising if Felicia feared that the same might happen to her. Charlotte felt that she would, in her place. In fact, her first thought was to picture their own mother, Caroline, strong and vigorous. A few years after Edward Ellison's death, comparatively young, Caroline had met an actor, of all things, younger than herself, and married him. She had embarked on a new life, full of adventures, and delighted in it.

Charlotte was happy for her mother, but she realized with surprise how much she was also happy for herself in the thought of it. Suddenly she felt quite differently toward Felicia Whyte, and ashamed of herself too. How easily she leaped to an emotional conclusion, when she knew nothing.

Emily was waiting for her to respond. Clearly, from the concentration in her face, her mind was following a different train of thought.

"How sad," Charlotte said gently. "For how many people does fear of the future take away the present as well?"

"Too many," Emily answered. "Do you want to meet again, or not?"

"Of course."

This next encounter was different. Charlotte knew she was reacting to the story of Felicia's mother, and what she imagined her own reaction might be, were it her life. How would she behave if she could see in her mind a time when she would age too much, and Pitt too little? What would be different between them? Social things, of course;

their value in other people's eyes. But what about more personal things as well, too precious and too private to speak of to anyone else?

"Good afternoon, Mrs. . . . er . . . Pitt." Felicia had nearly forgotten her name in two days — but then, Charlotte was of no importance in the social scene.

"Good afternoon, Lady Felicia." Charlotte smiled warmly. "What a perfect way to see the very best of it." She glanced at the blaze of flowers in the sun. "Do I have you to thank for this also?"

Felicia hesitated, then decided to accept. "I may have dropped a word or two," she conceded. "It is always interesting to get a new perspective on . . . things . . . It can all become so tedious, after a while." She gave a characteristic, elegant shrug.

"I find many things fascinating," Charlotte said, taking her chance when the slightest opportunity offered itself.

"Really?" Felicia obviously did not believe her — but then, it would be a terrible gaffe to actually say so. "Have you been abroad for a while?" It was the only explanation she could think of.

Charlotte thought rapidly. She had dug herself a hole. She needed to climb out of it with some degree of style. "Sometimes it felt like it," she replied. "I had forgotten how much interesting undercurrent there is in even the most charming occasion. Don't you agree? So much more is meant than is ever put into words. For example, the emotion behind people's comments on the most unfortunate and rather odd death of Sir John Halberd."

Felicia was plainly startled.

Charlotte wondered if she had gone too far. Pitt would be furious, and she had no excuse to give him. Then she remembered how restless he had been most of the night. He must be far more worried than he could tell her, and he could not even turn to Lord Narraway, Vespasia's husband, who had held the position in Special Branch before Pitt. Vespasia herself seemed to know so much that she would often guess what Pitt could not ask her, and tell him anyway. Charlotte realized how excluded she herself had been, by necessity. Pitt could not place her in danger by telling her what she should not know, or jeopardize his own position, on which all their well-being rested.

She remembered with a chill how frightening it had been when he was dismissed from the police, due to a conspiracy against him. Suddenly they'd faced being homeless and worrying about the next month's — even the next week's — security. For Pitt the worst feeling was not the fear of poverty or hardship, but guilt. She had hated that. He had seemed so vulnerable, although he had tried to conceal it, to protect her. Protection was the last thing she had wanted. She had felt not only more frightened, but shut out of his pain, and that was the hardest of all: the loneliness.

She had to do this. What was a little embarrassment, when the alternative was so much worse?

"Of course, they will be wondering why on earth he was in a rowing boat on the Serpentine after dark," she said clearly.

Felicia smiled and suddenly there was a real warmth to it. "I was wondering if he was really alone," she replied very softly. "I rather hope he was. He was a dangerous man, in some ways. He knew so much about so many people. I would rather believe it was an idiotic accident than that someone deliberately . . . let him drown."

Charlotte looked as regretful as she could, and spoke very quietly.

"Do you mean that someone deliberately stood by and watched him drown . . . or actually caused the accident?"

Felicia drew in her breath sharply. "Oh . . . I didn't think I meant that . . . But I suppose I do. That's terrible. I think perhaps I meant that someone else panicked. If it was someone who couldn't admit to having been there, then that might be . . . understandable."

"I suppose it would," Charlotte agreed. "If it was . . . shall we say, a woman of the night, she could have panicked."

Felicia stared straight at her. "Or a married woman, perhaps of his own social class. Then she would very definitely wish profoundly to not be seen. Whatever you said, everybody would believe that you were there for the least creditable of reasons. Whatever the truth, that would be the assumption."

Charlotte's mind raced. Was Felicia speaking of herself? A last affair with a magnetic older man, to prove to herself that she was still beautiful? It was not impossible to understand.

"Of course you are right," Charlotte agreed again. "What an appalling position to be in! And I suppose it might not have been for that reason at all."

Felicia waited.

Charlotte was not certain how to phrase the alternative she had been thinking. Emily filled the breach for her.

"Well, he did, apparently, know a great deal about very many people. So far as I know, he was always discreet. But perhaps some people, at least, made it worth his while to remain so."

"Oh dear. Of course," Felicia agreed. "How stupid of me not to think of blackmail. There is so much over which a person could be blackmailed, one way or another."

Charlotte's surprise must have been plainer than she intended.

"Oh, not necessarily a crime," Felicia said with dry, rather harsh amusement. "Life is full of indiscretions, at least a life of any interest is. And it isn't just that no one should know, or does know. It's that the wrong people shouldn't."

Charlotte's mind was teeming with ideas. Felicia mistook her silence for doubt.

"My dear, it isn't even what actually happened — or didn't happen, for that matter — it's what one makes of it."

Charlotte remained silent, in the hope that Felicia would continue.

Felicia glanced around, and lowered her voice a little. "Take Delia Kendrick, for example. She wasn't Kendrick's first choice, you know?" She raised her eyebrows a little. Charlotte's look of total incomprehension satisfied her. "He courted Arabella Nash, daughter of the Duchess of Lansdowne. Everyone thought they would marry. But they didn't. Of course it was said that she declined. But they always say that. A man never says he found out something about her. True or not, he would be socially ruined."

"And people assumed she had . . ." Charlotte left the sentence unfinished; the rest was not necessary.

"Naturally," Felicia agreed. "He was hell-bent on marrying her. A tremendous step up for him. He was clever enough, and most agreeable-looking, but came from nowhere! We all knew he would make money, of course, but that isn't the same thing. New money, and all that. It doesn't do . . . not socially."

"But he left her anyway?" Charlotte said with surprise.

"Not at all," Felicia answered impatiently. "The duchess cut off the relationship. New money wasn't good enough for her, when Arabella had the offer of a title. She's Marchioness of Something-or-other now. And not a penny to bless herself with, except what she brought with her."

"How very foolish," Charlotte said impulsively, then wished she had not. She saw Felicia's amusement.

"Not really," Felicia replied. "Delia is far more of a match for him. Even if he wasn't her first choice either."

Charlotte said nothing.

"Married before," Felicia explained. "Her first husband died in the oddest circumstances. Nobody seems to know what really happened. As I said, only the most colorless people have nothing in their lives they would prefer not discussed. Nothing *to* discuss, I suppose . . ."

"Or else they have kept it rather better hidden," Charlotte suggested. "Did Sir John Halberd really know more than other people?"

An expression crossed Felicia's face — a mixture of pain and anticipation — that was too complicated to read. "My husband was very fond of him. They both spent time in Africa. Up the Nile, you know. They are not memories you can share with everyone. Too many people haven't the faintest idea what the realities are, only romantic dreams. Walter would have found it painful to discover that Halberd was a blackmailer." She stopped abruptly.

Charlotte realized with a stab of pity that it had just occurred to Felicia that she had unwittingly given her husband an excellent motive for having made sure of Halberd's silence. Charlotte was certain from the stunned look in Felicia's eyes that it was unintentional. There was fear in her face now — fear of confusion, of betrayal, perhaps above all of loneliness.

"Why on earth would he hire a boat for such a thing?" Charlotte asked. "Surely a walk in the park would have been simpler, and far more discreet? It is much more likely it was an assignation that went wrong. One might very well use a boat for that!"

Relief flooded Felicia's face. She was probably not aware of how clear it was to see.

"Of course," she agreed. "Yes, of course. Let us talk of something more pleasant. Does your husband enjoy horse-racing, Mrs. Pitt? That was something Sir John had developed an interest in." She gave the graceful little shrug again. "Mind you, a lot of people have! It rather goes hand in hand with an acquaintance with the Prince of Wales." She smiled with a very slightly rueful twist. "That is one thing that excites his passion these days. Of course, his position requires a lot of him — attending balls, receptions, diplomatic dinners, and so on — but racing is different. That is a love, never a duty. What he wants more than anything else is to win the Derby again. And of course any other race that is really important. Then he'd put the animal out to stud, and its lineage would be priceless. Another Eclipse. My husband tells me all the greatest British racehorses are descended from Eclipse."

"I think my husband might be interested to learn that." Charlotte was not really lying. Pitt had never shown the slightest interest in horse-racing, but anything to do with this case would hold his attention.

They talked a little further, until they were interrupted by others joining them, and good manners dictated they change the subject to something more general.

By five o'clock in the afternoon, they were in Emily's carriage, taking Charlotte home.

"Well?" Emily asked with some urgency.

"Yes," Charlotte replied. "Very interesting. Tell me, Lady Felicia spoke quite a lot about the Prince of Wales. I think I noticed a change in her tone when she mentioned his name, but I'm not sure if I imagined it."

"You didn't," Emily answered. "I saw it in her face. It made me wonder what might have happened in the past. For one reason or another, I think she was fond of him, and perhaps still is. Of course, sometimes we remember the past as we would like it to have been. It gets a little gentler, a little sweeter each time we recount it to ourselves.

Perhaps when things are difficult, it's a comfort."

Emily drew in her breath and let it out again with a sigh. Charlotte wondered if it was for Felicia Whyte or for herself, just a fraction, but it would be tactless to ask.

"Thank you for your help," she said. "This afternoon has given me quite a lot to think about."

"Don't you want to meet Delia Kendrick?" Emily asked after a moment. "And Alan Kendrick too, perhaps?"

"Oh, yes! If you don't mind?"

Emily moderated her smile, not to betray herself too much.

"Not at all."

Pitt was very tired when he came home. He did not say anything, but Charlotte knew him too well for him to hide his anxiety, or the effort it took him to appear cheerful.

She decided to tell him about the garden party, and that she had been there with Emily. This way she would have been honest, but actually told him very little.

"Did you enjoy it?" he asked.

He was smiling as he sat back in the big chair and crossed his legs. He was too quick. He must have seen the excitement in her, even though she had tried to conceal it.

"Oh, yes," she said casually. This was clearly not the time to go into detail, certainly not about the facts and speculations regarding Lady Felicia Whyte and a possible relationship with the Prince of Wales. She realized he was looking at her, waiting for something further. He knew her at times uncomfortably well.

"There was a lot of gossip about the Prince of Wales and his love of horse-racing," she added.

"That's not gossip," he replied. "It is a fact that is in public knowledge." He was still looking at her very steadily.

"I know. The gossip part came in that it has replaced his love of women, for reasons of health."

"Oh." Then he smiled. "You are right, that is gossip, but interesting. It makes certain people less able to gain his favor, and others more so."

"That's what I thought," she agreed, keeping her voice level. Nevertheless, he caught something in it. "Charlotte . . . ?"

"I know!" she said quickly. "I did not ask for the information. I only listened, as one has to, to be polite. I repeated it to you because I understood at least some of the implications. Would you like a cup of tea?"

He smiled and accepted, but she knew the

discussion was not over.

At breakfast Daniel and Jemima were both at the table, Daniel hurrying so he would be at school on time. Yet Charlotte noticed him hesitate, look at his father, take another mouthful of toast, and then hesitate again. She saw his hand gripping the knife too hard.

"Papa," Daniel said at last.

Pitt looked up from his plate.

Daniel swallowed. "I've decided I don't want to take Latin anymore. Nobody uses Latin except Catholic priests. I'd rather do German." He was asking Pitt's permission, even though he made it a statement.

Charlotte looked at Pitt and saw the disappointment in his face. He had enjoyed Latin when it was taught to him by Sir Arthur Desmond's son's tutor. But that was by individual tutorial. Daniel was in a school class. There was no way imaginable that Pitt could afford to give his son the education he had received himself. But Daniel had a father, while Pitt had lost his so young.

"Latin is the basis of so many languages," Pitt argued. "Including our own. And it is an excellent discipline." Charlotte could feel her own stomach tense now. It would be so easy for Pitt to persuade Daniel, knowing how much his son wanted to please him. He would not have to do much, just a few expressions of his will. No punishment. No reward except approval, the only one that mattered.

Pitt hesitated. Daniel waited.

Charlotte ached to intervene, but that would diminish Daniel in his own estimation if it was Charlotte who actually swung the decision in his favor.

"German won't be easy," Pitt said, not even glancing at Charlotte.

Jemima also was waiting, her toast halfway to her mouth.

"I know," Daniel answered. "But I want to."

"Why?" Pitt asked.

"I think Germany is going to matter, a lot," Daniel replied. "They are getting stronger all the time. The kaiser declared nine years ago, in 1890, that he had plans for Germany to build a much larger navy, and to gain some more territories overseas." He was watching Pitt's face intently.

Pitt felt a coldness flood through him. The kaiser's *Weltpolitik* statement was meant as a boast, but it was also a warning only a fool would ignore.

He nodded slowly. "That is certainly true.

Have you thought yet about what you want to do?" Please heaven, he would have the choice, and another war would not rob him of it.

Daniel took a deep breath; his hand was still gripping his knife as if it were a life belt. "Not exactly. But if I'm good enough, maybe the diplomatic service, or . . . something like that."

Charlotte knew that what he meant was that he would like to follow in his father's footsteps in Special Branch, but he was afraid to say so, in case Pitt broke the dream.

She glanced at Pitt. Did he know that?

Pitt smiled. "Then German would definitely be of more use to you," he agreed. "But so would French. Don't drop that."

Daniel's face filled with relief, his smile wide, his eyes shining. "Thank you, Papa," he said very quietly, and took another mouthful of toast.

When both children were gone Pitt allowed the anxiety to come back into his face.

"Are you worried Daniel's going to move from one thing to another and not finish either?" she asked him.

"Is he?" He looked at her very gravely.

"I don't know. But I'm very glad you gave him the benefit of hoping. He would have stayed with Latin, to please you, if you'd insisted."

"I know." Pitt pushed his chair back and rose to his feet. She stood also, and reached up to give him a quick kiss, but she meant it very deeply. To have power, yet be able to not use it, was for her the most admirable strength.

Sensing the emotion in her, he turned and put both arms around her and kissed her more deeply, and for longer than she had expected. It felt extraordinarily good, like coming home. He wondered if she had any idea how much he loved her. Perhaps she did.

Emily managed to find another event a day later. This time she was quite certain that Delia Kendrick would be present. It was a much smaller affair, little more than an afternoon call, but well contrived in advance. Charlotte wore one of her own dresses, one that was quite glamorous enough for an occasion where she intended to look casual, almost incidental. It was mostly soft blues, a little toward the green, shades that suited her very well.

Emily called for her at mid-afternoon, glanced at her up and down, and pronounced herself satisfied. She herself was dressed in a delicate floral pattern that suited her surprisingly well. Lace would have been too much for this time of day. But she had a parasol. It was more decorative than of use, yet it commanded attention without the slightest effort. Exactly Emily.

The lady they were calling upon was the wife of another member of Parliament, whom Emily knew only slightly. Although titled and of considerable wealth, he was currently junior to Emily's husband, Jack Radley, so Emily sailed in with Charlotte beside her with great ease, introducing Charlotte as if she had been expected.

It was a beautiful house in Fitzroy Square, one of the classical Georgian squares, and eminently suitable for entertaining casual visitors. The marble-floored hall opened into spacious rooms, which in turn had French doors into a tiny garden.

They indulged for a few minutes in all the customary small talk, which gave Charlotte a good opportunity to observe Delia Kendrick, who had apparently arrived a few minutes before she and Emily.

Delia had an unusually dramatic face, with strongly marked brows and very handsome eyes, so dark as to appear almost black. Time had been kinder to her than to Felicia Whyte. Her more olive complexion and high cheekbones kept the brittle, slightly sagging look at bay. Her eyes met Charlotte's with boldness. Charlotte had either to smile at her or to look away. She chose the former. It was Delia who responded with a cool acknowledgment. But Charlotte did not dare to risk being caught a second time. That would require an explanation, which she did not have.

". . . so difficult with daughters, I always think," Mrs. Farringdon was saying, eyebrows raised.

Charlotte had no idea what the conversation had been. "I'm sure you are right," she agreed, hoping it was something reasonable.

"One of the most important days in your life," Mrs. Farringdon went on. "I think it should be as close to home as possible, don't you?"

"Whose home?" Charlotte inquired. She still did not know what they were talking about. Mrs. Farringdon stared at her.

"Why, the bride's home, of course!"

"I suppose so, unless of course there is a reason for . . ."

"Dear Mrs. Kendrick's daughter was married heaven knows where!" Mrs. Farringdon said in a whisper. "In fact, for all we know . . ." She left the rest unsaid, but very clear in its implication.

Charlotte was instantly annoyed by the spitefulness of it. She did not know Delia Kendrick further than the one deep stare, but leaped to her defense on principle.

"Perhaps the groom was of a different nationality, and if he was of a noble family, with huge estates, for example, it would be natural for them to marry among his people."

Mrs. Farringdon looked taken aback. Clearly that idea had not occurred to her, and she did not like it. She raised her voice considerably to be certain to attract Delia's attention where she was standing, half turning away from them.

"My dear, Mrs. Pitt mentioned that your daughter married into a foreign family of some considerable note. I must congratulate you. I had no idea. So modest of you not to speak of it . . ."

Delia turned to them, caught off guard.

Now Charlotte was really angry. "I apologize," she said to Delia. "I did not say so at all. Mrs. Farringdon said a couple should always marry close to the bride's home. I pointed out that there are exceptions. Apparently she considers your daughter, whose name I do not know, to be one of them. I don't consider it to be my concern, and I did not suggest it."

Delia's face softened but her body was rigid, as if, under the plum-colored silk, every muscle was clenched. She gave the briefest nod of acknowledgment to Charlotte, then faced Mrs. Farringdon. "Hardly a foreign country, Eliza, only Scotland. But yes, Mrs. Pitt is perfectly right, Alice married into an excellent family. They are titled, and of course they have thousands of acres of land. I believe he is the only nobleman left in the country who has the right to keep his own private standing army. Not that there is anyone to fight against. Wonderful land, but too far from here to travel back and forth easily. And of course now that she has young children, she would not leave them."

"How sad," Mrs. Farringdon said, with a tone that might have been sympathy but sounded far more like frustration to Charlotte.

"Do you think so?" Emily was not going to be outdone. "I think it sounds incredibly romantic. I know Her Majesty loves Balmoral. She goes there whenever she can."

"She used to," Mrs. Farringdon corrected her. "It is a long and rather tedious journey. As Delia has pointed out, not one to undertake lightly. I'm not sure I should allow my daughter to marry a Scot. I would worry what might happen to her, and I would not be able to go to her." She looked directly at Delia. "You don't go so very far north often, do you? Fearful about the winter. Does poor Alice find it very strange so far from home?"

"The climate is little worse than that of Derbyshire, or all the West Country," Delia replied, amid absolute silence from everyone else. "I have seen some terrible winters on Dartmoor. And since my first husband was a Scot, they are not alien people to her . . . or to me."

"Really?" Mrs. Farringdon said blandly. "I had no idea. Come to think of it, I cannot recall ever hearing you speak of your . . . first husband." Her hesitation suggested she doubted his existence.

Delia kept her composure, but there were two spots of color high in her cheeks and nothing could disguise the tension in her body.

Charlotte searched her mind for something to say that would silence Mrs. Farringdon. Why was their hostess not taking control of the situation? The answer was obvious: She did not like Delia either, whatever the reason. Could it lie with Alan Kendrick? Perhaps his sudden rise in the favor of the Prince of Wales was the subject of a degree of envy. When there is a new favorite, old friends lose at least some of their influence. The possibilities were many, and the undercurrent of emotion dangerously swift. Charlotte remembered what Felicia Whyte had said of Alan Kendrick's attempt to marry into the aristocracy. Was the duchess's refusal to allow her daughter to marry him because he was without title or heritage? Or something quite different? Was it a tragedy that marked his life, or merely a very ordinary happening that gossip had blown up beyond the reality?

It was Emily who interrupted the silence.

"I do not speak often of my first husband either," she said quietly, and looked at Delia. "Losing him was distressing, and I would not ask or wish to put anyone else to the pain of reliving such an experience. I hardly imagine that any of you would do so. It can only have been a slip of the tongue that suggested it."

Charlotte breathed a sigh of relief and shot a quick smile at Emily.

"We won't speak of such things," she agreed fervently. "Has anyone seen the new exhibition at the National Gallery? I hear there are some marvelously beautiful landscapes."

"Thank you," Delia murmured as she passed close enough to Charlotte to speak with no one else hearing.

"It's nothing," Charlotte said softly, but she knew very well that it was an interesting and excellent beginning.

Chapter 4

Pitt stood in the sun on the bank of the Serpentine, watching two small children playing with a miniature sailing boat. Their father had rigged it for them, and the slight breeze moved it across the bright surface of the water. They jumped up and down with excitement as the small craft hit a ripple, remained upright, then caught the wind again and finally made it to the farther shore, diagonally across from them, where an older boy was waiting for it.

This was how Pitt thought of the Serpentine, a peaceful place for children to play.

What on earth had made John Halberd come here alone so late, and get into a rented rowing boat? Was it even imaginable that he had intended to remain alone? The only explanation Pitt could think of was that Halberd had come here for reasons of privacy, safety, or anonymity, for a meeting. It was a well-known landmark, in the open, where no one could approach him unseen.

Had it been a woman he could not meet openly? A rowing boat seemed a chilly, hard, and uninviting place to make love — not to mention public, should anyone else be taking a walk in the dark. It had been a clear night and close to a full moon. The light on the water and the summer sky would make figures easily discernible.

Had it been to meet someone with whom he did not wish to be seen, even by a driver or a butler, let alone others dining in a restaurant? That was a darker thought. For what purpose? Blackmail? The passing of dangerous information? The handing over of goods of some sort?

Had he been meeting someone he did not know by sight? There were hardly likely to be others hanging around, unless they were courting couples.

There was always the possibility that Halberd's taste was for boys rather than women, but nothing Pitt had learned of him supported that view, and he had asked.

Pitt had been back to speak to Superintendent Gibson but had learned nothing more. Now he was waiting for the young man who had found the body, early in the morning, while walking his dog. Pitt was at the exact spot where Halberd's corpse had lain. At

least he believed he was; there was nothing whatever to mark it as unusual, just part of the gentle bank sloping down to the water's edge. There were bushes on the far side, many of them in bloom.

A few minutes after Pitt's arrival a young man approached him, a fox terrier on a lead held firmly in his hand.

"Mr. Pitt?" he asked nervously.

"Mr. Statham?" Pitt smiled at him. "I'm obliged to you for coming. Is this the right place?"

Statham looked around, blinking a little. The dog sat down obediently, even though she had not been specifically asked to. Her ears pricked as she watched the children twenty yards away.

"Look at the far bank," Pitt suggested. "Is that the same?"

"I . . . I think so. I don't know what I can tell you, sir." Statham was clearly unhappy. "I've already said all I know."

"Then try putting it into different words," Pitt suggested. He knew that when people repeat a story they are sometimes remembering not what happened, but what they said in recounting it.

Statham hesitated.

"Were you cold?" Pitt prompted him.

"Yes. Yes, actually I was. It was a cold

morning. No clouds, but a bit of a wind. Slices across the open park, it does. Not really a good time for walking Flora here, but got to do it." He bent down and patted the dog affectionately. "I was a bit surprised to see anyone out in a boat. I was a distance away, and I saw the boat first. Then . . . then I saw something on the edge of the water, and I knew it wasn't right. Flora began to bark and pull on the lead."

"Go on."

"She jerked out of my hand and ran over here." He pointed to a slight dip in the grass close to where they stood. "He was lying here, feet in the water, all sodden wet. Actually he was soaked all over, like he'd been in the water. I spoke to him, but he didn't move. Maybe I shouldn't have, but I tried to turn him over to see his face. Then I realized he was stone cold. He had to be dead. I'm sorry, sir."

"Was there blood on him?" Pitt asked.

"Not that I could see."

"Think carefully, Mr. Statham. Can you describe the boat, exactly? It was in the water, you said. How far from the shore? Where were the oars, precisely?"

Statham blinked. "Oars?"

"Yes, please."

Statham thought hard. "I saw only one. It

was floating in the water, this side of the boat."

"And the boat was the right way up, or capsized?"

"Right way up . . . I remember now, there was quite a bit of water in the bottom of it . . . as if it had been at least halfway over, and he'd managed to right it again. But I don't know what could have happened so close to the bank. He was a tall man. He could have stood up in the water easily. Must've been drunk out of his mind." He hesitated. "Sorry, sir, but it's the only thing I can think of. Unless somehow he fell overboard and the boat swung around and hit him when he was struggling to stand."

By accident? Pitt thought about it. "Stood up in the shallow water, lost his balance, fell and hit his head against the boat," he said. "Anything to suggest that? Which way was his head where he was lying? Toward the bank, or toward the water?"

"Toward the bank, sir, as if he'd crawled out. Only his feet were still in the water. I don't see how he could have fallen that way."

"If his head injury was serious he could have succumbed after he'd reached the bank," Pitt pointed out.

Statham gave him a dark look. "If the boat

hit him when he was struggling to stand up in the water, it's unlikely he'd have got that far . . . if it had hit him really hard, enough to knock him out, or . . . or to kill him."

"Did you look at the boat itself?"

Statham shook his head. "I didn't inspect it, but it was close in to the shore, and I pulled it to the bank, sir. In case it floated away. It seemed . . . right."

"It was right," Pitt assured him. "Then you called the police?"

"Yes. There was another gentleman walking a dog, a big sort of retriever of some kind. I told him there'd been an accident and to get the police. I waited here. I know it sounds stupid . . ." He looked away from Pitt and across the sun-dappled water. "I felt like I shouldn't leave him alone. Not that he'd care . . ."

"You were right," Pitt repeated quickly. "You said he was wet all over. Even his hair? His face? His shoulders?"

"Yes, he was all wet. Why?"

"So you secured the boat, in case it drifted away?"

"Yes. I thought . . . I don't know what I thought." Statham looked confused and unhappy. The little dog was intent on watching a small model boat on the water.

"You said the boat was wet inside?" Pitt asked.

"Not enough to make him soaked like he was," Statham said with assurance.

"But it was wet?"

"Oh, yes, quite wet. Very wet." He sounded certain, as if he were seeing it in his mind again.

"How about the sides? And the other oar?"

"One side was very wet, the other . . . I don't think so. But the oar was gone. I remember that now."

"Which oar was gone? Please be sure. Close your eyes and see it in your mind. What was wet, and what wasn't?"

Statham closed his eyes obediently.

"One oar was in the water, between the boat and the shore where he was. That side of the boat was wet . . ." His eyes opened wide.

"You mean as if it tipped over and somebody righted it again?"

"Yes . . . it was wet like that. Just quick, like. It wasn't all wet."

"And the oar? Did you see any blood on it? Please be exact. Don't say anything because you think I want it one way or the other. Just close your eyes again and tell me whether you looked at the oar to put it back. Describe it to me."

"It was just an ordinary wooden oar, sir. Quite a wide blade on it."

"Did you pick it up?"

Statham hesitated.

"Did you?" Pitt insisted.

"I put it back in the boat, sir. I remember now, the other one was still in its rowlock, and shipped safely, but that one was loose in the water. I don't know what the poor gentleman can have been doing. Why would he have stood up? He was too far out to climb ashore without getting wet."

"It's possible he struck his head. Did you see any blood on the gunwale? There was blood in his hair."

"No, sir, I didn't."

"Would you have, in the half light?"

"It was a clear dawn, sir. I didn't see any blood at all, and I reckon I would have. But I didn't really look at the other side."

"Did you see anybody else in the park when you first got here? Apart from the man with the retriever who went for the police?"

"No, sir. Just me and Flora. Bit early for most people. That's why I like it. Or I did. Doesn't seem so good now. Rather go round the other way." He indicated where he meant with a wave of his hand. Flora took it as a signal to go on, and shot to her feet.

"Thank you, Mr. Statham. You have been

very helpful. I would appreciate it if you did not discuss this with anyone else, anyone at all."

"No, sir, I won't. Let the poor gentleman rest in peace. And his family as well."

Pitt went back to the police surgeon, whom he'd questioned after his second visit to Superintendent Gibson, but he had nothing to add, except to repeat that Halberd had died from striking his head hard against something solid.

"Tall man," he said unhappily. "If he was standing upright in the boat and lost his balance, sending the boat rocking badly, he'd have hit his head damned hard on the side of the boat. Six-foot drop, and with his weight behind it, quite enough to crack his skull."

"And you say there was blood in his hair?"

"Of course there was blood, you fool!" the surgeon snapped. "Tore the skin and broke the bone!"

"Yes, that's what you said. Just wanted to be certain." The surgeon made a sound of disgust and walked away.

Pitt went to the owner of the few boats for hire on the Serpentine, a man named Dale. He asked to see the boat in which Halberd had died.

"You won't say nothing?" Dale said urgently. "That boat's no use to me if people won't ride in it. That's my living, that is."

"You'll probably get twice as much for it," Pitt said dourly. "But no, I won't say. Still, I need to see it."

"I dunno . . ."

"Yes, you do. You want the least fuss possible." Pitt gave him a bleak smile, rather more a baring of the teeth.

"It's been rubbed down, though, and repainted," Dale argued, not moving from the spot.

"Really? Why did you do that? Don't you keep them clean?"

"Course I do!" Dale said indignantly. "But people leave things . . . Dump things . . ."

"What did the man who died in your boat leave?" Pitt asked, staring hard at him.

Dale shifted his balance a bit. "A little blood. Fell and hit his head, they said. Bit the worse for wear, likely."

"Did he seem drunk to you?"

Now Dale was unhappy. "Not when he came and asked for the boat, sir, and I lent him the spare key. It wasn't the first time and I knew I could trust him. I keep the boats padlocked on a chain, or all sorts would be off with them and not paying. He came by to rent it an hour or two before he said he wanted it. He could have put away a few drinks in between. Or perhaps he just was clumsy? Or took a fit?" He sounded aggrieved. "How do I know?"

"Where was the blood? Exactly," Pitt persisted.

"On the handle of the oar, and a bit on the gunwale, starboard side. He must have taken a hell of a clumsy fall, poor devil."

"Thank you."

Pitt looked at the boat when it came in, but there were no traces of blood at all. As Dale had said, he had thoroughly cleaned it and given it a cursory new coat of paint. At Pitt's request, he showed him exactly where the blood had been.

"There," he said. "That tell you anything?"

Pitt did not respond, but he walked away with the answer in his head. It would have taken a contortionist to have stood up, tripped over the seat, and fallen in such a way as to strike his head on the gunwale, then the handle of the oar, and finally to topple into the water, taking the oar with him. The most natural answer that fit all the facts was that Halberd had met someone waiting on the bank of the Serpentine, pulled over, and shipped the oars. Then the person had leaned in, taken the landward side oar, swung it as hard as possible, striking Halberd on the side of the head and sending him overboard. Perhaps a second blow had finished him off; although his fall onto the gunwale and then overboard, when he was already unconscious, would also be possible. Whoever it was attacked him had let him drown — or possibly even held him down until he did — then pulled him partially out onto the bank. It would not have taken long, and Halberd was unconscious, unable to fight back. Just a few minutes. Then the assailant had walked away, and disappeared into the night.

They would have been wet, soaked up to the knees of their trousers — or dress! But who would notice? It might be worth asking, but no doubt the person would have a story ready by now.

But who? And why?

The next place Pitt went was Halberd's London house. By now he had no question in his mind that Halberd had been murdered. Despite owning a large estate in the country, Halberd spent most of his time in London, especially when the Queen was here rather than at her beloved Osborne House on the Isle of Wight.

This was one of the parts of his job Pitt liked the least, but it was also one of the most important. He could not afford to leave any decision to someone else's judgment. He knocked on the door early in the afternoon, and when there was no answer knocked again. It was opened by an elderly man with a pale, scrubbed-looking face, still quite clearly suffering from the shock of bereavement.

"Yes, sir?" he said with no interest whatever in his voice.

"Good afternoon," Pitt replied. "May I come inside, Mr. . . . ?"

"Robson, sir. Sir John Halberd has passed away, sir," Robson replied, his voice catching with emotion. "I'm afraid I cannot help you." He began to push the door closed again.

"Mr. Robson." Pitt pushed back on the door, hard enough to force Robson to let go. "I am Commander Pitt, head of Special Branch. I would like to talk to you about Sir John's death. I have reason to believe it was not as simple as it appeared."

"I don't wish to discuss it, sir. I cannot help you," Robson told him, still no expression in his face.

"I'm sorry, Mr. Robson," Pitt replied more gently. "I believe Sir John was murdered, and I have no choice but to investigate the possibility that is true."

Robson stared at him aghast, unable to speak.

Pitt stepped inside and closed the door behind him. He took the man by the arm. Ignoring the oak-paneled hallway and the magnificent carved stair, he guided the elderly servant gently toward the back of the house. "Where is your pantry?" he asked.

Robson blinked. "Pantry?"

"Yes. Your own private room, where you can sit down and perhaps have a quick sip of brandy to steady yourself. I'm going to need your help. Sir John was an extremely important man. I want to make certain that whoever killed him is found and dealt with. And that Sir John's reputation is not needlessly . . . damaged."

At last Robson saw a purpose in answering. "Thank you, sir," he said awkwardly. "Sir John was a good man. He doesn't deserve to be . . . slandered. People envy those with power. My father used to say that if you want money, or fame, or power, there will always be the men who would hate you for it because they will think it is at their expense. But if all you want is to be good, then you will not offend anyone."

Pitt waited. The man needed to be given a little time.

"He was wrong, sir." Robson looked up at him, composed again. "That is the greatest challenge of all. One man's compassion shows up other people's weaknesses. It's something you cannot get away from."

Pitt recalled a few of his past cases, especially that of the woman from Spain, the turbulent saint, the most uncomfortable acquaintance he had ever had. He could agree with Robson very easily, if Halberd had been as loudly and endlessly good as she. Power was a different matter.

"You are quite right, Mr. Robson. I am not fortunate enough to have known him, so I need you to tell me all you can. Who, in particular, did Sir John's goodness expose, whether he wished it to or not?"

Robson stared at him. "Do you think it was . . . personal, sir?"

"Yes, I do think so. Would you be good enough to make us a pot of tea? This may take some time."

They were still standing in the passageway off the main hall. Pitt guessed the kitchens were ahead of them.

"Yes, sir," Robson replied. "Would you be more comfortable in the housekeeper's sitting room? She's no longer here. Nor are the maids or the cook. They were all very upset by Sir John's death, even though we thought at the time it was an accident. But better for them they start to look for new positions as soon as they can." Remembering his duties and something he could actually do to help seemed to steady him. "I wrote them all good characters, and they had offers fairly quickly," he went on. A look of intense sadness filled his face, and Pitt could imagine he had in a single day lost his home and those who were in a way his family. Safety was gone, routine smashed apart, everything familiar dissolved, leaving only uncertainty and personal grief.

"Will you be all right?" Pitt asked him.

Robson was taken aback. "Me, sir? Oh . . . Yes, thank you, sir. That's very kind of you. I think I might retire. Sir John left me cared for. Out in the country, you know. Grow a flower garden, I think. And a few vegetables." The generosity of his employer had given him security, but it had not come in the way he wanted, and it was here far too soon.

"Did Sir John keep a diary of his engagements?" Pitt broke the momentary silence.

"Yes, sir. I can get it for you. We haven't disturbed his study at all."

"Who were his closest relatives? Presumably the house will go to them? And the estate in the country?" Pitt disliked asking, but it was not a subject he could ignore.

Robson looked appalled. “Oh, no, sir! You don’t think that anyone . . .”

“I don’t,” Pitt agreed. “I think it was far more likely fear, personal enmity rather than greed. But I would like to know, all the same.”

Robson began to lead the way through the baize door into the servants’ quarters.

“Sir John had a cousin, sir. Not close, I believe, but a good man. Doesn’t live around here. I’ve heard he intends to sell this house, in due course,” he continued. “Being very good about letting me stay here until . . . Well, another month or two. He lives somewhere up north. Would you like the diaries now, sir? Perhaps while I make us a cup of tea? I have some rather good cake, if you would like a piece?”

Pitt accepted, and while Robson prepared the tea he looked through the diary, starting with the day Halberd was killed and going backward from there. It was very little help in that Halberd had made no notes at all as to the nature of his engagements, only names. Pitt recognized many of them: members of Parliament, government ministers, aristocrats, judges, and the occasional bishop. Nothing was written as to the reasons for the meetings, whether social or business. As far as Pitt knew from Cornwallis, Halberd had lived very well off inherited money, carefully invested, and the income from his extremely nice manor house and lands. If there were anything else, Special Branch had seen no trace of it. It would be the interpretation of what was perfectly open that might lead to something further, although he doubted it.

There were the names he had expected to see: Algernon Naismith-Jones, Ferdie Warburton, Walter Whyte, and several other gentlemen who had time and money and little specific to do with either.

Why had Halberd spent his time with such people? They seemed so far from his own character and interests.

When Robson came with tea and excellent cake, Pitt asked him.

Robson took extreme care pouring the tea, to give himself time to weigh his reply.

Pitt waited. A lie might reveal as much as the truth.

"I'm not entirely sure, sir," Robson said at length. "I think he had some respect for Mr. Whyte. They knew each other in Africa, a long time ago. Gentlemen like to reminisce about adventures they had in their youth, especially with those who have seen some of those strange and foreign places. Have you been to Africa, sir?"

Pitt believed that what Robson was saying was perfectly true, but he was picking and choosing which parts to reveal.

"No, I haven't," he replied, pretending more interest than he felt. "Have you, Mr. Robson? Perhaps you were with Sir John, even then?"

"No, sir," Robson said very quickly. "But I heard the gentlemen talking about it a lot. Sounded like a wonderful place, but very dangerous. The heat, the diseases, the wild animals, people who have left civilization far behind. Some people seem to think that if a thing doesn't happen at home, where you are known, then it doesn't count. Sir John used to say that. But then he knew . . ."

Pitt waited.

"More cake, sir?" Robson offered.

Pitt accepted it, and changed his tactics.

"Were Sir John and Mr. Whyte in the army together?"

"Oh, no, sir. Mr. Whyte was, for a short while. He saw very fierce action, so Sir John said. Egypt, or the Sudan, or some place like that. Lost his brother out there, apparently. Nasty boating accident. Devoted to each other, they were. His brother, James, was something of a hero. Not sure of the exact circumstances, but saved several people's lives, they say. Mr. Whyte never really got over losing him. I think that was part of what they had in common."

"Sir John lost a brother, too?" Pitt asked with surprise.

"No, sir. Lost the lady he was going to marry." Robson took a deep breath. "Long time ago now, but I don't know as he ever looked at anyone else. Before my time with him. Sort of thing you don't talk about. Some kind of fever, I think it was. But I know he liked Mr. Whyte."

"And the others?"

"Nice enough, he'd say. Meant no harm. I think it was mostly the love for the horses, one way or another, that they had in common."

He was being evasive, Pitt was certain of it. Why? If Halberd gambled it was hardly remarkable. Many men did. There was no whisper that he lost more than other people, and certainly not more than he could afford. Did he profit in some way from other people's misfortune? Was this all about something as grubby as debt?

He decided to ask a question from a completely different angle.

"Did Sir John breed horses . . . on his country estate?"

"Hunters, sir, not racehorses. But lately

he seemed to be looking more into the really good racers, the sort Mr. Kendrick knows so much about. At least that's what Sir John says . . . said. He —" Robson stopped abruptly, his face a little flushed and acutely unhappy. He seemed to have considered himself to be telling too much.

"What is it, Mr. Robson?" Pitt asked quietly. "I think Sir John was murdered, and left in a place where people would make an unfortunate interpretation of it. Why did he go to the Serpentine after dark that evening? Was he in the habit of doing that?"

Robson looked startled.

Pitt felt a twinge of pity, but he had to know. He would like to be gentler, but there was so little time.

"I . . . I really don't know, sir. I . . ."

"Yes, you do know, Mr. Robson. You are his butler and his valet. You know what he wore each time he went out and at what hour he returned. Don't tell me you didn't wait up for him. I wouldn't believe you."

"I don't like to repeat —"

"I know you don't. He was murdered, Mr. Robson. Someone either made an appointment and then abused his trust in them, or caught up with him there and attacked him from behind."

"In a boat, sir?"

"Not likely," Pitt agreed. "It must have been someone he expected to meet but could not openly, in a more social setting. Either a man who was not of his circle, whom he did not wish to be seen with, or else a woman, perhaps a married woman . . ."

"Sir John wasn't —" Robson began, and then stopped abruptly.

"Attracted to women?"

"That's . . ." Robson let out his breath slowly. "That is not true, sir. He just never loved another woman deeply enough to marry her after Miss Rachael died. He had . . ." Robson was loath to say it.

This time Pitt did not force him. "But not, I presume, in a rowing boat on the Serpentine?"

A smile flickered across Robson's face and vanished. "No, sir. He . . . no, not like that."

"What was he doing on the Serpentine, Robson? Don't make me pull teeth, man. I'm going to find out. Let me do it discreetly, from you."

Robson stiffened, squaring his shoulders. "He knew a lot of things about a lot of people, sir. He kept an eye on the prince's affairs, for the Queen, in a way of speaking. She always trusted him. It was the memory of Prince Albert . . ."

Pitt was startled. "Sir John knew Prince Albert?"

"Yes, sir. He was kind of a favorite of the prince's, sir, since he was a very young man. That is what he's got against the Prince of Wales, but he looks after his best interest — did so, anyway, for the Queen's sake." Robson shook his head. "Now I've said too much. I swore I'd never be indiscreet, and I've done exactly that." There was guilt in his voice, but no note of blame against Pitt.

"As head of Special Branch, I understand discretion, and times when it has to be broken," Pitt said quietly, watching Robson's face. "I'm happy to let Sir John's secrets die with him, except the one for which he was killed. Now tell me some of his friends and, more importantly, some of his enemies. He knew a great deal about many people. Maybe more than anyone else. Whom did he trust? Who was afraid of him?"

"He didn't know more than anyone else, sir," Robson said with certainty. "He always said no one knew more than Lord Narraway did — or how to use it at exactly the right time."

Pitt felt a chill run through him, just slight, like a warning. "Victor Narraway?" he asked carefully.

"Yes, sir. Sir John said that if he wished to, Lord Narraway would be the most dangerous man in England."

Pitt hesitated. He did not want to hear more, yet he must. What was he afraid of? That he would learn something of Narraway that would undermine the trust between them forever? Or possibly worse: what Narraway had had to do in the course of the job that was now Pitt's, and that Pitt himself would have to do one day?

But that was for later. He could easily persuade this frail man — who had in one night lost his job, his home, his family, such as it was, and his purpose in getting up every day, knowing that he was valued — to give him the answers he sought.

He was behaving automatically now, still too stunned at the mention of Narraway's name to feel the full impact of it.

"Did he have political enemies?" Pitt asked. "His knowledge gave him great power. There must have been ambitious people in whose path he stood, men he could not let climb upward too far."

"Oh, yes," Robson agreed. "Knowledge is power, especially when the other person is not absolutely certain how much you know. I've seen it happen. The hesitation, the moment of fear, the retreat when someone realizes that he doesn't know. I used to wonder sometimes how much of it was a game, whether he really knew what he implied at all." He bit his lip. "But he would see fear in others, like a shadow in the eyes. If you know what I mean?" He looked at Pitt quite openly, one man to another, as if there were no difference in rank or power between them.

"Yes, I do know," Pitt agreed, almost in a whisper. "Who might they be, these men who could not read him, and needed to so much?"

"Oh, I don't know, sir. Except that Sir John wasn't one of them."

"I beg your pardon?" Pitt was confused. Where had he lost the thread of the conversation? Then he knew, like opening the door into the wind. Robson was not talking about Halberd, he was talking about Narraway.

"Sir John wasn't one of them," Robson repeated.

Pitt thought for an instant. He didn't want to betray his ignorance, nor did he want to know whatever this man thought of Narraway. But both pride and ignorance were luxuries he could not afford, certainly not now.

"And had Lord Narraway been useful to Sir John?" he asked.

Robson blinked. "Oh . . . yes, of course. I forgot. He got sent up to the House of Lords after that scandal, didn't he?" He gave a tiny shake of his head. "That's the thing about scandal: It doesn't matter if it's all lies, it still sticks to you. There's always some fool who will say, 'There's no smoke without fire!' " He sounded bitter. "There was no fire around Sir John, sir. None at all. He had his faults. Show me the man who doesn't. And he had enemies, people whose weaknesses he knew, but he couldn't help that. He was nobody's fool. He would read people like most men read a page of the newspaper."

"An uncomfortable ability," Pitt observed. "Especially if other people are aware of it."

Robson's chin rose a little. "He did what he had to, in loyalty to Her Majesty, and to the memory of Prince Albert, God save him."

"Indeed," Pitt said, hoping Sir John's motives were as loyal and as selfless as Robson thought. Most men had few secrets and even fewer heroics in front of their valets, who had seen them unshaved and in their underwear, hungover and bleary-eyed. Seemingly John Halberd was the exception. "If you are right, then it is all the more important that we find out who murdered him that night on the Serpentine, and that no scandal is attached falsely to that."

Robson's face was white. "I'll do all I can to help, sir."

"Good."

Pitt spent the next three hours going through all the papers and effects that he could find, with Robson's help. These included diaries from the last three years, earlier ones having been thrown away. Clearly Halberd had spent an increasingly large amount of time in the country, at his own stable and visiting others, mostly in horse-breeding areas. There were references to the Prince of Wales, but not more than were easily accounted for by Halberd's friendship with the Queen and his interest in horses. There were also notations on trees and flowers, especially roses.

There were a lot of social engagements. Clearly he enjoyed the opera, concerts, theater, and good conversation. Such information as there was painted a picture of a man Pitt would have liked.

There was a brief note lodged inside the front cover of the current diary, undated and unsigned: "Tuesday, not Thursday, please," which could have referred to anything. Pitt put it to one side to take away with him, but with little hope of it being useful.

Victor Narraway was referred to only twice, and so cryptically the entries offered nothing but more uncertainty. The first time it was merely, "Of course Narraway knew already. He would!" The second was longer: "I can't help wondering if Narraway has a part in this, but I don't want to tip my hand by asking."

There were notes about Kendrick, but they were mostly to do with horses and all self-explanatory. Kendrick had put a lot of money into good bloodstock, and was becoming successful. But that was public knowledge, as was the prince's love of the sport. There were several names of other breeders. Some large sums of money were noted, but briefly; horses involved high expense, and sometimes high rewards.

He searched thoroughly, not finding anything unexpected or out of the usual habits of a middle-aged man of good family and very considerable private means, but lacking any close relatives, which was merely misfortune.

Pitt asked to take away some of the papers he had seen, thanked Robson, and walked out into the warm afternoon street with a sense of failure.

And yet as he hailed a cab and gave the driver the Lisson Grove address, he was still certain that Halberd's death had been deliberate, violent, and planned. It had also been well concealed afterward. All the facts he had depended on testimony. There was no physical evidence that a court would see as proof.

Who had Halberd gone to the Serpentine to meet? And why? Why not meet in his own home, or the other person's home, or a hotel lounge, a café, the corner of a street? Or even under a tree in the park? There had to be a reason.

Perhaps the other person's home was not private enough. That might also apply to a café or restaurant. The park after dusk seemed good enough, but then one ran the risk of appearing to loiter. One might be accosted.

Had there been a third person involved, someone recognizable? Halberd did not live particularly close to the park. Did the other person live close by?

When Pitt reached Lisson Grove he spoke briefly to Stoker and a couple of other men, then went up to his office, but there was no time to make notes about his earlier interviews. There was a message waiting for him, requesting his presence at his earliest convenience to report to Her Majesty. A carriage was awaiting him. Apparently it had been there close to an hour already.

Pitt was conducted through the mews door into the palace. A footman showed him to the same room as before. Now that he was here, he would await her pleasure. There was no reason why he should not sit in one of the comfortable, overstuffed chairs while he waited, but he was too tense to relax. He paced back and forth like one of the sentries on duty. He could have been outside at the front, wearing a scarlet coat and the bearskin helmet of a Grenadier Guardsman.

He heard the door open behind him and whirled around. Victoria came into the room slowly. She looked old and very small. Had she been anyone else, he would have offered her his arm to lean on, but one did not touch the Queen, or even suggest it.

He bowed, and then watched as she made her way across the carpet, leaning on a stick, and sat down in the same chair as before. When she had arranged her skirts she told the maid at the door to go, and finally looked up at Pitt as the door closed with a barely perceptible click.

"Well, Mr. Pitt, what have you to tell me?" Her voice was firm but a little hoarse, as if her mouth was dry. She could not possibly be afraid of him, but perhaps she was afraid of the truth.

The least he could offer her was to be candid and not for an instant make her wait, or ask a second time.

"I can tell you the details if you wish, Your Majesty," he replied. His voice seemed loud in the quiet room. "But I have reached the conclusion that Sir John Halberd did not die accidentally as a result of standing up in the boat and overbalancing. I believe he was struck deliberately with an oar, and pushed over the side into the water. The boat was close enough to the bank for him to have reached the shore quite easily, had he been conscious. But the blow was hard enough to render him unconscious, and while in that state he drowned."

The Queen did not blink. "I see."

He waited a moment, but she appeared to have assumed that he would continue. She looked tired and deeply unhappy.

"I'm sorry . . ." He said it instinctively. It was true. What he had learned of Halberd was admirable, but he would have grieved for the Queen's sake, whatever Halberd had been like.

"Thank you. Why did the police not come to this conclusion, Mr. Pitt?"

Should he tell her the details? He hesitated.

"Mr. Pitt?" She spoke more abruptly.

"I tried to think of a reason why Sir John would be there at all, ma'am," he said awkwardly. "There were some unkind suggestions of meeting a type of woman he would not see openly." He saw the distaste in the downturn of her lips. "Nothing I could learn of him made that seem likely, so I looked for another reason, a meeting of a different sort." He was talking too quickly. Deliberately he took more time. "I spoke to the young man who found Sir John's body, then the man who owned the boat, and I looked at it myself, at the rowlocks and the oars. I found evidence that he was struck with the oar, then when he fell the gunwale caught him on the side of the head. From the place where the oar was found and the shape of the rowlock, that would not happen by accident. I cannot prove it because the boat has been painted over, but the young man who found Sir John had a clear recollection of what he found, and the police surgeon identified the injuries that correspond with my theory."

"I see." She took a deep breath and let it out soundlessly. "I was afraid of it. I wish you had proved me wrong. A simple accident. He was inattentive, stood up, and lost his balance. That is what I would like to have heard. And had you told me so, I would have believed it."

"Would you, ma'am? Sir John Halberd had experience with boats on the Nile, I was told."

She looked at him with a tight smile, but there was an unwilling amusement in it. "No doubt you were. Truthfully, I would have liked you to tell me that it was merely an accident, but I would have struggled to believe you. And I daresay that in the end I would not have. I would simply have thought you possibly kind, if a trifle patronizing." Her voice hardened. "Or else incompetent. Then I would have had to ask the home secretary to relieve you of your position. Victor Narraway would not have liked that. He thinks well of you. Or he did the last time I saw him, which was a while ago now. He would not have lied to me, whatever he had to say. A clever man, with steel in his soul. Have you steel in your soul, Mr. Pitt?"

This time he did not hesitate long enough for her to notice. "Yes, ma'am." Please heaven that was true. But perhaps not as much steel as Narraway. He wanted to, and yet he was also afraid of the price of it.

"Then you will find out for me who killed John Halberd, and why," she replied. "And you will tell me when you have proof of it. Do you understand me, Mr. Pitt?" Her voice was a little husky, as if she was battling against deep emotion.

"Yes, ma'am, I do."

"Regardless of who it is. Do you understand that also, Mr. Pitt?"

"Yes, ma'am."

"I have no time left for comfortable lies," she went on. "If the answer is one you do not like, you will bring it to me just the same. It is not your prerogative to decide anything for me. You are a nice young man. You have a wife and children, I am told. My friend Vespasia tells me you have a gentle heart."

He was startled, and moved that Vespasia would speak of him to the Queen.

The Queen gave a little grunt. "I am not your family, I am your queen and empress, and you will not be gentle with me! You are commander of my Special Branch, and you will bring me the truth . . . regardless of what you think I may do with it, or how unpleasant it may be. Will you give me your word, Mr. Pitt?"

He bowed very slightly. "Yes, ma'am. I give you my word."

"Good. Then you had best be about it. I shall expect you to report to me regularly. Good night, Mr. Pitt."

He bowed more deeply and left the room, moving backward to the door, then turning and going out.

A waiting footman conducted him to the rear entrance again, although Pitt was hardly aware of him. He walked out into the palace mews and found the carriage that had brought him still waiting. He asked the driver to take him to his home on Keppel Street, then sat back to go over and over in his mind what the Queen had said to him.

What was it she feared so much?

He knew. Why was he avoiding it? It was there at the edge of his mind all the time. She was afraid that in some way the Prince of Wales was involved. Not that he was directly responsible, but indirectly.

The prince's relationship with his mother had never recovered after the death of Prince Albert. Pitt had lost his own mother when he was a boy, but at least the memories were all clean. There was deep loneliness, a gaping sorrow where the rest of their lives together should have been, but there was no festering wound, nothing unhealed to poison the past.

And he had promised to find out who had

killed Halberd, and why, and tell Victoria! There was no way to escape it, except to fail, and so completely that she could not think he was lying to cover something he dared not tell her.

CHAPTER 5

Pitt began the day early, going to see Jack Radley at his office in the House of Commons. He did not wish to see him at his home, where Emily would inevitably learn about it. She was quick-witted enough to deduce that the case he was working on had turned more serious and was sufficiently political for him to seek Jack's help. It was something he had done before, but rarely, and only when it involved someone professionally connected to Jack. It had usually turned out unfortunately for Jack, with disillusion and a deep and painful lesson. In fact, on the last occasion, Jack had decided not to stand for Parliament again after his present term was finished.

Of course, he was free to change his mind, however unlikely that seemed now.

Jack was in a meeting, even at nine o'clock in the morning, and Pitt waited in his office, having sent a messenger to inform Jack of his presence in case he did not automatically return.

Pitt had been pacing the floor a mere twenty minutes when the door opened and Jack came in. His face was as handsome as always, time having marked it kindly, adding distinction as he began to take life more seriously. Now he actually looked worried.

"Sorry to keep you waiting, Thomas," he said warmly. "Some men seem to be able to talk endlessly without actually saying anything. I assume you have a case in which I can help?" He waved his hand toward the comfortable leather armchairs by the marble fireplace, which in the winter heated the office very pleasantly. He was no longer a junior member, sharing rooms with someone else.

Pitt sat down and crossed his legs comfortably, as if he intended to be here for some time.

"Did you know Sir John Halberd?" he asked.

"Slightly." Jack looked at him steadily. "I know the gossip regarding his being in a boat on the Serpentine, but I'm reluctant to believe it. I can understand if he had an affair. He's a normal man, and not married. It would take pretty good proof for me to believe he picked up a prostitute, or that he had an affair with a woman married to someone else, and conducted it like that." He smiled with a slight downward turn of his lips. "Awkward, uncomfortable, and completely unnecessary, apart from anything else."

"What do you think he was doing there?" Pitt asked curiously.

Jack frowned. "That's a question I can't answer, except that he must have been meeting someone. He wasn't going for a midnight row alone. Who on earth does that? Incidentally, how did he get the boat? Are they not locked up at night somehow? Moored with a chain and padlock, or something? Otherwise any fool could make away with them: young men a bit drunk; thieves just for the sake of it."

"I asked the owner. Halberd had a key to the padlock. The boatman gave it to him by arrangement."

Jack looked surprised. "What did he say Halberd wanted it for?"

"The man had not the nerve to ask him. Apparently it wasn't the first time," Pitt replied.

"I thought he was a pretty good man. Was I wrong again?" The sadness of previous misjudgments was clear in Jack's eyes and in the slight stiffness of his body in the easy chair.

Pitt thought for a moment, unhappy that he had been forced to disillusion Jack twice, and painfully. It would be an ugly thing if Jack was to lose faith in himself over this, and he had come very close before. Broken trust does not heal easily. Another time and it would become a habit to suspect, so that he would not see what was brave or good anymore. And yet evasion would not be kind either. It would be felt as condescension.

To begin with, Pitt had thought Jack a charming, empty man, too handsome for his own good or anyone else's. However, during the years of Jack's marriage to Emily, Pitt had come not only to like him but to see the best in him — the courage, the good humor, a gained self-knowledge of his original superficiality.

Now he was waiting for Pitt to answer.

"I don't think so," Pitt said seriously. "It is a private matter so far, although it will have to become public soon, because I am sure in my own mind that he was murdered. I don't know by whom, or why. Perhaps the *why* is what matters most."

Jack perceived the gravity of it immediately. "Murdered? And the head of Special Branch called in. By whom? The police?"

"No." Pitt hesitated. "As a matter of absolute confidence . . ."

Jack leaned forward a fraction. "Tell me only what you have to."

Pitt smiled bleakly. "I wouldn't tell anyone if I didn't have to. Narraway and Aunt Vespasia are out of the country, somewhere in Europe. I don't even know where. And I haven't told Charlotte. She knows I can't."

"But you have evidence?"

"I have now. Only because I looked for it. The young man who found the body told me what he saw. The boat concerned has been cleaned and painted since then. But it makes painful sense, with the police surgeon's report."

"Still, you must have had reason to look," Jack pointed out.

"I did. At the request of Her Majesty."

"Oh . . . Do you mean Her Majesty's Government, the home secretary . . . ?"

"I mean Her Majesty," Pitt said quietly. "Sir John Halberd was a personal friend, inquiring into a certain matter on her behalf. Before he could report his findings to her, he died. I believe he was murdered. It is possible it had something to do with her request."

Jack nodded, his face very grave indeed, the surprise still clear in it. "I see. So now you need to know what he found that someone considered worth murdering him to keep him from telling the Queen? And preferably with proof?"

"Exactly."

"I suppose you have thought of speaking to Carlisle? I know he's a very odd man; I've heard about the Resurrection Row affair." A bleak smile crossed Jack's face. "From Emily. I'm aware she and Charlotte both used to get themselves involved in your cases. She misses it . . ."

"I know," Pitt agreed quickly. "In several ways I miss it too. But this is more dangerous, and I can't tell them, even if it weren't. I would lose my job." That had happened once, and the recollection was sharp and painful. He had been afraid he would no longer be employed at the work he loved, the only thing for which he had any real talent. "I won't let it happen again," he said grimly. "I've exhausted the chances I'll get." The understanding in Jack's face was so plain, he let the subject drop. "Yes, I saw Carlisle."

"Was he helpful?" Jack asked.

"Quite a lot. I'll return to him if I have no other choice. But you are more connected to foreign affairs than he is. I've been through all Halberd's papers in his house. I managed to persuade his butler, who also serviced as his valet, to allow me access. He is very concerned that Halberd's reputation is not destroyed by gossip."

Jack shrugged and sighed.

"I know." Pitt settled back in his chair. "There seem to be a few threads to suggest a connection with Africa." He saw Jack's expression darken immediately. He waited.

"The Boers?" Jack said grimly. "I fear we are heading for another war. Please God, I am wrong, but I doubt it."

"Soon?"

"This year, unless something changes pretty radically," Jack replied. "This man Sir Alfred Milner is the worst kind of arrogant imperialist. Won't be told a thing. I don't know who the hell put him in charge, but it's heading for disaster. At worst, we would lose the southern portion of Africa, right from Johannesburg to the Cape — with all the land and resources. I don't need to tell you about the gold and diamonds in Johannesburg."

"That's the worst? What's the best?" Pitt asked. "Or more important, what is the most likely, in your view?"

"That we win, but at a terrible cost, not only in lives and reputation, but, to use an old-fashioned word, in honor. We could earn the hatred and the contempt of half the world."

Pitt had already proved Jack's judgment false twice, but he had a sinking feeling that this time Jack would be right. The miserable experience of the war against the Boers supported what he said.

"Do you know the name Alan Kendrick?" Pitt asked, turning back to the reason he was here.

Jack had been waiting for criticism. It was there in his bearing, subtly. Now he relaxed. "Close friend of the Prince of Wales. Opportunist, if you ask me. The Queen can't live forever."

"What else?"

"He has a damned good stables in Cambridgeshire, or Lincolnshire, somewhere like that. One really superb stallion. Could be a Derby winner. And of course he could make a lot more money if he put him to stud soon after. There's a rumor that he'll be restricting the horse's breeding on purpose."

"To send the price up?"

"Possibly. Or to keep him largely for the Prince of Wales. The best way to earn his favor. It's about the only thing he cares about passionately anymore."

"You know of an African connection?"

"Kendrick is a friend of Milner's. Can't

see how that would get Halberd murdered on the Serpentine . . . but you never know. Some circles are smaller than you think. Of course, you're right, I was meandering. Right now South Africa is very much on my mind." He smiled, a sudden, charming gesture, full of warmth. "My trade secrets."

Pitt acknowledged it with an answering smile. "Whose interests would be served by another African war?"

"Regardless of the outcome? Arms dealers," Jack replied without hesitation. "Big ones, perhaps German. The top of the field now. Heavy armor, certainly, from Krupp, in Essen. And Mauser. They export rifles all over the place. And they have a certain affinity with the Boers anyway. And we, like damn fools, are playing right into their hands."

"Thank you. Unless they start shipping them here, there's not much I can do about it."

"I assume you've looked into Halberd's friends . . . and enemies?"

"Yes. Two of them have connections with Africa, but so far it's North Africa: Egypt and the Sudan. And it's a long time ago."

"Is there an expiry date on blackmail?" Jack asked.

"No." Pitt stood up and straightened his

back. "No, there isn't, especially where the Prince of Wales is concerned. A lot of old debts could come due when he is king. And that can't be long." He felt a sudden tightening in his throat. It was not just the end of a long reign, the turn of the century, and a fast-dying world. It was also a little old woman who was tired, lonely, and afraid for an uncertain future she would not be there to guide. And now there was the dreaded possibility that the man in whose hand she was leaving it was not wise enough or strong enough to do it well. She had no choice except to do what she could in the remaining time.

"Thank you, Jack."

Jack rose as well and offered his hand in an instinctive gesture. Pitt clasped it hard.

That evening at home Pitt did not mention to Charlotte that he had seen Jack, and he knew that Jack would not tell Emily either. But the omission made him uncomfortable. Suddenly he had too little to talk about because he was thinking of what he must avoid; all his thoughts returned to the subject of Halberd's death.

Charlotte was sitting on the sofa opposite him, her sewing basket open as she chose threads to mend a dress of Jemima's where the hem had come down. Her fingers moved with certainty, stitch after stitch, the light from the gas lamp above her fiery on the needle, and the faint click of its tip rhythmic against her thimble. It was a sound he always associated with comfort.

She had not changed much. To him it seemed barely at all. He had always thought her beautiful. Perhaps she was not traditionally so, but the strength of character in her face appealed to him. He did not like prettiness. Obedience, far from making him happy, disturbed him. Constant, predictable agreement made him feel achingly alone, as if he were speaking to a mirror reflection of himself, not a living, passionate, thinking person whose ideas and emotions complemented his own, sometimes changed or completed them, never simply echoed.

He could not remember if he had ever told her so. Surely she knew anyway?

"There was a letter today from Aunt Vespasia," she said suddenly. "From Vienna. But it was posted over a week ago, and she said they were on their way south, not certain yet exactly where to."

He looked up and realized she was watching him closely. Did she guess how much he was missing Narraway's advice in this miserable case of Halberd's death? He tried to remember if he had said anything to her that he should not have. He hated not being able to confide in her. She understood the reasons, but that did not ease the loneliness of it.

"Would you like to travel?" he asked abruptly.

She looked startled. "I never thought about it. One day, perhaps. Why? Would you?"

"Perhaps in the rest of England. I hadn't thought further."

She started to say something, then changed her mind. She began to stitch again.

He continued to watch but she did not look up. He longed to be able to tell her what he was thinking, ask her what she thought of Halberd. She knew he had died; it had been in the newspapers, after all. He wanted to be able to tell her how much he missed Narraway's advice. And always at the back of his mind was that Halberd's butler, Robson, had spoken of Narraway's dangerousness, his unseen hand everywhere. A bit like Halberd himself.

Pitt had worked with Narraway on and off for several years. He even knew that Narraway had once been in love with Charlotte, but he had done nothing about it. How much did she know of that? She had never said anything to Pitt, but then, she wouldn't. What had been given words could never be totally forgotten. It was a dream, and now Narraway had realized that Vespasia was the woman he really loved.

Marrying her had changed him, in very subtle ways. To Pitt's mind, all were for the good. The brooding loneliness was gone, replaced by an infinite ability to doubt, to be wounded, like anyone else who cared with a whole, passionate heart. Pinpricks he would once have brushed off now drew blood — only a little, but sufficient to remind him of his own capacity for pain.

What had he been like before, when he was head of Special Branch? Harder, more willing to take risks because he could measure the cost? Or simply less aware of the chances of losing? He had been born to social position — not aristocracy, but to wealth, high intellect, and a university education in which he had excelled. Pitt had discovered only recently that Narraway's education had included a law degree, and then the right to practice in court. He had kept it current, and only recently used it again — brilliantly. A complicated man.

And yet Pitt had also seen how deeply he loved Vespasia, and, though rarely, the moments of uncertainty, the sharp knowledge of how much he had to lose if he committed a truly ugly act. It was the first time in his life anything had mattered so much, and it had come after he had been forced to retire from Special Branch, where the stakes were so high, and the loss perhaps irredeemable.

Who had he been before?

"Narraway knew Sir John Halberd," he said suddenly.

Charlotte looked up at him. So she had been right in her speculation. "Be careful, Thomas." She looked down at her stitching again. "I'm sorry. I know you will do." She felt she had trespassed where she was no longer able to tread.

At that moment he would have given anything he had to be an ordinary policeman again, except for the trust placed in him by Narraway, by the Queen and, above all, by Charlotte herself.

He could not think of anything to say that was not trite, and they had never exchanged the meaningless.

Pitt was surprised to receive in the morning post a brief note from Somerset Carlisle inviting him to have lunch at a very distinguished gentlemen's club. Carlisle would meet him at the front door at one o'clock. It was signed in the elegant, flowing hand that Pitt recognized. It was not quite a summons, but it had that ring to it.

At another time he would have resented the peremptory tone and lack of explanation. But Carlisle knew that Pitt considered Halberd's death to be the most important matter he was dealing with, and Carlisle had never wasted Pitt's time.

Pitt dressed carefully, so as to fit in with the type of people who would dine at such a place, rigidly restricted to members and their guests. He was a little self-conscious doing it; making an effort to be tidy did not come naturally to him, as it did to Narraway, who was always elegant.

He also took care to be at the steps leading up to the club's front door at two minutes before one.

Carlisle, another of those men who have valets to make sure they were elegant, came out of the door, saw Pitt and smiled broadly. It was more than a welcome; it was bright with humor and anticipation.

"Glad you could come," he said quietly. "Food is excellent. I'm partial to the duck pâté, followed by roast lamb." Typically, he made no reference to the late invitation, which Pitt had accepted without question.

The doorman inclined his head graciously to Carlisle, looked more closely at Pitt to make sure they were together, then opened the inner door before they reached it. "Good afternoon, sir."

"Good afternoon," Pitt replied, following Carlisle into the large dining room with its chandeliers, Adam fireplaces, and a thick carpet that enveloped their footsteps in silence.

A steward showed them to a far table by one of the windows. Its view onto an inner courtyard was pleasing. He pulled out their chairs for them and made sure the table napkins were opened and placed on their knees. The wine menus were offered.

"Thank you, Benton," Carlisle said. "I'll have the duck pâté, and then the lamb. I think Commander Pitt will have the same?"

"Yes, thank you," Pitt agreed.

The steward offered wine, and Carlisle declined it, then after a brief glance in Pitt's direction, decided for him as well. "Better not," he said as the steward withdrew. "This invitation was not for your enjoyment. You may find something interesting." The gleam of amusement was still on his face.

Pitt had been placed where he had the wider view of the room, and it was a moment later that he saw the home secretary come in and join a member of the House of Lords and the German ambassador.

"Is this for my general education?" Pitt asked very quietly.

"Not at all," Carlisle replied without glancing around. "Quite specific. You can linger over the port, but I suggest you begin with the pâté as soon as it arrives."

Pitt raised his eyebrows. "Am I going to be put off the rest?"

"Quite possibly."

The pâté was all that Carlisle had promised, and served with slices of brown bread lightly toasted. He was glad the rack of lamb was there before he saw Alan Kendrick come in, Ferdie Warburton close on his heels. Whether it was at Carlisle's request or not — and Pitt could easily believe it was — they were shown to the next table, and without effort Pitt was able to observe them yet appear not to.

Kendrick settled himself as if perfectly at home. He ordered without bothering to look at the menu. The steward did not ask if he wished for wine. It was also clear from his manner that Ferdie Warburton was Kendrick's guest. He looked at the menu briefly, squinting at it a little, then chose something without making any deliberation. He accepted the steward's suggestion for wine. He sat very upright in his chair.

Pitt wondered if it was his gambling that made him nervous, or Kendrick himself. He thought the latter.

Kendrick, on the other hand, was almost complacent. He led the conversation. Pitt caught snatches of it while eating his lamb and spring vegetables.

"I don't know if I can get it for you by then," Warburton said unhappily. "I don't know the man well enough."

"For God's sake, Ferdie, you can charm the birds out of the trees when you want to." Kendrick did not bother to hide his impatience. "I need to know if he's running the damn horse at Ascot or not! I need to know if it is in top form. If it is, it'll win."

"He's not going to tell me!" Ferdie protested.

Kendrick leaned forward across the table and spoke so softly Pitt could not catch the words, but the hard, suddenly ugly lines of his face made his meaning plain. Then he straightened up and leaned back, his old smile wiping away the darkness. "You're a good man, Ferdie. You have an obscure talent, but a very valuable one. Shall I send the steward for some more wine for you?"

Ferdie accepted.

Pitt looked across at Carlisle and met his

steady gaze.

"Thank you," he said quietly.

"We'll retire to the lounge when we've finished," Carlisle said quietly. "That should be more interesting. Prepare yourself. The port is excellent, but pretty heavy stuff. I suggest you play with it rather than drink it. You ought to be in your best form if you cross swords with Kendrick."

Pitt had had no intention of doing so, but he realized that to retreat now would not only signal his cowardice to Kendrick but, more important to Pitt, it would also signal it to Carlisle. The rack of lamb was tender and delicious, but it had lost its appeal. Now it was just food. He declined dessert.

"Nonsense," Carlisle told him. "The apple pie is perfect with a little cream." His smile widened. "Fortify yourself, Pitt." Twenty minutes later, when Pitt was sitting in a large, leather-covered armchair and Carlisle was relaxing opposite him, a glass of brandy at his elbow, Kendrick and Warburton came into the room.

"Hello, Kendrick," Carlisle said cheerfully. "Care for a brandy? It's one of the best. Napoleon would have been happy to see his name on it. You know Pitt, don't you?" He waved his hand in Pitt's direction. "Head of Special Branch. I believe you knew Victor

Narraway, his predecessor."

Kendrick was caught off guard but he recovered immediately.

"Yes, of course. Good afternoon, Pitt." His manner was cool, but amiable enough.

Ferdie Warburton smiled more affably and accepted the seat nearest Carlisle, leaving the one near Pitt for Kendrick, who had little choice but to sit also or deliver a noticeable rebuff. He might not have cared about Pitt, but Carlisle was a senior member of the House of Commons although he had never held political office and almost certainly never would. He was far too erratic politically, a man of too deep emotions to follow any government rules, but he was held in surprisingly high regard by people in and out of the Establishment. Only a fool would underestimate his influence. Pitt had learned that some time ago. Carlisle was a good friend to have, if he liked you, being both loyal and brave. He might be an equally bad enemy. Perhaps Kendrick could see that also.

The steward appeared at Carlisle's elbow, and he ordered brandy for both of the men who were now his guests.

"Not very good news from South Africa," he said ruefully, looking at Kendrick. "I believe you know Alfred Milner? What do you think he is going to do? He's not really going to go hand to hand against Kruger, is he?"

Kendrick smiled. "You overstate my knowledge of him, Carlisle. It is some time since we've had any contact."

"Has he changed from the man you knew?" Carlisle did not seem inclined to let the matter go. "Does he think Kruger will back down?"

From what Pitt had learned of Paul Kruger, president of the Transvaal, he would be the last man to back down, whatever the enemy or the cost, but he said nothing. This was not really about Kruger, or even about Africa; it was about Kendrick and what he was willing to say, or might let slip if pushed.

"Do you think he won't?" Kendrick responded. "Or are you suggesting that we should?" There was a thin vein of scorn in his tone.

"I think anyone with diplomatic skill of even the barest sort would have more sense than to put us in a situation where it was necessary," Carlisle said frankly. "Unless, of course, he had some interest in there being another Boer war?"

Kendrick raised his eyebrows. "That suggests you think we will lose."

Suddenly the atmosphere was different,

harder. Ferdie Warburton forgot about his own embarrassment, even about horse-racing and money, and stared at Carlisle earnestly.

Kendrick turned to Pitt. "Is that Special Branch's point of view, Mr. Pitt? You're afraid we could lose — against the Boers?"

Pitt gave him an honest answer. "Possibly not militarily, at least for a while. I mean a few decades. But economically is a different matter . . ."

"Have you even the faintest idea how much gold there is in Johannesburg alone?" Kendrick demanded. "Not to mention diamonds."

"A reasonable assessment, yes." Pitt met Kendrick's eyes unblinkingly. "What do you think a war that far away from Britain will cost us, in money, weapons, and men's lives? What about future trade? Not to speak of international goodwill? And if you reduce everything to money, you need to put a price on other nations' judgment of our morality and what we may have to do, fighting against a largely civilian population of farmers and their families. We may pay for that for a longer time than we imagine."

"You sound like a politician!" Kendrick derided. "Are you running for office?" It was a joke, not a question.

"I don't sound like any politician I've ever heard," Pitt answered him. "I hear 'expedient or not,' 'popular or not,' 'expensive or cheap.' I don't hear right or wrong so much."

"Then you should listen to Alfred Milner," Kendrick shot back at him. "He thinks it is our moral duty as a superior civilization to care for those less able, less wise, less advanced. It is a moral responsibility, and a good man accepts that and does his best. Counting pennies doesn't come into it."

"Well said by a man who has hundreds of thousands of pennies," Carlisle said bitingly. "Wait until your children lie awake all night, crying because they have nothing to eat."

"I don't believe Milner lives where he can hear that," Pitt replied before Kendrick could speak. "Or where he can send the butler for more brandy."

"In a club such as this, Mr. Pitt, he is referred to as a steward." Kendrick's sarcasm was knife sharp.

Pitt laughed. "Is Mr. Milner sitting around in a gentlemen's club? I thought he was in Africa arguing with the Boers. That could explain the lack of grasp on the details."

Kendrick swore under his breath. "Since you're not a member here, I'll get the steward myself." He raised his hand and the steward appeared almost immediately.

"Yes, sir?"

"Another brandy each," Kendrick asked. "Except Mr. Pitt here. He doesn't appear to drink."

While the steward fetched a further brandy for the three of them and served it, Ferdie turned to Pitt and asked a question about horse-racing. It was an obvious attempt to turn the conversation to something less contentious.

"Don't embarrass the man, Ferdie," Kendrick said with a quick, hard smile. "His experience lies with cart horses — sorry, perhaps I should say shire horses; it sounds less —"

"Rude," Carlisle supplied for him, his smile equally tight. "Actually, I think his expertise lies with knowledge of a different sort . . . more pertinent to . . . all sorts of things."

"Oh, yes," Kendrick turned to face Pitt. "Sorry. We horse-racers get a bit myopic where other subjects are concerned." He left the remark hanging in the air to be interpreted as anyone wished.

Pitt accepted the challenge. It was what Carlisle had asked him here for, and he would not get a better chance.

"Not really one to gamble my money on

winning," he said, looking at Kendrick and ignoring Ferdie.

There was a moment's silence. Kendrick waited, ignoring his brandy.

"More of a hunter," Pitt finished.

"Gamble my life, and yours, on winning . . . eventually," Kendrick replied.

Ferdie laughed nervously.

"So you are," Carlisle said with guarded eyes and a smile on his lips. "Told you, he took over from Narraway. You knew Narraway, didn't you, Kendrick?"

"Probably better than you think," Kendrick replied. "Or you," he added, including Pitt this time. "A great information collector, which is a dangerous occupation."

Ferdie looked increasingly uncomfortable. He shifted slightly in his seat.

"Usually personal and unpleasant," Kendrick went on. "I suppose it's necessary, grubbing around in other people's secrets, looking for something to use. It's hardly a gentleman's occupation. And as I just said, it's dangerous."

Pitt pictured Sir John Halberd lying senseless, facedown in the waters of the Serpentine, drowning. Quite suddenly he was deeply angry.

"Profoundly," he agreed, with no lift of good humor in his voice, no easing his face.

"When you find out something really ugly about some people, they don't face you openly as a soldier would, or on the floor of the House of Commons, to argue it out. They are more likely to stab you in the back, in some dark street where there is no one to help you. Or crack your skull and leave you to drown in a lake or river, so the unpracticed observer thinks it was an accident."

Carlisle's eyes opened wide. Kendrick's body stiffened.

"Oh God!" Ferdie let out a slow gasp. "Are you saying that John Halberd was murdered? He was a collector of all sorts of information. He knew everyone!"

"Don't be so damn stupid!" Kendrick snapped. "He's baiting you. Halberd probably had too much to drink and refused to buy a prostitute. Her pimp got into a fight with him and Halberd came off worst. I daresay it was an accident in that the man didn't mean to kill him." He turned to Pitt. "That's the problem with you people ferreting out all sorts of things. You can't leave even a decent man alone, you have to go sniffing around the midden and digging up things a better man would leave buried."

There was a hot silence. Even Carlisle was startled.

"Talking about knowledge," Pitt said

slowly and clearly, "it seems you know a great deal more about that particular incident than most people do. There is no evidence that there was a woman involved, or that she was a prostitute with an impetuous pimp. How do you know that?"

Another burning silence. Even Carlisle was rigid in his seat now.

Kendrick replied at last. "This time you are right, Pitt. It was only an uneducated guess, based on my acquaintance with the man. He was a clear example of one who gathers up every scrap of grubby knowledge about people, and still has no idea how the real world works. It was only a matter of time before he made an expensive mistake. It was his misfortune that it was also a fatal one."

Pitt's mind was racing, but he managed to maintain his calm, even his smile. At least he thought he did. Carlisle was sitting opposite him, just the faintest movement of his chest indicating that he was breathing.

"Knowing so much about it, I'm sure you must have warned him that trawling for prostitutes in Hyde Park was unwise," Pitt said slowly. "Apart from the awkwardness of a rowing boat out on the Serpentine for such adventures, there is the extreme likelihood of unintentionally bumping into someone you know."

Carlisle let out a guffaw of laughter.

Ferdie Warburton choked and went into a coughing fit.

Kendrick rose to his feet, knocking over his empty brandy glass, which rolled onto the floor.

"I thought Narraway was ghastly, but at least he knew what he was doing. You, sir, are a fool in policeman's clothing. You should leave the job to those who are capable of doing it at least efficiently, if not well!" He turned and walked out, leaving Ferdie Warburton to scramble to his feet and follow after him.

"Bravo," Carlisle said quietly. "You might be either brilliant or disastrous, but no one could call you a coward. I know a lot more about Kendrick than I did an hour ago. I hope you do too."

"Unfortunately Kendrick also knows a lot more about me," Pitt replied, his mouth dry.

"Then he'll either back off a little," Carlisle said, "or else he'll attack."

By late that afternoon Pitt knew which of the two it was to be. At five o'clock he was sent for by His Royal Highness, the Prince of Wales. Unlike the Queen, he did not send a carriage for Pitt, merely a hand-delivered message, formal and peremptory in tone. Pitt was to bring the note with him, and if presented to the prince's staff, it would gain him entrance to Kensington Palace, where the prince was presently staying.

Pitt told Stoker where he was going and caught a hansom cab at the end of Lisson Grove, giving the startled driver the address of Kensington Palace and the entrance at which Pitt was to present himself.

He sat in the cab, oblivious of the streets he was passing through and the delays caused by traffic jammed in the evening bustle. He had a considerable history with the prince, very little of it fortunate. It started when Pitt was thrown out of the police force and found Special Branch the only law-enforcement body that would employ him.

Narraway had been the head of Special Branch then, and the Prince of Wales had been deeply unpopular with a large section of London's inhabitants. The Queen was still very much in mourning for Prince Albert, even though he had been gone for years. In the eyes of many, she neglected her subjects. The Prince of Wales lived ostentatiously beyond his means and borrowed money from many people, never intending to pay it back. For one particular man it had ended in death, nearly closing his factory and losing employment — and thus livelihood and home — for hundreds of families.

The East End of London was on the edge of a revolutionary rising. It had not happened, but it had come far too close for comfort. The prince's self-indulgence had been a high contributing factor, and he was made aware that Pitt knew it.

Then there had been the tragic affair involving the prince's intention to back the building of a railway line from Cairo on the Mediterranean, through Africa — nearly all of which was British ruled, right to Cape Town on the southern tip. It was a marvelous dream — but again, it was Pitt's solving of a murder that had precipitated its collapse. And of course Pitt had interviewed the prince and witnessed his failure. That was unforgettable.

Now the prince had sent for Pitt. Edward would soon be king, but that did not affect the fact that Pitt's loyalty was to the throne itself, not to Edward or his frail, grieving mother.

The cab stopped. Pitt alighted and paid, then, drawing the prince's instructions out of his pocket, walked up to the guard at the side door and presented the card.

Half an hour later he was standing by the window of a pleasant sitting room when the footman told Pitt that His Royal Highness would see him now.

The second room was very like the one Pitt had just left, only larger. Edward was standing. He was looking very much his nearly sixty years, heavily built, much more than when Pitt had last seen him. His hair was thinning, and his beard covered almost all the lower part of his face. His eyes had a slightly downward outer slope, as always; usually they reflected clarity and humor, if not the joy of life.

Now he looked Pitt up and down with acute displeasure. Pitt knew better than to speak first.

"Alan Kendrick is a friend of mine," the prince began. "Do you suspect him of something criminal?" He was several inches shorter than Pitt, but still managed to look at him disparagingly. Pitt was startled. That was the last thing he had expected the prince to say.

"No, Your Royal Highness." There was no other possible answer.

"Then what the devil are you doing publicly insulting him as if he were some common hooligan? Have you no sense of who he is?" Edward demanded.

All the way here, Pitt had been trying to plan what he was going to say, but nothing in his mind fitted the interview at all. How could he say "He insulted me, and I insulted him back"? It sounded like something out of the school yard for ten-year-olds!

The truth, or at least part of it, was the only thing he could rely on.

"We quarreled over the death of Sir John Halberd, sir," he said quietly, trying to keep his tone and attitude respectful. "Mr. Kendrick believed that Sir John was with a prostitute and her pimp attacked him. I am looking into the matter —"

"Why, for God's sake?" the prince cut across him, his face red with anger. "Let the poor man rest in peace. How is it any of your business how it happened? Can't you keep your nose out of anything?"

Pitt clenched his hands at his sides. "If a loyal subject of Her Majesty, and one whom she trusted as an adviser, is first murdered and then his memory slandered, no, sir, I cannot."

"Murdered?" The prince was stunned. "Who murdered him? Do you think that? Are you sure?"

"I believe he was murdered, sir. There is no way he can have fallen accidentally and hit his head on both the oar and the side of the boat in the way his injuries and the blood on the boat indicated. I don't know who is responsible, or why, but I am doing all I can to find out, discreetly. I am also doing whatever I can to find out why he was there in the first place, in a rowing boat on the Serpentine, after dark and apparently alone. But it is not easy to do so without ruining his reputation. It is not made easier by Mr. Kendrick's loudly expressed opinion that Sir John was there with a woman of the street."

The prince pulled his mouth into a tight line of displeasure, as if someone had broken a bad egg near him.

"Why the hell was he such a fool?" he demanded. "Do you know, Pitt?"

Pitt found himself defending Halberd with some heat. "I know of no reason to believe he was doing anything of the sort. I think he may have been meeting someone, but it could have been a man or a woman, and for a variety of reasons."

"Such as . . . what?"

Should Pitt tell him anything close to the truth? That it was for Victoria? No. He did not have to question himself to know that the prince was the last person who should even guess at Halberd's task.

"I don't know, sir. The more I look into

his life, the more I see he knew a great deal about people and affairs."

"Whose affairs?" the prince said suspiciously.

"Business and political matters, sir, not personal, so far as I know."

The prince considered in silence for several minutes. Pitt stood to attention, waiting.

"Then I suppose you had better get on with it," the prince said at last. "But Alan Kendrick is a friend of mine. Good with horses, really very good. Never knew a man who judged his bloodstock with more skill. And loyal! I don't forget loyalty. Or disloyalty, Pitt. Remember that."

"Sir." Pitt stood to attention, meeting the prince's eyes. One day this man would be king. He had waited for it all his life. Now he was portly, gray, and far from the young man he had been. His accession to the throne would change a lot of things, far more than anyone could foresee.

It might change the whole of life for Pitt as well.

"All right," the prince said abruptly. "I suppose you had better find out what happened to Halberd. Don't charge around like a bull in a china shop! You can do that . . . ?"

Pitt drew in his breath, and let it out. "Yes, sir."

CHAPTER 6

Charlotte had a restless day. She saw that Pitt had dressed unusually formally and knew that he needed to go somewhere that required it of him. He had no interest in clothes for style, only for comfort. The only article he cared about was boots. He greatly appreciated if they were also smart. Recently he had dropped his old habit of stuffing all kinds of things into his pockets because he realized that he needed more than the affection of his men; he needed their respect. He must look like a commander of Special Branch, even more for the general public and the aristocracy he quite often had to deal with. He would never match Narraway for elegance, but he moved with ease, and that was a kind of grace.

And so she knew that wherever he was going to lunch today, he was nervous about it. She had nearly said something to reassure him, but just as she was going to speak, she saw how unwelcome it would be. It was not a superficial tension in him: The anxiety was deep.

And yet he could not tell her anything about the case. He should not even have mentioned Sir John Halberd and Narraway. Of course, this lack of information had only succeeded in driving everything else out of her mind. She was worried for him. He could not triumph in everything — nobody did — but he had to win all the big ones. There were enough people who thought Victor Narraway had entrusted too much to Pitt in promoting him so far, so quickly. Having a brilliant career as a policeman solving murders was not the same thing as heading a whole force that deals with treason, sabotage, and bombings. The stakes were often ideological rather than personal, and the perpetrators were anyone from foreign refugees without a penny to their names, living on whatever they could find around disused warehouses, up to the landed aristocracy whose loyalty to the Crown might be suspect and whose ambitions outgrew their places.

If Pitt was worried about this case, then it mattered very much. Behind it was someone important, probably someone in society, or he would not have gone to the party attended by Lady Felicia Whyte. His brush with Kendrick there was significant, it had to be, or Pitt would have walked away from it.

But there was nothing she could do, because he could not tell her! Why on earth was she spending her day on small chores, like cleaning the pantry, as she was doing now, when Minnie Maude could have done them very well? Minnie Maude had replaced Gracie when Gracie had at last married Tellman and started a family of her own. Apart from adopting a stray dog and, to begin with, hiding him in the cellar, Minnie Maude was an excellent maid, and Charlotte had already grown fond of her. The dog, Uffie, took more time to get used to. Once discovered, he had been allowed upstairs, and now he had practically taken up residence in the kitchen and was thoroughly at home. Even Pitt agreed that he was here for life, and often stopped to have a word with him and stroke him and admire his soft coat. He had no idea Charlotte did exactly the same. Sometimes she actually sat with him on her knees. He settled his warm little body immediately, and it was comforting.

But Charlotte longed for the days when she had been able to give Pitt more practical help. They were not so long ago. Even when Pitt first moved to Special Branch she had been involved. When Narraway was running for his life, Charlotte had gone with him to Ireland and played a major part in solving the case. Pitt had been in France, chasing and assessing a fugitive who had fled London, leaving a man lying in the street with his throat cut.

It felt like a long time that she had been kept out of cases. It might be partly to protect her, but she thought it was mainly because Pitt had been promoted beyond what he was sure he could handle. He was keeping rules he would not have been so bound by before. In the past there had always been someone else as a final arbiter. When he was in the police it was assistant commissioners, and in Special Branch it had been Narraway. Now there was no one.

She was afraid for him. He had never had such enormous weight of responsibility before. It would take a great deal, many successes, to become used to it, if he ever did. He was a man who seldom took anything for granted. He had been very well educated in terms of knowledge, but not when it came to the gentlemanly grace and manners that were a birthright. And he would never have the natural arrogance of being born to lead.

She ached to be able to protect him, and knew even before the question formed in her mind that there was no way she could.

And she was also lonely. She had seen that so clearly in Emily, just a little while ago, when she believed Jack no longer found her interesting. The same fears stalked Charlotte herself now. Had she become predictable, like a favorite comfortable piece of furniture, eventually completely taken for granted, just part of the room where you feel at home? When do you look at it and suddenly see how shabby it has become?

She kept up an appearance of calm contentment when Daniel and Jemima came home in the mid-afternoon, and even through dinner. But when the children were gone about their own various interests for the evening, she sat in the parlor with the curtains drawn back and the French doors open onto the garden. She remembered the children playing in it when they were younger: Pitt teaching Daniel how to catch a ball; Jemima at about three, bent over next to Pitt pulling weeds, thrilled because she was helping him. Charlotte had stood inside watching, aching with love. The light breeze ruffled the leaves on the poplars and there was a sweet smell of roses drifting inside.

All was at peace.

Pitt was in the armchair opposite her. His eyes were closed as if he were asleep, but she knew from the tension in him that he was not.

"How was your luncheon?" she asked suddenly.

He opened his eyes. "Duck pâté and a rack of lamb," he replied. "It was excellent."

She looked for laughter or slight mockery in his expression, and saw none. Was that his way of telling her not to ask? Was she expected to interpret it and obey? Did she risk creating a stupid quarrel if she was tactless enough to pursue it? She was being childish, and yet the sense of exclusion was as sharp as a physical pain.

"Who did you dine with?" The minute the words had escaped her she regretted it. But adding something now might only make it worse. She had nothing to say herself. She had been nowhere and met no one. Was she turning into the kind of boring woman she despised, who could talk about nothing but gossip?

"Somerset Carlisle," he answered. "I thought I said so?"

"No."

"Oh. Well, it was Carlisle."

"How is he?" This was absurd. Carlisle

would not have asked Pitt at a couple of hours' notice except for something he believed of intense importance. She remembered how closely he had been involved before, and it had been hard to say on which side of the law. What he believed was morally right, always, but not everyone would agree with him. "He is involved in your case." She made it a statement. When he did not answer she became much more afraid.

"Thomas! Be careful! He's a complete . . ." She did not know how to finish.

Pitt's eyebrows rose sharply. "Isn't that why you like him, because he's an 'outsider,' to use the colloquial term? Unpredictable, outrageous, but always brave."

"Is that what you think I like?" She was surprised.

"I think you have a natural affinity." For the first time he relaxed a little and smiled.

"I'm not as extreme as he is," she protested. "Not at all!"

"You have been," he pointed out. "And I don't have any doubt that you will be again, if you think the occasion warrants it."

With both pleasure and pain she remembered some of the cases she had helped with in the past. There had been tragedy, danger, intense pity, but always a sense of fighting side by side, of sharing passionately in something that mattered.

"I will," she agreed fervently. "I don't have to step sideways out of life just because I'm married. That isn't the end of everything. It's supposed to be the beginning."

He looked at her very steadily, and she was carried in memory back to when they had first met, and he thought her so protected that she had no understanding of what life was like for most people. She had never wondered where the next meal was coming from, or if there was any coal for a fire, if she would keep the job that gave her a few pennies or lose it. She never had to make do and mend. Her father had both wealth and position.

And none of it protected Charlotte's family from having their eldest daughter murdered. At that terrible time he had seen her courage and strength of will. At least he had thought her capable then. And she was willing to learn. They had taught each other.

"We're well past the beginning now," he said ruefully. "Jemima is eighteen already."

She knew that — very well! She now had a daughter who was no longer a child but a young woman looking toward marriage herself. It made her feel suddenly old, as if ten years had passed while her attention was somewhere else. She didn't feel anything like it, but she was over forty. Not exactly a romantic image. What did Pitt see when he looked at her?

"You're right," she said a little sharply. "I do like Somerset Carlisle. He has passion, courage, and honor, and is never afraid to do what he believes is right, whether anyone else agrees with him or not!"

"I think you would find it a little unnerving to live with," Pitt observed.

"I've never thought of living with him." She looked up and blinked back a sudden stinging of tears. "Or did you mean that I am unnerving to live with? Or I was, when I did anything unpredictable?"

Now the conversation was out of control, and she had not meant it to be this way at all. She wanted to help, not make everything worse. What could she say that would mend it?

"Is he helping you . . . with the case you spoke of?"

"I think that is his intention," he said slowly.

She looked at him, sitting back in his chair. He looked so tired, and worried. The last thing he needed was a wife who needed to be told that she was still beautiful, at least to him, and that she could help, be at the heart of things, not out on the edge.

She made a guess, based on what she had heard at the party with Emily.

"Was Sir John Halberd murdered?" He froze, his eyes wide. She knew she was right. "Oh dear," she said softly. "What a mess."

He stood up and she rose also, automatically. He was half a foot taller than her, although she was tall for a woman.

"There is a great deal of speculation," he said gravely. "Most of it unkind, and of the sort I imagine you can guess. You will not add to it. Do you understand?"

"That's unfair!" she said angrily; it was better than showing her hurt. "I have never gossiped like that, and never repeated gossip except to you when I thought it could be helpful."

He sighed. "I know that. But Halberd was a man who moved in the highest society — the very highest — and he knew a great deal about a lot of people. Whoever killed him will not be squeamish about killing again, if they think anyone is a danger to them. And that could include you."

"I'm in less danger than you are!" Now she was afraid for him not only professionally but personally. She forgot about her own feeling of being shut out. She stepped forward and put her hands on his chest, gently. "Narraway and Aunt Vespasia are not here to help, Thomas. I'm going to, whether you want me to or not. I shall be very careful indeed. I do know how to be careful, you know."

"Do you?" he said skeptically. "This person is very dangerous, Charlotte. He or she killed someone very clever, who knew he was in danger."

"What on earth was Sir John doing alone at night in a rowing boat on the Serpentine?" she said quickly. "Do you know the answer to that already?"

"No, I don't."

"Perhaps he didn't expect to be attacked. He was meeting someone else. Are there two people involved?"

"I don't know. Possibly. Sir John knew a lot of things about a great many people. Charlotte, please! I can't afford to spend my time worrying about whether you are safe or not."

"I will be perfectly safe. I will do nothing but watch and listen. And you can't afford not to solve this case, can you?" It was a hard thing to say, but as soon as she met his eyes, she knew that it was the truth. "I'm not asking you to tell me anything," she went on. "I already know that Alan Kendrick is involved —"

"No, you don't!" he retorted. "You don't know —"

"Oh, Thomas. Please! I was with you at Lord Harborough's party. You would never have stood there politely talking to Kendrick if you didn't have a reason to. By the way, did you know that Delia Kendrick was married before she met him? I don't know to whom, but he was a Scot, I know that. And apparently she wasn't Kendrick's first choice either. He courted the Duchess of Lansdowne's daughter, and the duchess declined him as not good enough for her family."

Pitt winced. "Did you ask someone this?"

"No, of course I didn't. Give me a little credit for brains."

"She told you?" he asked incredulously.

"Of course not! Someone else did. I just listened. Delia Kendrick is the sort of woman people gossip about."

"Is there another sort?"

"Of course there is. Principally the sort that never does anything that is worth retelling." She thought she was one of those herself, but it sounded so self-pitying to say so. "You only talk about people you envy," she added.

"Who envies Delia Kendrick?"

"Felicia Whyte, for one."

He looked puzzled. "Why?"

"Because they are of a similar age, and Delia looks ten years younger, at least," she said with a wry smile. "Can't you see that?"

"I never thought of it."

"Oh, Thomas! Whether you want to accept help or not, you need to!" She turned away before he could remonstrate with her. She was going to help — for her own sake, yes, but mostly for his. "I'll be discreet," she added.

He did not reply to that.

She was at least fairly discreet. She went to see Emily again, this time asking in advance what would be a convenient time. Emily replied immediately that afternoon tea would be excellent. Thus at about four o'clock they were together in a small sitting room that looked onto the garden. They ate cucumber sandwiches and very small chocolate éclairs stuffed with cream.

The elegant pewter teapot was piping hot. It would be refreshed at regular intervals with more boiling water.

Emily did not waste time in niceties. "Have you learned anything more?" she asked. "You have! I can see that you are even more worried. What is it?"

"Sir John Halberd's death." Charlotte was

finding it difficult to tell Emily what she needed to know, keep certain facts discreet yet not so discreet that Emily would prompt her to say or do anything that would give away her knowledge. It could forewarn some guilty person, or even put Emily herself in danger.

"I assumed as much, didn't you?" Emily looked at her more closely now. "And what else? It matters to you a lot, I can see that."

"I know you can't do a job like Thomas's without making enemies, but all the same —" Charlotte began.

"You can't do anything much at all without making enemies," Emily cut across her. "You didn't just discover that." She put out a hand and touched Charlotte gently. "What is it really? You were always the one to be disastrously frank, and now you're going around in circles. If you're upset because Thomas doesn't tell you about his cases anymore, you shouldn't be. You'd have no respect for him if he told you things he shouldn't."

"I know," Charlotte said hastily. "And no, of course I don't want him to break anybody's trust. But how can I help if I don't know what it is about? Emily, it's terribly serious. Sir John knew all kinds of things about lots of people."

"Blackmail?" Emily asked.

"Good heavens! I hope not. He was . . ." She stopped. She had no idea what he was. Idealism was not going to be of any assistance to Thomas, and she was surely old enough not to be so unworldly.

"Oh, Charlotte!" Emily shook her head, a look of exasperation on her face. "You've been at home too long. You've forgotten what people are really like. You have been too comfortable, too safe, for years. Your common sense is in hibernation. Of course it could be blackmail, or the fear of it."

"Thomas knows an awful lot of things. It's part of his job to know. Victor Narraway knew even more." She had forgotten for a moment how much Emily knew about the treason at Lisson Grove, and Charlotte's travels to Ireland with Narraway, when Pitt's life was in danger in France — or, to be more honest, if Emily had known that Narraway had once been in love with Charlotte, or at least thought he was.

Emily's expression did not offer any answer. "Of course Narraway knew lots of things," she said impatiently. "And maybe Halberd wouldn't stoop to blackmailing anyone. But does everybody else know that? What on earth was he doing on the Serpentine at night anyway? Obviously something secret. Perhaps he tried blackmailing the wrong person? Is it someone Thomas needs to protect, do you suppose?"

Charlotte had wondered the same thing. "It could be. It would have to be a very bad secret indeed."

"There are very many bad secrets," Emily reminded her. "I could think of half a dozen quite easily."

"Well, it wouldn't be something everyone was gossiping about already," Charlotte responded. "What could be bad enough to kill over? Not an affair. Half the aristocracy is sleeping with people they aren't married to. One looks the other way. I haven't been so far out of society that I've forgotten that."

"If your son and heir to your title and lands is not your husband's, that will cause a little ill feeling," Emily answered. "But that's not what I had in mind. People care about money, or being made to look stupid in front of others. We all have something we care about; some possession, or reputation or appearance. Especially in society, you are what people believe you are, at least for the most part. No one wants to be thought a cheat, or a coward. No one wants people to know if someone jilted her, or she made a fool of herself with a man who found her boring, or ugly."

"But to kill rather than be blackmailed over such a thing?" Charlotte said skeptically, taking another chocolate éclair.

"No, probably not to begin with," Emily answered thoughtfully, taking one herself. "But maybe he tried too often. Or blackmailed somebody over a small thing, and they had something much larger to hide. Do you think?"

Charlotte considered for several moments. "Perhaps. But it sounds like an ordinary domestic murder, not something over which to call in Special Branch. There are all sorts of sad and grubby things that happen, sometimes to people you would least expect. But it's still not a government concern."

Emily raised her eyes, then looked back at Charlotte with exaggerated patience. "You have been out of society for far too long. You are beginning to become . . ."

"Ordinary?" Charlotte suggested. "Perhaps you are too considerate to say 'boring'?"

"Oh, my goodness!" Emily stared at her, but instead of derision in her eyes there was a sudden softness.

Charlotte was afraid to ask. She felt terribly vulnerable. Emily was her younger sister, and Charlotte had always been the elder, the taller, the leader in many ways.

Emily had the title and the money, but Charlotte had never envied her those. Charlotte had the emotional security of being with a man who loved her, and she had the adventures as well. She had the sense of purpose because she was involved in helping him in things that mattered, that touched on the highest joys and the deepest tragedies in life. At least it had been that way.

Emily had been through her crisis — feeling left behind, becoming an unnecessary appendage — and she had found herself a purpose again. Now it was Charlotte, passionate, indomitable Charlotte, who felt out of step and more ornament than of use.

But pity was the last thing on earth she wanted, particularly from her younger sister, who it seemed knew her too well.

"Oh, my goodness — what?" Charlotte demanded.

Emily bit her lip. "I was going to say 'too idealistic,' " she replied. "You have forgotten just how ordinary we all are. Under the extravagant clothes and the careful manners, we are as trivial and grubby as anyone else. I know it sounds absurd, but even dukes and duchesses get colds in the head, indigestion, and pimples, and other even more indelicate complaints."

Charlotte laughed in spite of herself, then realized how close she had been to tears. Was it that she was frightened and felt useless because Pitt was so much on his own, and she could not help? She could not even be told what it was really about.

"Nobody can blackmail you over that," she replied to Emily. "As you say, it is the common lot of human beings. If Thomas is involved, and Sir John really was murdered, then it is something that affects the safety of the state, and not someone merely being made to feel embarrassed, however deeply."

"Then we need to find out who felt so terribly vulnerable they lashed out that way," Emily said reasonably. "And I know a place to begin, right this afternoon. Have you ever been to a ladies' club?"

"A ladies' club?" Charlotte tried not to allow the disappointment to enter her voice, and knew she had failed. She could hear it herself.

"Not what you were thinking." Emily shook her head. "Heavens above, can you see me going to such a place, except under duress?"

"No."

"It is really very interesting," Emily went on. "We care a great deal about recent decisions in Parliament, current events, and plans for the future. I don't say 'hopes'; I really do mean plans. Big ideas, Charlotte. You would love it."

"Big ideas about what?" Charlotte asked skeptically.

Emily's eyes were alight with eagerness. "Improvements in health, changes in the law, in working conditions, prison reform. About a day when women have the vote just like men."

"The vote? You mean for Parliament?"

"Yes, of course for Parliament!" Emily exclaimed. "Why not? We are just as intelligent as men. We may not be as well educated, but do you know any woman who is not at least as good a judge of character as the average man? We have to be! We get by only because we see through most pomposity and understand what people really mean when they give these long, bombastic speeches. Of course there'll be the ignorant and the dreamers among us, just as there are among men. But most of us are a good deal more practical. We know that what matters is a roof over our heads, preferably one that doesn't leak, food on the table, and clean water to drink. For that we have to work. We have to make goods that other people will buy, and do it at a price that makes a profit. To survive, you have to make more money than it costs you to live. Idealism can come later, when you've got survival."

Charlotte stared at her. Everything she was saying made more practical sense than she had thought Emily possessed. Although, thinking back, she realized how pragmatic Emily had always been. Charlotte was the dreamer.

"You're right," she agreed fervently. "We should have a vote on who goes to Parliament. One day perhaps some of us will even represent the people ourselves! Why not?"

"Then you'll come to the ladies' club with me?"

"Yes. Yes, I will."

"Good." Emily stood up. "We are not really dressed for it. I'll change and find something for you."

"Now?" Charlotte said incredulously. "You truly meant this afternoon?"

"Certainly." Emily's eyebrows rose. "Why not? Have you time to waste?"

"What help could it be toward finding out who killed John Halberd?"

"We don't know until we try. Delia Kendrick will be there, I expect. And Felicia Whyte is a strong supporter. And there are others . . ."

"Then we'll go. But you are right." Charlotte looked down at her very plain skirt and pleasant but casual blouse. "I need to wear something better than this. I look . . . provincial!"

Emily hid her smile. "I'll find something." She was walking to the door. She had no need to clear away the tea table. She had servants to do that. "Come upstairs and we'll look."

In Emily's dressing room she very quickly decided on a late afternoon tea gown for herself. It was fairly formal but not dazzling. She knew the pastel bluish green flattered her fair coloring enormously.

When they were young, Charlotte had found it fun being the older sister. It was now very much less enjoyable. She looked at the suits and gowns in Emily's wardrobe. There were several she liked a great deal. She indicated a lilac-colored dress.

Emily shook her head. "Those colors are too pale for you. You'll look as if you're coming down with something nasty."

Charlotte winced. "What about the blue-gray one?"

Emily bit her lip. "It won't fit you."

"How do you know if I don't try it?"

"Because you are a couple of inches taller than I am, and you are a bit more . . . generously built . . ."

Charlotte let out a breath. "You mean fatter!"

Emily shrugged. "I mean . . . I mean you have more . . ." She gestured delicately at her own bust and slender hips. "More womanly. And don't pull faces like that! Most men prefer women with curves to those who don't have any."

"And how would you know?" Charlotte asked.

"Because I watch them, of course. What did you think? And you may not know how many men look at you admiringly, but I've seen it all my life. Now try this on. It's a suit, so it won't be too short in the waist for you. And wear this lace blouse with it, because I've never worn the two together, so it won't look like mine."

"It's gray!" Charlotte said doubtfully.

Emily rolled her eyes. "I can see that. But the blouse is dazzling white, and with all that lace it will look marvelous. Put it on, and stop complaining. We need to be there in good time."

Charlotte was amazed. The skirt was perhaps an inch tighter than was ideal, but Emily was right about the blouse: It was really extraordinarily flattering. It needed a plain-colored suit to show it off. She thanked Emily with feeling, and they set out in Emily's carriage to Albemarle Street and the most excellent club there, open to both men and women.

Charlotte felt nervous, but if she ventured nothing then she would gain nothing. Pitt believed that John Halberd had been murdered, perhaps because he knew something about someone who could not afford to have it made public. More probably, they didn't want it told to anyone in authority, especially someone who could prosecute them, dismiss them from office, or both. This was the sort of place where such people met. Vespasia would have been the perfect person to learn about it, thanks to her knowledge of such people, and all their dreams and nightmares. But she was not here. It was up to Charlotte, with Emily's help.

The club had the charm of a large, hospitable private house. There were big vases of fresh flowers, casual rather than formal arrangements, as if the hostess had chosen them out of the garden. The room they were shown to had a variety of paintings on the walls.

Charlotte could tell by Emily's face that she knew many of the women already there, and was quite at her ease. Charlotte must make the effort to appear just as much at hers. She needed to be, if she was to avail herself of anything that society offered. It was simply a matter of calling back memory, and speaking only occasionally, but as if she did this sort of thing every day.

At first Charlotte did not see either Felicia Whyte or Delia Kendrick. She watched and listened and was drawn into a circle where they were discussing with great seriousness the possibility of another Boer war by Christmas. It was a grim subject and feelings were powerful. One woman had lost a younger brother in the previous fighting in South Africa, and her emotions were understandably raw. He had walked out of their lives one day, off on an adventure to a place everyone had heard of, but very few had been. There had been a few letters home, full of vivid descriptions and tales of bravery. They had received the last one when he was already dead, and they never saw him again. The sense of loss was dreamlike; one forgot it and then remembered again, with new pain.

"It infuriates me that we have absolutely no influence in the government," one woman said fiercely. "If we were equal, we could put a stop to it."

"I don't think that will ever happen," another said wearily.

"Not equal."

"A new century, new ideas . . ." Her companion's voice lifted in hope.

"It is still about money," the second woman told her. "There are diamonds and gold in southern Africa, and who knows what else? We have barely touched the surface."

"No wonder the Boers want to keep it." Emily added her opinion with a look of both understanding and regret.

Charlotte had determined not to speak, merely to listen, but her emotions overrode the decision.

"It isn't only that we will lose the war," she said clearly. "It is the fact of who will get the resources if we don't." She took a breath. "Which will probably be the kaiser."

There was a moment's silence while the other women stared at her. It was Emily who broke it.

"I have already heard that suggested," she said gravely.

"By whom?" the third woman demanded.

Emily smiled, and remained silent, but there was a chill in the air that no one denied.

The thought forced itself into Charlotte's mind — was that really what Pitt was fighting against? Had he not said so, not because it was secret but because it was so very frightening?

It was then that they were joined first by Lady Felicia, and a moment later by Delia Kendrick. She was a woman of no more than average height and an unremarkable figure, but had thick, black hair that gleamed, and eyes so dark the sweep of her lashes seemed to shadow her cheeks.

Charlotte was more than happy to change the subject. The truth of what she had said was a bitter intrusion into the idealism of moments before. But the question of the Boers still dominated the conversation, even as Felicia and Delia joined them.

"I doubt it will come to actual war," Lady Felicia said comfortingly. "Mr. Kruger will back down."

Delia raised her black eyebrows. "Do you think so? He will lose the leadership of the Boers if he does."

"Nonsense." Felicia dismissed the very idea. "We would beat them. That can hardly be what they want."

Delia turned to look at her. "Would you wish to be governed by a foreign power thousands of miles away, who knew nothing about your life or your customs? Who had winter when it is your summer, and vice versa?"

"I would rather be ruled by Britain than be dead, wherever I was," Felicia replied, staring boldly at Delia.

Delia gave her the faintest possible smile. "I believe you," she said very softly.

It was a moment or two before anyone realized the double meaning of the remark; then suddenly they were all quiet. It was no longer a political argument, but personal, nothing to do with South Africa, war, or independence.

Felicia's face burned with color. "And I would rather have that for my family, regardless of my own pride." She was speaking only to Delia. "But perhaps you differ. You give me the feeling that family is of far less importance to you. I think your husband has some interest in heavy industry, doesn't he? Armaments, perhaps?" The implication was slight, but no one missed it.

Delia went rigid, with high spots of color appearing on her pale cheeks.

"I presume it was your husband who told you that?"

One of the other women was doing her best to interrupt, and realized there was no purpose. A change of the apparent subject would not bring peace.

"We will hardly be selling guns to the Boers," Emily said. "It would be treason, and I'm certain Mr. Kendrick would not do that. Surely the question doesn't even arise?"

"Of course it doesn't," Delia snapped. "I don't think that is what we are talking about at all."

"Not in the slightest," Felicia agreed. "This is a very . . . old . . . issue, a difference between us, if you like."

"Older for some than for others," Delia added, looking Felicia up and down, from the shining fair hair, the light catching a few touches of silver in it, past the pale skin, very finely lined around the eyes and mouth, and down the slender, highly fashionable figure in its perfectly tailored afternoon dress.

"About twenty years old," Felicia answered. "To change the subject completely, how is your daughter these days? Someone told me she's married and living . . . I forget where, in some other country? I do hope it is not South Africa? She didn't run away and marry a Boer, did she?"

Delia was white-faced. "She did not 'run away,' as you so coarsely put it. She married a Scot, which is not someone from another country. It is merely the north of this one."

"I wonder if we might return to the subject of what we can do to influence the government," one of the other women suggested, but no one took any notice of her.

"I doubt the Scots see it that way," Felicia responded, as if the other woman had not spoken. The corners of her mouth were turned down a little. "Although it is far enough from London. Does she like Edinburgh? I've heard tell it is a fine city. A little cold, perhaps. But of course a woman must live where her husband has his . . . occupation." Her choice of word implied it was some trade or other.

"She hasn't mentioned Edinburgh. It is not where she lives. And her husband's estate is farther north than that, nearer to Perth," Delia corrected her, her voice tight.

"I don't think I should care for that." Felicia shivered.

"You weren't offered it," Delia said acidly.

Felicia's eyebrows shot up. "My dear, I've been offered all kinds of things!"

Delia smiled. "I'm sure . . ." She let it hang delicately in the air, but her meaning was mercilessly clear.

Someone started to laugh, and choked it back immediately.

"I do think . . ." The woman who had spoken earlier made another attempt to regain the subject of action to influence the government.

Felicia was so furious she could hardly draw her breath, which was just as well.

Delia turned to leave.

Felicia found her voice. "You are fortunate to find *friends*" — she gave the word an odd twist of meaning — "who could help you. Mr. Narraway, was it? Lord Narraway now, I hear. But probably still up to his old habits. I can't imagine what you paid him, but it must have been handsome."

Charlotte heard Emily drawing her breath in sharply, and she felt a chill run through her own body. Could that be true? She had known Narraway for several years now. She thought she knew him well, even some of the sides of his nature that others did not. She had seen his regret in Ireland when he was obliged to tell her of the things he had done, of necessity, to catch the enemies of his country. He was ashamed of the lies he had told, the violent and desperate people he had betrayed, and hated himself for it afterward. But he would do the same again. The soldiers you fight against, military or civilian, are bound to their loyalties just as you are bound to yours. You are easily caught in a position where whatever you do, you turn on someone who trusts you. She knew it hurt him in a way that perhaps not even Pitt understood. A man will hide wounds in front of another man, but on occasion allow a woman he trusts to see them.

Narraway had trusted her: For a short time loved her, or thought he did. Now he loved Vespasia, truly and completely. And Charlotte loved Vespasia too. But what did Vespasia know of all the years before she and Narraway had met, the things that had taught him his wisdom and compassion? They were not easily learned. Would Vespasia love Narraway if what Felicia Whyte was suggesting turned out to be true? Was she right? Or just lashing out at anyone within reach, in an attempt to alleviate her own pain?

"What did Lord Narraway get out of it?" Charlotte asked. She would not let it pass. "Money? Did he need money so much?"

Felicia looked at her as if she'd only just noticed her.

"Not money, Mrs. . . . Pitt." Her scorn was razor sharp. "Of course he didn't need that. Power, and the ability to manipulate other people. That is always what it is about with men like him. Isn't that right, Delia? Power to use anytime he chooses, for the rest of his life. That's how such people work: knowledge, fear, the force of the mind. Really, you are too naïve!"

Emily was stung. She had loved Aunt Vespasia as long as Charlotte had, and Vespasia was actually Emily's aunt by marriage, not Charlotte's at all.

"She's not naïve," she said with a slight curl of her lip. "She just knows how to keep a still tongue in her head, and allow other people to say all sorts of things they might later regret . . . profoundly."

Felicia was shaking with a fury she could barely suppress. "You mean she listens and then goes away ready to repeat the gossip to all her little friends! God help us — I thought she was one of us, Mrs. Radley. You gave me to believe she was."

It was a devastatingly cutting remark, intended to close all doors to Charlotte from then on.

Surprisingly it was Delia Kendrick who came to Charlotte's defense, before Emily could think of anything to say.

"Good heavens, Felicia, if you thought for an instant that she was that kind of person, and you still said all you just did, what on earth might you have said if you trusted her? I can hardly wait for that display!"

Felicia clutched her glass of wine as if she might hurl it in Delia's face.

"If you do that," Delia said distinctly, "it will be you who is not invited here again. I will see to it. And believe me, Mr. Narraway is not the only person who knows a few choice things about other people."

"Is that a threat, Delia?" Felicia was ashen-faced. "Because if it is, I know a few secrets myself! And Mr. Narraway may accept money to be silent, but I will not!"

"Has anyone offered you any?" Delia retorted. "I didn't know you were so . . . financially embarrassed."

"He left you for me!" Felicia spat out. "Don't forget that!"

Delia winced. "I was with child," she said between her teeth. "Or had you chosen to forget that?"

Felicia turned on her heel and strode off.

Emily sighed. "What a shame. I thought we might discuss the battle for women's suffrage. I'm sure she has views on that."

"I should be most interested," Charlotte replied, surprised that while her mind whirled with all that she had heard, she still meant it quite honestly.

"Indeed," one of the other women said, regaining her composure with an effort, and grateful for the change of topic. "Let us tell you what we have done so far, and what we plan to do."

Charlotte smiled and listened.

CHAPTER 7

Charlotte stood in the middle of the sitting room. She had changed back from Emily's borrowed clothes into her own, and she had told Pitt most of what was important about the afternoon at the ladies' club.

Pitt was stunned, not that Delia Kendrick and Felicia Whyte had quarreled so openly — although that was surprising — but at Felicia's certainty that Victor Narraway had helped hide something for Delia twenty or so years ago. And apparently the secret was still dark enough and important enough to cause violent feelings now. Could he possibly have done it to gain money for himself, as they supposed? And more important, was it a secret with which to manipulate others?

Charlotte looked bewildered, hurt, as if something had bruised her when she least expected it. She cared deeply, perhaps because she had seen the vulnerability in Narraway, when to the rest of the world he seemed so effortlessly clever, elegant, always on the winning side, unscathed by the wounds that affected other people. But that had been how she was. She could lose her temper with a perpetual winner, but the moment she sensed real pain, she stayed her hand. She could not help it. She would never wound someone who was already hurt, even with a harsh word, never mind with an act. And she deplored duplicity and manipulation. Her righteous anger and passionate mercy were what had first made Pitt fall in love with her.

In the summer dusk with the lamp lit and the curtains still open, the light was slanted, full of gold, and she could have been the same young woman she had been when they first met, only six years older than Jemima was now! How fluid time was, as deceptive as a change in the light falling here or there.

"Did you ask Felicia Whyte what she meant?" he said.

"No, of course I didn't. I would have given myself away," she retorted hotly. "And I hated her for gossiping. I said something more or less to that effect. I don't think I'll be invited back."

"Is that all it was — gossip?" He wished as intently as she did that it was true, but his rational mind would not accept it.

"No." She shook her head. "Actually they spoke about all sorts of serious things. Votes for women — someday. And the likelihood of another war in South Africa. Do you think there will be one?"

He hesitated. She was only asking for his opinion, not facts.

"Yes, I'm afraid so. Milner has a high reputation. The colonial secretary thinks very well of him, and so does the prime minister, I believe. But he seems to be handling Kruger pretty badly. It's to do with empire, and what he perceives to be our duty toward the peoples in our charge all over the world."

She frowned, unsure of his meaning. "Haven't we a duty?"

"Not if we enforce it through violence. But whatever I think doesn't matter. We have to deal with reality, and it is very likely that Milner will put an ultimatum to Kruger, which Kruger will reject." He was thinking aloud, needing to share his anxiety with her. "A good negotiator never puts the other person in a position where they do not have an escape from fighting that leaves them with any dignity. Kruger will lose his own followers if he is seen to give in."

Charlotte stared at him gravely. "Doesn't the colonial secretary know that? Or does he want another war?"

"I don't know," Pitt admitted. "It may be he really thinks he has a duty to the integrity of the empire, our charge to protect all the citizens, of whatever race. And, of course, to build railways, harbors, all profitable industry, more work for Britain. And to enforce what we think is the law. Or it could be as ordinary as ensuring possession of the unimaginable wealth in gold and diamonds in the mines around Johannesburg. He may even think that if we don't hold on to them, someone else will come in — Germany, perhaps." For an instant Pitt thought of the kaiser's *Weltpolitik,* nine years ago. Perhaps they had not taken it seriously enough. Maybe it wasn't merely posturing?

Charlotte was silent for a moment. "Oh, and Victor? I wish I knew what he had done for Delia — and more than that, why he did it."

"So do I," Pitt admitted. Perhaps it was none of his business. Everyone, even Narraway, made mistakes; it was part of human nature. Pitt was painfully aware of his own errors, but they had sprung from his character; his wish to be a man who was not haunted by arrogance and hasty judgments that had caused him to hesitate when he shouldn't have, to give people latitude that others had to pay for. He was afraid of being considered cruel, a traitor to his own roots in poverty and necessary obedience. And of reaching beyond his abilities, and not being good enough in a position he was not heir to, or trained for from childhood.

Were those qualities the very opposite of what drove Narraway? Were his mistakes born of arrogance, the belief that his decisions were above question or weakness? He had always looked certain of himself. But then, he was a natural leader, and a leader must never be seen to doubt his own judgment, or how could anyone else believe in him? Surely, part of the very essence of leadership was that you took the burden of decision from others?

He moved toward Charlotte and gently put his hands on her shoulders. "I know you are afraid for him, and for Vespasia. But people do make mistakes, even people we love. This was a long time ago. I'll find out what I can, but it may be after I have found out who killed Halberd. That could be a good deal more urgent."

"Halberd knew something," she said, smiling ruefully now. "Please be careful, Thomas. Knowledge is very dangerous. I know you can't do anything without it, and you wouldn't be any use at your job, but just be careful! Halberd wasn't a foolish man, and yet someone managed to kill him, so he can't have seen it coming until it was too late."

"I promise I won't make any assignations on the Serpentine, or anywhere else, alone." He tightened his arms around her and held her very close, knowing that he would not necessarily keep his word.

The fear of what Narraway might have done was still with Pitt the next day. It was not so much the loss of faith in a man he admired as his mentor, someone who had given him protection when he had needed it and taught him a whole range of new skills; more so, he feared that the streak of ruthlessness Narraway had exercised might be a necessary part of the job he had passed on to Pitt.

Pitt was a detective, trained to get information, fill in the missing pieces, deduce the secrets, and, step by step, eventually understand the truth. He was, on occasion, diplomatic, but he despised the deceit of manipulation, the use of fear to make people do what they did not wish to. It was easier to accept if it was used to conceal guilt, but a lot harder if it caused pain to innocent people, and perhaps injury to someone they loved.

He sat at his desk at Lisson Grove and went through old records and papers of Narraway's. He was not looking for the work of twenty years past, but for records of information Narraway had gained, in order to calculate the pressures he had used to keep or break secrets. He had only spoken of generalities to Pitt, so Pitt had to study it all.

He had assumed in the past that Narraway's secrecy was to protect those who had revealed sensitive information. But it occurred to him now that it might have been less altruistic, maybe concealing the methods Narraway had used to persuade — or force — a revelation.

Were these tactics necessary? Was Pitt really too squeamish, too sensitive to his own conscience, to do this job well? And he could never afford to do it less than well. The price of failure was incalculable, and it was not only he who would pay it. The successes would never be known; they were the disasters that did not happen.

Looking through these files now, he memorized names, situations, relationships, movement from lower to higher positions. He noted particularly the scandals that never broke, the tragedies averted — or at least half-concealed, lied about for decency's sake.

Certain names stood out. He needed to learn as much as he could of what John Halberd had known, before he could deduce what had provoked his death. Which among all the secrets and weaknesses had moved someone to kill him?

The files were difficult reading. He found reference to several people within Kendrick's circle of friends. Algernon Naismith-Jones had several times taken the easy way around a potentially difficult issue, with a talent he never boasted about: an ability to create very clever forgeries, impossible for the average person to detect. He had been caught by Special Branch, but on Narraway's instructions not prosecuted. Was that out of mercy — a one-time assistance — or had the possibility of prosecution become a constant threat held over his head? Maybe even the occasional use of his talent by Narraway himself, as the need arose?

What about Felicia Whyte, the spoiled beauty now so clearly fading? There were very old notes on her mother, another fair beauty who had been dazzling in her youth, then dimmed so rapidly. By the time she was fifty, she was afflicted with dementia. She had died relatively young, alone, confused, and tormented by irrational fears.

Pitt sat with the page open in front of him on the desk. These were things he did not want to know, and yet even as he stared beyond the paper, he understood how easily the words could be true. Intrusive as they were, they were the means by which he could find the answers he needed. They were the path to preventing further tragedy.

He would far rather have at least given weakness the dignity of being private, but he knew why Narraway had kept the information. He was there to protect the safety of the state from those who would attack it, for any reason: anarchists, revolutionaries, industrial saboteurs, agents of foreign nations, including traitors with other loyalties or none at all.

What if Pitt's own home and family were the victims, and the man entrusted with the task of protecting them claimed his conscience was too delicate to take a difficult or uncertain step? His answer was a wave of fury. Never! Like any other soldier, you take the wounds, whatever they are, rather than betray those you are there to guard.

He heard footsteps along the corridor outside his office, but nobody interrupted him. His men all had their own tasks to do and would not disturb him. He was the commander.

When Pitt had been the junior, he had trusted Narraway, not wanting to know what he was doing or why. He had been happy to leave the difficult decisions to someone else. It had been difficult enough taking sudden, violent actions on the spur of the moment. He still remembered the decision to shoot a man when there was no other way to stop him. He had not hesitated, but he'd had nightmares about it afterward, wondering if he had been right, how big a part fear or anger had played, pointlessly second-guessing himself. He dreaded the day he found such actions sufficiently commonplace that they caused him no doubt or pain.

Now Pitt was deciding which information contained in these papers he would use to force people to tell him what Halberd had known. Pitt's was a deliberate decision, made in cold blood, or at least with a cool head. He was angry that Halberd had been left unconscious to drown in the Serpentine, and that people who had disliked him were free to make malicious speculation as to what he had been doing there, alone in the dark. It should not be so personal, yet if it did not anger him, where was his own humanity?

Had this something to do with another war in South Africa? He had no idea. Was the Queen right, and Kendrick was exercising a malign influence over the Prince of Wales?

He had given his word to the Queen that he would find out, and it was time to pick up the weapons that he needed to do the job, or else resign and leave it to someone who would not be forever looking at his own hands to judge their cleanliness.

Narraway had believed Pitt was the man for the task. Was he so wrong? If his conscience suffered along the way, what of it? Grown people, men or women, accept that there will be mistakes, pain, regret, but the shame lay in doing nothing, for your own comfort's sake, and letting evil happen because you were too squeamish to fight it, too afraid of the cost. Was that not the ultimate selfishness?

Was it not better that the leadership of Special Branch fall to a man whose conscience troubled him now and then, rather than one whose conscience was always at ease?

He picked up the next file and read it, and the next, and so on until he realized with a start that it was dark outside, and well after nine o'clock in the evening. But by then he knew what he was going to do the next day.

Pitt was in the office by eight and began immediately to search through the files, cross-referencing anything from the ones on Halberd that he had already read with anything known about all the other people Halberd had associated with in the last year. He began with those in Kendrick's circle: Naismith-Jones, Walter and Felicia Whyte, Ferdie Warburton, and, of course, Delia Kendrick.

Would Narraway have committed to paper anything to do with the help he had given her twenty years ago? Was it connected with Special Branch at all? Could it have been personal? Pitt did not imagine Narraway had led a cloistered life. He had been single; he could certainly have had affairs. Pitt knew of one or two already. Duty might require him to find out regarding Delia, but he felt grubby even at the thought of pursuing such a thing about the man who had helped him, trusted him, and was now perhaps his closest friend — apart, of course, from Vespasia, whom he regarded as family.

He learned little more about Ferdie Warburton, reading the notes on his various adventures, romantic and financial, the latter all to do with gambling. What emerged was his charm, his love of horse-races, and the embarrassing fact that when he drank too much, which was rather often, he was prone to long lapses of memory. It made him peculiarly vulnerable to blackmail or, at best, pressure from those who would take advantage of his easygoing nature and rather too much freedom with money.

Pitt smiled as he closed the thick file. He could well see how the Prince of Wales found him a good companion. Rather than helping each other's weaknesses, they mirrored them almost perfectly. Ferdie also was charming, sometimes even witty, and had an educated taste for the good life.

Had that given Kendrick any power that Halberd might have found dangerous? The prince had always had boon companions, people with whom he could enjoy himself, indulge his tastes, and know that at least most of it would go no further. Pitt had had one or two such friends himself, long ago, before police work took up so much of his time and marriage answered his emotional needs. He still found great pleasure in a good conversation with a man he both liked and respected, preferably one who understood the triumphs and disasters of his work and the thoughts that plagued him even after a case was solved. It was a delicate happiness to be able to share with someone who needed no explanations of the feelings for which it was so hard to find words, the self-questioning, the regrets, the painful wondering if it could have been done better, sooner, with more delicacy, and perhaps saved a life or a reputation.

For several years, Pitt's person had been Narraway. Maybe that was what was hurting Pitt now: the shadow over a man who was more than a friend, who in some ways stood in for the father Pitt had lost almost forty years ago. Not that he would ever have let Narraway know that. Even the thought of it was mortifying. He could feel the hot blood in his face.

A knock on the door interrupted him.

"Yes?" he said abruptly.

Stoker came in. His lean, bony face looked tired, his skin pale and drawn tight over his cheeks.

Pitt made up his mind in that moment.

"Come in, Stoker. And close the door. First, what did you come for?" He gestured to the chair. "Sit down."

"Just to report that that Marylebone business is all but closed, sir." Stoker sat down uncomfortably.

Pitt stared at him. "Is that all? You look awful!"

Stoker gave one of his rare sweet smiles. "Wondered about the case you're on, sir. You told us nothing, but you're putting in all sorts of hours, and you look awful too."

"Then perhaps it's time I did tell you, but it must go no further. You are the only one who will know. Lady Vespasia is out of England, Narraway also."

"Yes, sir. In Greece, I believe, or so you said."

"Somewhere like that. We get cards every so often, but they take a long time to get here, so the news is out of date by the time we get it. I'm investigating the death of Sir John Halberd, at the personal request of the Queen . . ."

Stoker's eyes were wide. "Then it was murder? How did she know about it?"

There was no point in telling Stoker a half truth. He would guess the rest anyway, and to evade now would insult him unnecessarily.

"He was investigating a certain matter for her, to do with Alan Kendrick, a friend and adviser to the Prince of Wales. Halberd was about to deliver his report to her, but that night he died in a rather ridiculous accident on the Serpentine."

"Except it wasn't an accident," Stoker finished the thought. "Is Kendrick a suspect?"

"Yes. The only one at this point. Although Halberd seems to have known a lot of people's secrets, or at least things they would rather not have had made public."

Stoker frowned. "Blackmail? Or fear of it?"

"Perhaps nothing as overt as blackmail, just discreet pressure?" Pitt replied, watching Stoker's face.

For an instant Stoker was puzzled, then he understood.

"Could have upset a lot of people," he observed. "Very powerful information. Have you looked through our files to see if Mr. Narraway ever used him?" He still found it difficult to remember that Narraway was "Lord" now, since his dismissal from his position, totally unjustly, and his subsequent elevation to the House of Lords, where his work experience could be useful.

"He doesn't appear to have," he said, "but they did know each other. There's no way to discover if he and Halberd ever exchanged information."

"Bound to have," Stoker assumed, "just didn't write it down. Do you know for sure if Halberd was murdered, sir, or is it only likely? What was he doing there anyway? Was it no more than a good opportunity to catch him alone and off his guard?"

"I'm sure he was murdered," Pitt replied, "but I'd have difficulty proving it in court right now. And I don't know what he was doing there."

"No witnesses yet?" Stoker asked.

Pitt bit his lip. "If there were, they were prostitutes and their clients, or other people going about business they'd sooner deny. I thought about looking, but if I do, as head of Special Branch, I might make the whole mess a lot worse. I don't think Her Majesty would appreciate that."

Stoker's face was bleak. "No, sir, I'm sure she wouldn't. And since Halberd was a friend of hers, it is hardly what she's looking for. And for that matter, Mr. Kendrick is a good friend of the prince's. I've got a few connections in the regular police, sir, who work that patch. I can ask very discreetly, and in these instances I don't mind stretching the truth of it. Can I tell them that no one will have to testify? We just want to know the truth, not necessarily use it."

"If that is necessary," Pitt conceded. He stood up. "I'm going to find out all I can about Mrs. Kendrick. I think she might be the key to at least some of this."

Stoker rose also. "Yes, sir, I'll start straightaway. You using any cover for this? I'm not going to lie to my own men. I'm nowhere if I lose their trust." He looked very steadily at Pitt, and Pitt knew that the message was as much for him, and that Stoker was right.

"Tell them it's a potentially nasty affair that has to be handled with the utmost discretion, in case it touches on the Prince of Wales. That won't be hard to believe."

Stoker's mouth pulled tight. "Not hard enough, sir. I'm not at all sure what it's going to be like under the new king. Lived all my life with her on the throne of England, and a lot of the rest of the world. I don't like change — not that sort."

"Nor do I, Stoker," Pitt agreed. In fact, with the dislike the prince had for him personally, he would be fortunate to keep his position. And he felt, as the reality of it tightened around him, how very much he did want to keep it, deserve it, succeed at it!

The fact that Ferdie Warburton was given to blackouts, and consequently the fear that he had done something seriously wrong, was the place to begin. Pitt loathed doing it and yet, he thought, as deeply as power can corrupt, so also does the abdication of power: the arrogance of misusing it, the cowardice of the failure to use.

Late in the afternoon Pitt found Warburton at a cricket match at Lord's Cricket Ground near Regent's Park. He was casually dressed and looked very much at ease. He held a tankard of beer in his hand. Other men crowded around him, laughing, slapping one another on the back. It looked as if the team they were backing had won.

Pitt felt a total outsider. He had never played cricket, nor had he wanted to, but it was the national game for gentlemen. The phrases for honor and fair play, courage in the face of the enemy, were littered with references to cricket. "It's not cricket!" for the dishonorable. "Last man in" when victory depended on you. "A straight bat" for the trustworthy. "Play up!" and "Play the game!" for life itself, for courage and honor to the last stand; win, lose, or draw.

He kept walking forward, not altering his pace in spite of the doubts in his mind. They would keep him an outsider forever, but perhaps he was that anyway. Would Narraway have done the same thing? Probably, but more cleverly, and he would not have cared what they thought of him. He would never be an outsider in their eyes, whatever he was in his own.

Pitt had almost reached Warburton when the others saw him. Naismith-Jones turned, hesitated a second, then remembered who Pitt was and where they had met.

"Cricket enthusiast, are you? Sorry, old chap, but it's all over. Great game. You'll have to come a lot earlier next time," he said with a smile. "Have a glass of beer?"

"No, thanks," Pitt declined with an answering smile. He hated this but forced himself to turn toward Warburton. "Could I have a private word with you, sir? It's a rather delicate matter."

"We're among friends." Warburton shrugged. He looked at Pitt's face. "But if you say so, we could go for a walk. Regent's Park is right next door." He waved his arm in the general direction of the park.

Pitt accepted, and they moved off together, feet silent on the close-cropped grass, a faint wind brushing by them. It smelled of warm earth and fresh clippings.

"So what is it about, then?" Warburton asked.

"Just a little information," Pitt replied. That was a disingenuous way of putting it.

Warburton's expression was puzzled, but it still held no alarm.

"About what, for heaven's sake? It must be urgent to bring you out here in the afternoon. Didn't Kendrick say you were somebody to do with the government?

What's gone wrong now?"

"Special Branch," Pitt replied. "I can't remember if he said that or not."

Warburton looked incredulous. "What, bombers and anarchists, and all that sort of stuff?"

"That sort of thing, and a lot more."

"Not exactly my field of experience, old chap."

"You may know a lot more than you realize."

"Doubt it. Memory like the proverbial sieve. Sorry." He smiled and came to a stop at the edge of the road, as if intending to turn and go back. He was a pleasant-looking man, standing there in his pale-colored summer trousers and white shirt. His face was freckled and very slightly tanned, probably by wind as much as anything. His expression was agreeable, even friendly, but there was an intensity in his eyes.

"Yes," Pitt agreed, trying to sound equally casual. "I had heard that your memory was liable to . . . lapse at times. It must be inconvenient for you."

Warburton shrugged. "A nuisance, not really an affliction."

"Except when something important has happened," Pitt replied, holding his gaze. "And you need to account for yourself, give evidence that perhaps you were nowhere near an event. Or, of course, swear that someone else was. Then it might matter."

Warburton was motionless for just a fraction too long for it to be natural. Then he made up his mind. "Are you referring to something in particular, old boy? If you think I've seen something in your sphere of . . . of things, you're wrong. I don't know anyone who isn't a decent and well-known member of society. Might have had the odd pint with a disreputable character or two, but who hasn't? Can hardly ask a chap for his political ideology before you let him have a pint."

Pitt drew in his breath, taking a second to decide how to play this.

"People will start to avoid you," Warburton added. He took a step away from Pitt, facing back toward the remnants of the match where people were beginning to disperse. "Sorry, but I can't help . . ."

"I haven't asked you anything yet," Pitt pointed out. "And your lapses of memory are fairly selective. I think some of them may be a kindness rather than the genuine absence of mind."

Warburton turned back to him. "What . . . what are you suggesting?"

"I'm not talking about sexual indiscretions, Mr. Warburton, or gambling debts that remain unpaid rather a long time. Or even about a few odd papers here and there that have been rather carefully re-created."

Warburton paled. He swallowed hard. "Are you threatening me with something?"

"I'm asking for your help," Pitt told him very carefully. "Anything you tell me would be used without your name, and only as necessary. I deal with murder and treason, Mr. Warburton, things I imagine you deplore as much as I do . . ."

"Well, of course . . . I don't know anything! I don't know people who would even think of such things . . ."

"You knew Sir John Halberd."

"He wasn't . . ." Warburton gulped, but his eyes did not waver from Pitt's. "He was as loyal to the Queen and everything she stands for as any man alive. I'd stake my life on that."

"I'm glad, because you may have to. I believe he did and, as we know, he lost it."

"Good God! Are you still thinking he was murdered? Why, for heaven's sake? I thought he just behaved like a damn fool, and overbalanced in that stupid boat and hit his head. Knocked himself out and drowned."

"Doing what, alone on the Serpentine after dark?" Pitt said quietly, yet his deep fear and sadness came through the words.

Warburton pretended to ignore it; still, the awareness of it was in his eyes. "God knows! Some . . . some damn silly assignation, I suppose. But I'm not going to ruin the man's reputation now that he is dead and can't defend himself. Anyway, what the devil is it the business of anyone else?" Now he was as defiant as he dared be.

"And what happened with this assignation?" Pitt asked curiously. "She was frightened and ran off? Is that the sort of woman Halberd met in the park, at night, in a rowing boat? You knew him, Mr. Warburton. Don't tell me that's something you have . . ." he hesitated, ". . . forgotten?"

Warburton blushed, cold anger solely in his eyes now.

"Of course it wasn't! But we all make misjudgments at times. Who knows why he went or what happened?"

"Whoever hit him over the head with the oar, and then left him facedown in the water to drown," Pitt replied, keeping his voice just as level as it was before, although the anger was rising in him too. Not against Ferdie Warburton, but against all the people who knew something and were silent for the sake of their own comfort. "I intend to find out who that was, Mr. Warburton. Who are you protecting? A friend? Or someone to whom you owe a certain loyalty, willingly or not? Someone you are afraid of, because perhaps they know what you did, where you were or with whom, in one of your blank spaces of memory?"

"You bastard!" Warburton said between clenched jaws. His face was now blanched white, his freckles standing out. "The fact that I can't remember everything doesn't mean that I did anything dishonorable!"

"Probably no more than foolish," Pitt agreed. "Embarrassing. But you can't be sure, can you? Tell me, what do you know about Walter Whyte? He has a rather interesting African background, as did Halberd. Did they know each other back then?"

"Not so far as I am aware," Warburton said aggressively. "What has that to do with anything? Walter Whyte is one of the most decent men I know. And he had nothing to do with Halberd. They barely knew each other."

He was lying; Pitt was sure of it.

"Really? That is not what Halberd's notes say."

"Then it must be in one of those moments I have forgotten," Warburton snapped back at him, bleak amusement in his face.

"Yes, I will have to look into the matter

much more carefully," Pitt agreed. "See if we can restore your memory. Someone will know . . ."

Warburton snatched Pitt's arm, and his grip was surprisingly powerful. It would hurt if Pitt pulled away, evidence of the depth of Warburton's fear.

"You swine," Warburton said bitterly. "Halberd knew about Walter's brother, and that Walter lied to protect him, for his fiancée's sake. There was a damned awful boating accident, on the Nile somewhere. Although a few people drowned, half a dozen were saved by Walter's extreme courage. His brother, James, got the credit, though, as the two men looked alike, and their identities were switched. Not that James took it on purpose, it was just a mistake. But Walter let it stand, for his brother's sake, and for the girl he was betrothed to marry. She thought it was James who'd rescued them and admired him for it. James never got over it. He was killed a couple of years later, trying to be the hero everyone thought he was. Walter never told anybody. It was only by accident that I knew. Even Felicia doesn't. I think she would treat him differently if she did." He stopped abruptly. "None of that is your business, Pitt. Still, Walter is a good man, and Halberd knew it and admired him for it."

"And pressured him?" Pitt said very quietly. "It sounds as if Whyte loved his brother very much. Was James the younger?"

"Yes, he was. But no, there was no pressure. Halberd wasn't the sort to pressure a decent man who gave so much to protect his brother. He admired Walter for it. If you don't believe that, then you know nothing of men. And you fail at your job. In fact, worse than that, you'll make enemies of anyone who is fit to know. I'll make damn sure of it."

"Are you saying Halberd didn't put to use all the knowledge he had about people?" Pitt was keen to hear what Warburton would say. It was the impression the Queen had of Halberd, but how realistic was she?

"Yes, I'm saying it." Warburton's voice was still harsh with anger.

"And about people who were less decent?"

"How the hell would I know?"

"The same way you know he decided not to use it for those he respected."

Warburton's shoulders slumped, as if he were suddenly exhausted.

Pitt took a step back, in case it was a bluff.

Warburton was still furious. "You think I would hit a policeman?" he said incredulously. "Or whatever you are! And if you want to charge me with something, or tell the world that occasionally I drink too much and can't remember where I was, go ahead. Most of the people I care about already know."

Pitt felt bruised by the accusation. "I don't want to tell anyone, Mr. Warburton. I want to find out who killed Halberd, and why. If it was over one of the secrets he knew, and was going to act on, then I need to know what they are."

"It would have to be something pretty bad," Warburton replied unhappily. "Halberd was an odd fish, but a decent man. I rather liked him, actually. He had a nice, dry sense of humor. Some tragedy back when he was young, don't know what exactly, but the woman he loved was killed. I thought from the way he spoke of it, just the once, he held himself to blame for it. At least to blame that she was there at all. She traveled there in the first place to be with him. It made him forgive other people's mistakes more easily."

Pitt tried to imagine it: the grief and self-blame of a man who had lost the one woman he loved. He thought how he would feel if some adventure of his had caused Charlotte's death. It was worse than anything he could grasp, a pain that would never stop.

Warburton must have seen this on his face.

"Mistakes," he went on. "But never did he forgive a betrayal, or any kind of cruelty."

"Doesn't sound like a typical courtier," Pitt observed.

"He wasn't," Warburton agreed. "Not much time for the Prince of Wales, but he was intensely loyal to the Queen. Of course he was a protégé of Prince Albert's and he admired him deeply. He came to the court to serve the Queen after Albert's death."

Pitt could imagine how the Queen would have cared for any man who praised her beloved Albert, who remembered him and kept his memory alive for her.

Perhaps if Halberd had shared her belief that the Prince of Wales's rashness and indiscipline had been at least in part contributory to his father's early death, then her passion to see Halberd cleared of any damage to his reputation, even to see his death avenged, was understandable. She would only be satisfied with the answer she could believe was the truth, which meant something Pitt could prove.

Was that a man who kept assignations with prostitutes in a boat in the park? Perhaps Stoker would turn up something, but Pitt profoundly hoped that if Stoker did, it wasn't anything that would disillusion the Queen about the man she had trusted.

"He sounds like a good man," Pitt said.

"He was." Warburton hesitated. "If . . . if you find he was with a woman of the street, do you have to let everyone know?"

"No, I don't," Pitt said quickly. "But I think he went there to meet someone whom he couldn't meet in a more comfortable or usual sort of place. Someone he didn't want to be seen with, and who didn't want to be seen with him."

"A woman?"

"It seems likely."

"Well, if Walter knows, he won't tell you."

Pitt did not answer.

Warburton started to walk back toward the cricket ground, then stopped. "Halberd was very loyal, not just to the Queen, but to the whole idea of empire," he said with urgency. "He wasn't militaristic at all — he had no love of conquering — but he did believe that we have a duty to look after the people we taught to trust us. He believed in the integrity of empire, the good we have promised to do, the trade, the law, the peace, and, of course, the building of great systems of jurisprudence and medicine, exploration, all the things that can be good."

"What did he think of Milner?" Pitt asked curiously.

"Disagreed with the general opinion that he is a fine man. He believes . . . believed . . . that he was too rigid."

"Did he think there would be another Boer war?"

Warburton's face crumpled. "Oh God, no! Do you think it was about that? He was dead against it, and didn't mind saying so. He'd have let the Boer states go rather than use the weapons and shed the blood to keep them against their will. He believed that in the future all sorts of places would become independent, but when they'd learned to stand on their own feet. Like a child growing up and leaving home. He thought we'd not see it in our lifetime. Do you think some bloody warmonger killed him?"

"I don't know," Pitt admitted. "But it's a possibility."

CHAPTER 8

Pitt came home a little later than usual, although because of the time of year it was still broad daylight.

Daniel and Jemima had already eaten and gone to separate parties given by their friends. Pitt and Charlotte took a light supper to the sitting room and sat before the open French doors.

Charlotte could see that Pitt had been outside quite a long time; the sun had caught his face and there was a warm glow to his skin. But it did not hide the anxiety, even deeper than before. She understood something of the issues far more deeply than she had only a few days ago. If Halberd had been involved with the possible war in South Africa, then his death could be infinitely more than a miserable, but very ordinary, scandal.

That brought it back to Special Branch again and explained why Pitt was involved so deeply. And she could not put out of her mind what she had heard said about Narraway.

Was Pitt just as afraid as she was that Victor Narraway had used methods that even he was ashamed of? He would not have wanted them to know, but Pitt had to. Knowledge was the material of his profession. Understanding people was essential in his work, not merely interesting, curious, uncomfortable. It was so much easier to allow yourself to believe what you wanted to and leave your own dreams undamaged.

Pitt could not afford that. Perhaps Narraway could not have either.

Was Pitt going to lose the part of himself that she loved most dearly, the gentleness, the understanding and even pity for those who had betrayed themselves and lost sight of everything but the darkness within? She remembered past cases, in which people had done terrible things and yet he had felt deep, twisting sorrow for them rather than rage. He took no joy in their punishment.

Was he going to lose that? Knowing frailty in people you love is part of growing up. Seeing weakness in everyone is cynicism, and it is poisonous.

"Thomas . . ." she said.

He looked up, and she saw the tiredness

in his eyes. If he had spent the day using his knowledge in a way he dreaded, she should allow him to do it without having to show her. He still needed her to believe in him, and to discover this part of his duty only when he was ready. Maybe even spend all her life looking slightly away, as if she did not see it.

He was waiting.

Now she had to think of something to say, but it must not sound contrived.

"There was another letter from Aunt Vespasia. They are going south, by train, all the way to Sicily," she told him.

He smiled slightly. "Sicily is an island; they'll have to go the last bit by sea. Did she sound well? Happy?"

In a letter one can sound however one wishes, but Charlotte did not say that. "Yes. Italy is marvelously beautiful, if one picks the places to look at. And the weather is perfect."

The question of Narraway hung between them, unspoken. She wished now that she had been able to think of some other subject to mention, but it was too late. Neither of them said so, but they were both wondering about Narraway. Perhaps he had changed. People could, but then, too few actually did.

Would Pitt change too? Charlotte had

cared about Narraway very much, but Pitt was woven into every thread of her life, and that was totally different. It could not be unpicked.

If she had changed, begun to lose what was best in her, would he intrude, regardless, and try to save her? She knew the answer — of course he would.

But then, she would never be doing anything as important as he was. Nobody else's life would depend on what she said. Was that a good thought, or a bad one? Women didn't affect much, except their own children. And perhaps their husbands, or perhaps not.

She thought about the ladies' club that Emily had taken her to. Pity she might not be welcome there again. Was there really a battle to be fought in which women could gain the vote? It could change a lot of things. If as many women voted as men — which of course was not at all likely, she knew — if members of Parliament actually needed women's votes in order to be elected, then the possibilities were considerable! She allowed her mind to explore the thought for a while. It was far more comfortable than wondering what Pitt was thinking, feeling shut out and helpless.

■ ■ ■ ■

In the morning Charlotte telephoned Emily and was pleased to hear her voice. Emily, of course, also cared for Vespasia, so she would have been turning over in her mind the little she knew of Narraway's involvement in Sir John Halberd's life and death.

They knew each other well enough not to need prevarications, and clearly Emily had been thinking about the subject, and perhaps about their standing in the ladies' club.

"I'm sorry," Charlotte began. "I shouldn't have been so outspoken. Have I damaged your reputation with them? You could always promise never to bring me again." It was an apology she had to make, but the thought was painful, an exclusion she did not want.

"On the contrary," Emily said, full of energy, "I will probably be allowed in only if I do bring you. You have no idea how boring some people's lives are."

It was a flattering thought, if slightly absurd, but she found herself laughing at it. "Really?"

"Charlotte!" Emily said impatiently. "We must do something. Maybe we cannot help Thomas's case, but we must find out about

Victor Narraway."

"Do you really think he was involved with Delia?" Charlotte asked. "They seemed to be implying that she had some kind of affair with him. Even that he was the father of her child . . ."

"I know that's what they said," Emily agreed, "but I think that's just vicious tongues. In purely practical terms, Delia and Narraway are both very dark indeed. Before he was gray, Narraway's hair was as black as ink. Apparently Delia's daughter is fair . . . like the Prince of Wales!"

Charlotte winced, but this was no time for squeamishness. She must face the truth, even about friends.

"Then you mean that he used the situation, that he is far more manipulative and without conscience than we thought? And to what end?"

"Is that what you think we will find?" Emily's voice wavered a little.

Charlotte thought of everything she knew about Narraway, about their trip to Ireland. She had learned a lot about him then, both his emotions and his regrets. But he had still said little about his family, home, or early life before Special Branch. He had mentioned the army, but never in detail.

"No," she said to Emily, not entirely

honestly. "I just don't know . . ."

"Then we must make a plan," Emily said. "We must find out what really happened with Delia."

"How on earth are we going to do that? I don't know anyone who knows Delia Kendrick and is likely to even speak to either of us, let alone tell us anything."

"Don't be so feeble!" Emily snapped. "Pull yourself together and get ready. I shall pick you up in an hour."

"Ready for what?" Charlotte was stung because she felt a stab of truth in Emily's accusation.

"I don't know. Just look . . . ordinary." And with that the telephone clicked.

Charlotte put it back in its cradle.

An hour later Charlotte and Emily sat in Emily's boudoir drinking tea and eating chocolate cake, which was highly unsuitable at eleven o'clock in the morning.

"When you don't want to have a certain discussion, but you must, it is a good idea to indulge in something you really like." Emily excused it, and Charlotte entirely agreed. In fact she reached forward and took a second piece.

"We need to find someone who knows as much as possible," she observed.

"Of course, that's obvious." Emily took a second piece as well.

"And who is willing to tell us," Charlotte added. "That makes it much more complicated. I think Lady Felicia Whyte has known Delia for years . . ."

"And hates her," Emily agreed. "But that doesn't necessarily mean she would be willing to talk about her. She would need to have a reason, so she could feel she was doing it justifiably . . . Maybe even to help, which doesn't seem likely."

Charlotte had a sudden idea, or at least part of one.

"Perhaps we could merely ask her to reminisce? If we can get her to recall that time, Delia is bound to come into it."

"Excellent," Emily said enthusiastically. "But of course, if she knows any secrets about Delia she would have told them already. And I really don't want to be known as a gossip . . ." she bit her lip, ". . . if it's avoidable. And people who gossip about people they don't like very seldom tell the unvarnished truth. Which is what we need. If we can find anyone who even knows it."

"Servants," Charlotte replied without hesitation. "And if they ever want to work again, they don't repeat it."

Emily sighed and stared through the

windows at the sunlight outside. "You're right. Especially lady's maids. They know more about you than you know about yourself. If my lady's maid was to gossip, I'd be ruined!"

"Then we need a servant who has retired," Charlotte reasoned.

"And is not dependent on a pension from her past employer," Emily added. "A word about gossip and that would disappear like snow in a rainstorm."

"Don't you mean sunshine?" Charlotte asked.

"No. Sun doesn't necessarily melt snow, but rain always sweeps it away. You must come out to the country more often. Where do we start?"

"With snow? Hardly at this time of year."

"With finding someone who will talk to us about Delia! Pay attention."

"I loathe doing this."

"I know," Emily said more gently. "The only thing worse would be not doing it. Nasty things don't go away just because you don't look at them. Are you so afraid that we'll find something dreadful?"

"I'm afraid of what being in Special Branch, in charge of it all, can do to people."

Emily put down her cup and looked at Charlotte very gravely. "That's part of what women are supposed to do: be strong enough to make a place where sanity and kindness always matter." She looked at Charlotte's expression. "Not deny everything," she said quickly, "just keep proportion. Believe the good is better and can win in the end, even if that's not always true."

Charlotte straightened up. "What is it we want to know, exactly? Eventually, who killed Halberd and why, but before that, what Narraway did for Delia that she was so grateful for, and that Felicia thinks was somehow dishonest. And whether they are connected or two quite separate things? Delia's daughter was born about twenty years ago. We should find out when she got married, where, to whom, what was odd about it, and what Narraway had to do with it. Also, maybe how Felicia Whyte knows anything about it."

"Yes," Emily agreed. "It's not easy to be subtle, is it!" Then she smiled widely. "Not that, as far as I know, you have ever tried."

"Then it's going to be up to you, isn't it?" Charlotte had the perfect riposte, and she saw it in Emily's face immediately.

Emily shrugged. "Oh, sometimes I am so subtle I don't even know what I'm doing myself," she said with a short laugh. "We will begin immediately with the most difficult part. I happen to know where Lady Felicia will be taking luncheon."

"Oh, no! Emily . . ."

But Emily had risen to her feet and was already halfway to the door, beckoning Charlotte to follow her.

The lightness and a few words of teasing were only to disguise the real fear underneath, and Charlotte knew that. They were both uncertain how to proceed without doing real damage, not sure what they would find that might hurt more deeply than they could take. And the disillusion would be not only for them but also for those they loved. Still, once the seed of doubt is sown, it has to be plucked, however sharp the thorns.

They spotted Lady Felicia quite easily. Her bright, fair hair and her distinctive clothes marked her in any crowd. Charlotte felt a stab of pity. To take the trouble to stand out in such a way was brave, and possibly a mark of desperation.

Believing that Felicia might wish the scene at the ladies' club had never happened, Emily behaved as if it had not.

"Marvelous hat," she said quietly, sitting down beside Felicia at the small table as if she had been invited, leaving Charlotte to find her own place. "Of course, you need to be tall to look so graceful," she went on, although there were only a couple of inches' difference between them.

"Thank you," Felicia murmured. One had to acknowledge such compliments, otherwise it might discourage any more.

People were moving around them. At any moment they could be interrupted. Emily quite shamelessly introduced the conversation she wished.

"I so admire your grace," she said quietly, her face absolutely serious. "I enjoy hearing you reminisce about your days at the court. I know you were presented to the Queen at your coming out." She regarded Felicia a trifle wistfully, and Charlotte wondered for a moment what it would be like to have belonged to the class of young lady who "came out" around the age of eighteen. One was officially welcomed into the adult world, and was open to being wooed by appropriate young gentlemen. There were balls, parties, dinners, trips to the theater, where one was seen by all society that mattered. As the daughter of a marquess, Felicia had enjoyed all these privileges and duties. She had probably had little choice in the matter.

Charlotte would have hated it. But Emily

might not at all. She had married Lord George Ashworth anyway. And Charlotte had married a policeman, which at the time was the social equivalent of a rat-catcher or a bailiff, at least in some people's eyes. The status of the police was higher now, twenty years later, and Pitt was no longer junior, but a far more powerful figure. Respect, at least outwardly, was more easily given. What people actually thought was a different matter. And she knew that Pitt was perfectly aware of it.

Felicia was delighted to recall what had been her happiest years. Her face lit and there was a softness in it as she spoke.

"Oh, yes," she replied easily. "At the time it seemed ages, days and nights going by like a dream, but of course one's first season is actually so short, and if you have not had an offer, you feel such a failure."

Charlotte knew that the pressure was unbearable. She imagined buying horses, each animal paraded up and down to be chosen — or not! The horses had no say in it at all. She wondered how much say the young women had.

Emily and Felicia were still talking. Charlotte managed to look as if she were listening with admiration. Actually, the pleasure in her face was relief that it had not happened to her. She had been married in what was to others a social disaster, but to her at the time had been an impossible romance and, in her middle years, brought far more happiness than most women ever knew.

She interrupted them, knowing they could be cut off by any of the other people passing by, nodding and smiling.

"Did you get to dance with the Prince of Wales?" she asked eagerly. "He must have been younger then, of course, and so charming." She tried to sound ingenuous and was not sure if she succeeded.

Emily gave her a quick glance, and then looked away. There was a faint flush on Felicia's cheeks. "Once or twice," she said. "It was far later than that, when I was in my twenties, that I knew him better."

There was a moment's complete silence. It was Emily who broke it.

"Oh!" She stared at Felicia with wonder. "Do you mean . . . ?"

Felicia glowed. She lowered her eyes. "I suppose it's not really a secret anymore, and you are friends. Yes, I knew him . . . very well." Something in the angular lines of her face softened. "You are right. When he is allowed to be himself, not stared at by everyone, not expected to be a diplomat or a prince, he's funny and generous and . . .

and a man one cannot help liking." She used the word quite clearly as a euphemism for a feeling far deeper.

Charlotte wondered if it had been love, or if that was merely how Felicia liked to remember it. The prince had had many mistresses, as far as she knew always married women. Like many men of high rank, he conducted his romances with discretion, although in his case everyone knew about them, but it was said that he never took a girl's virginity or risked getting her with child. Whether he did that out of morality or self-preservation did not matter.

"Is that why Delia Kendrick is so envious of you?" Charlotte asked. "Clearly she is!"

Felicia gave a secret little smile, sweet as if she were sucking on honeycomb.

"How quick of you to see that. Yes, I'm afraid it is. She was his . . . favorite . . . before I was. She did not take gracefully to being superseded. Very foolish. It could never have been more than . . . fun, and affection. I think she imagined something . . ." She left the word unsaid, for the imagination to fill in. "It was like expecting the same butterfly to be there next summer. Of course they are still as pretty and as brief, but they are different, for all that."

Charlotte looked at her with a surge of

pity for a woman who saw so clearly and yet missed the laughter and the joy that mattered, the moments of beauty. No wonder the years had marked her unkindly. She wanted to say something gentle.

"Most of us are never butterflies at all," she pointed out. "I believe tortoises live for a hundred years — but who wants to be a tortoise?"

Felicia gave the first totally genuine laugh Charlotte had heard from her. There was no time to follow it up: a moment later they were interrupted.

"It's a place to begin," Emily said hours later when they were back in her home. "But where does it connect with Narraway?"

"We can find out," Charlotte replied, making herself more comfortable in the boudoir chair. The windows were open and the scents of the garden blew in. There was a bowl of yellow roses on the small table between them. "It will take work but it will be possible. We can find out which year Felicia was having her affair with the Prince of Wales, and when she replaced Delia. That could be when it started, whatever it is. Where was Victor Narraway twenty years ago? That was long before he was head of Special Branch."

"You don't know?" Emily looked slightly surprised.

"No, I don't!" Charlotte held her temper back. It should not have mattered to her so much to realize how little she knew of Narraway before he had been Pitt's superior. "But what we really need is someone who knew Delia Kendrick then. I wonder when her daughter was born."

"Yes, of course. It could be the same time," Emily said quickly. "If she stepped out of society for a while, giving Felicia the chance to take her place, that could be why. What about her husband then? Perhaps he matters."

"It's all in the feelings," Charlotte said, as much to herself as to Emily. "We need to find someone who observed the private moments, as a lady's maid does, and yet is not involved themself. How are we to find who was Delia's maid then? With luck, it will not be the same one as now, and we can get her to talk. I wonder how difficult Delia was to work for. She doesn't seem to be particularly gentle or agreeable."

Emily considered that for several seconds. Then they each suggested possibilities, discarding them one by one.

"I could ask my maid to make some inquiries," Emily said at last. "But the moment she mentioned my name it would be as bad as if I was asking myself. In fact worse, because it would look so underhanded."

"But a lady's maid would be a good idea," Charlotte replied. "One maid to another. She could say that her aunt or cousin had known Delia's maid twenty years ago, and she was trying to contact her, for family reasons."

"But it would be bound to come out that she is my maid," Emily argued.

"Yes, I know. I wasn't thinking of your maid. I don't have one. Minnie Maude would be game enough to do it, but she couldn't pass herself off as a lady's maid. She's far too" — she searched for a kinder word than "blunt" — "individual. And apart from that, she would tell Thomas. She would be bound to, sooner or later. I was thinking of asking Gwen, Aunt Vespasia's maid. If one of us told her most of the real reason, she would do it. She does anything if she thinks it is for Vespasia's sake . . ."

That was the worst part of all this. Thomas's disillusionment she could try to heal, but Vespasia's would be terrible — and unreachable. She forced it out of her thoughts.

"Isn't it for Vespasia's sake because of

Narraway?" Emily's eyebrows went up.

"And Thomas's, yes." She nodded. "But she doesn't need to know at all . . . not yet."

"You are far more devious than I thought you were," Emily said with distinct appreciation. "I always believed you were a bit too straightforward."

"That's because I'm better at it than you are," Charlotte responded a little tartly. "The art of being devious is in not looking it."

"Then go ahead and be devious with Gwen. You probably know her better than I do."

Two long, difficult days passed before the plan worked, but it did so very well. Gwen proved to be inventive and quite a clever actress, a skill that pleased her immensely. She was devoted to Vespasia and willing to take any sort of risks to help, although she did ask that they not tell Vespasia herself of her role, except for such details as were absolutely necessary.

She returned to Charlotte and told her that Elsie Dimmock had been Delia Kendrick's lady's maid a great deal of her working life, and had been a housemaid before that in the home of Delia's parents. She was now living in a cottage outside Maidstone, in Kent, which she had inherited from her own parents and was able to keep up with a pension afforded her by Mrs. Kendrick. She seemed, in Gwen's opinion, a very obliging sort of person.

Charlotte thanked her warmly, refunded her the train and cab fares she had spent, and told her that if she preferred it, Lady Vespasia did not need to know of the matter at all.

Gwen accepted the money reluctantly, and thanked her.

It was early in the day still, and Charlotte knew there was no time to waste. She telephoned Emily to give her the news. She dressed in her most ordinary clothes — a simple white blouse with a dusky blue skirt and a straw hat — and set out to meet Emily under the clock at the railway station, where they would catch a train to Maidstone. They discussed their plans over the journey both in the train and in a hansom from Maidstone station to the street where Elsie Dimmock lived.

"I hope to heaven she is in," Emily said dubiously.

"Well, if she isn't we will have to wait." Charlotte refused to entertain the idea that they could fail, at least without trying a great deal harder. "We will ask the neighbors where she is, if necessary."

Emily kept in step with her, and when they went up the front path to the rose-surrounded door it was Emily who tugged on the bell rope.

A plump woman of at least sixty-five answered the door after a few moments. She had a homely face but the most beautiful silver-gray hair, which caught the light like a halo. She wiped her hands on her apron and looked at them with puzzlement.

"I am Emily Radley, and this is my sister, Charlotte," Emily said with a sweet smile. "Are you Mrs. Elsie Dimmock?" It was a courtesy on occasion to give an older woman the title of Mrs. even though she might never have married.

"I'm Elsie Dimmock, ma'am. How can I help you?" She did not move from the doorway, not expecting them to come in.

Charlotte swallowed. This was the most difficult part, the one over which she and Emily had had the most disagreement. She spoke softly.

"We are friends of Mrs. Delia Kendrick." She saw the swift recognition in Elsie Dimmock's eyes, and then instant concern.

"May we come in?" Charlotte asked. "There has been a little unpleasantness . . . rumors, you know? And as her friends we wish, vigorously, to stop them before they can spread any more widely. She won't do it herself; I suppose it is natural. We all have a little pride, and —"

"Oh, Miss Delia has that all right," Elsie agreed with something that was close to a laugh, but too tight in her throat to come out that way. "Her own worst enemy at times. But then, aren't we all?" She opened the door wider. "I don't know how I can help, but I'll do my best."

Charlotte and Emily glanced at each other, then followed Elsie inside the neat, lavender-smelling house. It was a cottage, one entered straight from the doorstep into the front sitting room, with its fireplace and comfortable furniture. There was a bowl of mixed flowers on the table, the first bright petals beginning to drop.

So Elsie was not surprised. Maybe there had been gossip before, from which Delia had not defended herself. Pride again, or perhaps because it had been true?

Emily sat with unself-conscious elegance on the settee, and Charlotte took one of the armchairs.

"Can I make you a cup of tea?" Elsie offered.

"No, thank you," Emily replied. "We don't wish to put you to any trouble."

"That would be so kind of you," Charlotte accepted. Emily might not know, but doing something familiar and useful, like making tea, would set Elsie more at ease. She would feel she had offered hospitality and was in some way in control of events.

Elsie disappeared about the task.

With obvious difficulty Emily refrained from saying anything. This was not the time for a disagreement.

As soon as Elsie had returned with the tea and poured it, she asked what the gossip had been about this time. While the kettle was coming to the boil she had cut slices of cake and she offered them now.

"Unfortunately there has been a death," Charlotte said as soon as she had swallowed the first mouthful. "At first it was seen as an accident, but now a question has been raised as to it being an attack."

"Oh dear." Elsie looked alarmed.

"The thing is," Charlotte continued, "he was a man who knew a great deal about other people, not always to their credit. The speculation is as to which particular piece of information got him . . . attacked. I'm sorry to say . . . killed. I'm sure you can imagine how many people are seizing the chance to make awful suggestions in order to take vengeance for one thing or another, real or not. And Mrs. Kendrick is a woman of whom many others are jealous. It's ugly, and so unfair."

"As if she hadn't had enough." Elsie looked truly distressed.

"Has it happened before?" Emily asked with sympathy, and before Charlotte could say anything.

"Some people just seem to attract tragedy." Elsie was staring wide-eyed into her own memory. Charlotte guessed that perhaps she spent a lot of time alone, since her retirement. She must miss the constant company of living in a big house, the other servants always coming and going, the banter and teasing, mostly good-natured: everyone's interest in the lives of the family they served. This cottage was comfortable, very much better than what most servants could retire to, but it might be too quiet at times, and all the freedom could also be lonely.

Charlotte accepted another piece of cake and bit into it with very clear pleasure, but she was subtle enough not to offer a compliment overtly, at least not yet.

"I believe she lost her first husband," Emily said sadly. "I understand how hard that can be, the shock. The wondering what you are going to do, how you are going to manage."

"That happened to you too, miss?"

"Yes. I know just how it feels. So . . . lost!"

"Poor Miss Delia, for all that Mr. Darnley was a bad one, he was handsome as you like, and could charm the birds out of the trees. I can see him as clear as if he was standing here. Played the piano a treat, and could sing too, all sorts of old songs, romantic ones. He used to tell a lot of tales, including that one of his ancestors was married to Mary, Queen of Scots, and was murdered for love."

Charlotte remembered that the tragic Mary, Queen of Scots, had indeed been married to a man named Darnley, and it was suspected that she herself had ordered him to be killed. But this was not the occasion to say so.

"How very sad," she commented. "And he was Delia's daughter's father, wasn't he? Not her present husband."

"Oh, yes, Miss Alice. What a sweetheart she was, such a lovely little girl. Reminded me of Miss Delia when she were that age. So happy. Bright as you like. Into everything. 'Please, Elsie, what's this? What's that? What's it for? Can I use it? Show me! Let me try!' " Her eyes filled with tears.

"That time goes so quick, doesn't it? Just a few years, and then they are all away. Seems like they were only babies the year before. Miss Delia married that Darnley when she were only twenty. It took him five years to spend all her money and then start looking around for someone else's. He was a — I shouldn't say what he was in front of ladies." She sniffed hard.

Charlotte was glad she had never had sufficient money to be worth marrying for. It was a blessing she had not considered quite so great in the days when she and Pitt had struggled for rent and economized on food. But that passed. The sense of being loved did not.

Emily took a piece of the cake and sipped her tea. "It must have been very difficult for her during those years."

"Oh, she had fun." Elsie's face brightened. "Always had courage, did Miss Delia. She could make people laugh, and gentlemen like a woman who enjoys life. She had courage, youth, charm."

"And she was beautiful," Charlotte added, being more generous than accurate.

Elsie gave a little shrug. "I thought she was, but then she was the closest I'll ever come to having a daughter myself. She wasn't ever beautiful like the Lady Felicia.

That girl was a real beauty, like a porcelain figure. Afraid to take it off the shelf and dust it, in case you dropped it and broke off a piece. But it all changed. The happiness went. And the friends."

"That's what happens when your husband dies," Emily said, biting her lip. "People change. Everything you relied on is gone. Even friends are different, like nobody knows what to say, so they avoid you."

"Yes, it was as if her life had stopped too."

"I remember," Emily said quietly. "How did Mr. Darnley die? Was it sudden? My husband died violently, and that was the worst part of it. People said some terrible things."

Charlotte recalled it with a sense of chill as bitter as if it had been very recent. She could feel the fear again aching inside, hear the voices who said that Emily had killed him. Some of them believed it. They wanted to, because Emily was prettier than they were, luckier, richer, all the things they wanted to be. And then she was suddenly, in one day, vulnerable as she had never been before. Title and money did not help at all; if anything, they made it worse.

Looking across at her, now talking quietly to this elderly lady's maid, the break was there in her voice, the fear back, the grief in the bend of her head. However deeply she had loved George, or not, the violence of the loss broke her life apart. In her new happiness with Jack she had not put it out of her mind, only into a far corner where it could escape her attention now and then.

"About you, too?" Elsie was full of sympathy.

"Yes. And even after all the truth was found, and things settled down, the invitations did not come anymore," Emily went on. "There is something about being a young widow that makes even friends nervous around you. With a man it is quite different. All the women want to look after him, make sure he is not left out, and friends invite him even more. My friends seemed to think I wanted their husbands' attention." Emily gave a tight little smile. "I could hardly tell them they had no need to worry, I would not have any of their husbands even with a diamond tiara attached. There is no price for boredom. But I felt terribly lonely."

"I watched Miss Delia just like that," Elsie agreed. "She wasn't beautiful like you, but she had a way with her. She was clever, and she could make people laugh. At least that is how it used to be."

"Before she was widowed?" Emily asked.

"No, not exactly. Mr. Darnley crushed something in her. He went after other women, and he wasn't always discreet about it, like a better man would have been. But when she took up with the Prince of Wales, it all became different. I thought as he was really fond of her. A nice gentleman, he was, for all that he is going to be king, and always was. Thoughtful, in his own way. And kind. Always very civil, he was. Here's me born in the East End slums, learned my manners after Miss Delia's mother took me in and taught me how to be a lady's maid. How to act, how to look smart, how to speak. And I'm standing there saying what a nice evening it is, just like it was nothing to me to be talking to the next king of England."

"And she cared for him?" Emily asked.

"Oh, yes. She was flattered, of course, but beyond that, she was real fond of him. Nearly broke her heart when she found she was with child, and had such a hard time of it she went off into the country. No wonder, poor girl: It was twins, and the little boy lived only a few weeks. It's a wicked cruel thing to lose a child like that. Don't see as she can ever really get over it. And loved that little girl like she was the whole world."

This time neither Charlotte nor Emily spoke.

"And then she came back to London with little Alice. She'd been gone a year, and the Prince of Wales had taken up with that Lady Felicia. I begged Miss Delia to tell him why she'd gone away, but she wouldn't do it. I thought it was pride, but I think now that it was fear that she would lose little Alice as well. Not that she wasn't a beautiful baby, and healthy as can be."

"And Mr. Darnley?" Emily prompted.

"Oh, it was about a year after that he was killed. Horse-riding accident, I think it was. Something like that. I don't recall the details anymore. I just see in my mind the man that came to tell her, all the way from somewhere in Buckinghamshire, he said, and terribly sorry he was. And there was Miss Delia with her son dead and now her husband dead, and all her friends gossiping about her when she was too down to fight back."

She looked at Charlotte. "And she didn't have a sister like you, miss, to be with her and fight the people who started all the whispers."

Charlotte tried to smile but she knew there was no heart in it. She could see the pain too clearly.

"Did Delia know Mr. Narraway then?" She had to ask.

"I don't know, but she certainly knew him

later, when it came time to find a good husband for Miss Alice. I thought she was too young, but Miss Delia said it was the right time. She was married to Mr. Kendrick by then, and I was just about to retire. About three years ago, this would be."

"Mr. Narraway was helping her to find a husband for Alice?" Emily said as if confused. "Not Mr. Kendrick?"

Elsie's face lightened and she sat up a little straighter.

"That's a different matter, miss. And I don't think I should be talking about it, if you excuse my saying so."

"No, of course not," Charlotte agreed quickly. "I apologize. I only asked because of something Lady Felicia said. I can see now that it's just . . . envy. But after what you have confided in us, and what I saw my own sister suffer at the hands of other people's gossip, I want to stop it all." She rose to her feet. "Delia is fortunate to have such a loyal friend in you. We will not mention who told us. I think discretion is better, don't you?"

"Yes, miss, thank you. But you will try to stop them, won't you?" Elsie climbed to her feet as well. "She don't deserve any more grief."

When they were outside, walking in the

sun toward the nearest main road where they might find a hansom to take them to the railway station, neither of them spoke for several minutes.

"I'm sorry," Charlotte said eventually. "I'd forgotten how bad that time was for you. I suppose I wanted to help. I just felt so helpless . . ."

Emily gave her a quick smile. "You helped me more than anyone else. You always believed I could not have killed George, in spite of what everyone else thought. But being a widow is always lonely because people are afraid of you. Apart from the fact that you remind them that death happens to all of us at some point, it can come suddenly, out of nowhere, and take away everything you thought you were sure of. They don't know what to say or how to help, and they do everything except behave normally. You're supposed to wear black for ages and sit alone in your house. It's like the worst punishment you can think of. Do you remember when we were naughty, Miss Hampton used to make us all go and sit separately in our rooms, no books, just sit there?"

"Enough to make you be good," Charlotte said grimly.

"Enough to make you and Sarah good,"

Emily retorted. "It just made me determined not to get caught."

It was the first time either of them had mentioned Sarah casually like that. They spoke of her, of course, but with thought, and memories. She had been murdered many years ago now. And it still hurt. She had been two years older than Charlotte.

"Why do you suppose Narraway helped get Alice married to someone in Scotland?" Emily asked. "Do you suppose she was the Prince of Wales's child, and not Darnley's at all? And if she'd stayed in London and been out in society, someone would have eventually realized it?"

"It is the obvious answer, isn't it?" Charlotte agreed. "The search for Alice's future husband was about three years ago, Elsie told us, and Narraway would have been head of Special Branch then. Who knows what the pressures were? I don't think Thomas knew about it."

"Are you going to tell him? Don't you have to?"

"Yes . . . I suppose so. He isn't going to be pleased."

"Why not? It's a lot better than some other things it could have been."

"That rather depends on what happened

to Alice," Charlotte said quietly. "Poor Delia!"

Emily said nothing.

"And then, of course, there's the other thing," Charlotte went on. "How did Darnley die?"

CHAPTER 9

Pitt listened with deep anxiety to Charlotte's account of her visit to Elsie Dimmock. Every new piece of information brought the prince further into the issue. For years it had been public knowledge that he had had mistresses. As long as he was reasonably discreet, and chose married women whose husbands were more or less compliant, it was accepted as a custom practiced as far back as records existed. Many had produced royal bastards, particularly in the previous centuries. The name Fitzroy, meaning "son of the king," was given to such sons. Some of them had even attained their own titles: Duke of this or Earl of that.

But Victoria's reign had been the beginning of a very different attitude toward the royal family, and a different standard of behavior was adhered to, at least in public.

Had Darnley been a compliant husband?

Very possibly not.

"Was Elsie sure that Darnley's death was a riding accident?" Pitt asked.

They were in the sitting room. As so often happened, it was late. Daniel and Jemima were in bed. The French doors were closed against the night air and the rain was pattering the panes.

Charlotte stared at Pitt, eyes wide. Her face was filled with apprehension. "No. I don't think so. What is this about, Thomas? The relationship between Delia and the prince? From what Elsie said, Delia had a difficult time carrying twins, and she retired from society and went into the country. During that time the prince found someone else — specifically, Felicia Whyte. Or she saw her chance and found him."

"That explains the dislike between them, but it is twenty years ago now," Pitt pointed out. "They must both have known their affairs with the prince would be brief. They could never have been anything more than that."

"Then what made you wonder if Darnley's death was really an accident?" she asked.

"I don't know. I'm not sure what kind of a man he was. Did he use his wife in order to gain access to the prince?" As he said it, he thought what a wretched situation it must be for the prince to live in, forever wondering if anyone — man or woman — liked you for yourself. Were they always weighing in their minds what advantage you could be for them? What a terrible loneliness. Pitt was overwhelmingly grateful for his own ordinariness. Charlotte had married him in spite of his position, not because of it.

"I don't know," she admitted. "It could be just Elsie's imagination. She seemed to care about Delia. She never had family of her own."

He saw a clear sadness in her face, weighing the loneliness of always being on the edge, needed, relied on, trusted but outside the glass wall, when the love was on the inside. All that was the way those excluded imagined it. Too often it was nothing like that at all. Sometimes it was colder on the inside; often there was no air, no room to stretch, to grow in.

"But Delia saw to it that Elsie had a home, and enough to live on, quite nicely, from your description," Pitt said.

Charlotte smiled. "Yes. A side of Delia Kendrick I hadn't expected. And even if she had a blazing affair with the prince, it doesn't explain what Halberd was doing, or why anyone killed him . . . does it?"

"No . . ." Pitt said, his mind trying to disentangle the emotion and the jealousies, the pride, and pull out of it all anything that still mattered over twenty years later.

"Do you think Delia's daughter could be the prince's as well?" Charlotte came straight to the point, as usual.

"Possibly," he conceded. "And maybe that's why Narraway helped her get married to a Scot and safely out of the way." He hoped that was true. But the question stayed in his mind, insistent and painful: Why had he bothered to? He had been head of Special Branch then. For whom was the favor really? For Delia? And if so, why? Or for the prince? If the latter was true, then there must have been a reason, perhaps much stronger than old affection, which might be long since faded and replaced by many new ones.

Had Darnley been murdered? Was that what Halberd knew? And why now, twenty years later? There did not seem to be any reason. Who might know — apart from the guilty person?

It was hard to believe, and yet the facts were there. He loathed the idea of opening up past pain that should have remained private, but he could not afford to ignore it.

He was not sure if he personally wanted to know what Narraway's part in the matter had been, but professionally he could not afford to look the other way. The thought of it tightened in his chest until he found it difficult to breathe.

"Thomas?" Charlotte's voice interrupted his thought.

He dragged his attention back. "Yes?"

"Do you think that's all Victor did?"

"Get Alice married to a Scot? It's a satisfactory solution, even elegant, in a way."

She was frowning. "That's all? Why couldn't Delia have done it herself? She'd be in a far better position, and certainly skilled enough. She didn't need Narraway. I don't see marriage broker as part of his skills. Do you?"

"No . . ."

"Then it was a cover for something else, which I presume he hasn't told you, or left you a record of," she said, not taking her eyes off his. "Was it not really about getting Alice married at all, but had to do with something much further back? Thomas . . . he would do all kinds of things when he was with Special Branch, in the earlier days. Maybe you don't know it all."

"You do?" It was not really a question.

"Not all," she said quietly. "But I do know

that some of it was very desperate, and he did things that saved some lives and cost others." Now she was looking at him very directly, a shadow of fear in her eyes. Was it fear for Narraway, and what they would both find out about him? Or even worse than that, fear for Pitt and what he might become?

This was all about responsibility again, and the need to act decisively, and alone. Make a judgment and trust it was the right one. Perhaps that was what growing up was about, accepting a certain aloneness and not drowning in it.

"But Narraway is very clever. If he meant it to be secret, it will be well hidden."

He wished he was sure that it would not be ugly, but there was no certainty of that at all. He could not banish the thought that Narraway might have been the father of Delia's child. Or uglier than that, and perhaps more likely, he may have used his knowledge of Delia's vulnerability to make her give him private and dangerous information so he could manipulate others, possibly the prince himself. He might even see it as his duty. That Pitt could believe, even though he hated the thought.

At Lisson Grove the next morning, Stoker

came into Pitt's office as soon as he arrived and closed the door.

"What have you got?" Pitt asked him.

"Been looking at where everyone was during the time Halberd must've been killed, sir: Walter Whyte, Algernon Naismith-Jones, Ferdie Warburton, and Alan Kendrick. Mr. Kendrick was at home with his wife; I checked with her, discreetly, and she backs that up. Mr. Naismith-Jones was with a woman, and gave me her name — very reluctantly — but I managed to confirm it. Mr. Warburton has no memory at all. Says he's subject to getting very drunk and blacking out now and then. Tight as an owl, sir. Passed out in one of the gentlemen's clubs. Steward put him in one of the rooms and let him sleep it off, well into the next day."

"You checked?"

"Yes, sir. Mr. Whyte is the problem. He won't say, and I haven't yet found out. I hope it's not him. He's a decent man . . . at least he seems to be."

"Thank you."

"I'm still looking for any witnesses in the park. Trouble is that being in the water as he was, it's hard to say exactly when Halberd died. For all that it's summer, it was pretty cold then. He could have been there only a short time. I'm trying to narrow it down based on what people didn't see."

"Good, it might still matter," Pitt agreed. "You could find someone who saw Halberd alive after he left his house, which would tighten it a little more." He did not feel a lot of hope; Halberd could have been anywhere in that space of time between leaving his home and his death.

Pitt turned to Stoker, who was lingering. "Yes? Is there something more?"

"I wondered if horses had anything to do with it," Stoker said a little awkwardly. "It's about the one passion the prince has never let go of, even though he's . . . slowing up a bit."

Pitt brought his attention back to the moment. "Go on."

"Well, sir, it seems he's doing very well at the moment. Had a few really good wins, and the best of his horses . . . one way or another, come directly from Mr. Kendrick's stables. Got a very good stallion there, doesn't use him all that much. Seems he keeps him for special friends, mostly the prince himself. Or else the prince made his purchases on Mr. Kendrick's advice. That's how Mr. Kendrick is in so well with him. He's either very lucky or very clever."

"Or both," Pitt added. "Thank you, Stoker. That's useful. At least we know what it's about. Anything else on Kendrick? I'd like all the details you have — dates and places."

"Yes, sir." Stoker pulled a pad out of his coat pocket and passed over several sheets to Pitt. It was all written down neatly, certain dates included, others merely guessed at, given approximations.

"Thank you," Pitt accepted. "I'm going to learn all I can about Kendrick's relationship with the prince. I want you to find out all you can, as discreetly as possible, about Halberd's last couple of months. Where did he go, who did he often see, and who didn't he see? Any change in previous patterns? I have some of his papers on file, but they haven't yielded anything useful yet."

"Yes, sir, I understand. If Halberd was looking into Kendrick, we need to know why."

"And what he found out specifically that got him killed."

"Be nice to know who actually did it," Stoker added. "Possibly not Kendrick himself, as his wife says he was at home all that evening. Presumably she would know if he got up in the night and went out."

"Not necessarily. People with that kind of money can have separate bedrooms, meet each other when they wish to. Although from observation, I think that may be fairly rare."

Stoker started to say something, but evidently changed his mind, having closed his mouth.

"Let me know what you find," Pitt finished. "I'm going to see if I can uncover some history."

In his job at Special Branch, and to a degree simply as a British citizen, Pitt already knew most of the public facts about the Prince of Wales. As the eldest son of the reigning monarch, he was automatically heir to the throne. At the age of seven he had begun rigorous training for this role. Pitt had heard rumors that the prince was a far less natural student than his elder sister, Princess Victoria, but he had been subjected to every possible effort in trying to meet the high expectations of his parents, most particularly his father. It was an effort doomed to failure: he was simply not of that inclination, although the pressure upon him was immense.

Pitt thought, with sudden sympathy, how he must have dreaded every day, every lesson never quite good enough. It was a miracle that he had passed his exams at all, especially in modern history, but apparently he had, at Trinity College, Cambridge.

Pitt sat back in his chair and turned it over in his mind. He himself had actually enjoyed lessons with the tutor Sir Arthur Desmond appointed to teach his own son along with Pitt, the son of a disgraced gamekeeper then laboring in the penal colony in Australia. It had not been goodwill alone; Pitt's abilities were a spur to Sir Arthur's own son not to be outdone by the son of their laundress! And as they grew older, Pitt had learned the wisdom of staying where he appeared to be equal.

He recalled one summer day in the manor's classroom when he had forged ahead in a mathematical problem, and then suddenly realized the fact and deliberately behaved as if he had found an obstacle he could not surmount. Only when they were finished did he realize Sir Arthur had been watching all the time. He said nothing, but Pitt remembered the gentleness in his eyes. To have withheld his answer to allow someone else the victory was a greater achievement than coming up with the right answer himself.

Had the princess Victoria ever done that for her younger brother? Or was she stung that she was the elder but could never inherit the throne as long as one of her brothers — or their sons, should they have them — was alive? Her mother had been queen only because there were no male heirs. Did that matter to her? Or had it been in truth a relief?

In 1860, at age nineteen, Edward had made a tour of North America, the first by an heir to the British throne. Here he had been a great success, possibly for the first time in his life. He had met all kinds of eminent people, in literature and art as well as law and politics. He was cheered by huge crowds and achieved many diplomatic benefits for Britain.

Apparently he had hoped to pursue a career in the army, but his mother had forbidden him to do anything more dangerous than the ceremonial duties, nothing of a genuinely military nature.

Edward had hoped to get some military experience and had been on many maneuvers in Ireland, where he had apparently spent some three nights with an actress called Nellie Clifden.

Prince Albert was ill, but he was so appalled by his son's behavior that when Edward returned to Cambridge, Albert rose from his sickbed and went to visit him, to issue what he felt was the appropriate reprimand.

Two weeks later, in December of 1861,

Albert died. Victoria was inconsolable. She wore mourning clothes from that day on, and she refused to forgive Edward.

Pitt thought of that too. His own mother had died when he was a boy, but all his memories of her were gentle. Many of them were touched with grief, the knowledge of how hard she worked and, in afterthought, the loneliness she must have felt at times. She had never told him how ill she was, never even let him see it. But it had not crossed his mind to doubt that she loved him, that she believed in his abilities to succeed and that he would become a good man.

He wished she could see what his life had become. Not his rank, but his family with Charlotte, how happy he was. She had never known that she would have grandchildren. The only good thing about it was that all his memories were sweet, there was no ugliness in them at all. If in reality there had been, he had been quite able to forget it.

The Prince of Wales had taken public life very seriously, presiding at the opening of great works such as the railway tunnel under the river Mersey in 1886 and the opening of Tower Bridge across the Thames in 1894. But Pitt knew from Narraway that only in the last year or so was the Queen allowing her son access to government papers, now that her health was failing and he must soon be king. There was an inevitability about it that was very recent.

That must be something else that hurt. Clearly she would let nothing go until age and infirmity forced her hand. Those around her must see her lack of trust. How could they then trust him, before circumstances gave them no alternative?

Pitt wondered how he would handle such a cutting away at his pride, his belief in himself, if even his own mother not only felt so little trust in him, but did it so all his friends knew, and his enemies — even his servants.

Was that what Kendrick offered? A wise man seeking the prince's favor would offer small comments of praise and trust, slowly, discreetly, not for the prince but for the man.

How many women had done so instinctively? Pitt had certainly seen women submit to a man, defer to him when in fact they were both cleverer and quicker-witted, and certainly as brave. He had caught Charlotte doing it only once or twice, and she had blushed, apologized, and they had defused it with laughter. But one did not laugh with a prince until he had agreed that it was acceptable.

The prince had sought the intimate company of women a great deal less of late. Pitt guessed that the overeating and the decline of vigor that went with it had damaged his health, and very possibly his virility. Now his love was horse-racing. He kept a stable in Newmarket, not so very far from his residence at Sandringham. Just three years ago, in 1896, his horse Persimmon had won the Derby, the ultimate prize. Had Kendrick helped with that too? Certainly he had helped celebrate the victory.

Was that all it was? A man diplomatic enough to say and do all the right things? If that was what Halberd had found, there was nothing to worry about; rather, something to rejoice in.

But there must be more, something stronger, and far darker, if Halberd had been killed to keep it quiet.

This was where researching public knowledge, even if applied with all the wisdom and understanding in the world, was not enough. Pitt sat still longer, unwilling to face what he knew was inevitable. It was time.

He could have found Walter Whyte more easily a couple of hours earlier, but he needed to speak with him privately, probably at length and definitely uninterrupted.

To catch him as he walked from luncheon at his club in Piccadilly, across Green Park toward the Mall, was too good a chance to miss.

Whyte was in his late fifties, slender, and still vigorous. Pitt had to stretch his legs to overtake him.

"Afternoon, Major Whyte," he said as he drew level with him.

Whyte stopped abruptly, startled by the sound of a military title he had not used in over twenty years. Some men like to remind people of their office for the rest of their lives, but Whyte was not one of them, and Pitt knew it. He was giving Whyte credit for his military service, while at the same time alerting him that Pitt knew much more about him that their casual acquaintance would justify.

"Good afternoon, Commander Pitt," Whyte said after an instant's hesitation. "how are you?"

It was a predictable response.

"Pleased to have run into you," Pitt replied. "I'm about a rather miserable errand." He was not going to pretend he enjoyed it, whatever Whyte thought of him in the end. "Your military record was brought to my notice. You showed remarkable courage, and loyalty far beyond what most men ever do. Of course, most don't have chance, or the necessity."

They were standing on the path, facing each other. Pitt was not comfortable, but he managed to disguise it. Whyte did not. His body was stiff, his eyes not moving from Pitt's face.

"I think you mistake me for my brother, Commander," he said quietly.

In the distance a dog barked excitedly and children cried out encouragement.

"It was he who saved people's lives in the boat accident on the Nile, if that is what you are referring to. I can't think what else. Unfortunately, he died only a few years later, again trying to save people." Now his voice was hoarse with emotion and the grief in his face was plain.

Pitt felt wretched. He even for a moment considered apologizing and going to seek the information he required from some other source. Except he knew of no other, and might waste time he could not afford in looking for one. Maybe he should simply have asked outright, without any attempt at pressure? Whyte might have told him. Unless he had lied to protect someone, not knowing the gravity of the matter. It must be grave, or Halberd would not be dead.

Whyte was making ready to turn away

from Pitt and continue his journey across the park. "Excuse me," he said.

"I wish I could, Major Whyte, but I'm sure you understand duty as well as I do. Sometimes it is expensive, as it was for you to have your brother take credit for your courage in saving the people in the Nile. I went to Egypt once, very briefly, over a case. A fascinating land."

"What the hell are you talking about?" Whyte demanded. He looked more narrowly at Pitt. "Are you sober, man?"

"Perfectly. And if this were not a matter of murder, and possibly treason, I would be happy to let it rest. But it is, and I cannot just walk away."

"Who's dead, for heaven's sake?" Whyte demanded abruptly, but he was pale now under the tan of his skin.

"Sir John Halberd, which you must surely know," Pitt replied.

"Is that what this . . . blackmail is about?"

"Blackmail? Is that what someone else called it?" Pitt spoke softly, with a lift of curiosity, wondering who else had pressured Whyte before.

Whyte did not answer.

"Halberd himself." Pitt let the words out with a sigh. "How very sad, but also how interesting. I find it hard to believe that

Halberd was blackmailing you, but if so, it raises the question, was it you who murdered him?"

Whyte froze, and there was a look of amazement on his face. Then it turned to utter loathing — the disgust of contempt, not fear.

"That is what I thought," Pitt said with a bleak smile. "And I very much doubt Halberd was blackmailing you. More likely he was forcing you to tell him certain facts that you would rather not. I regret having to do the same, especially since someone killed him to keep him from acting upon his knowledge. Does that not bother you, Major Whyte?"

"It should bother you a damn sight more!" Whyte snapped. "He's dead. I'm not!"

"Not yet," Pitt agreed. "But then, neither am I. What did Halberd want to know? And please be exact. And complete." Whyte stood in the sun for several moments, then seemed to slump a little. He turned to walk slowly in the direction of the street, but across the grass, not on the path. Pitt thought it was to reduce the chance of being overheard.

"He asked me a lot about the prince of Wales and his foreign diplomatic trips. The prince had been making those trips ever since the sixties. He's very good at it. Has made England a lot of friends in Europe, which we hadn't done so well with before."

"Is that all Halberd wanted?" Pitt said skeptically.

Whyte did not look at him. "He asked how often Kendrick went with him, and specifically where to."

"Interesting. And what was your answer? I presume he wanted an exact reply. Not a guess?"

"Yes. I looked up in my diary what I knew. Of course he had the prince's dates; anyone can find those. What he wanted was when Kendrick went with him."

"And you told him, I assume. Where did Kendrick go with the prince?"

"Only to France and, more often, to Germany. I think he might have family there, or something."

"I see. And did you go, Major?"

"With the prince? Only once. And I didn't go with him, I went a few days after," Whyte replied.

"And Kendrick went then?"

"Yes . . ."

"I see. And where did they go, specifically?"

"What the devil does it matter?" Whyte demanded, but there was a grief in his eyes as if he knew the answer. "The prince is closely related to the German royal family, which I presume you know. It's hardly a secret. Prince Albert was of the house of Saxe-Coburg and Gotha. And the prince's sister was married to the king of Prussia."

"I know. It is Mr. Kendrick I am interested in. Where did he go?"

Whyte stared at him, and slowly the color disappeared from his face.

Pitt waited.

"Most of the time he was with the prince, but he went to visit someone he said was an old friend . . ."

"The pattern, Major Whyte. What did you tell Halberd? You answered something he asked, and he realized what it meant."

"I'm not —"

"Yes, you are," Pitt insisted. "What did Kendrick go to Germany for? He went with the prince, I'm guessing to use his diplomatic élan, his name, his ability to create welcome anywhere. Kendrick made himself the prince's friend, right?" He did not need Whyte's agreement, he could see it in his eyes. "Where, Major Whyte? I need to know." He did not want to threaten to undermine the memory of Whyte's brother, but he had to be prepared to do it. He must make Whyte believe that he would.

They stood staring at each other.

Pitt wanted to tell Whyte how he loathed this, but he needed him to believe he would reveal the truth about the credit James Whyte had taken for someone else's act. That he had died trying and failing to be that man in truth. He hated the look in Whyte's eyes, the disgust.

"He went to the Mauser arms factory," Whyte said at last. "I didn't realize it until later. And I have no proof. If you take this any further I will deny it. Just think for a moment what it will do to the prince's reputation! If you have any loyalty to the Queen or to your country, you'll forget this."

"Kendrick is dealing in arms?" Pitt said slowly. "With whom?"

"God damn it, I don't know! The British Army, I presume. Or mercenaries somewhere."

"Somewhere like Africa?" Pitt said softly.

Horror filled Whyte's face. "Good God, no! You mean the Boers? He wouldn't."

"I think Halberd believed he would," Pitt argued. "But I need more than this to be certain." He thanked Whyte and left him to hurry on, with barely a glance at Buckingham Palace towering to their right, across the open space in front of it with its scarlet-coated guardsmen on duty, and then disappear down the Mall toward Whitehall. Not once did Whyte look behind.

Pitt turned to go back the way he had come.

Pitt owed it to the Queen to report his findings so far, before he set in motion the next inquiries, which would have to be with the Foreign Office, regarding the likelihood of war and the part Kendrick could be playing.

He told Charlotte none of this. She had helped very much with Delia Kendrick's background, and he had told her so, but she would find this further information a burden of fear, and she did not need to carry it. Nor did she need to know how he had forced Walter Whyte to help.

He was admitted to the palace in the middle of the following afternoon, in exactly the same manner as before, conducted by Sir Peter Archibald, who was looking very grave.

Outside the door of the room, Sir Peter stopped.

"Her Majesty is not feeling well today, Mr. Pitt. She granted this audience against my advice. I trust you will be brief, and as tactful as possible without directly misinforming her. I suggest that if it is unfortunate news, you tell her only the barest outlines, then afterward inform me of any issues I might deal with. Do you understand me, sir?"

"I do," Pitt answered. "But I will use my own discretion as to what I tell her. I give you my word it will be nothing I think unnecessary. That is the best I can promise." He met Sir Peter's eyes without blinking and saw the surprise in him, and then both anger and respect.

Sir Peter knocked and opened the door, leaving it for Pitt to walk through alone.

The Queen looked even smaller sitting in the large chair, her back as straight as she could make it, her lace-cuffed hands folded in her lap. As always, she was dressed entirely in black.

"You may approach, Mr. Pitt," she said quietly. Then, when he was standing in front of her: "I am pleased that you have succeeded enough to report to me again." The ghost of a smile sat on her lips, wry, full of regret for the friend she had lost. All the information he gave her would never replace Halberd, of the same generation as her sons and a deep admirer of Prince Albert. Pitt was an outsider, of a different social class entirely — indeed, lower than the servants who brought her meals or opened doors for her. And yet he had risked his life and his career to serve the same ideals she believed in.

"You may sit, Commander." She glanced at the chair a couple of feet away from him.

"Thank you, Your Majesty." He sat down, hoping he did not look as uncomfortable as he felt. Had anyone, except Albert, ever been totally at ease with her since she became Queen? The crown was not only physically heavy; mentally it must at times be almost unbearable. But no one had ever willingly laid it down.

"What have you to tell me?" she asked. "Do you know who killed Sir John, and why?"

He saw the grief on her face, and deeper than that, the fear. Did she really believe it possible that the Prince of Wales could, even indirectly, be involved? Maybe it wasn't such a stretch, since she had blamed him for Albert's death.

Pitt chose his words with painful care.

"I believe I know why, ma'am," he began. "You were perfectly correct in your assumption that it was because he had been successful in the mission you asked of him. I don't think it was Alan Kendrick in person who struck him. His wife says that he was at home." He saw her expression of disbelief and impatience. "Although that may or may not be true. But he could easily have paid someone else. It would be a risk he might have thought worth taking."

"Risk?" she said skeptically.

"That such a man might then blackmail him," Pitt answered. "Or of course, he could have . . . disposed of the man afterward. And the police would not connect the death to him because no one would know of their association."

"Continue, Mr. Pitt. You said that you believe you know why." Her face was pale in the soft light of this room.

Would it have been kinder to tell her straightaway that the prince was not involved, or would she see that as patronizing? Perhaps she might even disbelieve him or think that he was doing exactly what Sir Peter told him to. Better to do it well than hastily. He must be believed, or his words would not comfort her but instead arouse more fears.

"The Prince of Wales is extremely well liked in both Europe and America, ma'am. He accepts their hospitality, which is the greatest and most completely honest compliment one can pay to one's host."

She smiled, and for a moment there was

pride in her face. The years slipped away as if the darker ones had never been.

He had to break the spell. She was waiting for him to tell her the news that would hurt, the reason he had come here.

"Mr. Kendrick accompanied the prince on several visits abroad," he said, "most especially those to Germany. Because he was a friend of the prince's, people made him welcome and trusted him. He took advantage of this to make contact with the Mauser arms company."

"Indeed? To what purpose?" She sat perfectly still, her hands now locked together in her lap.

"My source cannot tell me the exact agreement, ma'am, but it has to do with a very large purchase of weapons, predominantly rifles."

"I see. And this purchase is intended to make a profit, of course. From whom?"

"I believe from the Boers in South Africa, ma'am, should there be another Boer war."

"Thank you, Mr. Pitt. I imagine that was not easy for you to tell me. I am an old woman and well-meaning people keep from me what is distressing. I would rather know. It is my duty to know." Again the ghost of a smile crossed her face. "Oftentimes what the imagination conjures up is worse than the reality."

He wanted to say something that might comfort her, and yet he dared not be too familiar. They must both always pretend that he did not see her emotions.

"It is so with many of us, ma'am. And the more informed your imagination, the worse the possibilities are. The only good things in the situation are Sir John's total loyalty both to his country and to you, and the fact that the Prince of Wales, although his generosity has been abused, is unaware of any of it."

She nodded very slowly. "I trust, Mr. Pitt, that as your inquiry proceeds, you will do what you are able to protect him from those who appear to be his friends but are not. It will be a heavier task when I am gone, but I place it in your hands."

There was nothing whatever he could do but accept. The weight of it was momentarily crippling.

"Yes, Your Majesty."

She nodded, but she did not say anything more, except give him permission to leave.

Chapter 10

After Pitt left the Queen, he went back to Lisson Grove and unlocked the files in the safe, which Narraway had placed where no one other than Pitt could see them. He needed to study them more closely. He must have his facts precise. Even so, they were written in a type of shorthand that Narraway had developed, and the key to that also was in Pitt's keeping. Narraway did not have Pitt's detection skills or his knowledge of the underworld on the borders of crime, the understanding of poverty and the role of petty crime in survival.

Instead, he had a vast network of connections in higher society, and the understanding of money, privilege, government, and military services. He knew how the men in them lived their lives, what they valued, and where their weaknesses lay. Some of it was instinctive, but most of it lay in these files, now for Pitt's use if he wished. Pitt did not want to even know the contents, let alone use them. But that kind of innocence was a luxury he could no longer afford. Other people would pay the price for his oversensitivity. His clean hands were not worth anybody else's life. Those who stand by and watch are complicit in what they could have stopped but chose not to.

It took him three hours of miserable reading before he found what he needed for this particular issue. If he was lucky, he would just catch Stephen Dudley before he left the Foreign Office for the evening. Distasteful as this was, like stepping into ice-cold water, it was better to do it straightaway. Finding excuses to put it off would make it worse.

He took a hansom cab and was at the Foreign Office three-quarters of an hour later. The traffic was wretched and his impatience changed nothing. He crossed the marble hall, his footsteps echoing, and climbed the huge staircase. He knew many people here at least slightly, and he nodded to them as he passed. He arrived at Stephen Dudley's door just as Dudley was about to leave.

"I'm sorry," Pitt said, then introduced himself.

Dudley was a handsome man, probably a few years older than Pitt, but with an ease of manner that betrayed a long line of forebears who had held high position in the courts of royalty since the time of Queen Elizabeth.

"Pitt?" Dudley said with slight hesitation. "I'm afraid I can't place you." He smiled very slightly. "It's late. Can this wait until tomorrow? I'd be delighted to see you, say . . . eleven-thirty?" He made as if to close the door, leaving them both in the corridor.

"We haven't met before," Pitt replied. "I'm head of Special Branch. Took over from Victor Narraway a couple of years ago." He spoke Narraway's name carefully and met Dudley's gaze as he did so. "And I'm afraid it won't wait until tomorrow."

Dudley was taken aback. They stood motionless, staring at each other in the wide, hushed corridor, with its formal portraits of past heroes on the walls. There was silence, except for the echo of leather-soled shoes on the marble floor, somewhere out of sight.

"Victor Narraway," Dudley said at last, still smiling as if to deny what he already knew.

"Yes, Mr. Dudley. It has been a testing position to fill, and I now find myself facing a difficulty in which I cannot consult him, so I'm obliged to go myself to some of his sources of information."

"He wouldn't tell you?" Dudley was turning the idea over in his mind, looking for an escape. "That doesn't give you pause for thought, Mr. . . . Pitt?"

"He cannot tell me," Pitt replied, still smiling pleasantly. "He is abroad at the moment and constantly moving, therefore impossible to contact. So I have come directly to you."

Dudley's body stiffened. He took a deep breath and let it out slowly, giving himself time to think, then led the way into his office and indicated Pitt was to sit while he himself took his seat behind his desk.

"What is it exactly that you wish to know? There is certain information I may not be able to share."

"If you know it, Mr. Dudley, you can share it," Pitt said carefully, not changing the quiet tone of his voice in the slightest. He knew what Dudley's vulnerability was, and he hated using it. But he could not imagine facing the mother of some soldier killed in a new war in Africa and telling her he had been squeamish over pressing a man in the Foreign Office, a man whose son was a cheat, of whom he was bitterly ashamed.

Dudley looked at him with distaste. "What is it you think I can help you with? You are hunting some demon Irishmen, I suppose."

"No, Mr. Dudley. I am concerned at the moment with the thought of another war against the Boers in Africa, and their being supplied with the very best of new German weapons."

"Oh God!" Dudley was startled out of his resentment. Now he looked drained of emotion and so weary, there seemed to be no energy left in him. "I don't know whether there's going to be another war or not. Depends on whether Kruger blinks, I suppose. Or Milner backs down a bit. But that's not likely, from what I hear of him. A winner, always a winner. Probably expects to be governor of South Africa; next step, prime minister."

"He has many admirers," Pitt pointed out.

Dudley's face filled with distaste. "Don't you know something nasty about him? That's where a little . . . leverage . . . would do some good."

"So there could well be war?" Pitt asked.

"My best guess, yes, and probably by Christmas. Now, what in hell is this about German guns?"

"Nothing yet. I need to know how often Alan Kendrick went to Germany with the Prince of Wales, and on which dates, and anything else you can tell me about those visits. You might know the names of some discreet courtiers, friends, servants I can speak to. And I need it immediately."

Dudley stared at him, his face grim. "What, exactly, is it that you suspect?"

Pitt must make the decision instantly. Narraway had left enough information about Dudley to embarrass him profoundly. Had he any connection with Kendrick, and would it outweigh his own standing?

"I suspect that Kendrick is setting up an arms deal with the Mauser company to supply guns to the Boers, should there be another war. And with the possibility that the kaiser is not only willing but actually able to carry out his *Weltpolitik* — a larger navy, the acquisition of major stakes in the lands in Africa, and more foreign territories in general — then an alliance with a vastly wealthy and individual Boer nation in South Africa is no longer unlikely." That was far ahead of where he was, and certainly nothing he could prove. Still, it was the worst possibility.

"God Almighty!" Dudley swore vehemently. "You've got to stop him! And using the Prince of Wales's connections to do it! Right under the man's nose. How can we prevent it? It would be tantamount to involving the next king in treason against his own Crown! Are you certain?"

"No," Pitt said sharply. "But I think John Halberd may have known more. I want to know if it is as bad as it looks. And if it is, I must stop it . . . or at least make certain Kendrick is stopped. Now, don't make us waste any more time in arguing it. Help me find out all I can about every visit the prince made when he took Kendrick along with him."

Dudley's whole manner had changed. He was as tense as an overwound spring, but his determination filled every part of him, his movements as he stood up like an athlete ready to sprint. He was going to be a good friend to Pitt in the future, or a bad enemy.

"You can't help," he said as Pitt also rose to his feet. "I'll work at it all night and have everything ready for you tomorrow morning at ten. I'll see whoever I have to, even if I get him out of a dinner party, the opera, or someone's bed!"

"I will be here at ten," Pitt said with considerable appreciation.

Outside he felt a wave of relief so intense it was like the ceasing of a physical pain. Would he have used Narraway's information to force Dudley, if he had refused? He would have hated it. It was personal and acutely embarrassing, and even though it was long in the past, it still had the power to injure deeply. In fact, it could put a stop to a glittering career, not to mention the possible damage to Dudley's personal life.

He thought of Daniel and the accusation he had told his parents about a few days previous, that he had cheated on an exam at school. Pitt had believed Daniel's innocence without question and admired the boy's determination not to sneak on the real culprit. Pitt hoped the matter had blown over, and yet the injustice of the false accusation still festered. Had Dudley also believed his son? What pressure had there been, what loyalties tested, what peer approval or damnation? Did anybody leaping to judgment even think of these things?

Tomorrow he must speak to Daniel and make sure this stain did not mar his future and arise again sometime when it was too late to prove his innocence. How naïve Pitt had been to believe it would be forgotten!

As he walked along the street looking for a cab, he wondered again if he would ever have carried out his threat against Dudley, and if he had, what he would have thought of himself afterward. Would he have taken responsibility for the damage, the pain, the loss of Dudley's service and skills? And the loss to himself! Perhaps the ruin of his son!

What would Charlotte think of him for it? When Daniel was old enough to find out, would he admire Pitt for it, or despise him? Would he perhaps even be afraid of him and not trust him again? He didn't know which was worse. If Daniel admired him, he could take it as permission to do the same, to gain what he wanted by manipulation, threat, emotional blackmail. He might do it not when it was the only way, but when it was simply the easiest.

The thought of any of these eventualities made his stomach clench with misery.

But if no threat were ever carried out, how long before threats stopped working? A paper tiger that frightened no one; Pitt would become a joke. What defense was a soldier who could not bring himself to fire his weapon?

It was time to accept the responsibility.

He was back at Dudley's office the next morning at ten o'clock exactly, and the moment he entered he knew that the news was grave. Dudley stood facing the door, his back to the window, the sunlight in a pool around him. There were two sheets of paper on the desk, covered in handwriting.

Pitt closed the door behind him.

"I'm afraid it is as bad as you thought," Dudley said. He looked tired, as if he had been up all night. Even his valet's best efforts had still left him looking haggard. "Kendrick has been to Germany five times, three of them this summer. The latest without the prince. It seems he has established himself well enough not to need royal backing anymore. I imagine you know that the Mauser M93 is one of the best rifles in the world, if not the best. At least equal to the Enfield. I can't trace any connection to the Boers, but I did make sure that he's not doing deals on behalf of the British Army. Not that I thought he was, but I had to be certain."

"Yes, of course you did," Pitt agreed, simply to fill the momentary silence, and to acknowledge that he was listening and understood. He had been hoping he was wrong. That perhaps Kendrick's trips involved a romantic affair, or even some sport he was following, not legal in England, although Pitt could not think what it would be.

"I tried to see if I could find any indication of Halberd following the same line of inquiry as I have," Dudley went on. "Sorry, but I couldn't prove it either way. If he asked anyone, they are not speaking of it." His smile was sad and a little bitter. "Perhaps it was someone else who could not afford to refuse an answer. Halberd seemed to know almost everything . . ." He did not finish the train of thought; they both knew what it would be.

Dudley glanced at the papers on the desk.

"That's all I know, and this is the only copy. I wrote down the details, and whether they were proved to have happened, or only possibilities. Dates and times, who was there, and so on. For God's sake, Pitt, do whatever you must to stop this Kendrick. Find something to silence him, and use it!"

"I should have asked you: Did Halberd go to Germany, that you know?"

"Yes, about two weeks before he died. I assume he was murdered?" There was an edge of distress in Dudley's voice, even fear.

"Yes. Although I can't yet prove by whom. It may have been Kendrick, but if so, we have his wife's word that he was at home, and I daresay that of his servants also. But beyond that, I can't imagine that Halberd would be caught unawares by him. If he planned to meet with him, it wouldn't be alone at night in a rowing boat on the Serpentine."

"Then he was lured there by someone else," Dudley concluded. "Don't try to persuade me he had another lethal enemy who just happened to do Kendrick's work for him," he added bitterly. "Putting him away for murder would be ideal."

"I'd still like to do that," Pitt replied vehemently. "But I can't afford to rest on that hope."

"We can't afford to rest at all," Dudley answered. "I'd be obliged if you would keep me up to date, as much as you can."

"I will," Pitt replied.

"We haven't got very long," Dudley warned. "The situation in South Africa is getting worse all the time. We may avoid war, but we can't trust that. It's damned unlikely."

Pitt knew he was right. He collected the notes Dudley had written for him, glanced at them, and then put them in his inside pocket, thanked Dudley again and left.

That evening Pitt finally made his appointment to see Daniel's schoolmaster. Perhaps it was the appalling vulnerability Pitt had seen on Dudley's face that had made him act. He was dreading it, having trouble preparing what he was going to say.

He had met Dr. Needham before, at school prize giving, but it had been a formal affair, agreeable but impersonal. The school was excellent, the best Pitt could afford, but he was acutely aware as he stood in the oak-paneled hallway with its portraits of past headmasters that most of the boys here were accustomed to wealth and its privileges. There was a part of him that still resented it, recalling too vividly how poor he had been at Daniel's age.

A boy of about sixteen came to conduct him to Needham's office, opening the door for him and then closing it behind him.

Needham was a lean, gray-haired man with a keen face, looking like a scholar rather than a sportsman. The walls were lined with bookcases, no trophies, no team photographs.

Needham rose to his feet and offered his hand. "Good evening . . . Commander Pitt, isn't it?"

"Yes. Good evening, Dr. Needham," Pitt replied with a slight nod, shaking the man's hand.

Needham waved to the chair on Pitt's side of the desk and resumed his own seat. "What can I do for you? I am happy to say that Daniel is progressing very well. I understand his desire to change from Latin to German, and I have your letter of approval."

Pitt smiled briefly. "He seems to have thought it through, and I couldn't disagree."

Needham waited, interest in his face.

Pitt swallowed hard. He must not waste the man's time, and yet he had to explain why he wished the favor of further investigation into a matter he had tacitly agreed was closed. He must make no excuses. Honesty was the only course with any dignity, for any of them.

"Are you aware of my profession, Dr. Needham?" he began.

"Daniel has said very little," Needham replied. "I gather it has to do with police work at a very high level." He looked puzzled.

Pitt filled the silence before it could become obvious. "Special Branch. I come across a great deal of information about people that is confidential . . ."

Needham frowned and his expression changed very slightly, but he did not interrupt.

Pitt could feel the heat in his face and knew he was blushing. Did Needham imagine he was going to attempt some sort of pressure, even blackmail? His mouth was dry and his heart beating too fast at the thought. He must be quick, and plain. He did not avoid Needham's solemn gray eyes.

"I have seen good men ruined by lying about an early mistake out of fear, and it being revealed at a time that destroyed them."

Needham still said nothing, but his expression grew darker. Pitt must get to the point. No more preamble.

"Daniel was accused of cheating on an exam recently. He told me he had not done it, but honor to the friendship of a classmate prevented him from telling the master that it was his friend who had cheated, not him. I believed him and applauded his desire not to be seen as one who told on others. I understand the code of loyalty, and the price of breaking it."

Needham pursed his lips and nodded very slightly.

"Since that occurred, I have seen a man I respect, in high office, manipulated into doing something he did not wish to, under threat of his own son being exposed and his career ruined, over just such an incident."

"I see. And you wish me to expunge this reference from your son's records?"

"No, Dr. Needham. I would like you to have the matter investigated, and blame put on whichever boy is at fault. And if that cannot be determined fairly, then the matter not to be recorded at all." He waited. He must not let nervousness make him talk too much. He had seen it so often in others, and had read it easily.

"That seems reasonable," Needham agreed cautiously. "I will ask Mr. Foster to reconsider the matter."

"And if he is unwilling to?" Pitt asked.

Needham smiled. "If I ask one of my masters to do something, Commander Pitt, it is very unlikely indeed that he will fail. If the head of Special Branch gives you a clear directive, do you not . . . Oh." His smile widened. "Your title of 'commander' means that you are the head of Special Branch! How foolish of me not to have recognized that. You are unusually modest, a rare quality."

"Thank you," Pitt said as graciously as he could. He was overwhelmingly relieved. And he was also embarrassed. This was a man he respected, and he would dearly like to be respected by him in return. That had nothing to do with Daniel's future.

He rose to his feet, eager to leave.

Needham stood also. "I shall write to you as to the outcome," he promised. "I cannot speak for the conclusion, but I believe it will not be unsatisfactory." He met Pitt's eye for a moment, then offered his hand again.

The following day Pitt was with Jack in the

same gentlemen's club as before, sitting in the smoking room after having had a good lunch. It was an excellent place to meet unobtrusively, and the chances were good of hearing a little news — and more than that, of seeing which people had business together, who was looking for whom, and whom they might be avoiding.

Pitt enjoyed Jack's company. He was agreeable and had a quiet, dry wit. Indeed, he had lived by his charm before marrying Emily. It had served him well, because it was quite genuine. They were talking quietly now about family, both watching men coming and going, glances, a moment's exchange, an avoidance here and there.

"Good afternoon, Pitt. Don't see you here very often." Pitt knew who it was before he looked up; the intonation of the voice was familiar.

"Good afternoon, Kendrick," he replied, deliberately leaving off the "Mr.," as Kendrick had with him.

"May I offer you a drink?" Kendrick asked, glancing at Jack also. "I know your taste, Radley. Single malt for you, Pitt?"

Pitt did not want to accept anything from Kendrick, and he did not particularly care for whisky, especially at this time of day. But this was nothing to do with likes or dislikes. He looked up at Kendrick. "Thank you, that would be very nice."

Kendrick sat down in the third chair and raised his hand for the steward, who was at his elbow almost immediately. He gave the order, then leaned back and crossed his legs.

"Pretty thankless task you have," he remarked to Pitt. "Any further forward with it?"

Pitt wanted to tell him that it was none of his concern, but it would sound offensive and would be taken as a clear indication that Pitt was floundering. This was the man who was trying to arrange the sale of the best rifles in the world to Britain's potential enemies. Half the men in this room would have relatives who could end up being killed by them! And worse than that, Kendrick was using the future king to do it. It would take a far cleverer game to beat him than self-defensive denial.

"At times," Pitt responded. "It can be slow going. But then there are sudden breakthroughs, and something becomes clear. Most secrets are a waste of time, but information does turn up in the oddest places."

Kendrick smiled. "Such as here?" he asked, looking around at the warm, deeply comfortable room with its soft armchairs, its oak and marble fireplaces, and carpets thick enough to muffle any footsteps. There was amusement in his voice, and only the slightest touch of irony.

"Especially here," Pitt answered, keeping exactly the same polite expression on his face.

"You think someone here might know who Halberd was . . . entertaining himself with? I assure you they are not in the least likely to admit it. And certainly not to you, my dear fellow. Everyone knows who you are. Just as we all knew who Narraway was. You are the last person to whom we would confide anything at all! The slightest misstep could end up being one's undoing. If ever there was a man not to trust, Narraway was it. Not that he wasn't hoist with his own petard now and then. A certain poetic justice to that."

"And yet he continued to come here." Pitt was too engaged in the conversation to withdraw now.

The steward returned with the whisky, and they remained in silence until he finished his duties and left.

Jack raised his glass. "Thank you, Kendrick. Here's to double-sided conversations. Perhaps Halberd liked the whisky?" He sipped his. "It's very good."

"I seem to remember he drank very little,"

Kendrick replied. "And when he did, it was brandy. Always too careful to be anything but sober. Have to be, when you have so many enemies."

"Are we to assume you were one of them?" Pitt asked, watching Kendrick's face over the top of his glass.

"Well deduced, Pitt," Kendrick agreed.

"Not particularly. You made it the obvious thing to assume. Not that he kept any record of it that I have found. Was he unaware, do you suppose?" He wondered why Kendrick was telling him. Was it a warning or bait?

"I'm sure he wasn't," Kendrick said, taking another sip of his whisky. "It was more personal than professional. And not, I imagine, something he was proud of. And something he would prefer his subordinates not to know."

Was that genuine spite, or said to make Pitt lose his temper and respond thoughtlessly?

Pitt smiled. "Then he would be very upset indeed to think what a man's servants know of him. Particularly a valet or lady's maid."

The faintest possible irritation crossed Kendrick's face, and vanished. "You are something above a valet, aren't you?" he asked with eyebrows raised.

"A different set of skills," Pitt said. "And actually I am employed by the Crown, as are all police, Special Branch, diplomats, judges, and other civil servants. And I suppose the army as well." He glanced at Jack. "And members of Parliament. In fact, one way or another, half the men in this room. I apologize, I forget, what was the point of this conversation?" He was interested. Was Kendrick going to take it back to Narraway again?

"Your progress, or lack of it, in learning exactly what happened to poor Halberd," Kendrick replied. "Or possibly we had moved on to how dislikable Narraway was, or maybe 'feared' is a more appropriate word. Dislike does not call for any action, except avoidance where it is possible."

"I think you were pointing out that men with power are often feared," Pitt replied. "Something of a truism. No one likes to be afraid. It robs one of . . . pride, or being free to do as you please, with no one to curb you. The loss of a certain kind of freedom that some people treasure rather a lot."

"Is that a kind of threat, Pitt?" Kendrick sounded as if the idea interested him, like a curious new species of insect.

"Of what?" Pitt raised his eyebrows. "In all the many papers Narraway left, your name was not mentioned."

"Really? So he has kept no record of it. How very . . . indicative."

"Indeed. Of what?" Pitt asked.

"That you would not approve, of course. And he knew that, because he knows you, and your morality." Now Kendrick was openly smiling. "Which doesn't make you unique, of course, just a little naïve for a policeman."

Pitt felt his temper rising. Perhaps that was exactly what Kendrick wanted. People who lose their temper lose control of the discussion and are more easily manipulated.

"You make it sound as if you actually know something." Pitt put his whisky glass down on the table. He had done no more than taste it, which was a shame because it was extremely good. "And I don't think you do."

Kendrick's eyes were bright, a wash of color in his cheeks. "Oh, yes I do. Do you know how Roland Darnley died? Horse-riding accident?" His expression was bitter. "Hardly. If you looked into it a little further you'd find it was no accident. You are so keen to find out what happened to John Halberd, but you won't reconsider what happened to Darnley. Why is that? Really — you have no idea? Too unimaginative? Don't care? Or would very much rather not know?" He leaned forward just an inch or two in his chair, his eyes not leaving Pitt's face. "And do you know that just after Darnley's death, Narraway began to pay his widow, quite regularly? And substantially. I see that you don't. What was it for, do you suppose? An affair? Blackmail? Hardly conscience money. If he paid that, he would be in the workhouse!"

Pitt was stunned, but he knew he must not show it.

"I suppose you know all this because she is now your wife?" he said softly, almost as if it amused him. "How disloyal of you to suggest that she is either a whore or a blackmailer. Fortunately, I have not been in a position to think such things of my wife, but if I were, I don't think I would tell anyone, least of all a man I disliked." He took a breath. "Or are you hoping I will investigate and prove you wrong? I don't think it falls within Special Branch's purview." It was a mistake, and he knew it the instant the words were said.

"Not in your purview?" Kendrick said incredulously. "The commander of Special Branch possibly murdered Darnley, and then paid blackmail to his widow, and you don't think it is your business? Good God, man, then what is? Some meddling idiot falls into the Serpentine while having an affair with a prostitute, in a rowing boat, for God's sake? And you waste everybody's time with that instead of drawing a veil over it, for decency. You can't even blackmail him into doing whatever you want, or telling you his secrets, because he hit his head on the gunwale and drowned. Let him lie in whatever peace there is after death! Stop muckraking."

Pitt felt every muscle in his body go rigid until it ached. He must control his temper, not think of his years of friendship with Narraway, all the hours they had spent fighting battles side by side, or of the pain Vespasia would feel if any of this was true, the appalling loss of all her newfound happiness. He must go forward, carefully.

"And I presume you can tell me how I should investigate it?" he asked as levelly as he could. "You know because your wife told you? Do you just choose to believe it, or is there some proof? You do not have access to Narraway's bank statements, but you do to hers. I don't. I have only your word, which is not proof of anything, except that you hate Narraway. Is that because you think he had an affair with your wife before you knew her? So, I believe, did the Prince of

Wales. It seems to be common knowledge. Except, of course, I don't imagine he paid her."

A tide of color washed up Kendrick's face, and Pitt knew that he had made an enemy for life. It was an uncomfortable thought, but that too was part of the price of making decisions and staying with them.

"Oh, yes, Mr. Pitt, of course I have proof," Kendrick said between his teeth. "I have her bank statements. It was considerable money, paid regularly. And if you look a little more closely at Darnley's death, you will see that it was murder, well disguised, cleverly done, but murder all the same. You would not expect Narraway to be clumsy, would you?"

Pitt kept his voice mild, but it was one of the most difficult acts of self-control he had ever undertaken.

"And I suppose you know why Narraway killed Darnley? It hardly seems to have been necessary in order to have an affair with his wife. It doesn't look like he wished to marry her himself."

The look in Kendrick's eyes was pure hatred.

"I imagine Darnley knew a few of Narraway's own secrets," he said, his throat so tight his voice was several tones higher. "I leave that to you to find out, if you have the courage to look!" And with that, he rose to his feet and stalked away without even glancing at Jack Radley.

Pitt let out his breath slowly.

Jack was staring at him, his face filled with apprehension.

"You've made a bad enemy," he said softly.

"I know. What did you expect me to do? Back away?"

"No. No, I think I expected you to do exactly what you did. Narraway has been a good friend to you, and regardless of that, he's Aunt Vespasia's husband, so we have to defend him all we can. Are you so sure he's innocent?"

Pitt's temper was instant, and evaporated as quickly. This was not the time for quixotic gestures.

"No, I'm not," he admitted. "He could have had an affair with Delia. Can't see it, but who knows? People are attracted to the oddest companions. It was twenty years ago. People change. But I don't believe he killed Darnley over it. Why the hell would he? She seems to have been available enough, regardless."

Jack did not look away. "Then what did he pay her for? And if you want to think he didn't, you're dreaming. Kendrick wouldn't say that if he couldn't follow it up."

"I know." Pitt pushed the whisky away from him. "First, I'll have to investigate Darnley's death. If it really was an accident, then it has nothing to do with this."

"Has it occurred to you that the whole issue is irrelevant to John Halberd's death, and Kendrick has only raised it to get you off that?"

"Yes, of course it has. Doesn't mean I can leave it alone." Pitt stood up. "Sorry, Jack, I've got a whole force at my disposal. I need to do both."

"Are you using the whole force?" Jack finished his whisky and rose to his feet also. "Is that wise? It signals that you're worried that Kendrick could be right. And you can be sure he'll be watching. He'll make an issue of it. I would, in his place — so would you."

"No. I'll just use Stoker. I haven't got anyone else involved in the Halberd affair either. But thanks for the warning. He's playing with emotions — fear, loyalty. I know that."

As soon as Pitt got back to Lisson Grove, later than he had intended, he sent for Stoker, and was told that he was out, though no one knew where. Pitt should not have been surprised. He had given him enough to do, and said very specifically that he was to inform no one else, either directly or indirectly.

He spent the whole afternoon going through all the files he could, dating from the year of Darnley's death to the previous two years. He did not expect to find anything of use. If Narraway had been having an affair with Delia, there would be no note of it in his office. But Pitt could at least find a good outline of where Narraway himself had been. If it was anywhere near Buckinghamshire, where Darnley had been killed, it was somewhere to start. Although it would be of help only if it was proved he was far enough away that he could not have gone there. It was not so far from London, and the train service was excellent.

After considerable cross-referencing, Pitt was surprised to find a copy of the police report on Darnley's death, clearly ruled an accident. In Narraway's small, handsome, but almost illegible handwriting, he found notes on it. With a magnifying glass he read them all, or as close to all as he could make sense of. He was still struggling with them when there was a brief knock on the door, and before he could answer it, Stoker came through and closed it behind him.

Pitt looked up, surprised at how pleased he was to see Stoker's bony face.

"Tell me what you make of this," he said, pushing the pages across the desk, along with a magnifying glass and his own notes.

Stoker read them all before looking up.

"Seems like he was sure Darnley was murdered, sir. And the note at the end implies he dealt with it, or someone did."

"That's how I read it," Pitt agreed. "But 'dealt with' could mean a number of things. What do you know about Darnley? This was all before your time. Is there anyone who would know?"

"Lethbridge might. He'd been here for thirty years when I came. But I am not sure how good his memory is. You could ask him, or I will, if you like?"

"Please do," Pitt said, "but be careful. I don't want speculation all over the office, and still less outside it. If Lethbridge asks, or perhaps even if he doesn't, don't overexplain. Just tell him the matter has risen again and we need to put it back where it belongs. Report to me as soon as you know."

"Yes, sir."

Pitt would have liked to go home and discuss it with Charlotte. They could have comforted each other, recalled memories of all the times they had sat at the kitchen table with Narraway and Vespasia and struggled to find their way through cases, prove the guilt or innocence they believed, work out what was true or false.

Everyone who had ever made decisions had been wrong at times. It was whether you owned up to it and how you changed that mattered, the degree of honesty, the courage and the will to face it.

Was Narraway the man Pitt believed him to be: clever, sarcastic, very private, when necessary manipulative, but still a man of his own integrity, able to feel both pity and guilt, and now deeply vulnerable in his love for Vespasia? How much did people change, for the better or worse?

It was time he changed and carried this weight of knowledge alone. He was afraid of what he would find, how it would hurt Charlotte — and even more, Vespasia. But would she ever have to know?

That was a foolish thought. She *would* know. Pitt's attitude toward Narraway would be different. The respect would be gone, and it was more than that; it was the kind of trust one has in a father, a man who has taught you his profession, at times exercised a kind of discipline. There was no sentimentality; but it was a kind of love. Either of them would risk his life for the other. Indeed, they had.

The truth was clear: He was afraid of learning something that would compromise forever his friendship with Narraway, but there was no escape. He knew enough that he could not turn away from the rest. The unanswered questions would always be there, growing darker, heavier, leaking their poison into everything else, as one drop of ink will turn a whole glass of water blue.

But Charlotte did not need to know that tonight. There might be another reason behind Darnley's death and Narraway's payments to Delia. Until he had found it, he would say nothing.

Determinedly, Pitt stood straight and smiled as he went in through his own front door that evening, and when Charlotte came out of the parlor to greet him, he kissed her gently, holding her only a single moment too long. When she looked at him more carefully, searching his face, he pretended not to notice.

He spoke to Daniel and Jemima, asking about their current projects, Jemima in more detail than usual. Daniel was quieter, and Pitt was on the verge of telling him that he had spoken to Dr. Needham, but knew it was still too soon. The answer could be that the charge remained on his record, false or not.

Daniel did not seem to notice, too withdrawn into himself. Only Charlotte detected a tension in Pitt, but he refused to acknowledge it. He admitted to a weariness after the children had gone to bed, though, and made it the excuse to go upstairs early himself. He avoided talking with her by pretending to fall asleep, when actually his brain was still going over and over the possibilities of why Darnley had been killed, and what on earth had made Narraway regularly pay his widow. He even wondered if Narraway could have been the father of her child.

In the morning he went straight to the hall table to see if the mail had arrived. He knew it as soon as he saw it. He opened it cautiously, then saw the school heading on the paper, and found his hand was shaking.

> Dear Commander Pitt,
> I am pleased to inform you that the matter we discussed has been looked into and resolved. I shall advise Daniel that in future his loyalty to the truth should supersede his loyalty to his comrades. A just man serves a higher cause than

concealing another's fault. One such action can become two, and then a habit. I believe that he will take my point. In the end, it will be the lesser pain. As you pointed out, a leader of men cannot be manipulated by popularity. Such a hard lesson for a child to learn.

Yours faithfully,
James Needham

Pitt folded the letter and put it in his inside pocket, his whole mind flooded with relief. Not only was the matter dealt with, but he was convinced that Daniel was in a school where he would be molded by a leader of both honor and wisdom.

He walked down the corridor to the kitchen, smiling.

For two miserable days Pitt attended to other Special Branch cases, and in any time left read all the reports he had on the current situation in South Africa. The more he learned, the more inevitable it seemed that a second Boer war would begin, possibly before the year was out.

Sir Alfred Milner might be a brilliant and honorable man, but Pitt could not like him. His view of empire, as a guardian of less advanced peoples and the supposition it should be enforced by arms if necessary, was repellent. It held an arrogance that seemed to carry over into every other aspect of life. Law can be administered successfully only with the consent of the people concerned. He had learned that in a very personal way during his years as a policeman. When the majority of people lose trust in you, you can rule only by violence.

Fortunately, his job had very little to do with the Boer question. It grieved him as a citizen, however.

When Stoker came in on the third day, it was late in the afternoon and he had obviously been hurrying. He was out of breath when he spoke.

"Glad you're still here, sir." His face was alight with more than satisfaction; it was positively joyful.

"What?" Pitt demanded. "Any good news would be welcome."

"Can't prove that Darnley was murdered." Stoker was gasping for breath. He looked at the chair but was too tense to sit in it, and would not have anyway without Pitt's permission. "The man working on the case at the time was quite sure he was, but it was damn cleverly done. Narraway didn't seem to want to make much of it, so he let it be —"

"Stoker!" Pitt's voice was hard-edged and louder than he meant it to be. "Get to the point, man!"

"He didn't look into it because Darnley was working for him when it happened — not regularly, just now and then."

Pitt sat upright. "Darnley was working for Narraway?" he said incredulously.

"Yes." Stoker glowed with satisfaction. "Narraway could never say so — it was a very discreet piece of work — but that's why he paid Darnley's widow. Killed in action, so to speak. The man was a bounder, slippery as an eel in some ways, but useful. This job wasn't the first one he'd done for Narraway. I came across a fellow who worked at the bank — he saw the money in Darnley's account. Nobody took Darnley seriously; best disguise there is. But he had nerve, I'll say that for him. No idea whether Narraway liked him or trusted him, but he stood by his widow. The record is pretty obscure, so it wasn't regular and there were no government funds to cover it. So it must have been out of his own pocket."

Pitt felt the warmth he saw in Stoker's eyes flood through him as well. He had not realized how deep the fear had been, how much pain he'd felt, until it stopped. He felt light-headed, euphoric.

Stoker was staring at him, his smile spread wide. "Like to go to the pub, sir? Pint of cider?"

It would be churlish not to. And besides that, yes, he would like it. He would like to spend a little time celebrating with someone who knew the reason and was celebrating as well. He stood up. "Yes, I would. First round is on me."

CHAPTER 11

Pitt was having breakfast a little later than usual the next morning, having slept well for the first time in over a week. He had just helped himself to a second cup of tea when the front doorbell rang. The bell itself was in the kitchen, so that a servant would be unlikely to miss it. He glanced at Charlotte, but both of them left it for Minnie Maude to answer. She came back, closely followed by a white-faced Stoker.

"Sorry, sir," Minnie Maude said quietly. "But Mr. Stoker says it can't wait."

Pitt nodded to her, then turned to Stoker. "What is it?" he asked.

Stoker never dragged things out for effect. "Mrs. Kendrick, sir. I'm afraid her body was discovered this morning. She must've got up in the night and . . ." He glanced at Charlotte, questioning whether he should say this in front of her.

Pitt hesitated only a moment. "What,

Stoker? I imagine we'll all know, sooner or later."

Stoker's voice dropped a tone. "She hanged herself, sir. At least that's what the local police say. She left a bit of a note. Not much, just — 'I deserve this.' When they questioned Mr. Kendrick about it, he was very upset, naturally, but he told them that when he thought about it, it wasn't so surprising. He blamed himself that he didn't see it coming and stop it. Least that's what they said. Lucky it was a pretty smart sort of man they had in charge. He told them to keep everything as it was, and sent a message to us. I came straight to tell you. The hansom is waiting, in case you want to go there . . ."

"I do." Pitt rose to his feet. "My coat's in the hall. We need to get there immediately." He gave Charlotte a wordless glance, saw the horror in her eyes, and wished he had the time to talk with her, but there was nothing that would make this better. He smiled bleakly, then followed Stoker along the hall to the door, grabbing his coat and hat as he passed.

It was a silent ride, made as swiftly as possible. Perhaps Stoker's mind was racing as fast as Pitt's, trying to fit this new, tragic fact into the picture to make sense of it.

They arrived at the Kendricks' house fifteen minutes later and noted that the mortuary wagon was waiting across the street. There was a constable on duty close to the front door.

Pitt showed his identification and a few moments later he and Stoker were in the large, handsome hallway, facing Inspector Wadham, a fierce man of perhaps forty-five, who looked deeply unhappy.

"Sorry to get you out on this, Commander," he said. "It may be no more than an ordinary suicide, but considering Mr. Kendrick is such a close friend of His Royal Highness, and that business with Sir John dying like that, I thought you should see it."

"Thank you," Pitt replied with sincerity. "Another man might not have seen the relevance. It may not be connected, but I'm afraid it is far more likely that it is . . . somehow. I see you've called the mortuary van. Have you taken her down?"

"No. I'm sorry, it seems indecent, but I thought you should see her as she was. I think the husband was too shocked to do it himself. Either that, or he had enough sense to leave her so we would find her exactly as he did. The police surgeon verified that she's been dead at least several hours, but I told him to wait to move her until you got here. Know you used to be regular police before you moved over. He is waiting for us in the back-kitchen storeroom, where she is."

Pitt was startled. "Back-kitchen storeroom?"

"Yes, sir. Only place with big hooks in the ceiling. I'm sorry, but it's pretty ugly. Husband is waiting in the morning room. Got one of my men with him. Doctor's waiting, sir." He turned and led the way across the hall and through into the back of the house, Pitt and Stoker following directly behind.

There was another constable in the passage outside the closed back-kitchen door. A third stood close by. Judging from his demeanor and a large leather Gladstone bag beside him, he was the police surgeon.

"Dr. Carsbrook, this is Commander Pitt, Special Branch," Wadham said briskly. "What can you tell us?"

Carsbrook looked at Pitt and clearly changed his mind about what he had been going to say, and possibly the manner in which he would have said it.

"She's still hanging there. From the body temperature and lividity I'd say she did this about midnight. That's as much as I can tell. I ought to know more after I get her to the mortuary and take a more thorough look."

"Are you sure she did this herself?" Pitt asked.

Carsbrook's eyebrows shot up. "Good God, what are you suggesting? A woman doesn't get up in the middle of the night, go down to the back kitchen, stand on a stool with a rope around the ceiling meat hook, and then kick the stool away by accident!"

"That is not the only alternative," Pitt told him wearily. "In view of another recent death that appeared to be accidental, I need to be sure."

Carsbrook stood very still. "The husband? Or are you suggesting one of the staff? There have been no break-ins, nothing stolen. The police have already established that. Or did they not tell you?"

"I am the head of Special Branch, Doctor, not the local burglary squad," Pitt said sharply. "I need to know, from the facts of the body, the nature of the death, whether you are certain she did this to herself."

"Then you'd better look at it and let me get the poor woman down," Carsbrook replied equally tartly.

Pitt walked round him and opened the door. The room was like any other back kitchen in a large house. It was designed mostly for storage, especially of things too big to put in the kitchen or larder: whole flitches of bacon or sides of beef, large sacks of grain or potatoes.

Delia Kendrick was hanging from the largest of the iron meat hooks, set deeply into the lowest crossbeam, about eight feet above the floor. The noose around her neck was made of knotted garden twine, thick enough to take her weight. It was tied in a slipknot such as an executioner would use. She was wearing a nightgown and slippers and her long black hair was loose, half covering her face. An old three-legged milking stool lay on its side a couple of feet away.

Pitt would have liked to have left her the decency of hiding her face from these strangers, but he could not. He walked over and touched her hand. It was cold, and he noticed that there were little bits of skin, just shreds, under the fingernails, but none of the nails was broken. He looked at the other hand, and none of those was either. He looked closely at her face, congested and blue. Her mouth was open, eyes bulging and dotted with the tiny red spots of minute blood vessels that burst when a person struggles desperately to breathe, and cannot.

It could have happened as the doctor assumed.

He turned and spoke to Carsbrook. "Take her down. I would like to see her neck when you get that rope off. And remove it carefully, please."

Carsbrook came forward and, with Pitt's help to lift her a little, climbed up on the seat of a kitchen chair, brought for the purpose, and lifted her down. With Wadham's help, they laid her on the stone floor. Very carefully Carsbrook eased the noose off and laid it beside his bag. He could do so without having to cut it.

Pitt looked at the skin of her neck. It was horribly bruised, but even the most minute examination could not find any torn skin. There was no tearing, no battle. Death had come quickly.

"What are you looking for?" Carsbrook asked.

"There's skin under the nails of her right hand," Pitt replied. Carsbrook frowned at him, looked at her neck again, then pursed his lips. "It must have come from some other place." As he spoke he pushed up the sleeves of her nightgown, but both arms were unmarked.

"If you find anything on the body, let me know," Pitt said. "In fact, let me know even if you don't."

"What are you thinking?" Carsbrook demanded. "What are you going to say to the newspapers? I know suicide is a crime, but in God's name, what is the purpose in telling every prying Tom, Dick, or Harry that the woman was . . . out of her mind with . . . I don't know. Grief? Fear? We don't need to know every damn thing about one another. Give her some peace." There was deep anger in his voice, his face, even the stiffness of his hands. Or perhaps it was just pity, deeper than he could deal with, that he dare not express.

"I need to know if she did this to herself, and if she did then I agree with you entirely," Pitt said more gently. "And I shall issue no statement at all, and answer no one's questions. But if someone else did this to her, then I won't rest until I find out who it was, and see they answer for it."

Carsbrook turned to look at him steadily. "Frankly, I don't know what you're doing here at all!"

"Fortunately, you don't have to," Pitt told him. "It's not my concern if she did this to herself, and it's not your concern if she didn't."

"Does this not tell you, man? It's clear enough, look!" Carsbrook picked up a paper from the floor and held it out.

"Yes, I see." Pitt took it from him. "It says 'I deserve this.' It is not addressed to anyone, nor is it signed. I expect it will be her handwriting, but it could refer to anything."

"Damn it, man!" Carsbrook's voice shook. "It's on the floor beside the corpse. What else could it refer to? It's hardly going to be that she deserves a new dress, or a piece of chocolate cake."

"Where is the pencil with which she wrote it?" Pitt asked. "Or the rest of the sheet of paper?"

Carsbrook looked confused. "Well, obviously she wrote it somewhere else and . . . brought it with her."

Pitt looked at Wadham. "Please be very sure indeed that you make a point of finding the rest of the paper; the pencil will probably be somewhere near it."

Wadham nodded. He understood exactly what Pitt was thinking — the note could have been written anywhere, at any time.

"The husband is in the morning room, Commander," he said.

"I'd better go up and speak to him. Stoker, come with me. Thank you, Doctor." Pitt walked out of the back kitchen and followed Wadham up the steps and through the passage, past the kitchen and into the hall again. Wadham knocked on the morning-room door and opened it.

Kendrick was standing in front of the fireplace and the embroidered screen that hid the hearth at this time of the year. He turned to face the door when it opened. From the look of shock on his face, he had not expected Pitt. Perhaps he had thought Wadham would take Delia's death no further.

Wadham spoke first. "Commander Pitt from Special Branch is going to handle the matter from now on, sir, so I will go and see to the other arrangements." That was a discreet way of saying the removal of the body, and perhaps the clearing up of the scene so the domestic staff could resume their duties, if they were in a fit state of self-possession to do anything.

As Wadham closed the door, leaving them alone, Kendrick stared at Pitt, horror marked deep in every aspect of him, from the pallor of his face to the rigidity of his body. His hands were so stiff, it looked as if movement might break them.

"Must you?" Kendrick said hoarsely.

"Yes, Mr. Kendrick," Pitt replied. "If I could avoid it and leave you to your grief I would do so. I will be as brief as I can.

Would you please tell me all you are able to about this?"

"I suppose it isn't obvious to you, or if it is, you still have to go over it like some . . . I'm sorry. Perhaps I should have seen it earlier, and I didn't. This is a total shock to me." Kendrick stared ahead of him, not at Pitt but at something within his own vision.

Pitt waited patiently for him to go on.

"Delia was always . . . a woman of deep feelings . . . and attractive to many men because of it. I knew all about her affair with the Prince of Wales, of course. It was before I met her, and while I was not pleased, it did not disturb me. It was Darnley she betrayed, not me. And I have many reasons to believe he was very far from faithful to her." Now he was watching Pitt, trying to judge his reaction.

"It all ended before she and I met, years before. She was a widow when I returned to London from various travels. All was well with us for many years. I treated her daughter, Alice, as if she were my own. She is a very sweet girl. I was pleased for her when Delia arranged a fortunate marriage with a Scotsman of good nature and background, who could look after Alice and offer her a life away from London."

Pitt wondered what else he was going to

say about Alice, or about Darnley, but he did not want to prompt him.

"She is very pleasing to look at," Kendrick went on. "Fair-haired, and with the most beautiful complexion. She resembles Delia's father, but not either Delia or Darnley. Unfortunately she also resembles the Prince of Wales, and Delia's courage and distinction have always attracted a degree of malicious gossip. Marrying Alice to a Scot and so getting her out of sight was a way of lessening it, in fact almost stopping it. Delia told me that your predecessor, now Lord Narraway, was of some assistance in the arrangements. I have no idea what his interest was in the matter."

Pitt guessed it went back to Darnley's service twenty years earlier, but he did not say so. He would allow Kendrick to get to his point by his own route, and in his own way.

"The gossip ceased," Kendrick went on. "But not the blackmail."

"Blackmail?" Pitt was startled.

Kendrick gritted his teeth. "Not merely for money, for . . . other things as well. Money I would have paid . . . Delia would have. But when she told him that it was over, I did not at first understand." He was staring directly at Pitt now, watching him.

He drew in his breath and held it for a moment before letting it out in a sigh, as if he had faced an immense obstacle and yielded to it.

"Halberd was not the man you thought, and what is uglier and far more dangerous, he was very far from the man the Queen believed him to be," Kendrick went on. "I think the prince knew that, but he would not grieve his mother by telling her. He hoped she would never have to know." He stopped, still searching Pitt's face, his eyes trying to judge whether he understood.

Pitt understood very well what he was implying, but he needed Kendrick to say it outright.

"Don't you understand, damn it?" As Kendrick lost his temper, his voice became shrill, his face flooded with color. "Don't stand there blinking like a damn owl!"

"I do understand, sir," Pitt replied. "But in case I am mistaken, I need you to be more specific."

"He wanted favors that were — repellent! When she could no longer bear it . . . she . . . killed him!" Kendrick looked desperate. "Does this have to come out? The Queen would be devastated. If it is in all the newspapers — and it would be — no one could keep it from her. She is old, but she is far wiser than many would imagine. Halberd had no family, but there are many who trusted him. Can't we bury it all? Who else, in God's name, has a right to know?"

Pitt was more shaken than he had expected to be. Nothing he had learned about Halberd indicated anything of that nature, but he had been a policeman long enough to know with a bitter certainty that the deepest vices are not just hard to recognize, they can be completely invisible. Victoria would not even have imagined them, let alone believed them of someone she had both liked and trusted.

But had they been true, or were they Kendrick's creation, in order to justify Delia's actions?

He must respond now. Kendrick was staring at him, waiting.

"No one," he said. "You're quite right, it is far better that we give nothing to the newspapers beyond the fact of her death. For legal reasons alone, it would be unwise to say anything about Halberd. It would only cause speculation of the most unpleasant sort." He watched Kendrick's face and saw the relief in it, even possibly a gleam of satisfaction, carefully guarded.

Was this the end of the question of Halberd's death? It made sense of both motive and the action itself, the place and the time of it.

"I assume Mrs. Kendrick was not at home, in your company, at the time you told the police she was, the night of Halberd's death?" Pitt asked. He forced himself to sound courteous, even sympathetic.

Kendrick hesitated. Apparently the question caught him off guard.

"Er . . . yes. I'm sorry. I was aware that she was out of the house late in the evening, but I truly believed it was an . . . innocent matter, at least innocent of having killed Halberd. Believe me, I had no idea of his . . . bestiality. She was obviously ashamed to tell me. If I had known I would have found a way to stop it. I don't care how powerful he was, or how well the Queen thought of him. She is old and very frail. Edward will be king within a year or two." His face was pale and haggard with strain, his voice catching in his throat.

Pitt nodded very slightly. It was not something with which he could argue, and he found himself surprisingly sad. It would be the end of a century, and of an age. Whatever the new century brought, there was a familiarity, even a love, of the old that would leave a kind of grief at its close.

"I apologize for misleading you," Kendrick

went on more calmly. "I believed I was protecting my wife from unkind gossip, not from . . . from the charge of having killed a man, even if she was driven to it by his . . . brutality."

Pitt was not certain if he believed Kendrick, but he must behave as if he did. He asked the question that would have come to his mind if he believed him.

"Why did you submit to this treatment from him at all? You could have ruined him, and surely you would have, had you known he had such things in mind? The Queen would've been appalled, but you could have handled it so that Halberd would simply retire to the country, claim ill health, and whatever other excuse he liked."

Kendrick smiled bitterly. For a moment he turned away. Was it to give himself time to think? Was he really so shaken he had not prepared this beforehand — at the very least, before Pitt came? Was it even conceivable that he was telling the truth?

Kendrick looked desperately uncomfortable, shifting his weight a fraction from one foot to the other.

"I . . . I knew she had a relationship with him, but I thought it was no more than a flirtation. He was aware of her . . . intimacy with the Prince of Wales, before her daughter was born, and before Darnley . . . died." His hesitation implied meaning. "Halberd used his knowledge to make it more than that. She only told me that in the letter she left me." Now his eyes were hot and defiant. He stared straight at Pitt. "I burned it. I have no intention of telling you what it said. You, or anyone else. They are both dead now. Nothing you say or do can bring them back. For God's sake, if you have any decency at all, let them rest in peace. They have both paid the ultimate price."

Pitt was taken aback, not yet completely believing. For now, he would appear to accept, but he would investigate. He must. He wished desperately that Narraway were in London. He knew them all so much better than Pitt did. He had been in the same social circles and known Delia at the time of her affair with the prince, and he had known Roland Darnley. He was born and bred in the same stratum of society and understood such people. Pitt was feeling so very like a blind man, not even recognizing what he saw.

Kendrick was waiting for his answer.

"I will do all I can to make that possible," Pitt said. Immediately he saw Kendrick relax. The man might not have meant to show it, but the language of the body, unintentional, was almost universal. Pitt understood that very well. Kendrick had been worried, even afraid. Pitt would not forget that.

He excused himself and went back to find the police surgeon. He had more to ask him. And he would ask Stoker to check in intense detail if Delia could have killed Halberd. He should look again, harder, for witnesses who might have seen a woman answering Delia's description anywhere even remotely near the Serpentine at the right time.

Charlotte had been present when Stoker had told Pitt of Delia Kendrick's death, but she wanted to learn more. She could see that he was moved by it, shocked because he had not foreseen even its possibility and grieved at the manner of it. There was pity in his eyes and in his voice. Even his choice of words showed distress more than merely discretion. But what Charlotte herself felt was guilt. She remembered the face of the maid, Elsie Dimmock, and the fierce compassion she had felt for a woman she had known since she was a child. Closeness does sometimes breed mercy, but there was more than simply long familiarity in her manner. She had seen both courage and pain in Delia, and she was moved by it. Delia had lost a husband, and — cutting far more deeply than that — she had lost a child. She had known both wealth and hardship. Certainly she had known loneliness. Perhaps in striving to be a prince's mistress, defeat is inevitable. But whatever the cause, rejection is a defeat, and a very public one. It was not as if she had chosen to step aside; she had been pushed, and when she was at her most vulnerable — widowed, grieving for the death of a child.

Charlotte felt a rush of gratitude for Narraway's discreet help to Delia, made as if it was a debt he owed, not a charity. It was a grace she would not necessarily have expected from him, and given entirely in secret.

What troubled her the most was a persistent fear that she and Emily might have contributed to Delia's despair, and thus to her taking her own life. Everything they knew of her, though, said that she was not a cowardly woman, the last person to give up on life.

What had happened that she felt was beyond her strength to fight?

Charlotte said nothing to Pitt, except to sympathize with his weariness and give him something simple to eat. He was not hungry, but he did not refuse freshly toasted crumpets with butter and blackcurrant jam and a cup of hot tea. They both went to bed as early as possible. She listened, held him in her arms, gently, and then after he had fallen asleep, lay awake herself and worried about what she could do, at least to vindicate Delia's reputation. What could be saved from this wreckage? Anything good? Anything to ease the news for her daughter far away in Scotland? Anything that would alleviate Charlotte's own sense of guilt? She was certain that Emily would feel the same.

When Pitt had left in the morning, Charlotte picked up the telephone to speak with Emily, telling her that she would leave immediately and be at Emily's house within half an hour. They must talk, and plan. She was relieved to hear in Emily's voice a trace of the same consciousness of the part they could have played in this, and the acute sense of having been too quick to meddle, too superficial even to weigh the possibilities of doing such harm.

She walked to the end of the street and found a hansom. In just over half an hour she was sitting in Emily's boudoir with a pot of fresh, hot tea.

"Did Thomas tell you what happened?" Emily asked. She looked distressed and very earnest. "Could it have been an accident?" Her voice lifted in hope.

Charlotte had not told her any details. They were not of the sort one relays over the telephone.

"No." She shook her head minutely. Emily looked ready to argue. Charlotte hesitated only a moment. "There is no way one can create a noose, put it over a hook in the back-kitchen ceiling, and hang oneself by accident." She ignored Emily's horror. "There are only two possibilities. Either she deliberately and hideously took her own life — executed herself, if you wish to put it so — or someone else very carefully murdered her."

"Oh . . ."

"I'm not sure which is worse," Charlotte said after a moment. "I wish I could think it was murder, because that might mean we had no part in it, but if it was, then how could it have been anyone except her husband?"

Emily's face was tight, her eyes bleak. "Why would she kill herself? I know people are talking about her, but they're always talking about someone, and she has certainly experienced it before. Did she really have something to do with Halberd's death?"

"I don't know," Charlotte admitted. "Thomas didn't say very much, and I don't know whether he believes she killed herself. Honestly . . . I didn't ask him because I was afraid of the answer. What if she did?"

Emily looked miserable, but she did not evade the answer. "Could it be anything we said or did, do you think?"

"We stirred up the questions as to who killed Halberd, rather than letting anyone go on thinking it was a stupid accident," Charlotte said.

"Did anyone really think that?" Emily's eyebrows were raised. "What did people think he was doing there?"

"It doesn't matter whether we meant to stir things up or not, or even whether we really did," Charlotte said very quietly. "We didn't care enough to think hard about what we said, or what meaning people took from it. Thoughtlessness is not an excuse. We aren't children, and we both knew what it's like to be the victim of other people's gossip."

"You haven't —" Emily began.

"I've seen it!" Charlotte said more sharply than she intended to. It was herself she was angry with, and she would not have excuses made for either of them. They had taken it too lightly, enjoying the involvement, the exercise of imagination, the swirl and color of being in society again. She was not going to excuse herself from blame. Delia Kendrick was dead, and people were assuming it was by her own hand, because she was guilty of having murdered John Halberd. "We have to find out if this is true," she said. "Even if she did kill Halberd, and then herself, what we did is still wrong, because we didn't care enough to think first. And if she didn't kill him, then we must prove her innocence."

"You're angry because you didn't like her, and now you owe her a debt," Emily pointed out. She bit her lip. "So do I."

"Then we had better think hard, and plan." Charlotte finished her tea and poured some more. "Where do we begin?"

It was later that day that Pitt was contacted by Dr. Carsbrook. It was just a brief note, delivered by messenger.

Pitt tore it open while the boy waited.

> I examined the body in detail, specifically looking for scratches that could account for the shreds of skin under Mrs. Kendrick's nails. I found nothing at all, not the slightest abrasion.
>
> I can only conclude that it is not her

own skin.

I have made a report to that effect. She fought for her life.

I am obliged to you for that knowledge.

Richard Carsbrook

"Thank you," Pitt said to the messenger. "There is no reply, except that I appreciate it." He gave the young man sixpence from his pocket, a generous tip.

It was half an hour later that he was sent for by the Prince of Wales. This time a footman had come, and sat in one of the offices until Pitt was free to accompany him. It was after five and the traffic was heavy. Nevertheless, before six Pitt was ushered into the room where the prince was waiting for him comfortably.

The prince was standing, as if too restless to sit. This mild summer evening he looked very gray, and all the lines of his face dragged downward.

"Ah, Pitt! Thank you for coming," he said as Pitt entered the room and heard the footman close the door almost silently behind him, just a soft *snick* as a latch caught.

Pitt had not expected to be thanked. In fact he had imagined the prince would show anger rather than what looked more like grief.

"It is a very sad occasion, Your Royal Highness," he replied gravely.

"I heard only the barest news," the prince said, brushing aside the formality. "Tell me what happened."

Pitt had thought on the journey here how much he should tell the prince, depending upon what he asked. If he had actually cared for Delia Kendrick, then he deserved as much truth as he wished to know. If he had merely used her for her wit, intelligence, and willingness to please him, then Pitt would tell him as little as possible, without appearing to concede anything of importance to a onetime friend.

Pitt looked at the prince's face, recalling what he had learned of him in the last few weeks. If it was not real grief he saw, then the man was superbly gifted at affecting it.

"I am not yet certain, sir," he said quietly. "Appearances suggest that she took her own life. There was a note that could be interpreted as a confession to her having been the one who killed Sir John Halberd . . ." He decided not to mention Carsbrook's message about the skin. It was an intimate detail that would distress, and he did not yet know where it would lead.

"Suggest?" The prince's voice was thick with emotion. "What the devil do you mean? Be plain with me, man! And how and why on earth could she have killed Halberd? That's preposterous! Who suggested anything so absurd? Halberd was a tall man, and fit. Very fit. How could Mrs. Kendrick have had the strength to kill him? The whole idea is ridiculous." It wasn't merely denial in his voice; it was genuine disbelief.

Pitt must choose his words carefully, not just because this was his future sovereign he was speaking to but, more important to him, because the prince was a man who clearly felt a real sense of bereavement, possibly even of guilt for a breach it was now too late to mend, whether he had ever intended to or not.

"She chose a particularly grim way of ending her life, sir, and the note she left said clearly that she felt she deserved it. But that is not yet proof. I find it hard to believe. Her reason for it is extreme, and I have only Mr. Kendrick's word for it . . ."

The prince's fair brows rose high. "Do you doubt it?"

Pitt looked at the prince's face, and it appeared as if he was struggling to find any answer other than the one Pitt had implied. It was not defense of Kendrick he seemed to want so much as simply a denial of the whole, tragic issue.

"I question everything until it is proved, sir. That is part of my job. And when someone unexpectedly takes their own life, or appears to have, I need proof before I accept it. Mrs. Kendrick seems to have been a woman of great courage. She had already survived the death of her infant son, then of her first husband, who apparently did not treat her well, then the financial hardship that was imposed on her, albeit temporarily." He did not mention her affair with the prince himself, or that she seemed to have cared for him more than he cared for her, but he saw a shadow in the prince's face and thought that perhaps he knew it, if not at the time, then now.

"Why on earth would she kill Halberd, even if she had the strength?" the prince demanded. He was angry because he was hurt and, Pitt was increasingly convinced, also feeling guilty for what was now irreparable.

Pitt answered the latter question first. "If Halberd was not expecting an attack he would be unprepared. Whoever killed him took one of the oars and struck him with it, across the head, extremely hard. But with so long an instrument, a full shoulder swing would have great momentum. He was knocked unconscious and left to drown. A determined woman could have done it without great difficulty, especially one from whom he was not expecting any trouble."

The prince flinched at the picture painted by Pitt's words. "I see. But why? Why on earth would Delia wish to attack Halberd at all, let alone kill him? Could it not have been an accident? And she had no idea that she had knocked him senseless and he would drown?"

"If the quarrel had been very fierce, and she was afraid of him, that is possible," Pitt asserted, but dubiously. "It still leaves the question as to why she was there at all."

"Yes . . . Why was she? And why would she be afraid of him?"

"Kendrick said she had an affair with Halberd, and then because of it, he blackmailed her into obscene practices, which she finally could bear no longer, and that was why she killed him . . . deliberately."

The last shred of color drained from the prince's face.

"That's . . . vile! I don't believe it, sir. I don't. It is totally . . . obscene!"

"I agree," Pitt said softly. "That is why I need proof, far more than one man's word, before I accept it as true."

The prince looked puzzled — when he spoke it was a genuine question, not a challenge. "What can you find? What would prove it? You said she left a note?"

"Only a few words, sir. Just that she deserved it. That could have meant anything."

"Sounds pretty clear . . ."

"That at some time, she felt she deserved something," Pitt said slowly, watching the prince's face to see if he followed the meaning. "We could think she was referring to her death."

"How did she . . . die?"

Pitt hesitated.

"How did she die?" the prince repeated more sharply. "For God's sake, man, tell —"

"She hanged herself, sir. In the back kitchen, from a hook in one of the beams."

The prince stared at him, too appalled to find words.

"I'm sorry, sir. I would rather not have had to tell you that." Pitt meant it. For these few moments they were simply two men grieving over the death of a woman they had both known, even if to a very different degree.

The prince nodded. "I forced you to. Poor Delia —" He stopped abruptly, choked with grief. Pitt saw in his face so many conflicting emotions. He imagined that other memories were running through his mind, other regrets, and perhaps a sense of his own mortality, and surely that of his mother and all that that would mean for him and the world.

The prince stared at Pitt. Was he wondering now what kind of a man Kendrick really was? That would cause grief as well, and a sense of betrayal. The prince might be used to them, but that did not lessen the hurt; in fact, perhaps it made it deeper.

"I'm sorry, sir." Pitt meant it.

The prince nodded, and for a few moments he remained silent.

Protocol forbade Pitt from interrupting.

"Er . . . thank you, Pitt," the prince said at last. "Please keep me aware of what you discover. I imagine Mrs. Kendrick will be buried as quietly as possible. I could send flowers, but I cannot go myself."

"Of course not," Pitt agreed. "But flowers would be excellent, something very simple. She will know, and no one else will."

"Will she?" It was a sincere question, full of both hope and fear. To sit in church, and to obey the rules, or most of them, was one thing. To believe, in the face of actual death, was another. It was beyond knowledge, a leap of faith when one was weakest.

"Yes, sir," Pitt said without hesitation.

Since the Angel Court affair he had given spiritual matters much quiet thought. Whatever conclusion he came to, this was not the time to acknowledge any doubts at all.

The prince gave a half smile. "Thank you, Pitt. I'm obliged you came."

It was permission to leave. Pitt bowed and obeyed. The footman who had come for him was waiting outside the door.

CHAPTER 12

Charlotte was deeply troubled, not only by Delia's death but by the manner of it. Had she really believed herself deserving of such an appalling end? Even if she had killed Halberd, surely there were some mitigating circumstances, some pain so deep that to her what she had done was justified? Anger, rejection after hope? Or fear? What danger would Halberd have been to her? Apparently he knew an inordinate amount about a lot of people. Pitt had said that much. Was Halberd blackmailing her? Hardly over her affair with the Prince of Wales. That was common knowledge, and always had been. No doubt those who were interested in such things could have named every woman in whom the prince had shown an interest over the last forty years.

Was there something else Elsie Dimmock would have told them, but had not?

Charlotte sat opposite Emily in her boudoir, the sun streaming in through the windows, which were open onto the garden. Birds chattered pleasantly outside and somewhere in the distance a dog barked.

"Why?" Emily said bleakly. "If she did it herself at all."

"Why now is the question we need to answer," Charlotte replied. "Whether she did it to herself, or someone did it to her, there was a reason it happened. It was something new, or something old that got horribly worse. Either way there will have been a change."

"Do you think she did it?" Emily's face was filled with unhappiness, deep lines across her brow.

"No." Charlotte had been thinking about it ever since she heard of Delia's death. She had to admit that it seemed strangely pointless. "I formed a very deep impression that she was a fighter," she replied to Emily. "Someone who turned her eyes outward, not in on herself."

"When we went to her former lady's maid and probed about the past, I didn't sense that Elsie Dimmock was deliberately evading anything," Emily said. "Did you?"

"No. I'm trying to find a place to start looking to see if Delia really did kill herself," Charlotte answered.

Emily bit her lip. "How likely is it?"

"Well, if it happened, very likely," Charlotte said with a self-mocking smile. "It didn't look as if Halberd was murdered either, to begin with. It seemed to be a rather ridiculous accident, the sort one doesn't talk about, it was so . . . undignified: A much-respected friend of the Queen falls out of a rowing boat while alone on the Serpentine at night and drowns in water he could have easily stood up in. Nobody hangs themselves from a meat hook in their own kitchen by accident! The point is that neither of them looks like murder, but one of them definitely is, and maybe the other one too."

"What did Thomas say, exactly? Or as close as you can remember?"

"That it looked as if she did it herself, but he is not at all sure it's so. Kendrick said Halberd was having an affair with her, and it was pretty disgusting. He blackmailed her into it, and when she couldn't take it anymore, she killed him."

"Then why kill herself?" Emily asked reasonably.

"Because she was afraid of being found out?"

"But did Thomas even suspect her?"

"Not that I know of. But I don't know

very much." Charlotte tried not to let the loneliness creep into her voice. Emily was watching her closely. She did not need words; Emily would catch even a change in tone, and understand it.

"Was Kendrick surprised when he knew she'd . . . done that to Halberd?" Emily asked.

"Yes, he was shocked . . . really horrified," Charlotte replied, recalling the look of grief in Pitt's face when he told her the very little he had. She even wondered if he would have told her at all, had she not known Delia personally. There were so many things he could not discuss with her. It would be wrong of her to try to persuade him to tell her more — a very selfish piece of cruelty. She wanted to know for her own sake, because she wished to be closer to him, to share and to be part of what mattered to him so much. But put like that, it sounded very childish. If she wished to share something with him apart from the daily details of life and home, then she should do something herself, and share that! Perhaps after all this was over, she would find something that mattered, a cause worth fighting for.

"If she didn't murder Halberd, what was it that made her kill herself?" she said. "It couldn't have been Thomas *suspecting* her of killing him. So it was something else. We need to find out what it was."

"A different affair?" Emily suggested. "She does seem prone to them . . ."

"The only one we know of is with the Prince of Wales, and everybody knows of that," Charlotte pointed out. "Halberd was what Kendrick said."

"Then we should find out if it was true. I suppose Halberd's death wasn't suicide, was it?"

"I don't know how you could hit yourself over the head hard enough to drown yourself!"

Emily's face was filled with doubt. "Are we sure they are even connected at all?"

"Maybe not. Who can we speak to, if we do it carefully enough?"

Emily thought for a moment. "Well, Felicia Whyte. And Helena Lyndhurst. She will talk about anything royal for hours. If we approach it that way . . ."

"Distasteful as it is, we had better begin while it's still a topic of interest and people remember things," Charlotte replied. She despised gossip in other people, but it had its uses. Sometimes nothing else served.

"Felicia will be at the ladies' club this afternoon." Emily rose to her feet purposefully. "We had better go. I'll find you something suitable to wear. Don't waste time going home to change, we must make plans."

"How charming of you to have brought your sister again," Lady Felicia said as soon as she saw Charlotte half a step behind Emily. Felicia's expression held just the right balance of warmth and amusement. Clearly she had forgotten nothing of the last meeting here. Charlotte liked her the better that she could find amusement in it.

"Thank you for making me welcome," she replied in just the same blend of amusement and pleasure. They had no time to waste. This could be a long and awkward task. "I wish the circumstances were unclouded by tragedy."

Felicia understood instantly what she was referring to. Surprisingly, there was a moment of real and deep regret in her eyes.

"Indeed. It is very sobering. One knows so much less than one imagines."

"You are right, of course." Charlotte said it with warmth that was purely tactical, but then immediately after she was surprised to find that she meant it. She did not know much about Felicia. The woman might have experienced her share of grief, of feeling frightened or lonely, or even betrayed.

It took another ten minutes before Emily

managed to steer the conversation to Delia.

"You knew her far longer than we did," she said with a sad little smile. "Were you surprised?" She seemed about to continue, but she was studying Felicia's face as she spoke, and something in it stopped her from asking her next question.

"Yes, I was," Felicia said quietly. "I can hardly believe it even now. Delia," she spoke her name gently, "was more full of life, for good or ill, than anyone else I've known. I can't imagine a despair so deep that she would" — she shook her head a little, quite sharply, as if to dislodge an image from her brain — "do something so hideously final."

Charlotte decided to take the risk. "There are all sorts of rumors flying about. One is that she was having an affair with John Halberd, and they had a terrible quarrel about something . . . too awful to say . . . and that it was she who killed him! And she took her own life because she felt they were about to arrest her." She bit her lip from guilt at speaking the words when she so despised loose and cruel gossip, as this was. But she had to see Felicia's reaction to it.

She felt the blood hot in her face at the anger in Felicia's eyes.

"Who says such a thing?" she demanded. "That's . . . vile! And complete rubbish. Sir

John may have been proud, and cold, and he knew a great deal more than he ought to have about almost everybody, but he was not the sort of man to have affairs of . . . a disgusting nature. He did not marry because the one woman he loved died tragically, in Africa, before they had a chance to marry. He never forgot her, or felt deeply about anyone else." She said it quietly, so as not to be overheard by others, but the certainty of her emotion was unmistakable. "I don't know that I liked him very much; he was too clever, too . . . self-controlled for my taste. He was one man you could not manipulate. I always felt somehow at a disadvantage in his company." She gave a rueful and very slight smile. "As if he understood me far better than I would ever understand him. Couldn't fault him for anything. And . . ." She took a deep breath, almost as if she was fighting for self-control.

Charlotte did not turn and look at Emily. She waited.

"And I happen to know that Delia had grown closer to him in the last few weeks of his life, but it was as an old acquaintance," Felicia continued. "She knew him very slightly, so she said, when she was still married to Roland Darnley. And that was years ago. I would have known if there were anything like what you are suggesting." The look of distaste in her face was profound.

Charlotte could not help defending herself, startled that she actually cared what Felicia thought of her.

"I didn't believe it either," she said. "I told the busybody who said it something close to what I thought of her."

"Close to?" Felicia asked.

"I couldn't use the kind of language I wished to."

Felicia's expression softened. "I see. The temptation must have been intense, but perhaps best not to . . . Although I agree."

"Jealousy destroys everything," Emily said. "Like a disease that eats you inside." She looked at Felicia. "You must have experienced a good deal of it, in your position."

Felicia chose to take it as a compliment. "You are very perceptive. Yes, it is like acid, corroding everything it touches."

It was Charlotte's turn. She felt a moment of real sorrow for this woman who had so much, and yet so little. "In the end I hope this will not touch the memory of Delia, just rebound on the people who think such things, whether they said them aloud or not. I'm glad Delia knew Sir John in a pleasant way, and that she received some regard from him before he died."

Felicia thought for a moment. "I rather think she was seeking his help for some purpose, although I have no idea what." She furrowed her brow in an effort to recall a thought that eluded her. "I know she asked my husband as well. He was in Africa for many years, you know? But not the south, I don't think. Or at least not much."

Charlotte gave a little shiver. "You mention Africa, and I am touched with fear of another war." She had begun the sentence intending a dramatic effect, but realized when she finished it that she really was afraid of another war. It was not that she knew so much about the implications, but she was concerned by the expression on Pitt's face when it was spoken of, and the diligence with which he read more and more articles about it in the newspaper.

Felicia was watching her closely now. "Do you think Delia feared it as well?" she asked. "What would Sir John know?"

"You said he knew a great deal about all kinds of things. Perhaps he knew something interesting, or dangerous?" Charlotte suggested. As she was saying it, she realized it made more sense. Many people were worried, particularly those who had already lost sons, husbands, or brothers in the first war.

But what was Delia's connection? Or was

Charlotte building something out of nothing? "Would Delia Kendrick be concerned about war, or know anything more than any other casual reader of headlines?" she asked.

"That depends very much on the conversations she overheard," Emily assured her.

"She might have," Felicia said after a moment's hesitation. "She was very inquisitive, even intrusive, in some ways. You know, at a glance her first husband was handsome, certainly in his own eyes, and not much use to anyone at all. He never appeared to have any interests apart from amusing himself. He wasn't in business of any sort, and he had no land, unless it was something in the wilds of Scotland. Delia had the money, but he spent a great deal of it. Not that that is unusual, of course." She seemed to be looking far away, as if remembering the past with more clarity than she had seen it at the time. "Once or twice I saw him act quite serious about things, and I know my husband had a degree of respect for him. And he is not one whose regard is earned easily." She seemed to lose her thread of thought and fell silent.

"Poor Delia," she said at last. "I wonder if we would all have been kinder if we knew what lay ahead for them." She gave a shudder and the color faded from her face. "Or for ourselves." She shrugged. "But then we would live in perpetual fear. Perhaps the only way to have courage is not to know. Tell me, Mrs. Pitt, are you serious about joining in the struggle for suffrage for women?"

Charlotte was caught completely off guard. "Why . . . yes. Yes, I am. It has to come one day. I am all for making it soon."

Felicia smiled, but it was clearly an effort. "Then I must introduce you to several people I know." She made a beckoning gesture. "Come."

Charlotte said nothing to Pitt about any of Felicia Whyte's comments, but she tried to persuade him, very much against his will, to attend a reception where Walter and Felicia Whyte would be.

They were sitting after dinner. It was past midsummer and the darkness was coming earlier. By nine the light was fading and color filled the sky.

"I haven't time," Pitt said, affecting regret. He did not wish to disappoint her, but clearly the last thing he wanted was to waste his time standing around making polite and totally artificial conversation. "I'm sorry," he added.

How much should she tell him of what

she and Emily were doing? As little as possible, of course, only what was necessary in order to find out more about Delia. She wanted to be honest. Pretense and manipulation were not the actions of friends. And yet sometimes one has to keep certain things secret, at least for a while.

"I'm learning to see Felicia Whyte in a different way," she began tentatively.

Now he was listening, puzzled. "Why? She is as unlike you as possible."

Was she so predictable? Should she tell the truth? If so, what part of it?

This was the moment that she told him the truth, or brushed it off and lost the opportunity forever.

The words came easily. "I don't really like her, but I can imagine very clearly the fear she feels. She understands Delia Kendrick better than anyone else I know, and she has, for a long time. She spoke about Delia's first husband, Darnley, and that Walter Whyte knew him and had a respect for him for which there did not appear to be any reason. And she was really angry about the gossip concerning Delia having had an affair with Halberd." She stopped, looking at Pitt to see if he was listening.

She knew from his face that he was quite aware she was trying to find out something, the way she had when they were first married and he had been able to share his cases with her. She'd been so much better than he at understanding the rules and shibboleths of society, and had a very sharp instinct for other people's emotions.

"What is it you are looking for?" he asked her bluntly.

"I don't know. I think Delia was murdered, and for something she saw, or heard. She understood its meaning, where other people didn't. Her death is connected with Halberd's, isn't it?"

"I don't know, but I believe so." He was very serious. "However, if looking into it got her killed very brutally, whoever it is won't hesitate to kill anyone else who seems to be following the same path. Don't give yourself any illusions that you are safe. If this issue is as big as I fear, no one is." He leaned forward. "Please, I can't do my job if I spend half my time worrying about where you are and what rats' nest you've just poked!" He said it with a slight smile, but only on his lips. It did not reach his eyes. He was totally serious.

"It's all been just social conversation," she began.

"Social conversation is all you need!" His voice was sharper.

She deliberately misunderstood him. "If Walter Whyte knows something about Delia, isn't it worth finding out? You don't believe she killed herself, do you?" She made the question very serious, because she knew he would not lie to her outright. He might refuse to answer, but that in itself was answer enough.

"No, I don't think so," he admitted. "And if she didn't, then it was Kendrick who killed her, and Halberd almost certainly had some connection with it. What I don't know is why, or how to prove it."

"Then we must find out what she knew." She said it as if it were simple, and she were out of danger here in this familiar room, in her own house. But Delia had been killed in her own home, either by her own hand or by someone else's. "Thomas, we can't let this happen and look the other way." She said it more vehemently than she had intended to, but it was reality, not affected by drama.

"I don't intend to leave it," he promised. "It was the Queen who asked me to find out who killed Halberd, and why. I can't leave it even if I wished to. And I don't."

Suddenly she had no breath. "The . . . the Queen? She asked you . . . I mean, in person? And you didn't tell me?" An enormous space opened up in front of her, vast, lonely, things she couldn't see and was not part of . . . and she couldn't help him.

He touched her face very gently with the tips of his fingers.

"I can tell you all of it when it is over. If I had told you she sent for me, but not why, it would have been frightening and misleading. It's not personal, it's part of my duty. If Narraway had been here, she would have sent for him. But he isn't."

Now she understood why he had been so withdrawn, telling her almost nothing. He was carrying the weight of this alone, and it was far heavier than just the embarrassing death of a much-admired man. The Queen had sent for him! A wave of fierce pride swept over her, followed quickly by a very sober fear of what failing a job for the Queen would mean.

"You must let me help," she said decisively. "I will be very careful, and always stay with other people. I promise. But I can ask questions that you can't, and overhear conversations. Women notice far more than many men realize —"

"Which may be exactly why Delia was killed," he interrupted her.

"Stop trying to shut me in the nursery," she demanded angrily, because she felt useless and she wished so badly to help.

"I'm afraid for you!" He was exasperated, as if she still did not understand.

"Of course you are," she retorted instantly. "And you think I'm not afraid for you? Or that I don't love you? Or maybe you don't care whether you solve every case or not?" Her words were sharper than she had intended them to be, but she meant them.

For once, he was speechless.

She felt guilty now. "Thomas, I love you. Please don't try to stop me from being the little bit of help I can be. I can get closer to the truth of some things about Delia Kendrick than you can. I didn't like her very much, but I understand her, and I'm sorry and angry at what happened to her. Oddly enough, so is Felicia Whyte, I think."

"We'll go to this party," he agreed, although she could tell from the strain in his voice that it was unwillingly. "But you will stay with me."

She nodded obediently.

"I mean it," he said, more sharply than before.

"Thomas, I've no more wish to get hurt than you do!" This time, it was he who nodded.

The party was very glamorous, and Charlotte went in one of her own gowns, plain dark blue but so exquisitely cut that it was remarkably flattering. It was easy to trim it with a variety of small additions: lace, a dash of something pale, or a silk flower. On this first occasion of wearing it, she chose just pearls. Even with his mind on so many other things, she saw Pitt's eyes widen with appreciation. That was all she needed. Now she would find out everything she could about Delia Kendrick, and do it very carefully.

She had known of the reception in the first place through Emily, and it was Emily who had obtained the necessary invitations for her. She saw her now standing close to Jack as if she was listening attentively to the conversation, but Charlotte knew she would also be thinking of the best way to introduce any subject that could lead to further discoveries.

The first half hour was taken up with introductions and polite formalities, and she could see that Pitt was as bored as she was herself.

"It's all necessary," she whispered to him in a quiet moment. "I've seen Felicia Whyte over there to our left. She won't be here alone. Mr. Whyte will be with her."

"I can't question him in front of other

people," Pitt replied. "In fact, I have no grounds to question him at all."

"Stop thinking like a policeman," she told him under her breath. They were being approached by Somerset Carlisle. Emily must have asked him to come. "You are Special Branch," Charlotte went on. "You don't have the same rules. In fact, are you sure you have any rules at all?"

Pitt had no time to answer because Carlisle was already there, with a smile that could have meant anything. He looked elegant and enigmatic, as usual.

"Rules? Seriously, which rules are you thinking of keeping, Pitt?" He smiled. "Or breaking only reluctantly."

"Only the ones I get away with," Pitt said. "I'm sure you are one of the best people at that. I've never known anyone who does it so frequently, and with such skill." He smiled back at Carlisle with exactly the same mix of humor and pretense at gravity.

"Are we still talking about Halberd's death?" Carlisle inquired with a like tone of voice, as if he had been considering the weather.

"Indirectly," Pitt answered.

"And directly, what else? Are you looking for proof that it was Delia Kendrick who killed him? I doubt you'll find it."

"So do I," Pitt agreed.

"Ah, you don't think she did!" Charlotte understood immediately.

Pitt hesitated only a moment. "No, I don't. I need to know who did, and why. More than that, I need to prove it."

Carlisle looked suddenly bleak. "Don't worry, Pitt," he said without a shred of humor now. "I won't upset it for you." He did not add any protestation of sincerity. He gave a brief smile, aimed at both Pitt and Charlotte, then moved away to speak to someone else.

It was a little after that when Charlotte separated from Pitt and quite easily drifted into conversation with Lady Felicia, and then with Walter Whyte alone. They had already mentioned the fact that Alan Kendrick would have been here but for Delia's death.

"Poor man." Charlotte tried to sound as if she meant it. "Not only has he lost his wife, but in such a terrible way. People can be so . . . so quick to judge. I blush when I think I disliked her, and allowed myself to show it."

Whyte looked at her with interest. "You are one of very few . . ."

"I'm glad," she said quickly.

"No." He shook his head. "I meant of the

many who disliked her, for one reason or other. There were several, but you are the only one who regrets it, and is not busy exercising your imagination as to why she would have done such a thing. I don't want to repeat their ideas." He seemed to be looking at something far away, beyond this gracious room with its marble pilasters and painted ceiling. His face still kept some of the color of old sunburn, and his eyes were remarkably blue.

Charlotte would like to have asked him about his adventures in Africa, but that would have to wait for another time.

"I can imagine," she said. "I have heard some of them. But I know from Lady Felicia that Delia had some very hard times. I believe she lost her first husband suddenly and very violently. I don't know how she bore it, except that one has to." She allowed her mind to consider how she would feel if Pitt were killed. Her throat was tight and she could hear the emotion in her voice.

Walter Whyte was looking at her, a gentleness in his face. "It was a long time ago," he told her as if trying to find some comfort himself. "And he was a difficult man. Elusive. I'm not sure how much she knew about him at the time."

"She learned after?" Charlotte did not

have to pretend either interest or a degree of compassion. Not all knowledge is better than uncertainty, but certainly some is.

"I'm not sure," Whyte admitted. "He disappeared quite often, sometimes for a week or so." He stopped abruptly.

She waited, not sure if it was some remembered pain of his own or discretion that silenced him. It could even be regret that he had raised the subject at all. She wondered what had been so painful for Whyte: Was there a mistress? Or did he drink himself insensible, and wait to sober up before coming home? Possibly he spent days and nights out gambling when she had no idea where he was.

The one thing Charlotte had not considered at all was what Whyte said next, very softly, a serious confidence not to be overheard.

"I suppose it hardly matters now, poor devil. They're both dead, but I want at least one person among the gossiping women to know the truth. He had some sympathy with a group of Irish rebels, but when their methods sickened him, he became a double agent."

Charlotte froze. It was as if the whole room had closed invisible doors on itself and she and Walter Whyte were utterly alone.

"He worked for Victor Narraway," he continued. "Appallingly dangerous stuff, trying to play both sides." He took a long, deep breath and let it out in a sigh. "He either made a slip, or someone betrayed him. His death was not accidental; he was murdered. Quickly, skillfully, and unprovably."

Charlotte's mind reeled first with grief for him, and for Delia and her baby; then she was drenched with fear for Pitt. It was irrational. He had never been a double agent; he was head of Special Branch. Everyone knew which side he was on. Then she was thinking of Delia, a new widow with a child to support, and her husband gone in one single act of violence.

Thank heaven Victor Narraway had at least helped her financially. It was a matter of honor, and possibly acknowledgment of some sense of responsibility, if it had been he who had persuaded Roland Darnley to play both sides.

Had Delia known that? Would she have accepted the money otherwise? How terrible for her that she could tell no one how or why Darnley had really died. Charlotte was not certain if she could have kept her silence all this time if she were so bereaved and had heard Pitt spoken of lightly, as such a wastrel.

She shivered and shook her head as if to free herself from the thoughts. Walter Whyte was watching her. From the look in his eyes, he understood at least something of what she felt. No doubt he also knew that she would tell Pitt all that she had just learned.

It occurred to her to wonder if she had elicited the information from him, or if he had created the opportunity to tell her, and if he hadn't tonight, then would he have as soon as the chance lent itself. Might he even have sought out Pitt and told him? Possibly.

The conversation moved to other things, and a few moments after that they were rejoined by Felicia and Somerset Carlisle.

Had Carlisle anything to do with Walter Whyte's sudden candor? Charlotte would probably never know, nor did it matter.

But there was considerably more, as she and Emily discussed the following morning.

"It's still possible that Delia killed Halberd," Emily pointed out. "I don't believe she did, and if she didn't, then she had no reason that we know of to kill herself. But how can we go about discovering who did? And if Thomas can't do it, there's no chance we can." She sat in her usual comfortable chair in the boudoir, looking anything but comfortable.

"No, we don't need to know who did," Charlotte argued. "Not if we can find where she was."

"Probably at home, and nobody but Kendrick can confirm that," Emily pointed out. "And since he's trying to blame her, or even if he isn't, he has said that she was not in."

"Which means that she could not have sworn he was in," Charlotte said emphatically. "Or that he wasn't."

"Unless the servants saw him, and will swear to it." Emily was taking up the position of devil's advocate deliberately. The stakes were too important to believe something simply because they wished to.

"Exactly." Charlotte's mind was racing at last.

"You're not going to ask them?" Emily was genuinely alarmed.

"Yes, I am. We are," she corrected herself. "Not if Kendrick was there, but to try to work out where Delia was. Her current lady's maid will still be in the house, with any luck. Or if not there, then we will find out where she's gone."

"She won't have a new position yet. It's been only days."

"Better still, we can promise to help her find a new position. Between us we must be able to exert enough influence to be of use," Charlotte said. "Well, you can anyway. Or perhaps Lady Felicia?"

"Delia may not have told anyone where she was going." Emily put up a last argument.

"Maybe not. That doesn't mean the maid doesn't know. And she will certainly know how Delia was dressed, whether her boots needed cleaning or not, if she got wet. Also, probably what hour she went out, then when she returned. Clothes can tell you a lot, if you know them well. And nobody knows them better than the person who has to clean and care for them."

"What are we going to tell this woman?"

"The truth. That people are saying terrible things about Delia: that she was having a very ugly affair with John Halberd, and she actually killed him that night." Charlotte was getting more and more convinced that their idea would work. "If Delia was anywhere near the Serpentine, the hem of her dress, not to say her boots, would show it. Maybe the maid would not testify to the police or the court, but if she can, she will help us learn where Delia was, if it will clear her lady's name now."

"And if Kendrick finds out? We can hardly cross-question his servants without his knowledge, and we certainly won't get his permission. We'll have to be . . . inventive." There was both doubt and hope in Emily's face.

Charlotte agreed that was a problem. "We might need help."

"Thomas won't help with this . . . will he?"

"I don't know. I don't intend to ask him, because it would involve his lying, which might compromise his position later. But Somerset Carlisle would do it in a moment . . . I think!"

Emily gave a beaming smile. "Of course! Why didn't I think of that? We will ask him immediately, and go as soon as he can arrange it."

It took a good deal of arranging, but Carlisle saw the point straightaway, although he required some persuasion and very definite restrictions before he would agree to come with them. He supplied both Charlotte and Emily with police whistles, or at least whistles that looked the same and sounded earsplittingly fierce when blown. Both of them had to swear they would use them if they felt in the least threatened.

Charlotte appreciated that they were running a degree of risk, because if they were correct in their beliefs, Kendrick had killed both Halberd and Delia, and so far had got away with both murders. To deal with two women at once might be very much harder for him, but it would still be, at the very best, an embarrassment if they were caught.

"Somerset is the one man who will be able to save us, even at risk to his reputation, or his life," Charlotte said earnestly.

"His reputation is beyond repair, but his life I care about very much," Emily replied.

Charlotte was not sure if she wanted to tell Emily that Carlisle was not coming unarmed to Kendrick's house. He had a very small pistol, but at close quarters it would be quite deadly.

"It could be terribly awkward," Charlotte admitted. "We will just have to succeed. After all, we are only going to call on a lady's maid and see if we can help her find a new position. I'm sure there is somebody we know — you know — who is looking for one."

It was nervousness that was making them talk. Charlotte had no intention at all of turning back. Of course, discovery would be, as she said, acutely awkward. But so would the inability to catch Alan Kendrick. Then Pitt would have failed the Queen. More important to Charlotte than that, he would have failed himself. She knew him well enough to have a good idea of what that would mean to him. This was not an ordinary case. Of course, he did not solve every case. Nobody did. Learning to accept defeat and not let it damage you was part of life, even for children. It was adults who sometimes forgot that.

They arrived at the back door of Kendrick's house a few moments after Somerset Carlisle had been admitted at the front. The scullery maid was reluctant to let them in, but Emily gave some rash promises she might later regret, and the woman who had been Delia's lady's maid came out of her own room and spoke to them in the housekeeper's sitting room. She was younger than they had expected, in her twenties, and clearly profoundly shaken.

Emily was very gentle. "You must be feeling quite ill," she said sympathetically. "The sooner you can get away from this house of tragedy, the better. Once you are no longer needed here, you may certainly come and assist at Ashworth House, until you find a new place where a proper lady's maid is required."

"But what can I do to . . . ? I'm not a parlor maid," the young woman stammered.

"I'm sure you are excellent at laundry

work, and can give my staff some help," Emily said easily. "But first you need to recover yourself a bit. This is probably the most awful thing you will ever experience."

Charlotte was willing to stand back and leave it to Emily. She was merely reinforcement if one of Kendrick's staff or Kendrick himself should come in. Still, this should be as quick as possible. Carlisle might be able to keep Kendrick's attention only so long.

Emily came to the point as soon as the young woman, whose name was Stella, had composed herself. Already her most practical anxiety had lifted. She had a temporary place to go. She would not have to return all the way to her parents in Devonshire, and then begin over again.

Emily mentioned that there were cruel rumors circulating about Delia, no doubt born of envy, but nonetheless it was better that they put an end to them.

The tears slid down Stella's face. "I heard them," she said wretchedly. "And I never thought as Miss Delia would do anything like that. Downright wicked, what some people will say. But she wasn't here the night Sir John was killed. They neither of them was."

"Do you know where she went?" Emily asked, her voice gentle.

"No, I don't," Stella admitted miserably. "But she wasn't in the park. That I know 'cause it were wet, and her boots didn't have any mud on them, nor leaves nor grass. Nor her skirt neither."

Charlotte smiled, then said, "Did she take her own carriage, or was wherever she went close enough to walk to? Or perhaps Mr. Kendrick took the carriage?"

"No, he didn't. He took a hansom," said Stella. She looked frightened now. Perhaps the valet had told her that Kendrick's boots had mud on them, and cut grass? Or she had seen them herself.

"What did Mrs. Kendrick wear?" Emily asked quickly.

"It was one of her more ordinary dresses," Stella said.

Charlotte could feel her stomach knotting. They were trespassing beyond anything excusable to Pitt now. She might as well risk it all.

"Do you know who she went to meet? If we could find the person she saw, they could clear her name of this terrible accusation. It is an awful thing when you cannot clear someone's name because the accusation is all in hints and whispers, and the person you are talking about is not here to defend themselves."

"I know he's a soldier, because she said so. His name is Joe Bentley. He is in one of them regiments named like electrics."

"Do you know his rank?" Emily asked.

Stella shook her head. "He's just young. He's maybe a sergeant, or like that."

"Electrical?" Emily frowned. "But is he a fighting soldier?"

"Fusiliers?" Charlotte asked.

"That's right, I think he knows a lot about weapons." Stella's face lit momentarily, then darkened. "It weren't no affair. It was about something! I don't want you to go saying she was having an affair with a man what was nearly young enough to be her son."

Charlotte put her hand on Stella's arm. "We only want to be able to say we know where she was, and it had nothing whatever to do with Sir John Halberd's death. And since she didn't kill him, she wouldn't have taken her own life in remorse for it. This Joe Bentley might have been the son of a friend, or maybe related to her son-in-law. There are all sorts of reasons that are no one else's concern, but perfectly respectable."

Emily pulled a card out of her reticule and gave it to Stella.

"When you are ready to move, please give the carriage driver this address. I should be ready to make you welcome, and my staff will see that you are given a room and sufficient duties for you to feel you are earning your way."

Charlotte stood up. "Thank you, Stella. You may have performed a last and most valuable service for your mistress."

Charlotte and Emily affected not to see the tears on Stella's face. She did her best to smile as they made as dignified a departure as they could. They went out of the back door, thanking the footman, then in the street went to inform Carlisle's coachman that they were getting themselves home.

"You will look after her, won't you?" Charlotte said, and instantly wished she had not. "I'm sorry, of course you will." Emily did not bother to reply, but took Charlotte's arm and they walked closely together along the street.

Chapter 13

Charlotte looked very contrite, almost as if she was afraid of Pitt's anger. She stood in front of him in the sitting room, her back to the French doors and the burning colors of the sunset garden behind her. Her face was grave.

"What is it?" he demanded.

"I broke my word," she said quietly. "Or maybe . . . Anyway, I took the risk."

"What did you do?" He was afraid to ask, but he had to. He found his mouth dry as he waited.

"I found out where Delia was the night Halberd was killed." She swallowed. "And I spoke to the young man she was with. It isn't what you think. Actually, she was very brave. She knew what Kendrick was doing and that it concerned getting guns for the Boers, though she couldn't prove it."

He felt fear for her, even anger at the risk she must have taken, and at the same time a swell of pride at her spirit. This was the Charlotte he had fallen in love with, but her courage had frightened him so much less then. She had been fascinating, exasperating, funny at times, but there was a distance between them. He was still separate. He could survive on his own. Now she was woven inextricably into the fabric of his being. She was the center of all that mattered to him.

"What happened to him, the young man?" he asked huskily.

"Nothing. He's perfectly well, for the moment," she said quickly. "But you must see him, Thomas. His name is Joseph Bentley. He was a soldier in the Boer War and is terrified there will be another one — I mean specifically afraid, not just generally. He now works for Wills and Sons. It is a gentlemen's outfitter; I have the address and where he lives in lodgings. Please, Thomas, he can prove to you that Delia could not have killed Halberd. Quite apart from having been somewhere else, which he will swear to, she was trying to do the same thing as Halberd! Just neither of them knew it of the other. We may never know, but I think she was closer than he to revealing the truth. It's just that Halberd must have tipped Kendrick's hand somehow." She went on, barely taking a breath. "He wasn't afraid of Kendrick, when he should have been."

"She was?" he asked, his voice catching in his throat. "He didn't save her, poor woman."

"We can save her reputation," Charlotte said quickly. "You can't let Kendrick get away with killing her so hideously, then making it look as if it were suicide! And you have to make sure nothing happens to Joseph Bentley, please."

Perhaps some other time he would tell her how foolish she had been to take such risks. Or he might simply tell her how much he loved her, and how empty life would be if she was killed by someone who caught her before she could catch them.

"I told him that you would find him, and he must speak to you," she went on. "But secretly . . . and very soon. Don't let him be killed too!"

"I won't," he promised. "I'll go to his lodgings tonight."

"Thomas, I'm —"

"Sorry. I know. We'll talk about it some other time . . . maybe." If he had any sense, he would tell her how recklessly she had behaved. Above all, she had broken a promise. He took a deep breath. "Thank you."

He saw the fear slip away from her like shedding a dark cloak and letting it fall to the floor. She smiled at him, widely, beautifully, then hurried past him and out of the door toward the kitchen.

Pitt found the address Charlotte had given him with little difficulty. He asked the landlady for Joseph Bentley, and was told he had gone out for supper and could probably be found at the local public house, the Triple Plea, a couple of streets to the east.

Pitt chose to walk, and it took him no more than ten minutes. Inside, it was crowded and noisy, as might be expected. He bought a tankard of cider, and while drinking it looked carefully around the room to see if he could find Bentley. Several young men were talking and laughing together. One, clean-shaven and with neatly trimmed hair, was sitting alone with a thick, crusty sandwich and a glass of ale. Pitt made his way over toward him, quite casually, as if looking for a place to sit.

"Bentley?" he said quietly when he was within a couple of feet of him.

The young man was startled, and looked as if he was going to deny it.

"My wife spoke to you yesterday," Pitt continued. "She and her sister."

The young man looked apprehensive, puzzled.

Pitt pulled a neighboring stool to the table and sat down. Now he looked at the young man openly, as though he had been invited.

"I am Thomas Pitt, head of Special Branch. Are you Joseph Bentley or not?"

"Yes, sir, I am," the young man answered as if he were still a soldier in front of a superior officer.

"Good. When I have finished my cider I'm going to stand up, and you are going to finish your ale, go out the door, and walk to your lodgings. I will follow you. Be as inconspicuous about it as you can. And don't run away. I don't want to waste time hunting you down — but I will." It was a warning, and he meant it to be taken as such. "It would make you very noticeable, and I may not be the first to find you."

"I've no intention of running away, sir," Bentley answered with a flare of anger.

Pitt smiled. "Good." He finished his cider, stood up, and made his way to the door.

Five minutes later, Bentley left also, walking past Pitt without turning, and continued on his way back to his lodgings.

A further ten minutes and they were together in the small, extremely tidy bedroom Bentley rented. The bed was made with military precision and the two or three dozen books he had on the shelves were placed according to subject, not size or color of binding.

"Tell me what you told Mrs. Pitt and Mrs. Radley," Pitt asked. "I already know most of it, but I want details."

"I have no proof, sir," Bentley said immediately. "I know Mrs. Kendrick couldn't have killed Sir John Halberd, because she was with me until about one o'clock in the morning." His face flushed a dull red. "It was for information, sir, nothing else. It was . . ." He stopped, uncertain how to continue.

"Special Branch, Mr. Bentley." Pitt looked into his eyes. "I'm interested in treason, not romance with a dead woman who was, I believe, betrayed and then murdered to hide whatever it was she discussed with you."

All the color drained out of Bentley's face, leaving him a chalky white.

"Yes, sir. I'm very sorry indeed about that. She was a brave woman and she cared a lot about what was right. I told her all I knew."

"Now tell me."

Pitt had already shown Bentley his identification. There was no reason to hesitate. Quietly, but very clearly, Bentley described how he had met Delia Kendrick through

Sir John Halberd, who had shopped at the gentlemen's outfitters where Bentley worked. His conversation with Delia had naturally turned to his own experiences in the Boer War. He told her he had served from beginning to end, only being lightly wounded; he had, however, known physical exhaustion and privation. And far more deeply marked into him than that, he had seen other men horribly wounded. Some had died quickly, others after hours — or even days — of pain. His face showed the grief of his memories, the friends he had lost, some to death, others to injuries that would heal over but from which they would never recover: lost limbs, lost sight. The devastation these weapons wrought on a man. In many cases, their wounds were deeper than that: destruction of the mind, their confidence in certain values torn apart. There were nightmares that made them afraid to sleep, irrational guilt about friends they could not save. Too often it was loss of faith in life itself that haunted them.

"We can't do that again, sir," Bentley said with passion sharp in his voice and his eyes unwavering. "I'm willing to fight for my country, sir, and die for it, if need be. But I'm not going to kill men and women again just because they want to rule their own land in their own way. So do I, sir. I don't want some Dutchman coming over here to England telling me what to do, or what I can't do. I'd fight him as long as I had breath. And I wouldn't blame him if he'd felt the same about me." He sat motionless, waiting for Pitt to respond, ready for anger, willing to argue.

Pitt was not sure he disagreed with Bentley, but that was not the issue now. "And Mrs. Kendrick felt the same?" he asked.

"Yes, sir, I think so. But she was upset because she believed her husband was helping the Boers to buy the best rifles in the world from the Germans — the Mauser company. She didn't know too much about them at first, but I told her what I knew. She thought he'd used his friendship with the Prince of Wales to get himself in favor over there. The Germans like the prince, as he is half German himself, I suppose. And he speaks their language, and likes their food and all. And of course Mr. Kendrick and he both love horses. Mrs. Kendrick said her husband was gifted like that. Almost the only thing he put before himself was a really good horse, and he's had a few."

"What about Sir John Halberd?"

"He knew about it too. Was right on the very tail of it, she said."

"Did you meet her after that fateful night? Did she say who killed Halberd?"

"She thought it could have been her husband behind it, but that he wouldn't risk doing it himself. But then, on the other hand, she thought he also wouldn't risk paying someone else to do it for him, in case they betrayed him later, or blackmailed him about it."

"It might have been one or the other," Pitt said thoughtfully. "Unless she was wrong, and it was someone else altogether. But I don't believe that."

"She seemed very sure it was him, sir. Said Halberd would have told the Queen, and that would have been the end of Kendrick." Bentley lifted his chin a little, meeting Pitt's eyes. "I know she's an old lady, but she's the Queen, and we have pledged our loyalty to her as long as she's alive. And I suppose to King Edward VII after her. I . . . I think Mrs. Kendrick was close to proving what she knew, Mr. Pitt. And that's not just because I don't want to think she did that to herself, although I don't."

"No," Pitt agreed. "Neither do I. She was sharp-tongued and opinionated, but she was brave. It seems she lost her first husband to betrayal."

"Yes, she said that," Bentley agreed, his

voice very low. "I wish she'd been more careful. Can you get him, sir? I'd like to see him on the end of a rope, the way he did to her. If I can help, I want to."

"Do you?"

"Yes, sir, I do."

An idea was beginning to form in Pitt's mind, not clear yet but the beginning of a plan.

"Then I think you can. Have you considered working in Special Branch?"

There was a flicker of emotion in Bentley's face, both fear and excitement. "I . . . I couldn't, sir. Not if there's going to be another war. I'd be called up again. I'd have to go."

"No, you wouldn't. I can deal with that, if you want. Sometimes the work is very routine, a bit like police work. At others it's fast, difficult, and dangerous, but it all matters very much."

"Bit like being a soldier, then," Bentley said with a smile. There was hope in his voice, and a fear of disappointment.

"I imagine so," Pitt agreed. "I've never been a soldier. The big difference is that there is no uniform, usually no weapons, and you can discuss it with no one, not even your closest friends or family." He watched Bentley's face, his eyes, the slight tightening of his lips. "Do you understand?"

"Yes, sir. Most soldiers don't talk about it, either, sir. Don't want your family thinking of you like that — dirty, scared, exhausted, willing to stick a bayonet into another man's guts. Better to say nothing than tell them a lot of lies. Just let it be, is my way."

Pitt nodded.

"Were you always Special Branch, sir?" Bentley asked.

"No, I was a policeman most of my life. Robberies, then murders. Now it's treason and anarchy, bombs, betrayals . . . and still murders."

"Yes, sir, I'd like to do that. Especially if we can prove to everybody that Mrs. Kendrick didn't kill anyone." The sadness was there for a moment, then he fought it away. "When do you want me to start, sir?"

"Tomorrow morning, send your current employer a letter of apology. Don't mention us. Just say urgent family business. Special Branch will make up what you lose in your salary. Report to Mr. Stoker at eight o'clock tomorrow morning at Lisson Grove. I will tell him to expect you. Take care of yourself, Bentley. Get yourself new lodgings. Give your landlady notice, but no forwarding address. Find a room nearer to Lisson Grove. If you have family, tell them you have changed jobs, but not the nature of the new one. Don't take this lightly, Bentley, I mean it." He looked at the young man's face to make certain he understood, and saw a momentary flicker of sadness.

"I've got no family, sir. My ma and pa died a while ago, and my brother was killed in South Africa."

"In the war?"

"Yes, sir."

"I'm sorry. Now tell me everything else that Mrs. Kendrick told you and then we'll start tomorrow to see what we can do to stop there being another war — or if we can't stop it, at least let it be without Mauser's guns!"

"Yes, sir. And . . . thank you, sir."

"I hope you'll still thank me in a year's time."

Pitt was at Lisson Grove early enough to tell Stoker that he had recruited Bentley. "We need him for this," he added. "And I think he may turn out to be a good recruit. We need someone to replace Firth."

"Firth was very experienced, sir," Stoker said cautiously. "This Bentley might need a lot of training."

"Then we'll give it to him. He's been in the army and served in the Boer War. I took a fresh look at his record late last night. Reclaimed a favor and woke up a few friends. He's a good man. And, Stoker, make sure he changes his lodgings, sooner rather than later. Nothing to be forwarded."

"Yes, sir. You think Kendrick will go after him?"

"Wouldn't you, in his place?"

"Yes, sir, I'll see to it today. Give him a hand. Get to know him a bit."

"Do it. He should be here in fifteen minutes. I'm going to look for more evidence. See if I can shake something loose, now we know Halberd's murderer wasn't Delia."

"Yes, sir."

Pitt re-examined witness statements and all the physical evidence of Halberd's death, but nothing new emerged. Almost anyone could have arranged to meet him at the Serpentine, or followed him there and made it seem like a chance encounter. The question was, had Halberd gone there expecting to meet a different someone? Who else knew, and could have intervened, preventing the right person from coming?

Surely it had to do with Halberd's knowledge of the Mauser rifle deal? Would he have gone alone to meet Kendrick? Did he imagine that in some way he was safe, just because it was a London park and perhaps not so very late?

What had he found that was so urgent? How had Kendrick learned of it? If Delia knew, had she spoken to anyone else? Had she gone out before Kendrick, or after? Pitt knew from Charlotte how she had dressed, but what about Kendrick? Had he gotten wet — even a sleeve or a trouser leg? Would Kendrick's valet tell Pitt? He had traveled to the park in a hansom, according to Delia's maid.

These were things to find out.

What evidence had implicated Delia? Since it was not her, then either the evidence had been misunderstood, or it had been deliberately manufactured to blame her. When, how, and by whom?

Pitt began the awkward task of mapping Delia's last few days alive. Before he could even begin, he had to obtain permission from Kendrick. Since Delia's guilt was all surmise and supposition, and she herself was dead and could neither confess nor deny anything, there was an element of decency that suggested the whole matter be left alone.

It would be different if Kendrick wished to prove her innocence. But he had presented himself as accepting completely that she was guilty and had killed herself in despair.

How should Pitt approach him? Kendrick was far too clever to outwit easily, and far too sure of himself to bluff. Pitt had no legitimate reason even to inquire into Delia's death, and Kendrick knew it. If there were anything to investigate, it would be for the police to follow up, rather than anyone from Special Branch. Kendrick had faultlessly crafted it to be precisely that way.

There was no evidence that Delia had killed Halberd — she hadn't! But with her connection to him, and her apparent suicide, everyone believed it. What decent man would not now bury her in peace and leave Kendrick to grieve, untroubled by intrusive and prurient questions?

Pitt still had the Halberd case to solve. He knew Delia could not have killed him, and he believed that Kendrick had. But what had Kendrick learned that precipitated Halberd's murder that night, not before or after? That question applied to all murders. Why at that time?

He could search for the answer in Halberd's life. Had he ever had an affair with Delia? If so, then someone would know of it. In searching her recent past, he might find what had really caused her murder. And if he was right, it would tie Kendrick to German guns and the ever-increasing likelihood of another Boer war. Apart from his murder of Halberd, and of Delia, Kendrick must be stopped for that reason alone.

If Pitt was to get the sort of information he needed, he would have to bring pressure to bear on people, more pressure than Kendrick could, or perhaps already had. The place to begin was Narraway's files. He must know what was in them, whatever it was; how it made him feel was irrelevant. A pre-emptive strike might be necessary. He must know all the vulnerabilities Narraway had known, and use them as circumstances dictated. He would protect anyone he could, and do his best to see that no information fell into other hands.

He spent several miserable hours sitting at his desk with tea and sandwiches. The records yielded what he had expected: meticulous details of errors, weaknesses, and misjudgments.

He had selected the files on all the people he knew might be of use in this case. The information, and the thought of using it, revolted him. The only thing worse was the weight of cowardice to stand by and do nothing.

There were several questions to which he must find answers. How had Delia learned of Kendrick's interest in South Africa, and then his intention to profit from it? If she'd had proof, would she have faced him with it, demanded he stop, or turned him in to Special Branch, the Foreign Office . . . or whoever was capable and willing to deal with the fact that a man so close to the Prince of Wales was a traitor?

Yes, she would have turned him in, and he knew it. Her death proved that. And perhaps Halberd's death proved that he was the one she had chosen to tell. That made excellent sense. But somewhere along the way she had made a mistake, because Kendrick had found out.

Had she trusted someone else, who had betrayed both her and Halberd? Or was it carelessness, something in her manner from which Kendrick had realized she knew?

It cannot have been absolute proof, or Halberd would have told the appropriate authorities straightaway, probably Pitt himself. But then, he might have been intending to do that after he'd told the Queen. And somehow Kendrick knew it. Deduction, or betrayal? Another loose end to be tied up.

Finally, Delia had found all the pieces she

needed and put them together. She had proof. But how did Kendrick know that, before she was able to tell anyone else? Maybe she had waited for one more piece, one more fact, and it had cost her her life.

Pitt might never know, but the study of Halberd's movements on the last two or three days of his life would be a good place to begin. He must go over in more detail the papers he had taken from Halberd's home. Something like this Halberd would not have done in even the most exclusive of gentlemen's clubs. He would have gone to a private office. He had his own carriage. Pitt would speak to the driver.

He might also speak to Kendrick's driver later, but to do so now would warn Kendrick, and he would very much like to avoid that.

It took him until the following morning to find Halberd's coachman. The man had naturally found a new position and was away from those stables, but was expected back in a little more than an hour.

Pitt thanked the butler and walked round the end of the block to the mews and the stable and carriage house. As in many large establishments, the coachman and groom lived above the stables. This one had room for four horses, but two of them were presently out.

The groom walked toward Pitt suspiciously, a pitchfork in his hand.

"Good morning," Pitt said agreeably. He did not intend to tell the man who he was. It would start speculation that could go anywhere. But he was a stranger, and gentlemen did not often come round to the mews at all.

"Morning, sir," the groom replied. "Something I can do for you?"

Pitt smiled. "No, thank you. I'm waiting for Mr. Spencer, your coachman. I believe he may have some information that would help me. Your butler suggested I wait for him here."

"Well, you just be careful, sir. Don't you touch nothing!" Pitt looked past him at the stables. They were well cared for, nothing out of place, and yet they had a comfortable, used look.

"Looks like the stables I worked in as a boy," Pitt remarked. "Except that was out in the country. But a good horse is a good horse, anywhere."

The groom looked warily at Pitt's clean and polished boots, and he mellowed a little.

Pitt breathed in deeply. The smell of hay, horse sweat, the lingering sharpness of manure, filled his nostrils, and then he smelled leather, saddle soap. It brought back memories, most of them good ones. Since then, more good had been added. He could not afford a mistake; he had so much wealth to lose.

He talked to the groom sporadically for the hour, mostly about horses. Then the carriage arrived, the horses were relieved of their harnesses, and the carriage itself put into its space.

The coachman was alarmed at first, but once he accepted that he himself was in no danger of suspicion, or of losing his new place, he was eager to help in any way he could.

"I'm very sorry about Mrs. Kendrick, sir," he said with feeling. "Sir John spoke about her once or twice. Said a few more with courage like hers, and we wouldn't have half the trouble we do. I am . . ." He hesitated, awkward with emotion. "I'm grateful as you never believed Sir John made a fool of himself over some woman, sir. He was a gentleman — I mean through and through, not just on the outside."

Pitt was quite frank with him. "I believe he was killed because he discovered something very shortly before. I need you to tell me everything you can remember about the five or six days before his death. Where he went, who he saw. And if you can, what his manner was, pleased or disconcerted, angry, whatever it was."

"Yes, sir," Spencer agreed. "I may even have notes of it."

Pitt left with far more than he had hoped for, putting him in the position to have to use some of Narraway's information. It appeared Halberd had spoken to exactly the sort of people he would have were he looking for the final proof of Delia's discoveries, and one of them had let Kendrick know, intentionally or not.

He hesitated, thinking hard of the pain he would cause. He would make enemies with power, people who might wait long and carefully for revenge. Narraway was a gentleman of similar social rank to those concerned; Pitt was not, nor would he ever be. Whatever professional position he might earn, to them he would always be a gamekeeper's son. To embarrass or humiliate any of these men would not be forgiven.

Was he looking for excuses because he was afraid? Was he still a servant boy at heart?

Possibly — there was nothing wrong with that. But being a coward was a poverty of the soul, and he refused to own that!

The first person he visited was General Darlington. He went to the man's office in

Whitehall and announced himself as the commander of Special Branch, on most urgent business.

Please heaven, he would not have to use the information he'd found out about Darlington. His wife's recent death was a well-concealed suicide. The man's grief must be appalling. Pitt could not even imagine it.

But so would the grief be in thousands of homes if there was another unnecessary war in South Africa.

Darlington saw him within a quarter of an hour. He was an upright man of military bearing, stiff-backed, still looking as if he faced an enemy who outgunned him. His shelves were filled with books, mostly military, but a couple on gardening caught Pitt's eye. There was little ornamentation, a model of a cannon in detail, an Eastern dagger with an exquisite jewel-encrusted scabbard. There was one haunting picture of a woman who must have been his wife.

The man deserved the truth.

"I believe Sir John Halberd came to see you the week before he died," Pitt began.

"It was a private matter," Darlington replied. "Of military concern. Nothing domestic, which I believe is your area of responsibility."

"Yes, sir. If you are willing, I will tell you what I believe, and you may tell me if I am correct." Pitt could feel his stomach clench at the thought of having to threaten this man, so proud, stiff, and yet appallingly vulnerable. He could never tell Charlotte what he had done. It was unfair to burden her with it. How poisonous secrets could be! Were they as heavy on Narraway's elegant shoulders?

"If you must," Darlington replied. He was looking at Pitt hard, summing him up.

"I believe Sir John came to ask your opinion of the Mauser rifle, and what difference it would make if a very large number of them were sold to Kruger and the Boers in South Africa, should there be another war. Will it make any difference in the likelihood of that, if they have such arms?"

Darlington paled, gray replacing white under the sun-and-wind burn on his skin.

"Where did you get that . . . idea?" he said hoarsely.

Pitt's stomach knotted even tighter. Darlington was going to deny it. Pitt must think of a way to persuade him not to — but without mentioning his wife.

"From information I have received, and followed up," he said slowly, choosing his words with care. "A great deal of bits and pieces come our way from various sources." He was fumbling. "I am afraid, General Darlington, of several things. Another damaging war is one of them, the loss of thousands more of our young men. I am also afraid of the effect of certain gun sales on the reputation of the throne. Is that sufficient information for you to tell me what Halberd told you?" He breathed in and out slowly. It was a matter of balance. He must not tip his hand too far. "I hope it is. I would very much dislike having to insist." What a tame word for the self-loathing he would feel if he had to use Narraway's information. It should be his job to protect the man from such things.

They stared at each other as seconds ticked by, then Darlington spoke.

"Halberd told me he had proof that a friend of the Prince of Wales was using the prince's frequent trips to Germany, and his contacts there, to set up a relationship with the Mauser company, and get a huge shipment of rifles to the Boers. He did not tell me who it was. He wanted information from me on the effectiveness of the weapons, strengths and weaknesses, what we had that was comparable. He left me this note that he said this friend of the prince's had made on the attributes of the Mauser and that he had acquired through a third party."

"In other words, the military capabilities of the gun in general. Is it remarkably good?"

"Yes. I wish I knew if he was correct, but I can find out nothing, and I dare not speculate because it is a charge that would ruin any man."

"And you never saw Halberd again?"

"No, he was killed that night. Now it seems that it was Mrs. Kendrick who killed him, and for a reason totally unrelated to guns, treason, or South Africa. I am grieved. I had thought far better of Halberd than to have anything to do with such a woman. I'm sorry. If any of what you say is true, I have been of no help to you, except to confirm your worst fears."

Darlington was vulnerable. If Pitt could pressure him, then there may have been other people who also could. And what he could use to his advantage could as well be used by them. It was something Pitt should never forget.

"Thank you, General Darlington." He wanted to tell him that Delia was not guilty, but it was far too soon to tip his hand. "Good day to you." He left with the note Halberd had given the general and an almost buoyant feeling of relief that it was over, without his having to use force. But he had been willing to, that was the thing. Or would he have balked at the final moment? He did not know.

Pitt studied the information he had received on the quality of the Mauser rifle. It was not what it said that held his attention, it was the writing itself, the characteristic formation of the *t* and the way it ran into the *h* when the letters occurred together in a word. He had seen it before, but he was not certain where.

Then it came to him. It was in the note sent to Halberd, which had been in the front of his current diary, changing an appointment to "Tuesday, not Thursday." It had been a Tuesday night that Halberd had been killed, and the night Delia had been with Bentley.

He looked at it again, carefully, with a magnifying glass. He needed more than memory, but if he was right, then he had Kendrick at last. He had changed Delia's appointment, and gone himself in her place. Pitt knew how and why. If he could find a note in her diary in Kendrick's writing . . . What Kendrick had been going to do with Mauser rifles would be irrelevant if he hanged for the murder of John Halberd.

And it would be some vindication for Delia.

But Pitt needed the right to search Kendrick's house. Done without a judge's warrant, anything he found would be valueless, regardless of what it was. How could he get it?

The answer was right in his hands. One of the men on Narraway's list was a judge whose son had embezzled from the company he represented in the City. His father had covered for him, granting favors to keep it silent until he could make up the money.

Wrong. Of course it was wrong. But how many people would not have done the same if they had the power and the means?

His hand stopped in midair, above the papers. He thought of Daniel, who had been accused of cheating and refused to defend himself because it meant accusing a friend. Could this happen to him one day? Since the charge was on his records? Anyone not knowing him would assume he was guilty, just as Pitt was assuming the guilt of this young man. And perhaps his father believed him as Pitt believed Daniel, but it was too late to make any difference now.

He swore in blind frustration. He must decide — now! And yet he understood exactly what the judge must feel. And he had caught himself making the exact judgment he so despised.

Then it was time to decide. He could not walk away and let Kendrick win. Every soldier shot by a Mauser rifle was somebody's son as well. He must do what Narraway would have done, and use the knowledge if he had to.

He caught a hansom and told the driver to take him to the law courts at the Old Bailey, where he would find Justice Cadogan.

He had to wait over an hour and a half before Cadogan was free and said he would give him fifteen minutes.

Pitt explained who he was and exactly what he needed.

"I'm sorry," Cadogan said immediately. "But you really don't have sufficient cause. And certainly not to search the house of a man of Kendrick's stature. Good Lord, man, he's just lost his wife in the most terrible circumstances. I don't care who you are. The man is a personal friend of the Prince of Wales! Find some other way." He said it politely, but with finality, standing straight as if for some kind of ceremony. He seemed almost unaware of pushing his hand over his white hair, smoothing it back.

"I regret this, sir." Pitt heard his own voice as if it were from a stranger. "I require this, as much in the Prince of Wales's interest as anyone else's. I don't wish to use force, but I will, if I have no other choice."

"Force?" Cadogan's eyebrows shot up. "What on earth are you talking about, man? I have told you I will not give you any permission to search Kendrick's house. Now get out! Before I call an usher and have you thrown out."

"On moral grounds?" Pitt said quietly. "You've let a good few people evade the law, covered for them, looked the other way. Now you can redress the balance a little."

"I have not! I don't know what you think you're talking about."

"Don't make this more unpleasant than it has to be. The interest of the state has to override the career or the well-being of one young man."

Cadogan stared at him. Gradually his belligerence turned into fear. Slowly, in a scrawling hand, he wrote out the permission Pitt had asked for.

Pitt checked it, then thanked him and walked out of the room. He hated what he had done. There was no sense of victory in it. Cadogan was not the only one frightened by the power of one piece of knowledge in the hands of someone willing to use it.

A year ago, he would not even have contemplated what he'd just done. Had he changed so much? Or was it only a matter of opportunity, and a reason to justify it?

He went first to collect a police sergeant. Special Branch had no power to arrest anybody. If he found what he was looking for, he would need to have Kendrick arrested immediately. Warned, he could so easily escape, possibly even to Germany.

The sky was darkening from the east, the light fading when they arrived at Kendrick's house and were admitted by a very nervous butler. They found Kendrick in the withdrawing room. He was relaxing with an open newspaper on his knee. He did not bother to stand up.

"What the devil do you want now?" he asked with exasperation, but no loss of self-control. He glanced beyond Pitt to the other man, but did not bother to ask who he was.

"To look a little further through Mrs. Kendrick's papers," Pitt replied. "Household accounts will do, and diaries. I'm sorry to disturb you."

"You're not going to disturb me," Kendrick snapped with a very slight twisted smile. He picked up the newspaper again.

Pitt told the policeman to remain in the hall, although he did not think Kendrick would run. He was still perfectly confident there was nothing Pitt could do that would damage him.

There was little to search. Most of Delia's personal effects had already been moved, given away, or otherwise disposed of. But the household accounts would be with the housekeeper and kept at least a year — for financial reasons, if nothing else. All Pitt needed was a verifiable example of Delia's handwriting, and of Kendrick's, and if possible someone's note of which night Delia had expected to be out in the park, and if this had necessitated some change of arrangements with any of the servants.

The handwriting was easy. Pitt had Kendrick's; the housekeeper had a note written by Delia two or three weeks ago; in fact, she had more than one. The hand was sloping like Kendrick's, the letters forward similarly, but the characteristic colliding of the *t* and *h* when they occurred together was not there, and both the *l* and the *g* were looped in the lower case, unlike the single, hard line of Kendrick's.

He thanked the housekeeper and put them in the inside pocket of his coat.

"Do you remember Mrs. Kendrick's diary from the week of Sir John Halberd's death, Miss Hornchurch?" he asked as casually as he could. "Perhaps you have notes on such things as who would be home for dinner?"

"Of course I have," the housekeeper said a little stiffly. "I don't know what good it can do now. You can't charge a dead woman, no matter what you think she did."

Pitt took a chance. "I don't think she did anything, Miss Hornchurch, at least nothing wrong. I think she gave her life in the service of her country, and one day I shall be able to prove that. Would you please look at your housekeeping book for that week, and tell me if there are any written notes of what was planned, and any changes? While you look, I'll go and speak to your coachman. I presume he has written notices of any engagements where he might be required to drive anybody?"

The coachman remembered very clearly that he had been requested to take Mrs. Kendrick to a restaurant near one of the entrances to Hyde Park, but it had been canceled. It was for the day after they heard of Sir John Halberd's death. He recalled it particularly because everyone was so upset.

"Mrs. Kendrick was upset?" Pitt asked with sympathy.

"Yes, sir. She had a high regard for the gentleman. She was very upset indeed." He sounded slightly surprised that Pitt should ask.

Pitt took the pages out of the coachman's notebook, thanked him, and went back inside the main house.

The policeman was still waiting in the hall. He looked at Pitt questioningly.

"Yes, Sergeant," Pitt said. He felt a bubble of elation inside himself. He had proof. It was subtle but quite definite. Kendrick was one of the few men he had ever had arrested for whom he had no sense of sadness. "Will you please come and place Mr. Kendrick under arrest?"

Inside the room, Kendrick looked up from his newspaper. He glanced at the policeman, then at Pitt.

"Really! For God's sake, Pitt, don't make such a damn fool of yourself!"

Pitt's nerve wavered. The man looked so confident, as if he were speaking to a tiresome child who had overstretched his patience once too often.

"Send your sergeant outside," Kendrick said curtly, "and I will explain to you why you should go away quietly and not embarrass yourself any further."

Pitt did not move.

Kendrick's face darkened. "I don't care if you make a complete ass of yourself, but you would be wiser not to. Get rid of him!"

"Wait for me outside, Sergeant," Pitt directed.

As soon as he was gone and the door closed behind him, Kendrick stood up, but he made no move toward Pitt, and still looked irritated but perfectly at ease.

"You should have just shot me. But I know you haven't the courage to do that. Narraway would have." He smiled. "You are not the man he was. If you bring me to trial, what are you going to charge me with? Killing John Halberd? I shall say he ruined my wife. I can't prove it, but you can't prove otherwise. She finally killed herself over it. Couldn't face living with it. Halberd was a libertine and sexual deviant. It would break the Queen's heart. She wouldn't thank you for that. Some loyal servant of the Crown you are."

Pitt felt cold inside.

Kendrick's smile widened. "And you dug up the whole thing about the Mauser rifles for the Boers. Are you going to accuse me of treason? You can't prove that without bringing the Prince of Wales into it. Another well-meaning ass who can't see beyond the end of his own nose. You would threaten the throne. And you won't do that, because you have enough sense to know I will do as I say. If I go down, so does everyone else. I don't believe you're an anarchist, just cleverer than the rest of them. You are a man who has been a servant and has been promoted far beyond his ability. You are still a servant at heart, and always will be. You are outclassed and outgunned. Leave, while you can do so without the whole world knowing."

Pitt felt sick, as if the room had tilted and he could no longer keep his balance. He could see no escape. He had never been so utterly defeated. It could only add to Kendrick's victory if he protested.

He turned on his heel and walked away.

CHAPTER 14

Pitt felt totally beaten, and furious with himself for so profoundly underestimating Kendrick. Was Kendrick right? Would Narraway have shot him? No, that was said to make Pitt feel inadequate, and it had succeeded. But knowing why it was said did not take the poison from it.

Narraway would not have given up, that was certainly true. And if Pitt did not solve this, then he did not deserve command of anything, let alone the service entrusted as the first line of fire against corruption, treason, and anarchy.

Whatever he felt, however much he was embarrassed and wanted to retreat and lick his wounds, there was no time for it. A person might understand self-pity, but no one admired it. To be beaten by shame was the ultimate failure. This moment came down to professional survival or defeat, and the end of his career. The end of self-respect.

All the people he loved, and whose opinion of him mattered most, would not be betrayed by his failure, but they would be if he gave up.

And he had to face the fact that if he allowed Kendrick to win this time, then he would win every other time as well. He could still ruin the prince whenever he wished. And he would do so if it served his purpose.

Perhaps even more important than that, this surrender would be another weapon in Kendrick's hands to use against Pitt whenever he chose. A long future lay ahead in which Kendrick could ask this favor or that, commit acts against men in sensitive office, and Pitt would be too vulnerable himself to protect them. He was setting himself up to be exactly the sort of man on Narraway's list of people to use when the need arose. Then what would the difference be between Pitt and, say, Cadogan? Both would have exercised a moment of weakness and become a prisoner to it forever.

If Cadogan had refused, would Pitt have made his crime public? It hardly even mattered, because he had made the man act against his will under the threat. There was an irony in the fact that he couldn't use the evidence now, not because it wasn't legally obtained, but because a more powerful and ruthless man had prevented him with a bigger threat.

He must find a way out, and there was no one else he could ask for advice on it. Isolation and loneliness were built into leadership.

He longed to be able to tell Charlotte about it, but he resisted, and he knew if he made his reluctance to talk clear enough, she would not ask. He was too tired to think now, or feel. He fell asleep in his armchair, and she woke him in time to go to bed.

The earlier sleep took the edge off his tiredness, and he lay awake long into the night. He had no idea whether Charlotte was sleeping or not. There had been times when she had been awake too, and not told him.

He did not consider simply killing Kendrick, as Kendrick had suggested. It had been a taunt, he realized now. And yet it had crossed Pitt's mind that the only way to stop Kendrick was to cause his death. He could not be imprisoned without trial, and any trial allowed a defense. Kendrick was guilty. He had no defense of justification. Neither Halberd nor Delia had threatened his safety, let alone his life.

He need not offer a defense. He could simply carry out his threat to bring everyone else down with him. Pitt had no doubt he would do it. He must be silenced, but not by Pitt, not directly.

He was tired, defeated, and — he admitted to himself while lying in the dark — afraid. Failure would cost him all his newfound respect, financial security, belief in himself and what he fought for.

Was respect worth so much? Was it worth anything if you knew you did not deserve it?

Delia had lost her son and then her first husband, then the man with whom she had fought against Kendrick's plans, and eventually her own life. And now, in Pitt, the man whose job it was to stop people like Kendrick, had she effectively lost the voice that was to speak for her, too?

He must have dozed off for a few moments because he let go of his train of thought. So many secrets. Darnley had been a double agent, in the end killed by his other masters. Kendrick had been simply a foreign agent, or a mercenary, a dealer in arms to anyone who would pay him. Where was he vulnerable? Nowhere.

Then an idea came to Pitt, just like a

pinprick. He had been wondering if he could turn any of Kendrick's strengths against him. He was an opportunist, without loyalty. But did Kruger's agents buying guns know that? What if they thought he was loyal to Britain, as perhaps Darnley had been in the end?

Darnley had been killed for it! Could Pitt arrange it so that either the Germans or the Boers thought Kendrick was a brave and very clever servant of the British Crown, prepared to risk his life to betray the Boers? They would kill him — wouldn't they? If the betrayal was bad enough? Yes, they would. Spies were shot. It was a risk they all took.

But how could it be accomplished?

Pitt lay with his eyes open, staring up at the ceiling. What facts did he have, what appearances that Kendrick could not deny? Pitt would have only one chance; Kendrick would never be caught a second time.

Pitt slept the couple of hours between three and five, but by morning he had the basis of a plan. Of Stoker's help he had no doubt at all. Bentley he believed would be more than willing, not only to accept something of a baptism by fire into his new job, but also to enact a kind of justice for Delia Kendrick.

The man upon whom it might well turn he could not take for granted. Somerset Carlisle had risked his reputation, his freedom, even his life on causes of his own, but this was Pitt's, and Carlisle could well refuse. It could be dangerous. Alan Kendrick would not be taken down easily.

He said nothing to Charlotte, but he had no need to tell her that he had a plan. She knew, and also knew better than to ask him what it was. She just whispered to him to be careful.

He went to see Carlisle first, early at his home, before he was likely to have left for the House of Commons, or anywhere else.

Carlisle was surprised to see him, and immediately interested. He was still at breakfast, but completely ignored it, forgetting even to offer Pitt anything.

"What can I do to help?" he asked keenly. "My God, Pitt, you'd better not be caught at this. You'll only get one chance. He's got some very powerful friends, you know? You do know, don't you?"

"Yes, I do," Pitt replied. "Great power, great passion, and quick tempers . . ."

Carlisle's eyes were bright, his concentration so intense now that he did not interrupt.

"It is precisely his friends' passions and tempers that I intend to use against him."

Carlisle gave a little sigh of extreme satisfaction.

"Do you remember Delia's first husband, who everyone thought died in an accident, but actually was killed by his masters when they discovered he was playing double agent and had betrayed them?" Pitt asked softly.

Carlisle smiled very slightly, but his eyes widened. "Oh dear, how very unfortunate. It could so easily happen to a man who was playing both sides of the line. Could happen to anyone, and I imagine it will, sooner or later."

"Sooner, I hope," Pitt answered. "If I can manage it."

"Be careful," Carlisle warned. "Do you know exactly who the other side is? I imagine you are telling me this for more than just my intense dislike of Kendrick and a desire to see him fall? What do you wish me to do?" It was more than a question, it was a distinct offer.

Pitt had no choice but to trust him completely.

"I must very carefully make it appear that he works for me, for Special Branch. And it must be observed by an agent of the Boers," he explained. "I have no idea who they are, but I imagine there will be someone at the Foreign Office who does. I need to meet with them and get that information, preferably not by force or coercion. I don't wish to make an enemy for life, but I will if I have to. If Kendrick survives, he could do more than merely sell the best guns in the world to the Boers; he could implicate the Prince of Wales in it, and if there is another war, which looks almost inevitable, the prince's ruin could bring down the monarchy."

To his surprise, Carlisle did not argue. "Worst imaginable supposition, but not impossible," he agreed. "Don't you have friends at the Foreign Office, or people who would be . . . shall we say, pleased to oblige you?"

"Yes, Morton Findlay. But does he have the information I need? And if I could manipulate him, who else might be able to?"

Carlisle sighed. "What a sad business it is. You've changed, Pitt. You used to have a kind of naïveté about you, at least in your view of people. You seem to have realized that in most of us it is no more than skin deep. Yes, I think I know someone who would be able to give you the information you need. Henry Talbot. And I'm afraid he is convinced that there will be another Boer war, so he will not take much persuading to help. Many people trust that Sir Alfred Milner will prevent that. I am afraid that the contrary is true. He is more likely to make a certainty of what is only a fear at the moment." He leaned forward a little. "Do you wish to speak to him yourself? I could do it discreetly, if you like, and bring you the information without your having to meet him. Explain to him what you need."

Pitt hesitated. He did not wish to compromise Carlisle any more than necessary. "It could become very unpleasant," he warned. "There is no guarantee of success."

"My dear Pitt, there is no guarantee of success in anything that is worth doing! And it could hardly compromise my reputation any more than it already is."

Pitt smiled; for a moment it was with real amusement. "On the other hand, if I get caught, and survive it, I might need you to bail me out! I will find myself with very few friends."

Carlisle's answering smile was very bleak. He took the point completely.

"I shall arrange for you to go to Talbot's home, and for him to give you the information you require there." He held out his hand and took Pitt's with a powerful, almost bruising grip. "Good luck, Pitt!"

■ ■ ■ ■

Two days later Pitt had most of the pieces in place. Henry Talbot had given him the information he needed. He knew exactly for whom the charade must be enacted. Stoker and Bentley were informed of the plan and all its possible variations. They knew not only their own roles, but enough of the purpose and the dangers to improvise, if necessary.

The opening gambit was played in the street, just outside one of the better restaurants. As Kendrick was exiting, closely followed by a prominent member of the House of Lords who had large financial interests in South Africa, specifically the gold mines of Johannesburg, Stoker walked up to Kendrick and furtively slipped a note into his pocket, giving him a very slight smile, just enough for His Lordship to see. The lord gave Kendrick a curious look and asked if he had been robbed. There was still time to pursue the man.

Kendrick looked puzzled. He kept nothing in such accessible pockets. He put his hand in. His fingers touched the note and he pulled it out, glanced at it, and immediately put it back again. He told His

Lordship it was a stupid prank, and to ignore it.

The peer pretended to be mollified.

The following day, Stoker did something similar while Kendrick was again with His Lordship with the South African interests. This time Kendrick was visibly annoyed, but there was nothing in his pocket except a gold guinea. He drew in his breath to deny that it was his but realized how absurd that would sound.

Shortly after, Kendrick was joined in his club by General Darlington, who to any observer might appear to be discussing something with Kendrick. He then thanked him profusely and looked far less anxious than he had for many months. Darlington might have enjoyed his part a trifle, but certainly he was happy to be doing something he thought was useful. He had told Pitt he never had a night when he did not think of some man he had lost in battle, and not a week without a nightmare of slaughter and death.

Bentley also played his part with enthusiasm, and more skill than Pitt had expected from him. The young man was still deeply angry over the horrible death of Delia and the misrepresentation of her in the gossip that Pitt had described. Pitt had done it on purpose, to spur him to action, but he still felt guilty for it. Not that what he told Bentley was untrue, regrettably. Delia had been resented. She herself had a sharp tongue and was raw enough and hurt enough not to curb it. Still, Pitt was playing on Bentley's emotions, and he knew it.

Dressed in his military uniform, unmistakably a British soldier from the Boer War, limping enough to notice, he walked up to Kendrick with a respectful smile.

"Just wanted to thank you, sir," he said quite distinctly. Kendrick looked puzzled, but not yet alarmed. He was in the street just outside his club. There were several other gentlemen either leaving or entering at the time, and able to overhear.

"Lost my brother in the last one, sir," Bentley went on. "And a fair few friends. I know a thing or two about Africa. And I'd want to thank any man who went out of his way to see we didn't have another war like that. Those Boers are hard fighters. We can't afford to give them any advantage. I don't want to be presumptuous, but I'd be honored to shake your hand." He held his hand out, respectfully, looking Kendrick straight in the face.

There were now at least half a dozen men on the footpath watching them, and Kendrick was caught. It would be inexplicably rude to refuse to take the young soldier's hand. He did shake it, his face frozen.

"Thank you, sir," Bentley said, with a huge smile as if he were thrilled. He nodded again. "Thank you, sir." Then he turned and walked away, his limp just visible but his head high and his back straight.

It was Pitt himself who delivered the final stroke. He had set it up with Darlington and Carlisle. It was prearranged that Kendrick had a luncheon at his club that he could not avoid, even though lately he had been frequenting clubs far less than had been his habit.

Pitt knew from his contacts in military intelligence that at least one Boer sympathizer was in the dining room. Kendrick was there and so was Pitt, invited by Carlisle, who had then made a discreet exit.

Kendrick afterward left for the smoking room, possibly with the intention of leaving altogether as soon as he could do so without drawing attention to himself. Pitt rose and followed him. As soon as Kendrick sat down, Pitt joined him, sitting immediately opposite.

Kendrick looked at him warily. His face was drawn, as if he had slept little, and the fine lines were pulling downward.

Pitt called for the steward's attention, possibly a touch too loudly, but he wanted to make sure everyone heard him. When the steward arrived, Pitt ordered a brandy for himself and whatever Kendrick would like.

Kendrick drew in breath to refuse, then realized that would be rude enough to draw even more attention.

As soon as the steward was gone, Kendrick leaned forward.

"What the devil do you want, Pitt? Haven't you troubled me and my family enough?"

"I thought it was supposed to be Halberd who hounded Mrs. Kendrick to her death?" Pitt said with a wide, charming smile, very far from what he felt inside. He would like to have hit the man as hard as he could, but instead he smiled even more.

"I wanted to thank you for all you have done for your country," he said quite distinctly. He had an excellent voice and knew it carried well, when he wished it to.

He did not take his eyes from Kendrick or cease smiling; he was aware of a very slight movement in the room, men changing position just enough to see who had spoken, and to whom.

"I've done nothing," Kendrick said ungraciously. He was so tense his voice was pitched a little higher than usual. "You are making something out of nothing."

"Your courage has saved many lives," Pitt said, lowering his own voice only slightly. In the motionless room it still carried. No one else fidgeted, nothing creaked or rustled. No one snored, even gently. No one turned the page of a newspaper or slurped a drink from their glass.

Kendrick glared at Pitt.

"It takes great courage to do what you have," Pitt went on. "I hope one day you are rewarded as you deserve. I imagine His Royal Highness will have much to say to you." Kendrick stared at him, his eyes hot and hard with rage. He was prevented from responding by the steward's return with two glasses of brandy, and the bottle from which they had been poured. He put it down on the small table, and Pitt paid him before Kendrick could.

Then Pitt raised his glass toward Kendrick. "We all thank you, Mr. Kendrick. You are a brave man. Most people will never know that you have risked your life for queen and country. Many will live now who might well have died in the heat and dust of a foreign land, but for you." He sipped the brandy.

Kendrick pretended to sip his.

"Now, I think we should not be seen

together longer than necessary," Pitt said, possibly a fraction less loudly, but clearly enough to be heard by the steward and the three or four men closest to them. Then he stood up, set his still full brandy glass on the table, and walked away.

He was at home and still too restless around midnight to go to bed. He paced the sitting-room floor, aware that he must be stretching Charlotte's patience to breaking. He had been sitting down and standing up again for the last three hours.

Would it work? Any more suggestions and half actions would be overplaying his hand; Kendrick could still win.

Should he have been bolder? Simply had the man assassinated? Or "murdered" would be a plainer and more honest word.

No, it wasn't. If the Boers believed he was a double agent, peddling lies he had deliberately played out in front of them, with the intent all along of telling their plans to Special Branch, then they would kill him as a traitor, even if he was in fact a traitor to Britain, not to them. If he had no business with them, then they would not care.

Morally, was it murder, or war? Pitt had no love of war, but he believed that sometimes it was necessary. If someone had broken into his home and attacked Charlotte or his children, he would have killed them of necessity, with regret but without hesitation.

He looked at Charlotte now, sitting quietly in her chair. She had abandoned her sewing. She had not asked him what he was waiting for, or what he was afraid of, but she watched him all the time, her face pale. She looked tired. Patience had never come naturally to her.

He thought back to their first meeting. She had been willful, ignorant of so much but always keen to learn even the tragic and ugly things most people preferred to pretend were not there. Exasperated or not, he had been fascinated with her, in love far too quickly.

And he still was.

He was startled, almost breathless, when the doorbell rang. He swung around and in three strides was in the hallway. He flung the front door open and saw Stoker and Bentley on the step. He had no need to ask. From Stoker's smile and the sudden ease in Bentley's previously rigid posture, he knew it was at least not a disaster.

He stepped back, and they followed him inside. Bentley closed the front door.

"Is Mrs. Pitt . . . ?" Stoker began.

Pitt glanced at the sitting-room door, which she had not fully closed behind him.

Stoker bit his lip. "It's pretty . . . gory, sir."

The sitting-room door swung open and Charlotte stood in the entrance, looking at Pitt, then Stoker.

Pitt went into the sitting room and signaled Stoker and Bentley to follow him. Again Bentley was last, and closed the door softly behind him.

"I'm sorry, ma'am," Stoker said to Charlotte.

Pitt's voice was rough with tension. "What happened? Where's Kendrick?"

"The police took him to the morgue, sir . . . what was left of him."

Pitt let out his breath very slowly. Charlotte was standing beside him, and he took her hand and held it so tightly he must have hurt her, but he realized this only afterward.

"Thought you should know tonight, sir," Stoker went on. "And I'd keep the newspapers where your family won't see them, if I were you. Not that the better ones will say much. They'll probably put it down as a robbery."

Bentley was shaking his head.

"Never mind," Pitt replied. "Thank you. You took risks." He was too drained of emotion now that it was over to make any appropriate response. He thought of Delia Kendrick hanging by the neck from the meat hook in her own kitchen, and it still distressed him, but this news did ease the knots in his stomach.

"Thank you," he said.

Stoker started to say something, then apparently changed his mind.

"Some soldiers die like that, sir," Bentley said quietly. "At least the enemy is in front of them, not behind. You've got to trust your own men. They won't always be right, and they may do some damn stupid things, but at least they're on your side."

"Thank you, Bentley," Pitt said again, with feeling. His voice sounded hoarse, even to himself. "Go home. I'll see you in a couple of days. And for God's sake, be careful!"

"Yes, sir. Good night, sir. Ma'am."

Pitt was too tired to dream, but he was deeply aware of Charlotte beside him, the warmth of her, and that she had turned toward him, not away.

He got up the following morning and sent a message to ask if he might speak privately to the Prince of Wales in a matter of the utmost urgency. Within the hour he was standing opposite the prince, the doors closed, and they were alone. It was obvious from the prince's white face that he had been informed of Kendrick's death.

"What happened?" he demanded. There was no preamble, no courtesies.

Pitt spoke equally frankly. "He was an agent for the Boers, Your Royal Highness. He was facilitating the purchase of the excellent Mauser rifle for their troops."

The prince was ashen-faced. "What? What did you say?"

"I regret it very much, sir, but he used his friendship with you, and your extraordinary popularity in Europe, particularly Germany, to effect a relationship with the Mauser factory, and . . ."

The prince was, if anything, even paler. He looked as if he felt sick.

"It was necessary to stop him, sir," Pitt said very quietly. He was worried in case the man should faint. "It was he who killed first Sir John Halberd and then his own wife, because both of them had learned what he was doing. They were loyal subjects of the Crown, sir, and paid for it with their lives."

"Do you . . . know that?" the prince asked. He seemed to be fumbling for words.

"Yes, sir, and in Sir John's case, I could have proved it."

"Then why didn't you?"

"Because Kendrick told me that if I brought him to trial he would say that Halberd was having an affair with Delia Kendrick, of the most obscene nature, and that she hanged herself rather than continue it any longer. And I could not charge him with purchasing guns for Britain's enemies without tarnishing your good name. He promised to do that."

"I . . . I see your point." He stumbled a step or two backward and sank into one of the elegant padded chairs. There were several minutes of silence, then he looked up at Pitt.

"And he's dead? Who killed him?"

"I think some Boer sympathizers, sir. They apparently had the idea that he was playing both sides, essentially betraying them to us."

"And was he? Don't lie to me, Pitt." Suddenly there was dignity in the prince again, in spite of his awkward position, half-slumped in the chair.

"No, sir, not so far as I know. He was an unhappy man. I think he felt cheated out of the position in society he thought he deserved. He may have had some loyalty to the Boers, or he may simply have wanted the financial profit and the power over the next king of England it would have given him. Those who once mocked him would have been obliged to court his favor then."

"But you made it look as if . . . ? You made the Boers think he had betrayed them, when really he had betrayed us . . . me?"

"Yes, sir."

"Thank you."

"May I suggest, sir, that you don't read the descriptions. It was . . . nasty."

"Thank you. I shall read what I choose. I knew the man." He rubbed his hand across his face. He looked old, and very tired. "I apologize. I'm very obliged to you, Pitt. I never thought I would say that, but I mean it."

"It is my privilege to serve the Crown, sir."

"Get out, man! Go get a stiff brandy. I'll have one."

"Yes, sir."

Pitt went straight from the prince's presence to Buckingham Palace and asked the guard to let him speak to Sir Peter Archibald.

Sir Peter appeared within fifteen minutes. He started upon seeing Pitt.

"God, you look awful, man. Sit down before you fall over." He turned to the waiting footman and ordered a brandy and soda. The man obeyed immediately.

"What has happened?" Sir Peter demanded. "Sit down! Tell me."

Pitt sat and when the brandy came, he drank it. He gave Sir Peter a brief summary of what had occurred. "I wish to report to the Queen. She asked me to find out what had happened to Sir John Halberd, and what manner of man Alan Kendrick was. I owe her the answer. She would be pleased to know that Sir John was the honorable man she believed him to be."

"And Kendrick the traitor," Sir Peter added. "I admit it is distressing to think how close he came to succeeding. Her Majesty will be most grateful that such a tragedy will be avoided, and no doubt will wish to tell you so herself, when she is in rather better health." His voice dropped a tone and his face was grave. "This has been difficult for her. I am sure you understand."

Pitt felt a darkness descend, as if a cold wind had blown out half the candles. Of course the room was lit by gas, and nothing had really changed. But he felt a sadness in him. He had taken it for granted that he would be able to tell the Queen himself, see her relief and her pleasure at what had been avoided, most particularly that there had been no guilt on the prince's part.

"Yes, of course," he said, recognizing

dismissal, polite as it was.

He went home immensely grateful that the matter had ended as well as it had. There would be no trial, no exposure of treason. He had done his job well. It was childish to wish he could have been the one to tell the Queen. He was smiling in self-mockery by the time he entered his own front door, and everything he told Charlotte was of his relief at the conclusion.

It was two weeks later that the letter came. Minnie Maude brought it in on a small tray, as if she did not dare to touch it herself. Her face was radiant.

Charlotte was at the kitchen door. Pitt was still at the breakfast table.

Minnie Maude stopped in the middle of the floor and stood absolutely still.

"What is it?" Charlotte asked her, then looked at Pitt and back again.

Minnie Maude gulped. "It's a letter, ma'am, from Buckingham Palace, from the Queen 'erself."

Pitt had been waiting, hoping, yet feeling ridiculous for it, as if he had presumed above himself. Now here it was.

"Thank you, Minnie Maude," he managed to say almost normally. His hand was quite steady when he reached for the letter and took it.

Charlotte stood motionless.

Pitt opened the letter carefully, without tearing the envelope.

It was not from Victoria. It was from Sir Peter Archibald. Pitt felt an absurd disappointment.

Then he read it.

It was very formal. Sir Peter advised him that as a mark of her appreciation for his services to the Crown, Her Majesty was pleased to offer him a knighthood. Should he accept, the investiture would be in just over a week's time.

There was a small handwritten addendum by Sir Peter, saying that it would be appropriate to bring his family, and such close friends as he might wish — for example, Lord and Lady Narraway, now that they had returned to England, if it pleased him.

"What is it, Thomas?" Charlotte said at last, no longer able to bear the suspense. "Is she thanking you? She should."

"Yes," he said, hesitating now, savoring the moment. "Yes, she is. You will need to have a new gown. And one for Jemima too."

She had no idea what he was talking about, but she saw the overwhelming excitement in him.

"What is it?" she said breathlessly. "What does she say? Thomas, tell me!"

He smiled very slowly, in amazement. "That if I should care to accept, she will be pleased to make me 'Sir Thomas,' " he replied. "And she will do so next week. We may invite Narraway and Aunt Vespasia as well . . ."

"We?" she asked.

"Of course 'we,' " he replied. "You have been with me all the way. Without you, I would have remained an inspector, at best. You are the one who created the dreams, encouraged me, sustained me when they seemed too big and too far."

"Sir Thomas and Lady Pitt," she said very quietly. "Good heavens!" Then she dumped the fresh toast she was carrying onto the table and threw herself into his arms, hugging him so hard she upset his empty cup and knocked his knife to the floor.

The investiture was a very grand affair, very splendid, as befitted such a high moment in anyone's life. As was customary, it was held in the Throne Room, one of the most magnificent in the entire palace. In earlier years, when Prince Albert had been alive, great balls had been held here. The Queen had loved music and dancing. Now it was carpeted in red, with paler scrolls in delicate patterns echoing the rich red, almost pink of the walls, which were interspersed with ornate gold pilasters and windows almost up to the vast ceiling, with its echoed circles. The thrones themselves, side by side, were up against the farthest wall. It was overwhelming for the first moment, then the beauty of it settled into almost a kind of peace. It was the heart of the empire. It should be glorious.

"I am very grateful to you for your discretion, Mr. Pitt," the Queen said quietly. "Your solution to the whole miserable affair was powerful and yet had a delicacy of touch that comforts me greatly. I hope you will long serve your country in what may be dark days to come. When Edward is king, he will lean on you as I have. He has promised me this. He agrees entirely that you should be so recognized. If you would be good enough to kneel now."

Vespasia had taught him how to do so with grace, on one knee.

"Arise, Sir Thomas," Victoria said with unmistakable pleasure.

He did so with dignity, blinking away tears of emotion and dazed with happiness. Then he walked across to where Charlotte, his children, and his friends were waiting for him.

ABOUT THE AUTHOR

Anne Perry is the bestselling author of two acclaimed series set in Victorian England: the Charlotte and Thomas Pitt novels, including *Treachery at Lancaster Gate* and *The Angel Court Affair,* and the William Monk novels, including *Revenge in a Cold River* and *Corridors of the Night.* She is also the author of a series of five World War I novels, as well as twelve holiday novels, most recently *A Christmas Message,* and a historical novel, *The Sheen on the Silk,* set in the Ottoman Empire. Anne Perry lives in Los Angeles and Scotland.

anneperry.co.uk
@AnnePerryWriter
Facebook.com/AnnePerryAuthor

To inquire about booking Anne Perry for a speaking engagement, please contact the

Penguin Random House Speakers Bureau
at speakers@penguinrandomhouse.com

The employees of Thorndike Press hope you have enjoyed this Large Print book. All our Thorndike, Wheeler, and Kennebec Large Print titles are designed for easy reading, and all our books are made to last. Other Thorndike Press Large Print books are available at your library, through selected bookstores, or directly from us.

For information about titles, please call:
(800) 223-1244

or visit our website at:
gale.com/thorndike

To share your comments, please write:
Publisher
Thorndike Press
10 Water St., Suite 310
Waterville, ME 04901